Sire

Beautiful Monsters Volume II

Jex Lane

This is a work of fiction. Names, characters, businesses, places, events, and incidents are either the products of the author's imagination or used in a fictitious manner. Any resemblance to actual persons, living or dead, or actual events is purely coincidental—or used with permission.

Sire: Beautiful Monsters Volume II © 2016 by Jex Lane.
All rights reserved.

JexLane.com

Edited by Michelle Rascon

Cover Design by Jay Aheer

Library of Congress Control Number: 2016917160

ISBN 978-0-9977533-1-8

For Jamie.
No bottle of wine is safe around us.

CHARACTERS INTRODUCED IN CAPTIVE

Matthew — Incubus turned vampire. Orphaned as a child; abandoned by his sire.

Incubi; ordered by social ranking:

High King Malarath — Monarch of the incubi people.
Queen Agleea — Social. Malarath's granddaughter.
Lady Rosaline — Social. Member of House Malarath.
High Lord General Tarrick — Warrior. Leader of the incubi armies.
General Tarquin — Warrior. Tarrick's eldest son. Leader of the Russian offensive.
Lord Ennius — Social. Queen Agleea's consort.
Lady Dennith — Warrior. Tarrick's "right-hand".
Lord Teleclus — Warrior. Retired. Lady Lillian's custodian.
Lady Sabine — Warrior. Lives a reclusive life in the Colorado Mountains.
Lord Vassu — Warrior. Largest of his people. Stationed on the vampire-infested West Coast.
Lady Talena "Lena" — Warrior. Tarrick's only living daughter. Rescued by Matthew.
Lord Tane — Warrior. Tarrick's youngest son.
Lady Lillian "Lily" — Matthew's daughter.

Hunters; ordered by hunter ranking:

Imperator Prescott — Leader of the Hunter Corps. Team leader of the Argonauts, High King Malarath's personal bodyguards.
Commander Hiroto — Assassin. Kitsune. Member of the Argonauts. Team leader of the Shadow Six.
Commander Cullip — Former leader of the Wardens.
Commander Silva — Team leader of the Wardens, Tarrick's personal bodyguards.
Fendrel — Dragonslayer.

Vampires; ordered alphabetically:

Ascelina — Vampire lord. Assisted in Matthew's escape.
Emilia — Ascelina's sired daughter. Matthew's former cellmate.
Stolus — Ascelina's sired son. Emilia's protective younger brother.
Victor Moreau — *Deceased.* Vampire lord. Ruled New Orleans. Killed by Matthew.

Humans:

Alyssa Callahan — *Deceased.* Matthew's wife. Mother of Lily.

One

DEVAK

Three Days After Matthew's Escape. Pennsylvania.

Devak rolled down the window of his rental sedan and sucked in the cool fall air as he drove down the two-lane road. The asphalt was exceptionally well maintained considering this road led to seemingly nowhere. Long and winding, it cut through the middle of a forest filled with tall, autumn trees.

There were no houses or structures. He hadn't even passed another car in over an hour.

He rubbed the back of his head, his dark curly hair too short to be bothered by the wind. He wasn't quite sure where he was, other than somewhere in Pennsylvania, nor did he know why he had turned down this specific road. He only knew that he had to find *him*.

And soon.

A few months ago, Devak had been closing up for his oh-so-glamorous job as a bank teller when he was struck with intense pain and rendered unconscious. When he came to on the bank floor, he had no idea what had happened to him.

Since that day, he felt as if he was being drawn somewhere. He ignored the feeling. Then his memories—his real memories—began to return. Not all of them, but enough to know he should not have ignored the feeling for so long.

And now, as he sped along the road, he hoped he wasn't too late. He was certain he was close now.

When he rounded a bend in the road, his heart sank.

Before him was an old rusty gate, and set back a ways were the crumbling ruins of what looked to be a once-great mansion. Only the stone foundation remained, and the wall surrounding the place had collapsed into nothing more than stone piles. The forest had begun to reclaim the area and the grey clouds that blanketed the sky, covering the sun, only added to the bleak visage before him.

He stopped the car and got out. Touching the gate, his fingers buzzed as if a low electric current flowed through the metal.

Magic.

This was the correct place. But he wasn't sure what waited for him, and he couldn't remember how to use all of his powers yet. He needed to be careful.

"Hey there!" a female called out to him from down the road.

Devak took a few steps away from the gate and faced her. She looked to be in her late twenties, her brown hair pulled back into a bun, and she wore jeans and a long-sleeved flannel shirt that was buttoned all the way up. She was petite, not that Devak was tall at five-six, but she was five-nothing.

"Hello," Devak said, trying to sound friendly so he wouldn't frighten her. It was hard for him; his co-workers would rib that he was always too serious.

"Car break down?" she asked as she approached.

"Uh, yeah. I was just about to call a tow truck."

She shook her head. "Don't bother—you won't get reception out here. Let me take a look. I know a thing or two about cars."

"Sure. Devak, by the way," he said and held out his hand.

She took it. "Mary." When she broke the handshake, her eyes lingered on him, as if she was looking for something.

Devak slipped into the driver's seat and popped the hood. "You live near here?"

"Yeah, not far. I was taking a walk when I saw your car. Turn it on, let's see what it's doing," she said.

"Not many people out this way." Devak turned the key, the engine starting perfectly.

"Nope, we like it like that. I'm not seeing anything wrong here."

"Give it a moment, the engine will shut off randomly," he said and walked around the hood to stand next to her. He pointed at the ruins. "Do you know who owns this place?"

She chuckled. "Yeah, he has a house further back. I wouldn't go on the property. The man who owns it is old and grumpy. He's likely to shoot any trespassers."

"Ah." Devak touched the side of the car and forced the engine to stop. That was something he could do now—break technology. He had found out the hard way when his electric razor went up in flames in his hand. Then later when his car stalled on the way to work. And again when he was with a customer and the computers in the bank all crashed at once. It took him a few days to figure out how to stop zapping the electronic or mechanical objects around him.

Mary pursed her lips as she studied the engine. "I don't see what the problem is."

Devak shrugged and pulled out his phone. She was right, no service. "Do you have a landline somewhere? I'll call the rental and have them pick it up."

"Even better, my brother has a flatbed. He can drop you back in town with the car."

"I couldn't put you guys out like that."

"Really, it's no trouble. He's heading to work anyways—he should be along any moment," she said, her smile looked genuine but her body was taut. She kept her hands on her hips and feet planted on the ground as if she was expecting to defend an attack at any moment.

Devak didn't know what she was. Human for sure, but she had magic. Not the power of a witch or bruja, but magic all the same. It felt...borrowed. Judging from her stance and the careful way she maneuvered around him, always keeping a few feet away, she was a fighter of some sort.

Mary shifted to look more natural when she noticed him staring at her. "What brings you down here? Wrong turn?"

"No. I'm looking for someone." Devak glanced back at the ruined estate.

"Who you looking for? We don't get many people this way. I know almost everyone who passes through here."

He ignored her question, walking back to the gate and touching it again. "I'd really like to talk to the owner of this place."

"What do you want to talk to him about?" She moved her hand behind her back, to grab a weapon no doubt.

Devak considered summoning in his own weapon but he didn't want to have to fight his way to the answers, not when he was certain he could convince the one he was looking for to speak with him without the need of violence. Well, not much violence anyways.

Devak moved fast, appearing behind her. He hadn't expected her to be as quick as she was, as she spun around and slashed at him with a silver dagger.

He took a step back to avoid the attack and when she thrust at him again, he grabbed her wrist firmly and plucked the dagger from her hand, tossing it away.

The green light of magic outlined her body. Teleport spell. Devak absorbed her magic and the spell failed. She tried to twist out of the grip and he allowed her wrist to slide in his hand so that she wouldn't be hurt, but he didn't release her.

"I don't wish to fight you. I wish to speak to the master of this estate," Devak said.

Her face hardened and she scowled. "What are you?"

"I wish to know the same about you." He ripped open her flannel shirt. She struggled against him and seemed surprised by his strength when she couldn't get away. He was small for a male, his body lean; his strength always caught people off-guard.

"Relax, you aren't my type," he said. "I just want to see how you are using magic."

She threw a punch and he caught it with his other hand.

"I said I didn't wish to fight you, do not take that to mean that I'm above killing you if you persist."

She stopped moving. He pulled open the ripped shirt to get a better look at her chest, it was covered in silver runes. Each one was a spell. Interesting.

Devak tightened his grip on her wrist. "Are you important enough that your master will speak with me in exchange for your well-being? Or do I need to find another?"

"I will speak with you. Silva, bring him in," said a deep male voice from out of her other wrist. Devak pulled up her sleeve to reveal a metal band, some sort of communication device.

"Mary, huh?" Devak said to the human.

He released the woman. She dove for her dagger and scowled at him when she was back on her feet.

"Your magic will return to you momentarily, *Silva*," he said to reassure her.

"What are you?" she asked again.

"You tell me."

"I don't know of anything that can suck away magic like that, except maybe an elf. You move like a vampire lord but you're warm. And it's day time but you have no ring. Unless it's hidden."

"I wear no magic. I'm certain you will work out what I am eventually." He didn't have all his memories back but at least he knew what he was.

Protector.

He didn't deserve to be called that. He'd lost a battle. He couldn't remember the details, but he knew he'd failed when it had mattered most. And now he had to make it right.

Devak motioned for her to lead them onwards into the ruins.

She kept her dagger in her hand and backed up to the gate. The rusty iron creaked open with a push, and she stepped through, disappearing before his eyes. He had expected that, though.

Devak wondered again if he should summon his weapon, but he decided against it since it'd take too long to arrive. These were allies anyways.

He followed after her, passing through a magic veil. The other side was completely different from the ruins he had been looking at. An impressive stone estate, reminiscent of a castle, rose four stories above him. Fierce, unmoving gargoyles guarded the roof.

The grounds around him were flawlessly maintained. The stone wall that encompassed the estate was high and thick.

Surrounding him were two dozen armed humans; all with borrowed magic and wearing different style leather outfits. Their weapons varied, though it seemed silvered longswords and crossbows were popular. Each of them armed with at least one stake, most had several.

Vampire hunters.

Devak had never seen so many gathered together on this planet. Then again, in his day only a handful of humans ever dared to hunt vampires and none of them had magic like they did.

Silva walked backwards, keeping a crossbow trained on Devak and leading him up the gravel driveway to the estate. The other hunters kept their distance but maintained a circle around him.

As they walked, clouds grew darker and a sprinkle of rain wet their faces and shoulders.

Near the entrance to the house, Devak saw them. Incubi. There were three. Each profoundly beautiful.

The one he was looking for stood in the center, wearing a dark suit and tie. He made Devak's tan slacks and light button-up shirt seem casual in comparison. The leader was near impossible to read beyond his veil of confidence.

A chill ran down Devak's spine as piercing blue eyes studied him with calculating scrutiny.

To the leader's left stood a younger male incubus who looked like a slightly smaller copy of the leader, with the same short dusty blond hair and strong jaw. The leader's son, or brother perhaps, held a claymore with the tip resting on the ground and wore a full set of metal armor. Unlike the leader, he was letting some of his incubus form show through; his eyes were purple and he had black horns that started at his forehead and curved back, ending with purple tips.

To the leader's right stood a female warrior, also armored. Her blue tipped horns curled around the sides of her short black hair and her wings spread out behind her. In one hand, she held a polearm; in the other, a massive club-like weapon with heavy metal spikes.

"I am Devak. Who do I address?"

The leader nodded to Silva, who had taken up a spot next to the succubus. The hunter stepped forward and spoke, "This is High Lord General Tarrick." She motioned to the incubus in the center, then the other two. "Lord Tane, Lady Dennith, and I am Hunter Commander Silva."

A faint green glow appeared off to the side and a human male appeared. This one looked like a knight in shining armor, complete with shield and sword. Devak recognized the ancient sword: Dragon's Bane. The knight studied Devak for a moment, then shook his head.

Devak scoffed. "Did you think I was a dragon?"

"You have ten seconds to convince me not to have you killed," Tarrick said, his features severe.

"You can't kill me."

"I assure you, I can."

"Feel free to try, but you—" Before Devak finished his sentence, the leader gave a signal to his humans. Bolts flew from their crossbows. Devak raised his hand and made a barrier of energy around himself. The bolts smashed against it and clattered to the ground. When they were done shooting at him, he lowered his hand and the barrier with it.

Devak raised an eyebrow at the leader whose eyes widened for the briefest of moments before returning to their cold analytical gaze.

"Demon..." Tane whispered.

Devak's eyes narrowed and he took a step at the younger incubus. The humans around him tensed, ready to attack.

"Call me 'demon' again and those will be the last words to ever leave your lips," Devak warned. It wasn't a bluff. He would kill him for such an insult.

Devak felt a change in the incubus general's tactics since he now realized a show of force wasn't going to work. Tarrick released pheromones to try and sway Devak's emotions and make him more forthcoming. Devak was immune, but he wasn't going to tell him that.

"Tell me what you are," Tarrick said.

"The Prince will tell you if he wishes you to know."

"The Prince?"

"That is why I have come. To serve him."

The general looked back at his house, then to Devak. "There are no princes here."

Devak studied him for a moment. An incubus Tarrick's age would have been able to sense the Prince for what he was, or at least know he was different. Maybe his prince had been cursed as he had been. Maybe his prince didn't yet know who he was... He hoped that wasn't the case considering Devak wouldn't—or, more accurately, couldn't—tell him.

As he studied the incubus he couldn't help but feel attracted to him. Then again, Devak always had a weakness for strong incubi. Especially generals.

"My prince was here recently. His scent still lingers." Maybe Devak had arrived too late. The scent was a few days old.

"I'm telling you that there are no—" Tarrick paused as some piece of information fell into place. "What is your prince's name?"

Devak could not speak his true name, but he knew the name

his prince was given. He was the one who had chosen it after all. "Matthew."

A cold wind swept the late afternoon air as the incubi and humans stilled. He heard hearts pounding violently against their chests and shallow breaths, heated with anger. Not a single person spoke, but many glanced to Tarrick, waiting for an order.

Devak had been wrong. He had misread the situation. These were not allies. He should have summoned his weapon. Now it was too late; if he tried they'd be on him before it arrived. "I thought he was here as a guest, but he wasn't, was he?"

Tarrick remained silent. His face betrayed nothing, but his subordinates were not as controlled. Hunter Commander Silva bared her emotions the most; her eyes narrowed and lips pressed together, her crossbow trained on Devak's head. The smell of anger rolled off her.

Devak clasped his hands together behind his back so he wouldn't be tempted to lash out at one of the surrounding creatures. "You mistreated him, didn't you?" Again he received no response. "Didn't you know he was different? That he was born as one of you? Or did you think he was just a regular vampire? A prisoner of your endless war, maybe."

"Everyone knows he is an abomination," Tane spat out.

Tarrick held up his hand to silence the young incubus.

Abomination? His prince? They had no idea who he was—if they did, they wouldn't dare speak so callously. Devak allowed the feeling of preeminence to seep through him before running his fingers through his short hair.

"If you did mistreat him, then I pity you and all that comes next. I assume you no longer know where he is." Devak allowed a long pause to float between them—they didn't know. "Thank you for your time, General." Devak turned to leave. The circle of hunters closed around him, not letting him pass.

Devak sighed and turned back to Tarrick. "I didn't come here to fight."

"Then surrender and there will be no fighting," Tarrick said.

Devak rubbed his fingers across his forehead while he thought about what he wanted to do next. He really didn't want to kill any incubi; it would displease *her*.

The general waited patiently while Devak made his decision.

"There will be no fighting today," Devak said, but he wasn't surrendering.

The hunters standing behind him grew uneasy as they saw what Devak was doing.

"Sir," one of them said, "his back—"

For the first time today, Devak smiled. He loved this part and the reverence that would follow. It was wrong to feel this way—he should be humble, like the others—but he wasn't like the others, and he couldn't help it.

"—he's bleeding," another hunter finished. And he was. Two red blotches formed and spread across his light shirt until his back was drenched in blood.

Devak launched himself high into the air with a powerful leap. He focused on the blood pouring out of two long openings on his back and willed it into shape.

Massive wings snapped out. Bloody tendrils weaved and twisted as he levitated above his would-be captors. He stretched his wings out farther; they spanned impressively behind him.

The dark clouds above him parted and a bright ray of sunlight fell upon him.

He looked down at Silva. "Have you worked out what I am, little human?" he asked, his true voice reverberant, causing the ground to tremble with each word.

Silva's mouth hung open and her eyes darted up and down his body. "It can't be..."

Devak turned to the High Lord General who maintained a composed demeanor. "If you find my prince before I do, know that I will come for him. And know that the next time I will be prepared to fight."

Devak rose higher into the sky. As the incubi and humans disappeared below him, he heard them say:

"Should we chase?" the female incubus, Dennith, asked the general.

"No. Get me the High King. We have a serious problem."

Two

MATTHEW

One Year Later. Chicago.

Three days. For three fucking days, Matthew had been in incubus territory, dodging hunter patrols, and trying to track down a vampire who might have some information about his sire.

He shouldn't have been surprised that his lead turned up nothing. For a year now, he had been searching for some information—any information—that would lead him to his sire, or his birth parents, but every clue hit a frustrating dead end.

From the dark shadows of an alleyway, Matthew watched as a hunter team swept the block. A low growl drew his attention. At his side, an oversized Rottweiler hunched its back and bared its teeth at the hunters.

Matthew crouched down and patted the huge dog on its head. "Hush, Jet. We're not killing these hunters." Jet didn't seem to care. The Rottweiler lunged forward only to be yanked back by the skin of his neck. "I said no."

The black and tan dog snapped at Matthew, who tightened his grip on Jet's skin.

"You want to throw down? Right now?"

Jet stopped growling.

"Yeah," Mathew said, releasing him. "Thought so."

The big dog huffed and skulked away, disappearing into the shadows.

"Aw, come on." Matthew stood. "I'm sorry, but killing hunters will only draw attention we can't afford right now." But it was too late, Jet was gone.

Matthew frowned. The last year had been hard on him, but Jet's presence had made it a little more bearable. After escaping captivity,

Matthew stayed with the vampires for four months until he couldn't stand them any longer. Most hated him and voiced their opinion every chance they got, despite Ascelina's ruling to leave him be.

Since then, he traveled across the country in search of any clues that might help him discover who sired him, or who his parents were. So far he had come up with nothing. Almost every lead fizzled and every supernatural creature he had questioned knew jack shit.

He had heard rumors about ancient vampires that slept deep in the ground for thousands of years, said to be older than even the Queen. Ascelina thought it could be possible he was turned by one of them, but—if they existed at all—it was unlikely something so ancient and powerful could remain hidden.

Matthew watched as the hunters radioed in that the area was clear and moved on. He hated being in incubus territory and after finding nothing, he was considering leaving.

It wasn't the high level of hunter patrols that he hated—for a vampire as powerful as he was, they were easy enough to hide from—it was each time he'd catch a glimpse of an incubus, a deep, longing desire to talk with them would bubble up. He wanted to be around his people. He yearned for it.

It was awful and it didn't help he wasn't feeding on sex often. Within him, his empty soavik cramped.

Of all his shit luck, he had the downsides of being an incubus without many of the perks. He didn't have their wings or horns, and if he didn't feed he was crippled with pain. At least he could sway emotions a little and evoke pleasure with his touch. And, he could make lube ooze from his skin...because that's not disgusting or anything.

Unable to resist feeding any longer, he put his search for the vampire on hold and made his way to a gay club in Boystown. Normally he'd have Jet guarding outside the club, but it seemed his dog was going to throw a fit tonight. He wasn't too worried; Jet would show up eventually...he always did.

Matthew watched the crowd, thankful there were no incubi here right now, and honed in on an attractive looking couple nursing drinks and chatting at a small standing table.

He approached them and slipped his hands around each of their waists.

"Hey, what do you think—" the slightly smaller of the two men began to say. He stopped when he saw Matthew, and blushed.

Matthew flashed a sexy smile at the two of them. "Would you two like to join me in my private VIP room?"

The couple exchanged glances, silently communicating with each other. "Yeah," said the slightly taller one as he placed his hand on Matthew's chest.

That's all it took. Just a touch and Matthew could have any human eating out of his hands. Well, not a hunter, they were trained to resist it. But any of the horny men in here.

He had chosen these two because he heard them discussing the possibility of having a threesome. And they were hot. The taller of the two had dark brown hair and dark eyes while the other had brown hair a few shades lighter than Matthew's and blue eyes. Both were lean and fit.

Matthew led them into a private VIP room on the second floor of the club. He compelled the current occupants to leave and shut the curtains behind them. The club was loud enough to cover any sounds they were about to make and no one should be coming in to bother them.

He took a seat on one of the couches and spread his arms along the back.

"Come," Matthew said.

They sat down, one on each side of him, and began rubbing their hands over his clothes.

"You boys want something to drink," Matthew offered. The taller man answered by leaning in and kissing his ear, the other by undoing the top button of his jeans. Guess not.

Matthew wrapped his arms around them and drew in a little bit of the sexual energy they were releasing. Both of them tasted amazing.

The one kissing his ear grabbed the bottom of Matthew's turtleneck and peeled it off while the other pushed Matthew's pants open and rubbed his hard cock through his boxers. Matthew moaned in response.

The taller one eyed the now-exposed metal collar around Matthew's neck. "Kinky," the man said with a grin.

It wasn't. Not to Matthew. It was a constant, painful reminder of his time as a prisoner to the incubi, but the witches hadn't been able to figure out a way to remove it without it killing him so he was stuck with the damn thing around his throat. It's why he always wore turtlenecks these days, even though he wasn't a fan of them. At least the witches removed the tracking spell.

Matthew pulled the taller man in for a kiss while the other grabbed Matthew's cock and wrapped his lips around it.

The shorter one worked his skilled mouth and tongue down the shaft. Matthew grunted as the man on his cock took as much of it as he could before pulling away and sucking in a deep breath.

Matthew leaned his head back and let himself enjoy the pleasure of being blown.

"He's good, isn't he?" the taller one said as he worked his lips up Matthew's chest.

"Very. Undress. Take your cocks out," Matthew ordered.

Both pulled their shirts off and unzipped their pants, pushing them down to reveal their own hard erections. Matthew stood and finished taking his clothes off as well. He grabbed their lengths, one in each palm, and secreted a silky-smooth lubricant onto their dicks. Wanting to draw this out and feed for a while, he ran his hands up and down at an unhurried pace.

Matthew pushed pleasure into both of them and fed off their desire. He enjoyed the feeling of their heated skin against his and had to suppress an unhuman-like purr when they pressed against him.

They were close, but before they came Matthew dragged them over to the couch and had the lighter-haired one kneel on it. Matthew fingered his backside, slipping a wet finger into his hole to ready him. The tall one handed him a condom, but Matthew shook his head. "I want to watch you fuck him."

The human looked confused for a moment but Matthew touched his shoulder and increased his desire for his partner. He didn't blame the man for the confusion, it had looked like Matthew intended to be the one entering, but the truth was he didn't want anything more than a blowjob.

Ever since his escape—ever since his heart was broken—he'd sometimes lose his erection. It didn't happen all the time, mostly when he thought of Tarrick and his betrayal, but it happened just often enough to be embarrassing. Limiting his encounters to blowjobs helped a bit.

But he was troubled by more than just losing an erection; he could never feed enough. Feeding deep on these humans was an acknowledgment of the monster he was. Matthew *hated* incubi and it pissed him off that he was one of them.

Matthew watched as the dark-haired human worked his way into his partner. Breathy moans escaped them. The bottom grabbed Matthew's muscular thighs and wrapped his wet lips around Matthew's thick cock, moving up and down the shaft while he got pounded from behind.

It wasn't long before the movements of all three men grew urgent.

An intense orgasm rolled through Matthew as his cock thrust deep into the man's mouth. The dark-haired man followed next, his moans loud and heaving.

Matthew rested his palms on the lighter-haired man's shoulder blades and pushed him to climax as well. His cries were muffled as he cleaned Matthew's dick of cum and spilled his own on the couch.

Matthew peeled away and sunk into the cushions.

"That was amazing," one of them panted.

Matthew gave them a flirty smile to humor them. It had been pleasurable, yes, but not amazing. Amazing was...Tarrick's hand...Tarrick's tail...Tarrick's cock...Matthew closed his eyes and pushed the thoughts away. It wasn't healthy.

He grabbed the smaller man by his hair and pulled him up into his lap.

"Both of you look at me." They obeyed. "You don't fear me. I'm a vampire, may I bite you?" They looked confused, but the compulsion kept them relaxed. "Show me your pretty necks, and when I'm done you'll forget this happened."

Thanks to Ascelina's training, Matthew could now erase and replace memories without having to maintain a compulsion. It was a trick that had come in handy more than once. They bared their necks and he struck hard. His fangs sank in deep. Matthew took blood from them both, but not enough to weaken them.

When he was done, his two partners began making out and working their way to an encore. Matthew might have considered joining if he hadn't sensed something…strange…standing on the other side of the curtain, outside of the VIP room. The delicate scent of parchment and vanilla drifted past him.

He stood, still naked, and dragged open the curtain just wide enough to see who was out there.

It was a woman. She was average height with no makeup on; she had chestnut hair that hung limp around her shoulders and matching unexciting chestnut eyes. She wore a simple flower-patterned dress that was too big for her boney structure and small chest. She was maybe twenty years old at most, and that was being generous. She looked closer to seventeen.

If she hadn't been the only woman in a club full of men, Matthew wouldn't have even noticed her. She was the type of person that blended into the background, unassuming and diffident.

As far as he could tell, she was human.

When she saw Matthew, her eyes grew impossibly wide and fear pumped through her. "The blood of the sired seals the gate," she gasped and darted away into the crowd.

"Seriously?" Matthew sighed and snapped the curtains shut.

Three

Matthew, not happy that he now had to go chase down some girl, tossed on his clothes.

"Leaving?" one of the men asked, disappointed.

Matthew finished buttoning up his jeans. "Yeah. I have the room all night, everything's on me. Enjoy yourselves."

He left, found the manager of the club, and compelled him to take care of the two men in the VIP room and get them anything they desired at no cost.

Then he tracked the young woman's scent out of the club. She had a five-minute head start but she was on foot. It didn't take long for Matthew to find her. He stalked her unnoticed, watching from the rooftops of brick buildings.

She was agitated, walking at a swift pace, and talking to herself. It was a cold, fall night and she had no jacket on. She kept her arms wrapped tightly around her shivering body.

"I shouldn't have…so stupid…he could have killed me and then what would have happened? It must unfold correctly…but he could help…what was I thinking?"

Ooooooookaaay. She sounded as if the cheese had slid off her cracker a while ago.

Matthew watched as she hailed a cab. He took note of the address she gave and followed the car, bounding from rooftop to rooftop.

The cab came to a stop in front of a square, ten-story apartment building in a seedy area of town. He watched her enter.

Before the door closed behind her, he jumped off the roof and dashed into the building. He hid behind a pillar as she waited for the elevator. The lobby was trashy, with broken chairs and vandalized walls. Fluorescent lights flickered above him, threatening to die at any moment.

The ramshackle elevator arrived and the young woman got on.

Matthew waited until the doors were nearly closed then slipped in, moving so quickly she didn't see him enter. It wasn't until the elevator was passing the third floor that she noticed he was standing beside her.

Her eyes grew wide and she pressed herself into the corner. She said nothing.

He smiled down at her. "Care to tell me what you were doing back at the club?"

She shook her head as she trembled.

Matthew reached out and touched her arm. It was colder than his was. He tried to force her body to release chemicals to calm her down but it seemed to have no effect. Odd.

He looked at her eyes to compel her. "There's no need to fear me. Tell me what you were doing at the club."

She blinked at him.

Nothing.

He had no control over her. It wasn't that she was resisting his will—or even fighting it—but, rather, it was as if she didn't exist. He might as well have been compelling air.

"What are you?" he asked.

She studied him for a few moments then finally spoke. "Are you going to kill me?"

"I wasn't planning on it."

"I know."

Matthew tilted his head, confused. "Uh, if you knew, why did you ask?"

"I didn't know until you said it."

...Riiiggght...

The elevator doors opened on the ninth floor. She sidestepped away from him and walked out. He followed her down the windowless hall, with its fraying carpet and peeling paint, to a door near the end.

She reached into her dress and produced a key. Her hand shook so hard that it took her a few tries before she got the key into the slot.

Walking in, she shut the door behind her.

Matthew crossed his arms and leaned against the wall. He could have stopped her from going into her apartment, but he didn't want to frighten her even more. And, she had sought him out; there must be something she wanted from him. He decided to wait.

He listened as she moved around her small apartment. It sounded as if she was packing.

When she opened the door again, she wore pants along with a heavy coat, scarf, beanie, and gloves. This is what she should have been wearing before, not that dress. She also carried a stuffed duffle bag in her still trembling hand.

"Going out?" Matthew asked.

"Yes. You're taking me with you."

"Is that so?"

"Yes. You're going to save me and I'm going to save you."

Matthew laughed at the plain-looking girl. "What's your name?"

"Samantha, but you call me Sam."

"I'm sorry to disappoint you, Sam, but I'm not taking you with me."

"Yes, you are." She was determined.

"Do you know what I am, human?" Matthew asked her, amused.

"Yes, Matthew."

"How do you know my name?"

"Agree to save me and I'll tell you."

"I don't make agreements before I know all the details. It gets me in trouble. Why don't you invite me in and we'll talk about it?"

Samantha stretched her neck and looked down the hall towards the elevator as much as she could without actually crossing the threshold of her door. The elevator was coming up to this floor. "We don't have time. If he gets ahold of me, I'll be used like the others."

It struck Matthew that he wasn't the reason fear was pumping through her. "Who?"

"They'll be here soon to take me to him. I'm sorry I'm weak and I'm changing things. Please save me." Panic rose in her voice.

"Who is coming?"

"Darkness and dust."

"I don't know what that means."

She glanced down the hall at the elevator again. "He's here."

The doors to the elevator dinged and slid open. The smell of night and earth hit Matthew a fraction of a second before he saw who stood there. He blinked with disbelief; when he was sure what he was seeing was real, his breathing stopped as fear rose.

It was *Tarrick*.

The High Lord General himself.

Wearing a tailored suit and flanked by his team of six hunter bodyguards, the Wardens—or at least Matthew assumed that's who they were since they were all new members. Except for the team leader, Commander Silva, who was the shortest of the lot and wore a long black cloak that concealed her weapons.

His vampire side came forward and he snarled at them. This was bad.

Matthew was stuck in a windowless hallway surrounded by rooms he couldn't enter unless he was invited in. If he fought the hunters, if he fought Tarrick—the thousand-year-old incubus warrior—there was no way this wouldn't end with him chained in silver. No way this wouldn't end with him as a slave. Again.

For a moment, it looked as if Tarrick was equally caught off-guard by the sight of Matthew. Then, his eyes darkened and his jaw clenched as he said a single word: "Alive."

Matthew turned to Samantha. "I agree."

"You can come in," she said.

Green glowing outlines appeared in the air as the hunters teleported forward.

Matthew wasn't going to wait around. He ran into the room, scooping Samantha into his arms and kicking the door closed behind him. Hunters needed to have a general idea of where they were teleporting to, so the door would slow them down for a second.

He dumped power into his speed and ran at the window, shoulder first. Samantha closed her eyes and gripped onto him tight as he burst through the glass. The two of them soared through the air and landed hard on the roof of the neighboring building.

Matthew wanted to make the landing smoother but he wasn't used to carrying around an extra body. After making sure she was uninjured, he shifted her around to his back.

"Hold on," he told her.

She slung her duffle over her shoulder and locked her arms around Matthew's neck while squeezing her legs around his waist.

Matthew looked back. Tarrick was standing at the broken window scowling, his eyes glowing purple and his horns were out, the right one half-broken.

Tarrick raised a phone to his ear. "We've located Matthew. I want all available hunter teams, including the Argonauts, and all warriors to teleport to the North Chicago stone—*now*."

Shit. This place was going to be swarming with hundreds, fuck, maybe thousands of hunters in the next ten minutes.

Matthew took off sprinting over the roof, then jumped to the next building, and the next, rushing along at an inhuman speed. It wouldn't matter how fast he went, the hunters would be on his ass any moment.

All it would take was one or two lucky chain throws or a silver grenade to hit and it'd give them the opening they needed to bring him down. But his biggest worry was the fragile creature on his back.

Silva appeared alone on the roof before him and fired a bolt with her hand crossbow. Matthew dodged out of the way, careful to keep Samantha safe, and jumped to another roof.

She teleported beside him and slashed at his leg with a silver knife. It burned, but it wasn't a serious wound. Matthew healed it as he ran.

The hunter commander gave him no quarter. She teleported beside him again. Before he could react, she slashed his other leg then shot a bolt at him as he broke away from her.

Matthew dodged her bolt and jumped to another roof. She continued to teleport and fire, her bolts whizzing by his head.

She was corralling him, a tactic she was quite proficient in. He wasn't going to play her game—he changed directions and jumped over the side of the building, using the wall to slow his descent and landed in an alleyway. Samantha was still holding on tight.

The rest of the Wardens were down there waiting for him. She had *tricked* him. He shouldn't have underestimated her; she had helped train him after all. She knew his tactics as well as he knew hers.

Chains flew at him. One of the chains, with a collapsing grappling hook at the end, pierced Matthew's wrist and expanded once it was through his skin. Matthew, unable to pull the hook out, yanked on the chain and sent the hunter holding it tumbling forward.

He punched another hunter, sending her into the team. They scattered.

A stake hit Matthew in his chest, missing his heart by inches. He pulled it out, then jumped back up to the roof, bringing the hunter attached to the chain with him. Once he was up there, he grabbed the silver chain, ignoring the pain of his burning hands, and broke a link.

Samantha pulled the hook out, tossing it aside.

Outlines of green light appeared around him as Silva and the rest of the Wardens teleported onto the roof. Matthew was gone before they appeared, heading back towards the clubs. Towards humans. With over seven billion of them on the planet, neither vampires nor incubi could risk discovery. Going into a crowded area might stem the attack. At least until hunters erected veils and cleared out the bystanders.

Matthew needed a better plan, but he didn't know this city and he could only run until the sun rose; which was, thankfully, still some time away.

A hunter appeared next to him. Matthew kicked him in the chest, sending him soaring away. Another appeared nearby and tossed a handful of throwing knives at him. He dodged two and one hit him in his lower arm. He pulled it out as he ran away and licked the wound to speed the healing.

"Go down there," Samantha said and pointed towards an alleyway.

Matthew followed her instruction. Buildings and dumpsters blurred around them until they hit a dead end.

"Up," she said.

Matthew scaled the brick wall and was back on the roofs. Miraculously there were no hunters on this roof, but Matthew could sense them nearby. What had been a single team of hunters was now five teams. He sensed incubi approaching in cars too, but they probably wouldn't give chase until they were sure no bystanders could see them. One of the downsides of living in a major city as an incubus was that they couldn't fly around unless a veil was up.

"Move faster," she said, poking him in the ribs. "Drop down two buildings from here, into the street."

He pushed power into his speed and did as she said. They ended up in a narrow, empty side street, lined with townhouses.

"There. That one. The owner died last week," she said pointing to an unlit house.

He broke open the door with a shove and closed it the best he could. The inside was dark and packed with moving boxes. "We don't have long before they find me, a few minutes maybe. They have trackers," he said as he set her down.

Samantha tugged her scarf loose from her neck and wrapped it around her mouth and nose, which was red from the cold air.

He sensed hunters passing close by but none stopped. "I know you wanted me to save you but I'm not sure I can get myself out of this situation. I might have to fight, and once I start it's hard to stop until I'm…satisfied."

She nodded in agreement. "We need to give them a more important target than us to distract them."

"I'm open to suggestions."

"I have an idea." Clothes spilled out of her duffle bag as she opened it and dug around for something. She took out a dagger. It was jeweled with a gold handle and an intricate design etched on the blade. "Did you see that really tall building three blocks west of here? The one with the flat roof."

"Yeah."

"Can you get us to the roof?"

Matthew shook his head. "We'll be too exposed. Hunters would be all over us and incubi can fly. I'll be tossed around up there."

Samantha tucked the dagger into her jacket pocket before grabbing Matthew's claws and held them in her gloved hands. "I give you my word that this will work."

"I don't know you enough to trust your word, Sam."

"Isn't that what Tarrick said to you?"

Matthew's eyes widened. She was right. Tarrick had said that the night they had met…the night Matthew had been captured. How the hell did she know that?

Samantha squeezed his claws. "What would have happened if he had just trusted you? If the incubi had trusted you?"

Matthew looked away from her. Her words burned. That was the bullshit of everything, he liked the incubi as much as he hated them. At first, he was nothing more than a prisoner, but over time he grew to love their company. Incubi were social creatures and he was no exception.

He liked going to their parties: dancing, chatting, and being accepted as one of them. He even enjoyed fighting for them, and fucking them, and, on the rare occasions they let him, tasting their blood. He yearned to be part of that again, but it was no longer an option available to him. The High King decided he wasn't really one of them—that he was nothing more than a weapon to be used.

And now he was alone again, with only Jet to keep him company.

"I would have served them," he admitted. He would have been loyal if only they had trusted him, it didn't matter to him that he was undead.

She gently yanked on Matthew's claws to pull him closer to her, then pushed down the scarf she had so carefully wrapped around her face moments ago. "Give me a chance and trust me."

"Alright," Matthew said after a moment. "But at least tell me what you are."

She went up on her toes to kiss him on the side of his face, just a peck, and whispered in his ear, "I'm an oracle. And I've seen your future, Matthew."

Four

Matthew wasn't quite sure what an oracle was. He knew the Greeks had oracles, priestesses that gave prophetic predictions, but that was the sum of his knowledge. And he had learned that from human books—the reality might be something far different.

But there was no time to ask her for more information right now. Hunters were closing in on the area. They'd find their hiding spot soon enough.

Samantha was busy shoving her clothes back into the duffle bag and fixing her scarf around her face again.

While she did that, Matthew was planning their next move. Once they reached the building he'd take the stairwell up instead of scaling the outside. It was less of a chance of being picked off by a flying incubus and the hunters wouldn't be able to see up the stairs, making it harder for them to teleport.

"Ready?" he asked Samantha.

She flung her duffle bag over her shoulder. "Yes. The seal has been broken. And I will use it. He will be angry with me, but he forgives. You'll like him."

Matthew had no idea what she was talking about and had no time to find out. He kneeled down so she could climb onto his back again and waited until a team of hunters moved away before running out of the house.

He tried to keep to the shadows and hide as he ran but it wasn't long before a hunter finally spotted him. He dodged their attacks but it became increasingly hard as they converged on his location.

In a two-block radius, he could sense dozens, with more pouring in. Over the hunters' comms he heard calls for backup and positional changes. At least they didn't seem to have any idea where he was headed.

Samantha gave him instructions on where to run and it was making it hard for the hunters to teleport close to him.

When he arrived at the building—this one nearly thirty stories—

he ascended the stairs as fast as he could. He pushed extra strands of power into his speed to gain distance before the hunters figured out exactly where he was.

At the top floor, Matthew burst through the exit and went to the far end of the roof. Samantha slid off his back and took out the dagger from her pocket.

"Whatever you are going to do, do it fast," he said. He had bought them maybe two minutes.

"I need your blood. Lift up your shirt," she said, dagger in hand.

Matthew's trust in her was quickly fading. She didn't wait on him. She grabbed the bottom of his turtleneck, pulled it up, then drove the dagger into one of his blood pouches.

He roared and flashed fangs at her, but she seemed unfazed as she pulled the dagger out.

She rolled her eyes. "Stop it, it's not like you've never been stabbed there before."

He narrowed his red eyes as she cupped her hands under the flow of blood. When she had a handful, she walked forward a few steps and said words in a harsh-sounding language.

She made a fist with her hand and the blood oozed around it, falling to the ground. Small black fissures on the roof began to appear where each of the drops hit.

They weren't cutting through the concrete, but rather looked like they were forming into a portal devoid of all light. Pure blackness. The small drops began to spread, slowly.

Samantha took off her scarf, cleaning her hand and dagger on it. Matthew's skin was already mending, but it would take a while to heal a blood pouch.

Tossing the scarf aside, Samantha opened a side pouch of her duffle bag to pull out a flat bed sheet stuffed in there. She tossed it open and used it to cover up the spreading portal.

"Let all the hunters and incubi gather up here. You need to buy us some time," she said.

At the other end of the roof, the leader of the Hunter Corps and the High King's personal bodyguard, Imperator Prescott, teleported in. Prescott wore black plate armor that looked like something out of ancient Greece, complete with a form-fitting cuirass, arm and leg guards, and leather straps that formed into a skirt. His face was covered by a horned helm that made him almost look like an incubus.

Beside him, a white glow hung in the air for a fraction of a second and Commander Hiroto appeared. He was a kitsune assassin, a fox spirit, but right now he looked human enough; his black cloak and red mask covered everything but his eyes.

Two more members of Prescott's personal team, the Argonauts, teleported in. Considered the best hunters in the corps, Matthew had no hope in a fight against them. But he only needed to buy a little bit of time.

The hunters opened fire, sending bolts and silver grenades his way.

Matthew avoided their attacks, running back and forth on the roof. Hiroto teleported with a flash of white light. Knowing Hiroto's preferred tactic, Matthew turned and was already swiping with his claws when the fox appeared behind him. He ripped five deep grooves across the assassin's chest.

Hiroto, who was shorter than Silva and thinner, cried out as his skin split open. Matthew followed it up by grabbing him and tossing him from the building.

A huge bald hunter, wearing a set of massive silvered gauntlets, teleported in front of Matthew and punched him in the chest. It felt as if he had been smacked by a train and he went flying across the roof, bones broken. He stood and pushed power into healing.

More hunter teams poured into the area, opening fire on Matthew. He dodged the bolts and chains, but he had been pushing himself hard for a while and began to slow.

Prescott held out his hand and, with a green flash, a silver battleaxe appeared in it.

Matthew yanked a sword away from a hunter and kicked him into the Imperator. Prescott sidestepped out of the way and readied himself. Matthew was prepared to face him but the smell of human blood filled the air.

Samantha's blood.

He retreated back to her. She was on her knees, clutching her midsection. Something had hit her but her big coat made it impossible to tell how bad the wound was.

He wanted to pick her up but that might put her in more danger.

"Fucking careless hunters," he growled and charged at a group. He knocked three off the roof and stabbed two—one in the leg and the other in the arm—before the rest got away from him. Other hunters dove to save their friends.

Three silver bolts hit his chest and he snarled as they burned deep.

More hunters arrived. At some point a veil had been erected around the building, hiding the battle from human eyes.

Three incubi swooped down from the sky and landed on the roof. Two he didn't recognize, but one he knew all too well: Vassu. A large, black warrior incubus who had spent months training Matthew.

He was in his incubus form now, armored, ten feet tall with a wingspan triple the size. Terrifying black horns that ended in white tips twisted out of his head and he held a massive double-bladed sword in his hand.

Matthew had a hard enough time beating him when they sparred one-on-one. Now that it was one on…nearly a hundred, there was just no way. The roof was packed with hunters, and the sky above them was full of warrior incubi.

Matthew placed himself between the biggest grouping of hunters and Samantha.

"Stand down, Matthew," Vassu said, his deep voice rumbled through the air, silencing the others.

This was over. They knew it and he knew it. The hunters stopped attacking and surrounded him. Matthew knew what was coming. He knew what they were waiting on.

Gripping his sword tight, Matthew pulled the bolts out of his chest with his free hand. On the ground between them was the sheet, still covering up whatever the hell Samantha had done. Or failed to do since nothing happened and they were out of time.

He watched as Silva and her team teleported in behind Vassu.

A moment later, what they had been waiting on arrived. The High General dropped out of the sky and landed in front of the three incubi. In his full form, and armored now, he was a sight to behold. His black and purple dragonesque wings stretched impressively behind him.

Tarrick's irises blazed with violet fury when they set upon Matthew. It wasn't fair for Tarrick to be so angry, Matthew had saved the general's daughter, and saved both Cullip and Silva from a lifetime of being stuck under another vampire's compulsion...but all Tarrick probably saw was an escaped slave.

When he saw the weapon Tarrick was wielding, panic rose in Matthew's chest and he staggered back a few steps. The kanabō. A weapon that looked like a thick baseball bat except it was five feet long and adorned with square, silver coated metal spikes. Tarrick had beat Matthew to near death with it once. It was the only time Matthew had ever seen Tarrick fight—really fight—and it was the only time he needed to.

Matthew continued backing away until his heel bumped into Samantha's knee.

"There are several ways this can end, Matthew," Tarrick said, breaking the silence. "But none are with your escape."

Matthew swallowed a lump that had formed in his throat. His surrender was inevitable. He feared it. They were going to torture him for a long time and he'd be lucky if he would even be the same man once they were done. His eyes stung with both anger and fear. Although his body no longer required oxygen, his chest heaved. He shouldn't have trusted her. At least if he had run he might have had a chance.

"On your knees," Tarrick said, dark and commanding.

Matthew flexed his claw and held up the sword defensively. He didn't want to kneel before Tarrick anymore. Or anyone.

"No." Matthew stood defiant. They'd have to force him down.

Tarrick motioned to the elite hunters to take Matthew out. But before they could do anything a sensation of overwhelming power washed through the area. Matthew's skin tingled and his chest felt tight.

Tarrick held up his hand, halting their conversation, and looked for the source.

Whatever the hell Samantha had done, it had worked and something was coming. Something big. Something that gave Tarrick pause. Matthew didn't even think such a thing could exist. He fought the urge to smile.

"Fendrel?" Tarrick asked.

A hunter wearing full plate stepped forward. "Not a dragon."

"It's an incursion," Prescott said.

Tarrick shook his head. "It can't be, there hasn't been one in over two thousand years."

"I know, I was there." Prescott's battleaxe disappeared from his hand with a green flash and a longsword with a golden blade appeared in its place. On the hilt were scrolled holy symbols of the incubus goddess. "It's an incursion," the Imperator repeated.

"But the Pit is sealed," Vassu said from behind Tarrick.

Samantha, still bent over and holding her stomach, began to laugh. Guilt flooded Matthew. He had been so focused on Tarrick that he had forgotten about her. Her heartbeat was fading. She strained and said, "The seal has been broken."

Tarrick paused for a moment, his eyes on the oracle.

Matthew reached down and yanked the sheet from the ground. The black portal was only about the size of a door. He could feel creatures on the other side. He could *hear* them calling to him. They wanted to get through. The portal needed to be bigger.

He knew how to help. Instinctually—which was strange but he wasn't really in a position to question it right now—he reached down and touched the portal and poured energy into it. It began to expand at an accelerated rate.

"Impossible...wait, Matthew—" Tarrick said.

Matthew looked up at him with fierce red eyes.

"—I will let you go if you close the portal."

It sounded almost as if Tarrick was pleading with him. But Matthew knew better. He curled his lip at Tarrick. "How could I possibly trust anything you say?"

"You must stop. You have no idea what you're about to unleash."

Tarrick was right. Matthew had no clue, but he was about to find out. He stood and pulled his hand away, and the portal continued to grow at an accelerated rate. Hunters backed away from it.

He could feel the creatures coming.

Matthew squared his shoulders and glared at Tarrick from across the portal. "I've stayed out of the damn war, avoiding you and your army. But that changes tonight. If an incubi or hunter comes anywhere near me I will rip them apart. I'm not on your side, and I never will be, you manipulative fuck."

God, he had wanted to say that for over a year now, ever since

Tarrick had broken his heart. And now they had their warning: stay away or die. Matthew was done pulling punches.

Tarrick pointed his weapon at Matthew. "Take him down," he growled.

Before the hunters could attack, a hand burst through the portal—it was black, clawed, and over five feet in size. A massive arm rose high into the air then slammed down onto the roof, scattering hunters and cracking concrete. The colossal creature the arm belonged to was trying to rip itself free.

Around the hellish arm, human-sized twisted monsters came flying out of the portal. They had eyes of pure black and long claws. A few were wielding crude spears or polearms.

The incubi were in the air and attacking them before they could fly off. Hunters attacked as well, but every monster they cut down was replaced by three more.

"The world will break with his blood," Samantha whispered, and passed out.

Tarrick raised his comm to his mouth. "Dispatch, we have a demonic incursion in Chicago."

Demons. His blood had opened a portal to the Pit? Fuck. Samantha's idea of a distraction certainly had its flare.

It was time to leave. He carefully picked Samantha and her duffle bag up, cradling her like a child, then ran to the stairwell, passing hunters and incubi who no longer cared about him.

As he ran down the stairs, he heard Tarrick ordering all hunters and warriors to be pulled from their current assignments and sent there.

When Matthew exited the building he kept running for miles. Once he was certain that he wasn't being followed, he compelled a human to relinquish his van and drove out of the area with Samantha unconscious next to him.

As he drove, he dug his fangs into his wrist and pressed the cut to her lips in an attempt to heal her.

Still out, she didn't drink. He pulled over to the side of the road and peeled her jacket open to inspect her wounds.

There were two bolts lodged inside of her. One in her upper chest and one in her belly. Her skin was pale and her lips blue, her heart a whisper now.

He cut his wrist deeper and bled on her wounds as he pulled the bolts from her body. The wounds healed as the blood seeped into them. Shoving his wrist into her mouth, he filled it with his blood.

She choked and swallowed a mouthful, then no more. The remaining blood flowed over her lips and down her chin. He hoped that would be enough.

Her heart stopped for a moment and Matthew was getting ready to give her chest compressions when it started back up again. Giving her blood had worked—she was healing.

He waited until he heard her heart get a little stronger, and continued driving.

It was a few hours until sunrise and he had to put as much distance between him and Chicago as possible. With one hand, he dug through her duffle bag until he found her cell phone and tossed it out the window.

He had come to Chicago for some answers about his parents and instead helped open a demon portal, and had an injured human in his care. Nothing had gone as planned. He cussed. Then sighed.

In the rearview mirror, Matthew glanced back at the city's skyline. A part of him, much larger than he cared to admit, hoped that Tarrick wouldn't be killed by the demons.

Five

The next night, Matthew woke with Samantha in his arms. They were in a motel off interstate 80.

She had been in bad shape when he went to sleep, but he couldn't do anything for her other than give her more blood and let her rest. He held onto her as the sun rose and his body shut down for the day.

She wasn't any better at nightfall. Her skin was cold and grey and he was unable to rouse her. Matthew wasn't sure what he could do for her. He had been a firefighter when he was human so he knew basic first aid, but this was beyond that.

Desperate, he drove her to the hospital. The ER admitted her right away. Shortly after, he was waiting outside a room while the doctors worked on her.

Anytime someone tried to move him to a waiting area or comment on the dried blood that ran down his shirt and pants, he'd compel them to go away. He was hungry and irritable. At one point, he considered going to feed, or even stealing some blood packs, but he didn't want to leave in case there was an update on Samantha.

He had agreed to save her and he was failing miserably on that front.

A doctor came out of the room to speak with him.

"Your sister—" the doctor started to say.

Samantha was too old to pass as his kid since she looked just under twenty and he looked like he was in his early thirties. He could have said wife but it felt wrong. So he went with sister. The two of them looked nothing alike except that Matthew had brown hair as well. If anyone questioned it, he'd just compel them to believe whatever story he told them.

"—had to be put on a ventilator. Her major organs are shutting down and we haven't found the cause yet. We're waiting on some lab work now. It should be back soon."

"Thank you, Doctor," Matthew said as the doctor went back into the room, leaving Matthew alone.

She was going to die and it was Matthew's fault. Normally the death of a human didn't concern Matthew too much. He didn't enjoy killing them, and avoided it for the most part, but if one died he'd shrug and move on. But Sam was different. He felt...connected to her. And the longer he was around her, the more his concern for her grew.

He needed help.

Annoyed by the handful of humans buzzing around, he compelled everyone to empty the area, but not before taking a phone from one of them. He sat down on a bench and dialed the number to a vampire call center.

It turned out that the incubi had people everywhere, including phone companies. Hell, they probably owned the companies. They could use a phone's GPS to track vampires down and dispatch hunters to kill them during the day.

It was clever.

In response, vampires had to swap their phones and numbers often, but that made it difficult to get ahold of anyone. So, the vampire general had set up a call center that had a way to keep their species connected. All a vampire had to do was call in with their current number and it was updated in their system.

"6843 Delta," Matthew told the woman who answered the call. "Put me through to Ascelina."

The call rang through.

"Yes?" a male answered. He sounded as irritable as Matthew was.

"Stolus, I need to speak to your mother."

"Matthew. What do you want?"

Matthew didn't respond.

When Stolus finally realized that Matthew wasn't going to answer him he said, "I will get her."

"Matthew, are you well?" a firm female voice asked him. Ascelina. The only vampire lord who had been kind to Matthew. Then again, he had been trying to kill the other lords when he met them so it was a little bit his fault.

"Are you alone? I have something private to ask you." He heard Ascelina ordering people to leave her. Vampires' hearing was sensitive enough to hear each side of a phone conversation and Matthew didn't want Stolus listening in.

"I am alone now. What is wrong?" she asked.

"I have a young woman in my care. Human. She was badly injured. I gave her my blood to heal her but it didn't work and she's dying."

"Did you inject her with your venom after giving her your blood?"

"Venom? What venom?" Matthew asked, confused.

"Did her heart stop at any point?"

"Yeah, why?"

Ascelina ignored his question. "Where are you now?"

"I took her to a hospital. I don't think they're going to be able to save her. Is there anything else I can do? Maybe the witches—"

"Get her out of there," Ascelina said, cutting him off.

"She's in critical condition. If I remove her—"

"She's becoming a vampire, Matthew."

Matthew froze and let long moments pass as he wrapped his brain around her words. Finally, he managed a delayed, "…What?"

"You gave her your blood and she died. You've sired her."

"But her heart restarted," he protested.

"As does yours when you ingest blood. How much did she have before her heart stopped?"

"Not much, just a mouthful, if that."

"Then she will be a weak child. Under normal conditions, we spend the night feeding them blood to prepare them for the change."

It hadn't been like that when Matthew was turned. A vampire overpowered him, shoved his wrist into his mouth, and forced him to swallow a few gulps of blood before the vampire snapped his neck and left, leaving Matthew to change on his own. He never even saw the bastard.

Matthew couldn't believe he was responsible for making a vampire. This was a nightmare. "How can you be so sure that I've sired her? Maybe she's just dying…"

"Matthew," her tone was one of kindness and compassion for his situation. "You feel the connection to her, don't you? And a strong desire to protect her? Why else would you call me over a human?"

He leaned forward and rubbed his forehead. Ascelina's words hit him hard.

"You were right to call," she said. "I have sired many children. Are you near? Can you come to my home with your child?"

"No, I'm not close right now. And I have a child, it's not her." He had a daughter, Lily, that he abandoned the night he was turned. She was a succubus who didn't even know Matthew was still alive. Well, undead anyway. His biggest fear was that the incubi would one day use her against him. It was one of the many reasons he didn't want to fight in the war.

"You don't have to call her 'child'. Some vampires don't when they sire their lover or a friend. But the bond is the same regardless of the name you use."

"Explain this bond to me." Matthew never had any connection with his sire…this was all new to him.

"You'll be able to feel each other's emotions. She will be compelled to follow any direct commands you give her and you'll be able to summon her from anywhere. If she's able, she will travel to you. If you two are near each other, you'll be able to lend her power through the bond so that she can break a feed early or heal quicker.

"The worst of it is that you will become fiercely protective of her, and obsessive in your desire to keep her safe. It will fade in time. Normally it takes about a century for the bond to weaken enough that you can release her. If she dies while a bond is strong, it'll be the worst pain you've ever experienced. Oh, she'll want to seek out her immediate family and kill them. It cannot be prevented, even if you command her."

"This sounds awful."

Ascelina chuckled. "I used to think the same when I was young. But having a child is rewarding. You should keep her away from humans for a few days. When she fully turns, her hunger will be insatiable."

"I remember that. I…slaughtered whole families when I woke."

"Let her feed from you. It'll help. You'll have to teach her to hunt eventually. "

"Jesus. I don't know how the hell I'm going to do this."

He could hear Ascelina's amused chuckle on the other end of the phone. "You survived being a prisoner to the incubus and wiped out the vampire lords of New Orleans…does one little girl scare you so?"

Matthew smiled and leaned back against the wall. "Well, when you put it that way…"

"Do not worry. It'll come naturally. Besides, you don't like being alone and you need more than Jet as company. This could be a blessing for you."

Maybe she was right. He craved company just as any incubus did. But forcing someone into this life by turning them into a vampire was something he *never* wanted.

"In the future, if you give someone your blood, you can inject a venom with your bottom fangs that will prevent a human from turning if they die. I would have taught you this but I assumed you knew."

Matthew had no idea he could inject anything with his bottom fangs, but he would test it out next time he fed.

"I have another question…what can you tell me about oracles?" he asked.

"Have you found one?" She didn't conceal the excitement in her voice.

"Uh, well…the girl…"

"You turned an oracle? Oh. Well, perhaps she will keep her powers because she is weak. Sometimes a weak vampire is able to use a little magic…" She trailed off then remembered his question. "There are quite a few different types of creatures that can see the future, but oracles are the most powerful. They are incredibly rare. It's been many centuries since one has appeared. They see the past and future as a riddle they have to decipher. If they interpret correctly, they know what is, what has been, and what will be. The last one we have knowledge of was seduced and killed by High King Malarath. He used her death to put the dragons to sleep."

"Damn. Malarath knows about her. I ran into Tarrick last night. He was there for the oracle."

"Was he? Our reports say that Tarrick spent last night fighting a demonic incursion in Chicago…she opened the portal?"

"Yeah. It was so we could escape."

"The Pit is unsealed then?"

"That's what she told me. Should I be worried?"

Ascelina said nothing for so long that Matthew thought she might not answer. Then she finally spoke. "Demons are a…difficult foe. Don't let her open any more portals. If a demon gets through, it might expose us to the humans. We can't fight against the demons, the humans, and the incubi, we'd be wiped out."

"Okay, no more portals."

Matthew rubbed his hands through his brown hair and across the stubble on his chin. There was one last thing he wanted to know. Matthew slipped his fingers under his shirt to feel the metal collar at his neck.

"Did your report say if...if Tarrick..."

"He is still alive," she said.

"I'm sorry." He was ashamed that he even asked. Tarrick and Ascelina were old enemies.

"You do not have to be. You are not the first vampire to fall for an incubus. You will not be the last."

Matthew didn't bother denying it. If it had been anyone else but Ascelina he would have. She always understood. If he ever had a reason to fight for the vampires it would be to repay the kindness she had shown him. But he didn't want to fight in a war where he'd be nothing more than a pawn.

"You should come to my home again. I will empty it of any who bother you and help you with your child. I will even send Stolus away for a time."

"I'll consider it. Give me a few nights to sort things out and I'll let you know."

"Be safe," she said and hung up on him before he could say 'bye'. Considering her age, over half a millennia old, her phone etiquette was much better than some of the other vampires he had spoken with. Vampires, unlike incubi, didn't always make an effort to keep up with the times.

Matthew leaned forward on the bench and placed his elbows on his knees while he plotted out what to do next. It'd be easy enough to remove Samantha from here—he'd compel the doctors and nurses to destroy her charts and forget her, and he'd make a security guard wipe the camera footage from the past few hours.

Then he'd acquire a new car and drive for a while to get more distance from Chicago. At some point, he'd find an empty house for them to stay in. He'd make sure she was safe before he went hunting so that he had enough blood for her when she woke.

Drifting across his nose, the faint scent of sweet wine and fragrant oil caught his attention. He looked up and saw a man standing at the far end of the otherwise still empty hall. His skin was dark bronze, so unblemished and smooth that it almost shined. His eyes were golden, and his black hair was short. His face was as humorless as stone.

He was so beautiful and appealing that Matthew would have thought him an incubus if not for the fact his heart wasn't beating and he drew no breath. He had to be a vampire.

How long had the vampire been watching? Had he overheard the phone call?

Samantha…he had to protect her. Matthew's vampire side came forward as he sprung to his feet.

"Whoever you are, I'm not in the mood to deal with anything else right now. Leave or I will kill you," he growled at the man.

"But I have come to—"

"I will not repeat myself."

The man froze for a moment. Then he bowed deeply and left.

If it had been any other night, Matthew would have gone after him to find out why the hell the vampire had just bowed to him. But tonight he had to get Samantha to safety.

Tonight, he had to take care of his *child*.

Six

Sitting in a chair beside her, holding her hand, Matthew watched as Samantha's eyes began to flutter. She had been unconscious since they left the hospital the previous night. It was a few hours after sundown and she was lying on a king-sized bed, still wearing a hospital gown.

He only had one small lamp turned on in the bedroom because he knew her eyes would be sensitive for a while.

Her lids slid open and looked around, confused. "Where am I?" she asked, her voice hoarse from having been intubated.

Matthew put a hand on her forehead affectionately. "You're safe."

"In a house?"

"Yes." He had compelled the owner to invite him in, then sent him away for a few days. "You're safe," he repeated, wanting to assure her that she was in no danger.

She nodded once and drifted back to sleep.

Matthew had covered many miles the previous night before reaching an unclaimed territory. Ideally, he wanted to be in vampire territory, but that was still a few states away. He had fed on the neighbors while Samantha slept and was surprised to discover that if too much distance separated them, his body began to ache.

And the longer he was away, the more he desired to return to her. He ignored the instinct and stayed out late teaching himself how to inject the venom into a person…the last thing he wanted was to turn another human into a vampire. It was strange at first, but he got the hang of it. Once his bottom fangs were in, he pressed his tongue against his lower gums and the venom released. Despite the name, the fluid didn't seem to have any harmful effects on the human.

Before he returned, he stole some fresh clothes for himself and was now in tan slacks and a dark button-up shirt that exposed the metal collar around his neck. He covered it with a scarf, wanting nothing more than to rip the damn collar off, but it would explode and he liked his head in one piece.

With Samantha still sleeping, Matthew went through her duffle bag and laid out all the contents on the bed next to her.

It was mostly clothes, but it also had the dagger and sword he had taken from the battle, along with a simple gold ring that had witch runes inscribed on it, a lighter engraved with the words 'Samantha Bree', a small copper bowl, a wax-sealed glass vial full of a clear liquid, and a bag of toiletries.

He had just returned to his vigil by Samantha's side when he heard scratching at the front door downstairs. Bringing the sword with him, Matthew went to the door and opened it.

A Rottweiler was looking up at him with big brown eyes.

"Where have you been? I could have used you two nights ago," Matthew said.

Jet growled at him.

"Alright. I'm sorry I yelled at you. I've decided we can kill hunters now. But I need you to follow my orders or I can't have you around. Understand?"

The huge dog walked past him. He stood at the base of the stairs and sniffed, then looked back to Matthew, cocking his head.

"I, uh, sired a child."

Jet barked and went up the stairs into the master bedroom. Jet licked Samantha's hand and jumped onto the bed where he curled up next to her. Matthew took his seat again and waited.

He studied her as she slept. He found it strange her features had changed slightly. Her body seemed to fill out a bit and she wasn't quite as boney. Her hair had a luster that it lacked before and her scent of parchment and vanilla was stronger, and far more pleasant to him. Overall, it wasn't a major change—she was still fairly average looking— but there was something different about her. More appealing. The longer he looked at her, the more interesting he found her.

He wondered if this was part of the bond or if others would notice the same thing.

Just past midnight he felt her rouse.

"Hungry…" she said, so quietly that he wouldn't have heard it were he human. She opened her eyes, revealing scarlet irises.

Breathing hard, Samantha struggled to sit up. Matthew helped her while Jet jumped off the bed. She started screaming and put her hands over her mouth.

"It's alright," Matthew said. "Your fangs are emerging for the first time. The pain will pass in a moment."

"Fangs?" she asked, and bit herself on her lip, bloodying it. She whimpered in pain and held her hands out in front of her. She watched as her fingertips began to change into claws. "What is this...?" she asked, and began to cry.

Matthew sat down beside her and grabbed her small wrists. He leaned in and gently licked her lip so that his saliva would heal the puncture marks. Her blood was delicate and sweet.

"I'm sorry, this is my fault. I gave you blood to try and heal you," he said when he pulled back. Her lip already healed. "I-I turned you... you're a vampire."

She didn't seem to care as her eyes settled on his neck. "I'm so hungry."

Matthew unbuttoned his shirt and slipped an arm out of it, exposing his neck and shoulder.

She didn't wait for an invitation. She pushed up onto her knees and wrapped her arms around Matthew to hold him in place as if he was prey. A quiet growl escaped her as she sunk both her top and bottom set of fangs into his shoulder.

Matthew held her close while she drank greedily from him, pulling his blood at a rapid pace. He wanted to tell her to slow down but he remembered how hungry he had been that first night and it had taken him years to control the speed at which he drank. She would be a slave to her instinct for a while. But maybe with his help, she could learn faster than he had.

When she was full, she removed her fangs and sat back, resting against the pillows. She hadn't taken as much blood from him as he thought she would. Ascelina had said she would be a weak vampire, meaning she probably had only one small blood pouch.

"Do you feel better? Did you get enough?" Matthew asked.

She nodded. She held up her hands and watched as her claws drew back. She wiped the last of her tears away from her once again brown eyes. Her fangs receded back into her gums and she touched her teeth, just to be sure.

"It's not your fault," she said. Her vocal cords had healed and her voice sounded strong.

"What's not?"

"It's not your fault I'm a vampire. It's mine."

"I'm not sure how you figure that—"

"I changed the future."

A confused expression crossed Matthew's face.

She looked as if she was about to start crying. "I don't get to see my own future very often…but sometimes I get a prophecy. I saw that… darkness and dust…"

"His name is Tarrick."

"I saw that Tarrick would take me to the tyrant and he would use me. I changed the future by asking for your help. When I change things, Fate demands a price. The price, this time, was my death."

"I don't believe in this fate shit. It wasn't your fault. It was mine—I should have protected you."

She looked down. "The only other time I changed my future was when I was fifteen and I gave my parents the winning lotto numbers. It was only a small pool but I knew they could use the money. They won, and then died in a car crash the next day. Fate hates being messed with. There is always a price."

Matthew still wasn't convinced that it was anything but a coincidence, but he wasn't going to argue with her. "I'm sorry. That must have been hard for you. Do you have any other family?"

She shook her head. That was one minor relief.

Jet jumped back onto the bed and licked Samantha on the cheek. She scratched behind his ear and he plopped down and put his head in her lap.

"This is Jet," Matthew said.

"It's not really a dog, is it?" she asked.

"No. He's a gargoyle. They can change into animals, I guess. I didn't know that until he showed up a year ago and refused to leave me alone. Be careful around him, he can be temperamental."

When Matthew was plummeting down to the ground, facing death at the hands of a vampire named Victor in New Orleans, Jet had caught Matthew midair and saved him.

After Matthew escaped the incubi, Jet had shown up at Ascelina's house a week later. The other vampires weren't so happy to have a strange gargoyle around, but he wouldn't leave…and trying to force a gargoyle to do anything they didn't want to do was pointless. They were stubborn creatures.

"He won't hurt me. He likes me," Samantha said.

Matthew raised an eyebrow. "Is that something you've seen in the future? That Jet likes you?"

"No. I'm just guessing." She patted Jet on his head and he wagged his tail.

"Can you still see the future now, as a vampire?" Matthew asked.

"Yes, but everything's fuzzy right now."

"What happens if you tell me something and I change it?"

"Nothing. Everything I tell you is what will be, so long as I interpret it correctly. I'm the only one that can change things. But I won't. Not anymore. I don't have anything left for Fate to take, other than my soul." She looked Matthew up and down. "I feel strange around you."

"We share a bond now."

"I…can feel it. I can feel that you're worried about me."

Matthew squeezed her arm. "I am. I want to keep you safe and I am not a safe person to be around."

"You're strong. I think you can protect me. The other one will help too."

"The other one?"

Samantha looked around. "You sent him away."

"I haven't sent anyone…oh. Do you mean the vampire in the hospital?"

She settled down onto the bed and closed her eyes. "I don't see everything. I'm tired."

Matthew wondered if she knew anything about his own sire or his parents. But he could find out later. "Rest. I'm going to go out to hunt. Keep her safe, Jet."

The dog barked.

★★★★

Samantha slept until well into the next night. Matthew made sure he was at her side when she woke. He could feel her hunger as if it was his own and found it curious that he cared so much for her well-being.

He took off his shirt as she stirred, so she could bite him wherever she pleased.

Her eyes opened and she studied him for a few moments before rubbing her hands along his chest, tracing his defined muscles.

He chuckled. "What are you doing?"

"Everything feels different now. And you smell really good."

"Yeah, all your senses are heightened. And I smell good because I was born an incubus. From what I was told, I would have been a powerful one too if I hadn't been turned into a vampire. But you knew that, didn't you?"

"That you're a vampire? Yeah."

"Vampubus? How about Incupire?" Matthew laughed.

She giggled.

It struck Matthew that he hadn't seen her smile or laugh once since he first met her. It brought him joy to see her smile; the same joy he felt when Lily laughed for the first time as a baby.

She stopped and her eyes turned red as she watched the pulse on his neck. He tilted his head to the side as an invitation. Her fangs came forward and she fed from him, again holding him possessively.

"Lick the wound," Matthew instructed when she was done. She did and watched with wonder as the skin stitched together.

"We're going to be together for a long time, aren't we?" she asked as she ran her finger over the new skin.

"Yeah, so I've been told. I didn't have a sire bond so I don't really know what to expect. I might mess things up with you. I'm sorry,"

She let her fingers slide down his arm. "Well, this is my first time being a vampire so even if you did, I don't think I'd know it," she said with a smile, her hand moving across his pecs.

"Enjoying yourself?"

She snapped her hand away.

He laughed. "You don't have to stop. I'm an incubus, I enjoy being touched."

"But, it wasn't like that..." Since she had just fed, a hint of red colored her cheeks and she looked away.

"I know. You don't need to be embarrassed."

Samantha studied him. "Will it always be this way?"

Matthew had seen young vampires without their sires, but they were at least a few decades old. "I think it'll fade with time but I'm not sure how long that'll take. I'll ask next time I speak to Ascelina. Do you know who she is?"

"No."

"I thought maybe you might because of your oracle powers. She's a vampire lord. I'll give you her address. If anything happens to me, you are to go to her. Do you understand?"

She nodded. "I'm not all knowing. I only know what Fate allows."

"How old are you?"

"Nineteen. You?"

"I was thirty-two when I was turned and that was nine years ago. By vampire standards, I am still a child. Oh, and vampires count age from the day they were turned. So you are...two days old. Two nights old? I don't know, that sounds strange."

As he rambled, Samantha slipped off the bed and grabbed some fresh clothes Matthew had left out for her. She walked into the bathroom, Matthew following.

She went to shut the door and stopped. "I've never, um, showered in front of anyone before."

"I'll wait out here." Matthew pushed away disappointment. He wanted to stay close to her, protect her.

"No. It's just...I don't think I'd mind if you were in here," she said. "But, uh, I don't know. This is frustrating. I've never felt anything like this before."

"I know what you mean. I think this bond will take a little getting used to." Matthew grabbed the chair by the bedside and dragged it over to the open door, facing it away to allow her some privacy. "I'll just sit here."

While she showered, he told her the basics of being a vampire; stuff that had taken him years to figure out on his own. Silver burned, don't go in sunlight, beheading was the easiest way to kill a vampire but massive damage could do it, stake to the heart rendered a vampire unconscious, there were some plants that affected vampires in strange ways, like foxglove slowed healing and hawthorn could knock a vampire out, what a vampire lord was—she was excited to find out that one day she might sprout wings but that would be centuries away.

"Where's Jet?" Samantha asked as she dried off.

"Keeping watch on the roof. What were you doing on your own in Chicago? Going to college?" he asked as she dressed behind him.

"I, uh, no. I dropped out of high school after my parents died. I'm doing okay right now but sometimes I have days where the visions flood me and I have a hard time knowing what's real or what's an echo of the future. They were talking about putting me into a long-term psychiatric hospital, but I knew what I was. I ran away from the group home they stuck me in."

Matthew winced. He had been in his fair share of group homes as well. When she came to stand before him, he stayed sitting so that he wouldn't tower over her.

"I like it better when I'm alone. There's no one to judge me," she said with a shrug.

Matthew grabbed her hand. "I won't judge you. I have my own fucked up shit too. And you don't have to be alone anymore."

She squeezed his hand. "You don't have to be either."

Matthew smiled at the thought. He really had been isolated during his search to find his sire.

Samantha eyed him up and down. "Can you put a shirt on?"

Matthew laughed. "Why? Are you worried you won't be able to control yourself around me?"

She yanked her hand away. "Ew. No." But she was happy, Matthew could feel it. And, for the first time in a while, he was happy as well.

After Matthew put on a new shirt, they spent the rest of that night talking about vampires and what life might be like for both of them now. Matthew told her about his past: the family he left behind after he had been turned, his wife who had passed on, and his time as a prisoner with the incubi. Samantha seemed to already know most of it, but she allowed him to retell it anyway.

They talked until just before sunrise.

Matthew double checked the curtains a half-dozen times before he was satisfied no light could come through. He sat down in the chair beside her.

"Are you sleeping there?" she asked, her voice tired as dawn approached.

"Yeah. Would you rather I sleep with you?"

She nodded.

Matthew lay down next to her and pulled her into his arms so that they were pressed together, spooning. She sighed against him and fell asleep before he did.

He affectionately stroked her hair and brushed it away from her face.

It was becoming clear that he had messed up the turning and left her frail by vampire standards. She could never fight in a battle. Hell, a single cadet vampire hunter would be a threat to her.

The irony that he was one of the strongest vampires around and had sired one of the weakest was not lost on him. He would do everything in his power to keep her safe and god help anyone that harmed her.

Seven

The next night, Matthew fed Samantha and left her with Jet so that he could go hunting. Once he was done feeding, his plan was to move on from this place. He wanted to get her into vampire territory, which in the States was most anything west of the Rockies, save for Vegas and a small part of Southern California.

Matthew went a few blocks over and found a family sitting around watching a movie. Once he was finished feeding on them, he walked back at a slow pace. He felt the pull to return to Samantha but he also wanted to enjoy the clear night, studying the many stars that filled the sky above him.

A black SUV speeding down the road grabbed his attention. Matthew hid in the shadows as it passed, but he knew right away that hunters filled the car...and they were headed to the house. To Samantha.

Matthew's vampire came forward. He pushed red strands of energy into his speed and rushed after the hunters.

The SUV pulled into the driveway of the house they co-opted. A team of six hunters piled out of the car, joining the two other teams already surrounding the house.

Imperator Prescott, trailed by Hiroto and the rest of the Argonauts, exited the home.

Matthew came to a halt and hid behind a wall. He couldn't sense Samantha inside. Anger bubbled within him. If they had taken her captive, he would kill every incubus and every hunter to get her back.

But before he moved in on them, Prescott gave an order to his hunters. "Alright, pack it up. The house is clear. They're gone."

Gone?

"How long?" a warrior incubus asked. Matthew didn't know him.

"Not long," Hiroto answered. "Less than an hour head start."

"We should have this bastard by now," a man with a southern drawl said. He wore a long leather duster and had two revolver crossbows on his belt. He looked like something out of a western.

"Hush, Lock," Hiroto said and held his hand up while sniffing the air. "We're being watched."

Matthew stilled.

Hiroto sniffed the air again and pointed off in the direction opposite of Matthew. "That way."

Confused, Matthew sniffed the air as well. He could smell a trail of his own scent, going off in the other direction.

As he watched, the hunters teleported away, and he felt a pull inside of him. Samantha. It was as if she was calling to him.

He bolted in her direction. Every part of his being needed to get to her. He had to make sure she was okay and he had no choice in the matter.

He pushed himself to go faster, covering miles in minutes. The houses became sparse in number while low trees and rocky outcroppings blurred around him.

He came upon a single, empty ranch house and sensed Samantha on the far side...along with the scent of sweet wine and fragrant oil.

Matthew's eyes narrowed as he came around the house at full speed.

Before him was Samantha, and next to her, with his hand on her shoulder, was the bronze-skinned vampire he had seen in the hospital.

Matthew lost all control and roared, mad with the need to protect her.

He ran to the vampire and grabbed him by the neck, slamming him into a tree with all his might. Bones cracked and the vampire cried out.

Matthew hoisted him into the air. Small compared to Matthew, the vampire was easy to hold in place. "How *dare* you go near her," Matthew spat the words out and dug his clawed hand deep into the vampire's skin, drawing blood.

The vampire stayed limp and pliant, not resisting. Trying to punish the creature, Matthew pressed his other claw into the vampire's lower abdomen, cutting through flesh with ease. Hot blood dripped out around his clawed fingers. Matthew was going to make this creature suffer for a long time before he killed him.

When the vampire tried to speak, Matthew clamped down tighter, allowing no air to pass through his throat.

A soft hand rested on his arm. Samantha peered up at him, her eyes wide. "I'm okay. He didn't hurt me."

Matthew flashed his fangs at the vampire.

"Please stop," she said.

He would do no such thing.

"Father…" she said. Tender. Pleading.

Matthew growled. He tossed the vampire to the side, sending him sliding across the dirt and crashing into a rocky wall.

He grabbed Samantha and pulled her back, closer to the house. Then, he looked her over checking for any sign she might be hurt, careful not to cut her with his bloody claws.

"I'm okay," she repeated.

Matthew pushed her behind him so that he was between her and the other vampire.

He watched as the vampire healed at an incredible rate, faster than even him. The vampire stood, took several steps away from Matthew, then fell to his knees and prostrated himself, his head so low it bumped the ground.

He said nothing. Matthew wasn't able to tell how old he was. Most of the time he could feel a vampire's age by the power they radiated, but this vampire didn't give off anything. Even lords, who could suppress their aura, gave off something.

"He is fueled by the divine and his wings betray him. Have you seen them? They are beautiful. You will think so," Samantha said from behind him. That made no damn sense and he was too angry to figure it out.

"Who are you?" he growled between his fangs.

"I am Devak, my prince," he said, his face still pointed down at the ground.

"Look at me," Matthew said.

Staying on his knees, he obeyed and looked at Matthew. His dark, golden eyes wide. He didn't breathe and his heart didn't beat, and, again, Matthew thought he could easily be mistaken for an incubus. He was exquisite.

It was strange that his blood was so hot. Even after Matthew fed, he never got that heated.

Matthew flexed his claws. "Explain what you were doing with

Samantha. If I don't like what you have to say, I'll kill you."

"Please forgive me, my prince. I didn't mean to upset you. I...I have been following you in hopes you would call for me. I saw the hunters approaching while you were out—"

"You led them to us?" Matthew stepped forward only to feel Samantha tug on the back of his shirt and he stopped.

"No, I would never, my prince. I overheard them say they were tracking the car you took. Something about cameras in the parking structure."

Fuck. That was careless. He hadn't thought to tell the guard to wipe those as well.

"I knew you had a newly sired child in the house so I led her away from there before the hunters could find her. Your gargoyle came with us." Devak motioned with his head towards the house.

Matthew turned and, sure enough, Jet sat on the roof. Right now he looked like a Rottweiler with black stone wings coming from his back, and he had two rows of short spiky horns running down his body.

Matthew's rage subsided a bit and curiosity stirred. If Jet didn't attack this guy, then he didn't think he was a threat. "Why are you kneeling? And why do you keep saying 'my prince'?"

"You are my prince and I was sent to serve you."

"By who?"

Devak said nothing. His gaze left Matthew's as he looked back at the ground.

"Who sent you?" Matthew demanded.

"He carries a curse. It ties his tongue," Samantha said.

A curse? Matthew didn't know those were a thing, but he was hardly surprised. "Can you at least tell me what I am the Prince of?"

This wasn't the first creature to refer to Matthew as 'prince'; in New Orleans, the vampire lord, Victor, had uttered the word before he died. Since Matthew had no idea who sired him, or who his parents were, he didn't count the idea that he was a prince of some kind out of the realm of possibility, even if it sounded ridiculous.

Devak, again, said nothing. His face twisted with distress.

"Do you know?" Matthew asked Samantha.

"You are the Prince of Princes," she said and offered nothing else.

Great.

Devak looked past Matthew and shifted around on his knees a bit. "My prince, I do not mean to speak out of turn, but we should leave. I set a false trail for the messenger spirit to track, but he would have figured out the deception by now."

"We? Do you think you are coming with us?" Matthew still had no idea who this guy was or what he was doing here. Something was *off* about him and Matthew didn't trust him, even if he had just saved Samantha.

A pained frown painted Devak's lips as he bowed his head. "I made an assumption, my prince, but I shouldn't have. Forgive me. I know I am unworthy to be your guardian, but I will serve you loyally. Should you need me, just call my name and I will find you."

"Guardian?"

"Yes, my prince." Devak dipped his head lower. He didn't seem to understand what Matthew was asking.

"No. I mean, what is a guardian?"

Before Devak could answer, Matthew caught the scent of a fox. Hiroto. It was faint, but approaching. Jet and Devak turned their heads in the direction of the smell.

"If you desire it, I will fight them for you, my prince."

"Stop calling me that. 'Matthew' is fine. And no. I don't want to fight on their terms. Is there a car around here?"

"I think, my pr—" He stopped himself. "—uh, around the back."

"You stay here," Matthew said to Devak, then pulled Samantha along with him to check out the car. There was an SUV parked next to the house. Samantha picked up her duffle bag. Matthew was relieved she brought it since it carried the weapons and extra clothes.

"Devak will drive," Samantha said.

"I haven't decided if he's coming with us."

She crossed her arms and stood her ground. "He will drive, Jet will sit in front, and we'll be in the back together."

Matthew sighed. "I suppose you've made up your mind on this."

"I see the future."

"I think you're bullshitting me right now. Okay, fine. Go sit in the car, but you should know that I'll kill him if I feel like it so don't get too attached."

When Matthew came back around the house, he found Devak still on his knees. "I once had to kneel before another and wasn't allowed to rise until they told me. Is that what you're waiting on?"

"Yes, my prince."

"Alright." Matthew paused for a moment, finding this situation ridiculous. "Okay, here are some rules. You seriously need to stop calling me 'my prince', it'll make us stand out and—really—since I don't know why you are doing it, it's pissing me off. No more kneeling either. If you touch Samantha, I'll kill you. If I find out this is some sort of sick trick, I won't kill you. I'll torture you until you wished you were dead and then I'll keep going. Do you understand?"

"Yes."

"Good. Then get the hell up. Apparently you're driving, and you—" Matthew turned and pointed up to Jet on the roof, "—are in the front seat. Put your wings away. And no, you cannot roll the window down."

Jet whimpered.

Moments later the group was underway, the scent of the hunters fading behind them.

They didn't have keys for the car, but Devak touched the hood and the engine revved to life by itself. Matthew had never seen a vampire do that before.

He put his arm around Samantha and she leaned against his chest. Jet pawed at the button to roll down the window but Matthew had locked the windows from the driver's side before they left.

Devak took the job he had been given seriously and stayed focused on the road, heading west.

Once the danger of the hunters seemed to have passed, Matthew broke the silence. "If you have a phone, ditch it. We'll pick up new ones later."

"I've enchanted my phone so it cannot be tracked but I will toss it if you desire," Devak said and pulled it from his pocket.

"You can use magic?"

"In a way. I need a power source in order to manipulate magic that comes from the earth."

"Alright, keep your phone for now."

Devak nodded and set it in the cup holder beside him.

"What is a guardian?" Matthew asked again, wanting a damn answer this time.

"I...cannot say. Please forgive me."

Samantha sat up a bit. "It'll be made clear tomorrow."

This was getting old. "This curse you have, can it be broken?"

"Yes," Devak said. Matthew could tell he desperately wanted to tack a 'my prince' onto the end of everything he said.

"You know about me? What I am?"

"Yes. I have all the answers you seek."

Matthew watched him drive. A year of dead ends only to have some vampire come along who held the answers he wanted. It felt a little unbelievable. This guy could be lying to him, but he couldn't help the swelling of hope that filled his chest.

"And if the curse is broken, can you tell me about my parents? My sire?"

"Yes. I will be able to explain everything."

"Do you know what we have to do to lift the curse?" Matthew knew nothing about curses. Maybe witches could help.

Devak frowned. "I wish I did. The one who put it on me also erased many of my memories. For a time, I forgot even who I was. It wasn't until last year they began to return to me. I've been looking for you for a long time."

"Do you have any ideas how we could break the curse, Sam?"

She chewed at the inside of her cheek as she thought. "Hmm. Maybe, but the time isn't right yet."

"What does that mean?"

She shrugged. "I don't know, but it'll come to me."

Matthew tried his best not to be frustrated with her but right now he was struggling. He noticed that Devak kept glancing in the mirror at Samantha.

"Is there something you wish to say?" Matthew asked.

"Yes. Opening a demon portal is extremely dangerous for you. If they find out what you are they will not stop until you've been captured or killed. Having both the demons and incubi after you puts you in too much danger."

"You can relax. We won't be opening any more demon portals."

"Not true," Samantha said.

Matthew rubbed his face. "Alright...then we will do our best to not open a portal if we can help it."

Devak accepted the response with a nod.

The drive passed in silence until they reached Nebraska. Matthew knew of at least two smaller incubus households in this area, but he wasn't worried because they were owned by social incubi with only a few hunter teams stationed at each.

"That one," Matthew said as they drove around a neighborhood. He picked out a townhouse that had only a single occupant who was awake.

They parked in the driveway and Matthew knocked on the door. Samantha was behind him with her duffle bag, with Jet by his leg and Devak in back, keeping an eye out for danger.

A middle-aged woman answered.

"Don't be afraid, we're your old friends, invite us all in," Matthew said.

"It's wonderful to see you all again, come on in," she said with a warm smile as the compulsion washed over her.

Once inside, Matthew gently grabbed the woman's chin and met her eyes. "You're going on a much-needed vacation. Go pack and call your work to let them know you'll be out for the next three days."

Samantha tossed the duffle on the living room couch while Jet scratched at the door to go back outside. Devak opened it for him to let him out.

They waited in the living room for the woman to finish the tasks Matthew had given her.

"She smells like fresh bread and butter," Samantha said as she watched the woman walk to the door, ready to leave. Her eyes had turned a light red and her fangs were out.

Matthew set his hand on Samantha's shoulder. "You fed already tonight. Are you still hungry?"

Samantha was practically drooling, her eyes fixed on the woman. "Can I taste her?"

"You won't be able to stop once you start. Are you sure you want to kill her?" If Samantha wanted it, he'd let her—she was a vampire after all—but he was hoping to spare the pain and guilt of taking a life.

Samantha didn't answer. Her pink tongue darted out and licked her lips. She stalked forward as a lust for blood consumed her.

Matthew grabbed her shoulder and *leant* her power. It was an odd sensation. For a split second it felt as if the two of them were one—Matthew slightly weaker and Samantha slightly stronger. It was enough that Samantha stopped thirsting for the woman's blood. She blinked hard several times and took a step away.

"No," she said. "I don't want to kill her. I want to taste her. I've only ever had your blood."

He had an idea, something he had once seen another sire do with their child. Matthew cradled the woman's face in his hand and looked at her eyes. "May I take a little of your blood?"

"Anything for a friend." The woman smiled and tipped her head to the side to expose her neck.

He sunk his fangs into her and pulled on her blood, holding it in his mouth without swallowing. He drew back and leaned down to Samantha, pressing his mouth to hers. She kept her mouth sealed as if confused by what was happening, but Matthew stayed there until she parted her lips. He filled her mouth with the blood.

He broke away. "How was that?"

She looked dazed for a few moments, then she looked away and shifted about.

"Is something wrong?" He worried he had done something incorrect, that he had hurt her somehow.

"No. It's just…I've never been kissed before," she whispered.

Matthew had never even considered that she had never been kissed and that she was probably a virgin. "I'm sorry, I should have thought of that."

"No. It's okay, I just…I have bugs in my stomach. Can I go rest?"

"Yeah, of course."

She grabbed her duffle and ran upstairs to the master bedroom.

"Are you hungry?" Matthew asked Devak, who had taken up an unobtrusive spot in the corner of the living room and watched in silence.

"Thank you, but no."

Matthew licked the woman's neck to seal the bite marks, erased her memories of what had just transpired, and sent her on her way.

Now that he was alone with Devak, he studied him closer. Devak's skin showed no sign of the wounds Matthew had caused. His shirt, a light button-up, had dried blood and rips in it where Matthew had pressed his claws in.

He was a head shorter than Matthew. His amber eyes were watchful of every movement Matthew made, and when Matthew stilled himself, Devak went about analyzing the room.

Matthew knew what he was doing—he was looking for escapes, memorizing objects, identifying potential dangers. Matthew had been trained to do the same. Devak was a warrior.

It looked as if he wanted to speak, but he stood silent, his body primed to take action against any dangers.

"You don't need my permission to speak. If you have something to say, say it," Matthew said.

"I am surprised you've chosen to sire a child when you are still so young yourself."

"Yeah. I don't want to call her an accident, but..." Matthew trailed off and Devak nodded his understanding. "Does the curse prevent you from answering everything? Like, how old are you?"

"Not everything. But that is not the easiest question for me to answer." He bit his bottom lip to hold back a 'my prince', then continued. "I have been to places where time is not always consistent. I was born in Egypt, and not yet an adult when the Pyramid of Giza ended construction."

"That puts you at around, what? Forty-five hundred years...Jesus, you're *really* fucking old. Ancient Egyptian..."

"Yes."

Matthew took a step back. He had never been around a creature so old before. He knew they existed, there was the vampire Queen, and the incubus High King, both of whom were older than that according to rumors.

Now Matthew regretted threatening him; he had to be incredibly powerful.

"You don't need to fear me, I'm your servant. Yours to use as you see fit. I'm sorry it took me so long to find you."

"We'll see, I guess," Matthew said and looked at the window. The space around the curtains was beginning to lighten.

Devak took a step towards Matthew. "I can sense your incubus side is hungry. Would you like to feed from me?" His voice, much like his eyes, reminded Matthew of honey: thick and sweet.

It was a tempting offer since Matthew hadn't fed on anything but blood since Chicago. Devak was mouthwateringly attractive, even if he never smiled, but Matthew had a feeling he might be around for a while. He didn't want to make things more complicated than they already were. For now, he'd stick to sleeping with nameless humans that he cared nothing for. Also, he didn't trust Devak yet, even if Samantha did. "No, I'll go out tomorrow when the sun sets."

Devak nodded. "I will keep guard during the day."

Matthew blinked. "Don't you need to sleep?"

"No."

"But the sun..."

"I can go out in the sun."

"As a vampire?"

"I am not a vampire. I am a guardian."

"Any hints as to what that is? You seem like a vampire. Kind of."

Devak bowed his head. "I am sorry, my prince."

Matthew groaned and rubbed his eyes. "Alright, I've had enough of this shit for today. You do whatever it is you do, I'm going to bed."

Matthew marched up the stairs and crawled into bed next to Samantha, who was already asleep. He hoped that someone could give him some answers tomorrow night.

Eight

When Matthew woke, he was sitting in an antique clawfoot tub full of hot water, naked except for the collar wrapped around his neck. Surrounding the bathtub, fine white and red cloth draped from the ceiling and cascaded down to the floor. The delicate material glistened as if catching the sunlight from unseen windows, but it couldn't be day because Matthew could move around just fine.

A breeze rolled through the room, causing the cloth to sway gently. The pleasing scent of incense and cherries filled Matthew's nostrils and he relaxed into the water and closed his eyes.

"May I join you?" a youthful voice asked.

Languid, Matthew opened his eyes and smiled. Standing next to the tub was Hiroto, and he was completely naked.

This wasn't real. Matthew shouldn't have gone to sleep so hungry, but at least this dream was pleasurable.

Slender, with subtle muscles, Hiroto had bright red lines on his face and body that were a striking contrast to his ivory skin. They looked as if they were painted on by quick brush strokes. His chest had no hunter runes, but it did have five healing slash marks across it.

Hiroto's brown eyes had a long black slit down the middle, the irises were so big Matthew could no longer see white around them. Fox eyes.

Matthew's gaze drifted to Hiroto's cock. It rested among a small nest of white hair. It was smaller than average but it was well proportioned for his stature. Hiroto's fluffy white fox ears twitched while he waited for an answer.

"Yes. Please join me," Matthew said and sat up a bit to make room.

Hiroto stepped into the bath, his feet between Matthew's legs. He eased himself into the water and sat on Matthew's lap.

Matthew used the edges of the bathtub to pull himself up fully and began caressing Hiroto's shoulders, tracing the red markings with his fingers.

"Little fox." Matthew's breath hit Hiroto's neck and he followed it with a gentle lick.

"You've wanted to do this for a while, haven't you?" Hiroto asked and pressed his butt back. Matthew's cock rose in response.

"Mm," was the only sound Matthew made as he ran his fingers over Hiroto's chest, lightly tracing the scarred claw marks he had given to Hiroto back in Chicago. "I am sorry about these."

"Are you?" The fox sounded more surprised than angry.

"Yes. I didn't want to hurt you but you know what will happen to me if I'm captured."

"Perhaps if you turn yourself in—" Hiroto stopped when Matthew's fangs came down and he growled. "Are you just going to hold me, or are you going to fuck me?" the fox asked instead.

Matthew pressed a kiss onto the back of Hiroto's neck and squeezed one of the fox's perfect ass cheeks.

Hiroto arched his back in response, turning up his ass and giving Matthew better access. Matthew rubbed the outside of Hiroto's hole, gradually working an oozing lubed finger into it.

Hiroto moaned.

"You're so tight, I don't know if you can take me," Matthew said. Assuming his cock would even stay hard. It'd be pretty shitty to lose an erection in a dream, but so far his dick was behaving.

"If you go slow, I'll be able to."

Matthew gradually worked a second finger into Hiroto, whose whole body began to tremble. Matthew reached his free hand around and gripped Hiroto's cock. He slid his palm up and down it, eliciting breathy sighs from the small fox.

The sighs turned to pleading whimpers when Matthew pressed his fingers against Hiroto's prostate.

"Little fox...may I bite you?" Matthew asked. He hated that he asked. He always asked. Even the humans who couldn't say no because of his compel...he always asked.

He should just sink his fangs into his neck and take what he wanted—he was a damn vampire after all. But he couldn't bring himself to do it, not without permission. He feared that if he didn't ask there would be consequences, even though that wasn't the case anymore. Fuck Tarrick. This was his doing.

"I will let you, if you answer a question for me."

Matthew pressed against Hiroto's sweet spot once again to punish him for not giving up his blood. Hiroto squirmed and his breathing became labored. Matthew's own hard dick pressed against the fox's smooth ass. "What is it you wish to know?"

"Why did you take the oracle?" Hiroto asked between heavy breaths.

"I…" Matthew looked around the area again. Everything felt off. He rarely dreamed and when he did, it was never like this. It was never so vivid. He removed his fingers from Hiroto. "This isn't a dream."

"Never said it was. Don't stop, we're both enjoying this."

Matthew didn't want to stop, but something was wrong. "What's going on here?"

The smell of the incense and cherry blossoms drifted back to Matthew. His whole body felt heavy. He leaned back and let his arms drift around in the water.

"Why do you still have her with you? Are you taking her to the vampires?" Hiroto asked.

Matthew's eyes turned red but he had grown too weary to bring his claws forward. Why did Hiroto want to know about Samantha? "No. She's mine. You will never get her."

Hiroto swiveled around on Matthew's lap to turn and face him. He ran his hands along Matthew's face. His eyes smiled as always. "No need to be angry. You care for her for some reason, I was only wondering why."

"Is it so astonishing that I care for someone? Or do you think as the incubi do: that I am a soulless weapon, to be locked away until I'm needed?" Sorrow broke his voice.

"Shhh," Hiroto said and ran his fingers through Matthew's hair, then across his collar. "I don't believe that. I know you care for people and I know those people hurt you. I can feel you suffering even now."

Matthew tried to lean forward so that he could rest his head on Hiroto's chest, but he found it too hard to move and instead sank deeper into the water. Everything but his face was submerged. Hiroto sat weightless on top of him.

At the edge of the bathtub, a dark figure appeared wearing skintight black clothes adorned with many leather laces. The figure's face was blurry.

"Move away from him," a deep voice said.

Matthew squinted and tried to focus on the figure.

Hiroto's eyes widened. "So it's true…"

The figure raised his hand and a blast of bright light came from it, hitting Hiroto and sending the small fox tumbling out of the bath and into the hanging cloth. He fell to the ground, tangled in it.

Matthew sunk under the water and looked up at the figure.

"Give me your hand and I will lead you from here," it said to him. The words sounded distant and distorted.

Matthew tried to raise his hand but he couldn't move.

"Fight it. Samantha is in danger."

Sam…he had to save her.

Matthew surged out of the water, sending waves over the side. The figure was clear now—it was Devak, who held his hand out to Matthew. The moment their skin touched, a blinding light surrounded them.

Matthew gasped and sat up. Confused, his brain struggled to process what was going on. Bit by bit he pieced together his surroundings.

It was nighttime and had been for a while. He was dry and in the same clothes he had fallen asleep in, slacks and a button-up shirt.

Samantha stood at the foot of the bed, watching him, her face wet with tears. In front of her lay the duffle bag, all packed and ready to go. The silver longsword rested on top of it.

Devak stood beside him, grasping Matthew's hand and wearing the same outfit Matthew had seen in the dream. Leather laces ran down the sleeves and the front of the fitted shirt. His dark pants were also tied by laces. The clothes suited him but Matthew wondered where the outfit came from.

"What happened?" Matthew asked.

"The spirit fox can track anyone. He can pull you into his mind and use it to locate you. If there's a leystone nearby, they will be here soon. We must leave," Devak said and released his grip.

"How did you get me out of there? What did you do?"

"I am a guardian. He is only a messenger. His power is no match for mine. I would have intervened sooner but I didn't know he had you until Samantha—"

"Sam," she corrected, drying her eyes.

"—until Sam came down and told me you weren't waking. We must leave this place. Now." Devak grabbed the sword and tossed it to Matthew, who caught it as he stood.

"Where are we going?" Samantha asked.

Matthew gripped the hilt of his sword tight. "I don't know. There's an incubus estate not far from here, we don't have much of a head start."

"We should go there, to the leystone," Devak said, following Matthew and Samantha as they ran down the stairs.

Matthew glanced back over his shoulder. "You're kidding right?"

Devak shook his head. "They won't expect us to go to it, that'll give us an advantage."

"I don't see the point. They'll be here before we can break it…"

"We won't be breaking it, my prince, we will use it," he said as they ran outside. The moon was almost new and clouds covered the stars.

"How?" Matthew asked. "Vampires or incubi can't activate the runes. You have to have magic…oh. You can do it?" Devak had said he could use magic if he had a source.

"Yes. And after, I can scramble the leylines so that no one will arrive at their intended destination for a few hours."

Matthew ushered Samantha into the back seat. Jet hopped off the roof and joined her in the back.

"Keep your head down," Matthew told her, then turned to Devak. "I'm driving." As soon as he was behind the wheel, he tore out of the driveway and raced down the road. "Going to the stone is too risky, we're better off just driving out of here. I'll try to lose them."

Devak shifted in his seat to better face Matthew. "Because of the mind breach, the fox will have your trail for a while. We need to teleport out of their range or kill them. I know their leader—if we are to kill him his armor must be removed first, otherwise he is nearly invincible."

"Seriously?"

"Yes. It holds magic that is beyond my power to manipulate."

Devak looked just as somber as ever, and Matthew realized that he hadn't ever seen the guardian smile. Not even once. "How do you know him? Or is that something you can't tell me either?"

"I can, and will…but is this the appropriate time? We must settle on a plan."

Devak was right. Matthew would ask him later.

"Alright." Matthew gripped the wheel while he considered their options. "Let's say we use the leystone. The incubi estate has two teams of hunters and if they know I'm here, they'll send more. The stone is outside, in a courtyard. I've only been to this place once, for a party, but I didn't see any vamp traps or wards by the stone, but that was over a year ago. And the incubi that live there aren't warriors. Can you choose the destination?"

"Yes. Do you know of a safe location to teleport to?"

"All the ones I know of are in the middle of incubi houses. There's one in Colorado that's hidden up in the mountains, there aren't even any roads leading up to it. The incubus there is a warrior but she only has one team of hunters. If you can fight, we'll be able to handle them."

"I can fight. When we are closer to the stone, I'll summon my weapon."

"Summon your weapon?"

Devak nodded. "You will see."

This plan might work. Maybe.

"I'm putting a lot of trust in you right now and I don't even know you. If you fuck me over I'll do everything in my power to hurt you," Matthew said.

"I give you my word—I will not fuck you unless you wish it."

Matthew glanced over at Devak. He wasn't sure if the guardian had misunderstood or was joking around. He got his answer when a sly smile pulled at the corners of Devak's full lips. Then it was gone again almost as quickly as it arrived.

Matthew shook his head and looked in the rearview mirror. "Jet, will you be fighting with us? You can kill the hunters this time."

Jet barked and the fur on his body pressed into his skin, turning into hard black rock. His face twisted into a terrifying snarl that was frozen in place. Two sets of spikes ran down the length of his body, ending where his wings would emerge once he was out of the car.

Samantha reached out and patted his head. He wasn't moving but Matthew could sense he liked it.

"Sam, they don't know you are a vampire yet, or that I sired you.

I'd like to keep them in the dark about it. Can you try and keep your vampire side hidden?"

"I'll try."

"Do you have ear plugs in the duffle by any chance?"

"No."

Damn. The alarms were going to hurt her. He had mastered shutting down his senses, thanks to Ascelina, so they shouldn't be too bad for him, but he worried for his child.

"There they are," Devak said and pointed at a pair of headlights in the far distance coming down an otherwise empty road.

"Think we could drive by them without them knowing it's us?"

Devak closed his eyes, raised up his palms, and said, "La'mast. Na'mori." He opened his eyes. "No. But I will destroy their car and slow them. Keep moving to the house and I will meet you there. Stop the car."

Matthew slammed the brakes. "Why did we stop?"

"I need a moment for my armor and weapon to arrive."

"...Arrive?"

"Yes." Devak offered no further explanation as he got out of the car.

In the back, Jet pawed at the door and Samantha let him out. He jumped onto the roof of the car and finished morphing into his true gargoyle form; his stone wings sprouted from his back and his front arms made snapping sounds as they transformed into limbs that looked less like a dog's, and into something that looked more humanesque.

The night sky grew lighter. Matthew looked up and watched as a jagged line of pure light formed high in the clouds. The sky split open and from the light came two meteors, one right after the other, plummeting towards the earth.

Devak stood a few feet in front of the car. The scent of powerful blood filled the air but Matthew couldn't see a wound.

A few seconds later, the area became as bright as day when one of the fiery meteors veered off course and rocketed at the hunters' SUV.

Green light filled the car as all six of them teleported out right before the meteor hit and turned it into a ball of fiery, twisted metal. The sound was deafening.

Devak leaped into the air and massive wings burst from his back.

Matthew's jaw dropped. They were made of blood, Devak's own blood. They weren't like incubi or vampire wings; these ones had a dozen individual tendrils that curled and coiled behind him.

He had never seen anything like it.

The second meteor slammed into Devak and engulfed him in bright light, blinding Matthew for a moment. He blinked hard and, when his vision cleared, Devak was levitating in front of the car, wearing impressive black armor. With his wings floating behind him, he looked downright intimidating.

Once again, Matthew really regretted threatening Devak. He had no idea what the hell a guardian was but it was clear he outclassed Matthew.

Devak flew at the wreckage of the hunters' car. He dove down and grabbed the object that had been encased in the meteor.

It was a maul. A massive sledgehammer-like weapon with a thick handle and an oversized black metal head.

Matthew, so engrossed with watching Devak, had forgotten that there were hunters out there. That is until Hiroto teleported next to the driver side door in a flash of white light.

Matthew kicked open the door, forcing Hiroto to dodge out of the way. Jet leaped from the roof and swiped at Hiroto, hitting him in the leg as the hunter retreated. Jet pressed his advantage and savagely clawed and bit at the kitsune assassin until he was forced to teleport away from the area.

Matthew could run faster than a car, and they were less than two miles away from their destination. "Grab the bag, we're running the rest of the way."

Samantha slid out of the car with the duffle and he scooped her up, holding her protectively against his chest. He took off down the road, pushing power into his speed. Flying above them, Jet and Devak followed.

Imperator Prescott appeared in front of Matthew, holding a silver battleaxe.

Shit.

Matthew had left his sword in the car.

Devak swooped down and swung his maul at the hunter leader. He missed; Prescott dodged out of the way, but it gave Matthew an opening to get the fuck out of there with Samantha.

The Imperator charged at Devak and the two of them became locked in combat. Prescott parried Devak's swings and countered; the silver battleaxe hit the guardian's upper arm, leaving a deep, gaping wound behind.

Devak roared and his eyes turned red. But it wasn't like a vampire where only the irises changed color. Rather, his entire eyeball became a deep pool of crimson. He flashed long fangs and his soft fingers transformed into horrendous claws.

For a creature that wasn't a vampire, he sure looked like one right now.

Matthew gripped Samantha tighter as he rushed away from the battle. Desire tugged deep within him. He wanted to join the fight, but Matthew ignored the urge. Protecting Samantha was his only goal right now.

As he ran, he glanced back. Devak was still on Prescott—both seemed equally matched warriors. Devak would land a blow, Prescott would shrug it off and land one of his own, which Devak would, in turn, heal.

Unfortunately for Devak, Prescott had a team trained to fight together. The cowboy hunter opened up with his hand crossbows sending a volley of bolts at Devak. Devak whipped them out of the air with his wings, but Prescott used the distraction to land a blow deep into his side. It slowed Devak just long enough for a different hunter to move behind him and land a half-dozen cuts along the exposed skin of his neck. At the same time, Hiroto tumbled by and drove a dagger through a weak spot in Devak's armor on the shoulder.

Matthew came to a stop. He considered going back but Devak broke away from the fight by leaping up into the air.

Jet dive-bombed into Prescott, pinning him under his heavy body. The gargoyle wasn't able to bite through the armor but he was trying his hardest. He didn't see the rest of the hunters converging on him.

Matthew whistled. "Come, Jet. There's more this way." The gargoyle swiped at Prescott's helmet one last time then flew away.

Matthew turned to resume the sprint to the house when a green outline appeared in front of him. Devak dove down and was already mid-swing with his maul as the hunter teleported in. The head of the weapon smacked hard into the hunter's chest with a *crack* and the hunter went flying away.

"Fall back," Prescott barked at his team.

"Where the fuck are they going?" one of them asked.

"Dispatch," he heard Prescott reporting. "Matthew, a blood guardian, a gargoyle, and the oracle are headed to Lord Kristok's house. Get the incubi to safety, and we need gargoyle busters."

"They goin' for hostages?" the cowboy asked.

"No," Hiroto said. "Guardians can activate stones."

"Well, shit."

Matthew no longer bothered to listen to them. It was using too much energy and he needed it to keep his speed up.

Alarms filled the air as a midsized mansion came into view. Samantha squirmed at the sound of the alarms.

"Stop," Devak said.

Matthew slid to a halt.

Devak held out an arm. "Let me take her. They have no warriors in the air right now. I can protect her and you can focus on getting to the stone."

Matthew pulled Samantha away from Devak instinctually.

Devak frowned. "I won't let any harm come to her and it will free you up to fight."

He was right. With no small amount of reluctance, Matthew handed Samantha to Devak who grabbed her in one arm and held his weapon in the other. He took off into the air, Jet flying behind them.

Matthew flexed his claws and surged forward.

They were at the house in moments. Four hunter teams were there waiting for them. Matthew let out a growl and sped up, running at one of the teams.

He hit the first hunter with a blow to the chest, ripped the heart out of the next, the throat of the third, and stole the sword out of the fourth's hand, kicking him in the knee, shattering it. Matthew cut off the head of the fifth, and the sixth teleported away in reaction to watching five of his team members go down in a fraction of a second.

The sixth hunter didn't live long—when the hunter reappeared, Jet was there waiting for him and ripped him apart savagely with bone-crushing jaws and sharp claws.

Matthew had warned Tarrick that he'd kill any that stood in his way, and he hadn't been lying. He bounded onto the roof while avoiding bolts, and cut the arm off a hunter who foolishly tried to stake him.

Devak landed near the stone in the courtyard and held up his hand to form an invisible shield around him and Samantha. Chains and bolts dropped harmlessly to the ground when they hit the barrier.

Samantha had her palms pressed against her ears, curled up in pain from the alarm.

The stone glowed as a team of hunters tried to teleport in. Devak dropped the barrier and touched the stone. The glow faded.

"Jet!" Matthew called as Jet tore into the chest of a hunter. "Come."

Matthew jumped and landed beside Devak and Jet followed behind.

Around them, the Argonauts appeared.

Devak said something to Prescott in a language Matthew didn't know and Prescott sneered, looking right at Matthew. "Don't get too used to your freedom. Not even a *blood guardian* will be able to protect you from me."

Before Matthew could respond, Devak touched the stone and they teleported away.

Nine

Matthew, Devak, Jet, and Samantha appeared in a basement that housed a teleport stone. This was Lady Sabine's home, a warrior succubus that Matthew liked quite a bit. He had been here for a dinner once when vampires had attacked.

They were alone and it was quiet until Samantha began to vomit up black blood. Devak rubbed her back to comfort her. Matthew had completely forgotten how terrible teleporting was the first time.

Alarms sounded. Samantha sobbed in pain between heaves.

Matthew took her from Devak and pulled her into his chest once she had stopped vomiting. He shared his power with her through the bond and her pain subsided.

"Is that better?" Matthew asked.

She nodded but still covered her ears.

Devak, whose wings were receding into his back, set his maul down and put both hands on the stone. He closed his eyes and the green runes began to flicker. When he opened his eyes again, they were back to his dark, honey color. "It is done, the leylines are scrambled. They will not even be able to teleport to a nearby stone, if there is one."

"There might be anti-vampire wards on all the exits to the outside, can you handle those?" Matthew asked.

"Yes."

Matthew set Samantha down in the corner. "Stay here, don't come out until we tell you to. Jet, can you stay with her?"

Jet growled at him. It sounded like rocks tumbling together.

"You're a damned gargoyle, don't act like you don't love babysitting. There will be plenty of other battles for you to kill whatever you want."

Jet sat down and froze in place in front of Samantha.

Matthew heard two hunters running down the hall to see what had caused the alarm. Chances were they had no idea what had happened back in Nebraska.

Matthew waited until they were by the door and kicked it open. It smashed into the hunters.

He ran out and killed them both with quick stabs of his sword. Over their comms he could hear requests for a report. Matthew picked one up and pressed a button to shut off the alarm.

Devak headed towards the ward on the front door but two hunters appeared in front of him, cutting him off. He swung his maul into the head of one, bashing it in, and kept his momentum going, smashing the second hunter in the chest, bringing the hunter down.

The remaining two hunters of the team teleported between Matthew and Devak.

Devak rushed at one while Matthew took the other, skewering the hunter on his sword and cutting upwards. The human's torso slid in two different directions. Devak knocked the legs out from under the other hunter with a swift swing of his weapon and stomped on the hunter's neck with his armored boot. The human choked to death with a gurgling sound.

A gasp drew their attention.

They turned to find Lady Sabine standing in the hallway wearing nothing but a silky slip. She was tall and beautiful, with a warrior build.

"Matthew...what have you done?" Horns grew from her head and her eyes turned a glowing blue.

"I..."

"These hunters were my friends." Sabine's body grew in size and claws came forward.

Matthew looked around at the dead hunters. He had never wanted to kill them but they were a threat, and now that it was more than just his life at stake, he would do whatever was necessary to survive. But it still pained him. "I didn't want it to come to this. I wanted to be left alone but Tarrick and your High King won't let me be. I'll let you live if you stand down."

"You killed my friends," she said, her voice quaking with rage.

"You have no weapon, no armor on, and you're outnumbered. You know what I'm capable of. You don't have to die."

Sabine studied Matthew. She was a skilled warrior, surely she'd see that it was a hopeless fight for her. When it looked like she was starting to accept the fact that this was not a fight she could win, a quiet growl came from the smashed doorway that led to the basement.

Samantha stood there. Her vampire form was out.

Matthew didn't blame her for coming up but he wished she hadn't. She had done well up until this point, considering she hadn't fed tonight and the amount of blood she had been exposed to during all the fighting. But the smell of the incubus was the tipping point for the fledgling vampire.

Sabine looked back and forth between Samantha and Matthew. "You turned the oracle into a vampire? Now she is useless."

"My *child* is not useless," Matthew growled. Samantha was his, and he would let no one harm her.

The moment Sabine saw Samantha as a vampire Matthew knew he'd have to kill her. He couldn't risk Tarrick knowing he had sired a child. Tarrick would target Samantha and use her to bring him to his knees.

Sabine saw the opportunity to control Matthew. She dove at Samantha. Jet, with his arm-like limbs, pulled Samantha back down the stairs into the basement while Matthew dropped his sword and rushed at Sabine.

He was lost in frenzy. How *dare* she even think about hurting his child.

Sabine was strong, but no match for Matthew's rage. He ran his claws deep into her body again and again. She clawed him back but he ignored every wound as he tore her to shreds. He didn't stop when she was dead, tearing her body apart until a strong hand touched his back.

He swung around and swiped at Devak who stepped out of the way, then dropped to his knee and bowed his head to Matthew.

Matthew snorted at him, then paced back and forth until his head began to clear.

Samantha reappeared with Jet.

"Are you okay?" Matthew asked her, his voice deep. Angry.

"Yes. Hungry. Can I have her?" she asked, eyeing what was left of Sabine's shredded body.

"Take what you can," he said. Her heart wasn't pumping and most of her blood was on the floor or in spattered ribbons on the wall. Samantha wouldn't get much, but incubus blood was strong; it'd be enough to sate her hunger for a while.

Matthew needed to eat as well. He eyed the hunters.

"I wouldn't, my prince, they poison their blood against vampires. I can smell it," Devak said, one hand propping up his blood-covered maul.

That was something the hunters had never told him. Guess they wanted it to be a surprise in case he ever bit one.

Samantha struggled to pull Sabine's body up. Matthew went over, lifted the body off the ground, and sunk his fangs into one side of her neck while Samantha fed from her arm. The blood was like a drug, enhancing their senses and sending pleasure through their veins. They fed off what they could, and once they were done, Matthew gently set the body down.

He sliced up the skin where Samantha had bitten so Tarrick wouldn't find her bite marks, then Matthew closed Lady Sabine's eyes. "I wish this had gone differently." He stood and looked down at Devak. "Go break the stone."

Devak nodded and went into the basement. The sound of his maul smashing apart the stone rang in the air. He came back a moment later, carrying the duffle bag, and dropped it by Samantha.

He walked to the door and drained the ward of its magic. "They will still come once they figure out where we went, but we have some time. It'll be a few hours before a team can get here."

Matthew nodded in agreement. "If we head north we'll hit a highway by tomorrow. We'll take a car and head to Salt Lake. That'll put us in vamp territory. Hunters might come after us but they'll have lords to contend with as well."

"You are still injured," Devak said.

Matthew hadn't taken much blood from Sabine, only a few mouthfuls, leaving the rest for Samantha. His blood pouches were almost empty and the stored energy in his soavik was low. He had overdone it in his effort to protect Samantha, and he wouldn't be able to fight anymore tonight.

"Feed from me, my prince. I have strong blood and much of it," Devak said.

"I'll be fine until tomorrow."

Devak waved his hand and with it, his armor and weapon crumbled apart, disappearing into the light, and leaving behind only his tight, laced outfit.

Matthew couldn't help but rake his eyes over the powerful man who had only ever been submissive towards him. His cock grew hard and he fought the urge to wrap an incubus hold around the guardian.

Devak raised his clawed hand and scraped it along his neck, leaving behind two deep grooves. Blood poured out. It smelled better than incubus blood.

Matthew took a step towards him, his feet moving without command. "I thought you were supposed to do what I told you to."

"Yes, my prince. You can punish me later, once you have fed."

Matthew couldn't resist the smell. He was on Devak in an instant, holding him by the back of his head and his waist. Matthew licked the blood from the wounds, sunk his fangs into his neck, and pulled the blood into him.

When it filled his mouth, he moaned. It was erotic; potent. Matthew could feel strength returning to him and his wounds sealing. He drank deep but only filled a single blood pouch, not wanting to diminish Devak.

Reluctantly, he removed his fangs, licked the puncture marks, but didn't release Devak from his grasp right away. Matthew wanted more. And not just blood. Being this close to such a strong creature was maddening.

"You did not have to stop, my prince. I am yours," Devak said. He pressed into Matthew, removing any doubt of what he was truly offering.

God, it was tempting.

"What happens to you if I take all your blood?" Matthew asked, his lips hovered above Devak's skin.

"I will be unable to make my wings, but I will survive until I have the opportunity to acquire more blood."

That didn't sound too bad. Maybe he could just take a little more... maybe he should just start kissing Devak's neck...

The moment passed when Samantha grabbed his arm and pulled it off Devak's waist. She brought it up to her mouth and began to feed from Matthew.

Matthew released Devak. "No. I'd rather you have your wings in case they track us down during the day and you're forced to fight."

Devak watched Samantha feed.

"She won't take much," Matthew said. And she didn't. A few moments later she released Matthew. "Let's get away from here."

"Wait, there's something we need," Samantha said and wandered back into Sabine's room, duffle bag in tow.

Matthew and Devak followed her while Jet sat guard by the door.

Sabine's room was moderately decorated for an incubus. It had a large bed, some art, and weapons hanging on the walls. Nothing outlandish.

Samantha disappeared into the walk-in closet while something else grabbed Matthew's attention. It was a miniature marble figurine of the goddess Ilertha—the incubus goddess of sex—displayed on a side table. The figurine was her whole body, but it was small enough to fit in the palm of his hand.

Matthew picked it up and his eyes slid to Devak.

The wings, the way his weapon and armor appeared from the heavens, the powers he had all made sense... "You're an angel."

"I am a guardian."

Matthew gripped the figure and rubbed his thumb along it. "A guardian angel?"

"Just a guardian."

"Alright, how does one become a guardian? Were you born as one?"

"I was a vampire once and now I am a guardian. I cannot answer your questions beyond that. But...there are others that know the answer. Ask any older incubus or vampire, they should be able to tell you. My prince—"

"Matthew," he corrected.

"—please believe that this is as frustrating for me as it is for you."

"I believe you. We'll find a way to break your curse." Matthew studied the small statue in his hand. "She used to sing to me. Every night before dawn."

Devak said nothing but it seemed as if he wanted to and the words wouldn't form for him.

"She stopped when I went to live with Ascelina. Isn't there anything you can tell me? I have to know more."

"If you order me, I can tell you about my life when I was a human and...what happened after."

"Only if I order you?"

Devak averted his gaze from Matthew.

"He's embarrassed," Samantha said, emerging from the closet. Matthew noticed that the duffle bag was back to being stuffed full of items. And she was holding a sword of high quality, with a sheath and belt.

"Did you find what you were looking for?"

She held up the sword. "Yes, and I got you a new weapon. One you can wear."

"Very thoughtful, thank you." Matthew set the figurine back down on the side table and took the weapon, putting it on. "What did you say to Prescott before we teleported away? And how do you know about his armor?"

"I told him that so long as I live, he will never capture you. And as for the armor, I have battled against Prescott before. Although I was not a guardian at the time. He doesn't know it is me. My body…has changed."

Samantha disappeared back into the closet. When she emerged again, she held out a plain grey t-shirt for Matthew.

"Thanks," he said as he tore off his bloody one. Before he had a chance to put on the fresh shirt Devak came forward and touched Matthew's collar. The guardian's hand brushed against the skin of Matthew's neck and he fought back a moan.

"I can remove this if you wish," Devak said.

"Can you really? Why didn't you say so before?"

"You did not trust me before."

That much was true. He still didn't completely trust him, but Devak was powerful enough to kill Matthew at any time and hadn't yet. "Are you sure it won't explode?"

"I can drain it of its magic, then we can rip it from you. The metal itself will not be very strong once the magic is gone."

"Sam, go wait with Jet," Matthew ordered. She frowned and stomped out of the room. "Alright, do it. I've had this fucking thing on me long enough."

Devak placed his hands on each side of the collar.

A questioning look crossed Devak's face as Matthew grabbed his wrists. "Why are you embarrassed about your past?"

"I…" Devak swallowed and tried to pull away from Matthew, but he held him tight. "I am the cause of this war between the vampires and the incubi."

Matthew released him. He wasn't sure what to think. "This war has been going on for thousands of years."

"And I am the reason it started. It is painful for me to speak of it but if you order me to tell you, I will obey."

"Tarrick once told me the war started over love…"

Devak winced, his face full of torment. "It did," he whispered.

Matthew could feel Devak's anguish. "I won't force you to tell me if you don't wish to speak of it."

"Thank you, my prince," Devak said, softly.

He put his hands back onto Matthew's collar and closed his eyes, absorbing the magic into himself. When he opened his eyes, they glowed green for a moment, then it dissipated. Devak took a step away and nodded.

Matthew poured power into his strength—far more than he needed—and ripped the collar off. It split into two pieces. A feeling of freedom washed over him as he looked at the metal.

"Let's get out of here." As Matthew turned to leave the room, he could have sworn he saw Devak touch the figurine before following after Matthew.

Matthew set the broken collar down on a table, where the hunters would find it. It was a message for Tarrick—he was free.

Four hours to dawn.

"Would you like to run or would you rather I carry you?" he asked Samantha.

"Run," she said and gave him the duffle to carry.

They'd have to go slower so she could keep up but they'd be far enough away that the hunters would be no threat when they arrived.

Before they left, Matthew eyed the collar one last time, wishing things had been different.

Ten

The party of four arrived in Salt Lake without any incident. They had run until just before sunrise. Matthew did end up carrying Samantha for a few hours.

Before the sun rose, Matthew had made a pocket deep in the ground for them to stay in, the dirt obeying his command. Samantha, who had no idea vampires could do that, spent the final minutes before sunrise trying to get the dirt to move. She was unsuccessful but Matthew promised he'd teach her soon.

Devak and Jet, who was back to looking like a dog, stood guard above them all day.

At nightfall, they took off again and made it to the freeway. They acquired a car and drove through most of the night, stopping once for Matthew to get a blowjob at a rest stop. Devak and Jet kept an eye on Samantha while he took the human somewhere private.

It wasn't great head but he was hungry enough not to be too picky. Feeding was unsatisfying. He didn't take enough, and what he did take felt thin and weedy, like eating a bag of chips and expecting it to fill him. It didn't. Not even close.

At least he could still feed on blood just fine. He drank from a few humans—leaving them alive—before they continued on. Samantha fed from him in the back while Devak drove.

Every now and then, Matthew would touch his neck just to make sure the collar was really gone.

They rolled into Salt Lake a few hours before sunrise, stopping at a nice hotel. Matthew compelled the lady at the desk to comp them the room, one with two queen beds.

Jet, who had been cooped up in the car all night, left to go fly around the city. Or at least, that's what Matthew assumed he did, but really, for all he knew, Jet was sitting on some corner watching traffic.

"What is the plan for tomorrow night?" Devak asked while moving to the other end of the room and checking for any possible dangers. Once he was satisfied there were none, he sat down in a chair. He was rigid, ready to stand should Matthew ask him to. Devak never seemed to relax.

Matthew shrugged. He wasn't sure where he wanted to go from here. "I don't know. We might be heading to California. I know a lord there who is willing to take us in. It'd give me time to teach Sam how to hunt, and she can meet other vampires."

"I'd like that," Samantha said. She plopped down on one of the beds, turned on the TV with the remote, and turned it off almost immediately. "Watching that hurts."

"Yeah, until you can better control your senses, anything with bright lights will hurt your eyes. Tomorrow we can hit the bookstore before it closes."

"Okay. I'd rather read anyway. And we can go get you both fitted for tuxes. I already have a dress but it needs to get hemmed." She picked up one of the hotel magazines and flipped through it.

Both Matthew and Devak turned their attention to her.

"Sam...?" Matthew asked, an eyebrow raised.

"Yes?"

"Why do we need tuxes?"

"For the vampire party, of course," she said as if he were being dense.

Did vampires even have parties? With a few exceptions, the incubi always made it sound as if vampires never gathered together. "Samantha..."

She went back to flipping through her magazine. "Relax, it won't be until next month."

"Samantha..." Matthew said again. She paid him no mind.

"You'll have fun. Well...kinda."

"We are not going to any parties. It's not safe for us."

She looked at him and smiled. "I see the future."

Matthew considered lecturing her to stop using that as an excuse to get what she wanted.

"I enjoy parties," Devak offered.

Matthew had a hard time believing that. The guardian couldn't even relax in a chair; it was hard to imagine him enjoying anything.

"But," he continued, "I haven't been to one in a few thousand years. I will not know current dance steps until I study them for a while."

"We aren't going," Matthew said, trying to quash this idea before everyone got their hopes up. "It's too dangerous."

"Whatever you say," Samantha said.

Matthew folded his arms. "Most vampires hate me. I fought for the incubi and I've killed a lot of them. They want me dead. We're not going. That's final." He was the one in charge here and he would *not* let her manipulate him.

"'Kay." Samantha's expression didn't change as she worked her way through the magazine.

Matthew narrowed his eyes and began to strip off his shirt as he walked into the bathroom to shower.

"But if you want to break Devak's curse we have to go."

"God damn it!" Matthew tossed his shirt against the wall in anger. "SAM!"

Devak started to stand but stayed put when Matthew shot him a glance.

A wily smile crossed Samantha's face. "I see the future."

Matthew growled and rubbed his temples, trying his best not to yell at her. "You set me up for that."

She smiled wider.

"Alright. Talk."

"It came to me last night when we were sleeping underground. I need to go to Delphi. It's a place of power for oracles. The last of us—before me that is—died there. I can break the curse in what's left of the temple, but I need the offering."

Samantha stood and unzipped the duffle. She dumped all of the contents out on the bed and went to the closet to get some hangers.

A designer dress that once belonged to Lady Sabine was among the items. It was baby pink in color with a high-jeweled waist, made for a woman much taller than Samantha, but Matthew thought she would look stunning in it once fitted.

She hung it up along with some other clothes she had taken.

Matthew saw a pair of bracers among the mountain of items and clothes. He picked them up. They had been part of Sabine's armor and they sparked of magic.

He placed one around his forearm. It was a little snug but manageable. He ran his finger down it. It reminded him too much of his time as a prisoner and he ripped it off again.

"Why did you take these?" Matthew asked, putting them back in the bag.

"Because you learned to fight with bracers."

That was true. But he wouldn't put them on unless the situation was dire.

"What offering do we need?" Devak asked, sitting forward, clearly eager to break the curse.

"I'm not sure yet. All I know is we'll find the one who owns it at the party. Oh, and we need to impress the general. He can help us get to Delphi."

For a moment, Matthew thought she was talking about Tarrick but that made no sense. Then it came to him. "The vampire general? He'll be there?"

Only a few vampires had ever seen him or even knew who he was beyond 'the general'. He stayed in the shadows so that the incubi couldn't find him. He was protected because for the first time in centuries, he was giving the vampires a fighting chance. He was starting to convince his people that working with humans, mercenaries, and witches wasn't below them. He knew incubi tactics and how to counter them. The general was bringing the vampires together.

Matthew, out of sheer curiosity, wanted to meet him, but in no way wanted to join him. He didn't want to be part of this war, especially now that he had Sam.

"He'll be there. He thinks no one will see his face." Sam laughed and shook her head as if she found her own words amusing.

"And why doesn't he think anyone will see his face?"

"Because of the masks. Oh, we need to get masks, too."

Devak looked intrigued. "The Solstice Masquerade? It is still held?" Samantha shrugged, but Devak looked almost excited. "It is something that has been done since my time, celebrating the longest night of the year. Where will it be?"

"Washington, a few hours outside of Seattle."

Matthew shook his head. He couldn't believe they were even still talking about this. "This is a terrible idea. How many lords will be there?"

Samantha fiddled with the corners of her magazine. "I'm not sure. Lots."

"I took out eight in New Orleans but I had time to plan and I got lucky. If there's more than that there and we're discovered, we'll be killed."

"I can take many out as well, my prince. I will be the oldest in the room…unless…will the Queen be there?" Devak asked Samantha.

"No. She's sleeping."

Devak looked relieved to hear that.

Matthew sat down next to Samantha. "Tell me the truth," he commanded, knowing she would be unable to disobey. "Is there really something there that can help us break the curse or are you just telling me that so you can go to a party?"

Hurt twisted her face and rippled through the bond. "Going there will lead us to the offering. I do not yet know what it is, perhaps because I'll play a part in acquiring it and as I've told you before, I rarely see my own future."

"I'm sorry, you have to understand, with all those vampires, I don't know if I can protect you."

Matthew could feel her frustration and anger. She slid off the bed and grabbed a fresh shirt and leggings. "I'm not lying to you. You don't have to force me to tell the truth. And I'm not as fragile as you think I am."

"That's not what I—"

She didn't let him finish as she marched away and slammed the door to the bathroom. The shower turned on.

Matthew sighed.

Devak leaned forward in the chair. "You are right."

Matthew looked at him.

"She is fragile," Devak said. "But that doesn't mean she's powerless."

"I can't help how I act around her. It's this damn bond."

"I do not think it is just the bond," Devak said, his words careful.

Matthew didn't think so either. It was in his nature to try to protect those around him who needed it. "Can you teach me how to prevent Hiroto from tracking me again? I don't want a repeat of what happened the other night."

"Of course, my—"

He stopped when Matthew glared at him. He had let it slide too often and right now he was sick of being called 'prince'.

"And Sam as well?" Matthew asked.

"Unnecessary. If the fox tried to enter her mind or pull her into his, he would be driven insane by what he saw." Devak, seeing the concern on Matthew's face, quickly added: "Because the mind of one who can see the future is nearly impossible to navigate. Did you try to compel her before you had a bond with her?"

"Ah. I did, I wasn't able to."

Devak gave him a look of 'well there you go' but said nothing.

Matthew stood to repack the duffle bag. There were some new items inside: jewelry, makeup, and a decorated rod which felt as if it held powerful magic—the damn thing practically electrocuted him when he touched it. Samantha was collecting some strange shit. "How long do you plan to stay with me?"

Devak stood and paused, as if to make sure Matthew wasn't going to order him back into the chair. When that didn't happen he approached Matthew. It looked as if he might kneel for a moment but decided against it. "I do not plan to leave unless you dismiss me. I hope that you won't. I hope that you will allow me to serve you. If you would permit it, I would like to train you."

"I know how to fight."

"You are an excellent warrior, but there are creatures you will face that are far more powerful than incubi or vampires."

"Like demons."

Devak nodded. "Other guardians as well, dragons, champions, many will want you dead. I think you should learn how to fight in full armor, not just bracers, and master all weapons, not just swords. To train you correctly will take a long time."

Matthew had little to lose by having Devak train him, and anything to make him stronger was fine by him. In fact, he found the idea of taking down powerful creatures enticing. "Alright, I'll let you train me if you agree to one thing—consider it an order if you have to."

"Anything," Devak said.

"If the choice comes down to saving me, or saving Samantha, you will save her. And you will protect her."

Devak glanced at the bathroom door then back at Matthew. He

didn't look happy. "I will follow your command."

"Alright, so our plan is this: we'll go find an out-of-the-way cabin. I'll train Samantha how to hunt and resist some of her instincts—I don't want her trying to bite every human she sees. Any time I have left in the night, you can train me to fight. We'll go to this masquerade, get the offering we need, and then go break the curse."

Devak nodded and returned to his chair. The shower turned off in the bathroom. Matthew went and knocked on the door.

Silence.

He sighed heavily. "I'm sorry I forced you to answer. I didn't mean to hurt you. Please forgive me. I only want to keep you safe."

Samantha opened the door and glared at Matthew. "Okay. But you need to shower before coming to bed, you still have dirt all over you."

Matthew smiled and kissed the top of her head. She scooted around him and pushed him into the bathroom.

After he'd showered and they were in bed together, he thought he heard the angelic female voice singing to him. But when he sat up, there was nothing.

"Stop moving around so much," Samantha said from his arms, her voice sleepy as the sun rose.

"Did you hear that?"

"Hear what?"

"Nothing. Never mind, sleep well."

Matthew frowned, he had missed the song more than he realized.

Eleven

Matthew stood alone on a hill. Across a grassy plain, a great army had assembled in the night—a sea of incubi and vampires, all armed and ready to fight. The armor most of them wore looked ancient Greek.

Anticipation hung in the air as the multitude stood on the precipice of battle.

Thousands against one.

They charged. Leading them from above was an incubus—wearing armor of gold—riding a great black dragon. The incubus held a massive gold bladed sword that glowed against the night sky.

A swarm of bats swirled around the dragon and a mass of vampire and incubi flew behind them.

On the ground, humans charged forward.

Matthew laughed. As if this army could stop him. He was invincible.

He raised his hand and watched as hundreds of incubi and vampires fell out of the air with a flick of his wrist.

He squeezed his fist shut and their bodies burst apart. Matthew pulled the blood to him. Long streams of the crimson life liquid floated through the air and twisted around him in a hypnotic pattern.

As the army neared, he held his arms out and sent the blood forward like long, pointed spears. The blood spears hit the front lines and a wave of his foes dropped to the ground.

"Focus, Matthew," a honeyed voice said to him.

Matthew looked over to see Devak standing beside him.

"I must kill them all," Matthew said and continued his attack.

"No. Focus. This is not your mind."

Not his mind?

That's right.

Matthew took a step away.

"Do you know where we are?" Devak asked.

"We're inside your mind," Matthew remembered now. Devak was teaching him how to resist Hiroto's tracking ability.

"Good. And what should you do next?"

Matthew wanted to turn and fight the army. To destroy them all but he fought the urge. He pushed it away and focused on following strands of memory back to his own mind.

White light swallowed them and when Matthew woke, he was lying on a bed. Matthew shot up and looked around. He was in the cabin they had called home for the past few days. It was nestled in the mountainside and not far from a small college town.

Matthew could hear Samantha in the front living room with Jet. She was reading to him.

"What the hell did I just witness?" Matthew asked.

Devak clenched his jaw. "I don't know how you ended up at that memory. I did not intend it."

"That was a real event? You took on an army by yourself?"

"Yes."

"Thousands of years ago, in Greece?"

"Yes."

"How? I've never seen anything control blood like that. It felt so… invincible." Matthew swung his legs over the side of the bed to face Devak.

Devak turned away and opened the heavy curtains of the master bedroom. The moon was hidden by clouds tonight. Snow fell on the ground.

"Do you know what a Sanguine Dominar is?"

"No. But…Tarrick, uh, the incubus High General, mentioned it once. He thought maybe people called me 'prince' because I might be one."

"No. You're not going to be a Dominar. There have only ever been two that have walked this planet. I was one of them. The other had been killed long before I was born." Devak turned and faced Matthew. He ran his hand through his short black hair. "A Sanguine Dominar is a vampire that possesses the ability to control blood at a distance. As you saw, I could rip it out of bodies and manipulate it into weapons. Or I could move a man around like a puppet if I desired it. I could…*I did*, kill entire cities with a flick of my fingers."

"The wings you have now…"

"No. The wings are because I am a guardian."

"So you're not a Dominar anymore?"

"I am a guardian now and it is for the better. Having such power brings with it a desire for destruction. I nearly wiped all incubi and vampires."

"What stopped you?"

The lean muscles in Devak's body tensed under his bronze skin and his eyes darkened. Matthew waited for him to answer the question. Finally, Devak said, "I was killed."

Matthew stood. "You're...dead?" He walked around Devak, studying him. He didn't look dead—well more than a vampire looked anyway.

Devak nodded. "I am a guardian."

"I know you love saying that but it means shit-all to me. I thought angels were made by God or something."

"I am not an angel. I am a—"

"Guardian. Yes, I know," Matthew said, cutting him off with a wave of his hand. "I'm sick of hearing it. Do you have your phone still?"

It had miraculously survived the run-in with the hunters. As Devak pulled the phone from his pocket, Matthew's eyes traced the lines of the fingers and drifted upwards to the delicate bones of his wrist. It was hard to believe that such a delicate structure could wield a heavy maul with so much proficiency and strength.

He lingered on Devak's skin for so long that his body got the wrong idea and his dick throbbed for attention. God, he was hungry. And with the way Devak looked—his irises blown open with need, his hips pressed forward, his lips parted slightly—it wasn't only Matthew's body getting the wrong idea...

Clearing his throat, Matthew grabbed the phone, dialed the number to the call center, and asked to be put through to Ascelina.

While the call rang, Devak said, "I would not even whisper the words 'Sanguine Dominar' to either vampires or incubi. If they thought I was still a Dominar, or knew who I used to be, they would try to kill me and that would put you in danger."

"Yes?" Stolus answered the phone before Matthew could reply to Devak.

"Put your mother on," Matthew said, sitting back down on the bed.

Devak watched in silence from his place by the window, but he seemed to strain against his own body, as if he wanted to speak and was unable. Or maybe Devak had hoped the touch would lead to something else. Matthew couldn't let himself get caught up with another man, not when he was such a mess. Besides, it wasn't like he could have sex right now anyways...

Over the phone, Stolus growled. "Matthew? Fine."

Matthew could hear Stolus walking around and handing the phone over.

"Have you made a decision about joining me?" Ascelina asked.

"That's not why I'm calling. Can we speak privately?" He heard Ascelina dismissing those who were around her.

"No one will hear," she said.

"What is a guardian?" he asked, hoping to finally get some answers.

She laughed. "That is a topic of great debate among us. The most popular belief is that they are creatures that fill the ranks of a god's army."

That wasn't very useful. He was already guessing Devak was an angel. "I need more details."

"Do you?" She sounded amused. "Have you seen a guardian?"

"Something like that," Matthew said and glanced at Devak, who averted his eyes as if he had been caught looking at something he shouldn't have. Matthew wasn't sure why. He found himself pleased by the way Devak looked at him.

"The mythos is that when we die our souls go to our god," she explained. "Strong souls are sometimes restored to form—resurrected in a fashion—and made into eternal servants. A guardian's powers, appearance, and role differ from god to god."

"Are there a lot of gods?"

She sighed. "Are you having a religious crisis so young?"

"No...I don't know. Maybe. I don't really believe in this stuff but I didn't believe in vampires either and then I became one."

She paused. "I suppose we all go through this at some point or another. We have religious texts that list hundreds of gods. They all have different domains."

"What about the human gods? Or...God?" Matthew had never been very religious but he had gone to church a few times growing up, depending on the family he was living with.

"I do not concern myself with humans. You will have to ask one of them."

"Do you worship the vampire god?"

"The Blood God? I suppose but I am not as devout as I should be. It is difficult for me to worship one who has never walked among us. We know so little about him. My sire is devout. She could better answer your questions. If you would let me tell her of you—"

"No," Matthew cut her off. "I appreciate that you have kept what I am hidden from other vampires, and I'd like to keep it that way for now."

"Alright." From her neutral tone, Matthew had no idea if she was angry or not but suspected she wasn't. It took a lot to piss off Ascelina, unless it concerned her children. Then she was like a mother bear.

"What do the Blood God's guardians look like?" Matthew had a feeling he knew what the answer was going to be, but asked anyway.

"Like vampires with completely red eyes and wings of blood. They wear black armor."

It was the answer he expected. Devak, who could easily hear both ends of this conversation, said nothing as Matthew stared at him.

"At least that's what I've been told. I've never seen one personally. There are those older than me that have, would you like me to ask around for more details? I will be discreet."

"No. But thank you. There's something else I wanted to talk to you about…the bond I share with my child—"

"It pleases me to hear you are calling her 'child'," Ascelina said warmly.

"Yes, well. You were right about that. But the bond, it's…dangerous. All it takes is for someone to look at her wrong and I lose all sense of control. Is that how it'll always be?" He hated how he lost himself to rage when he killed Sabine.

"The bond will remain for a century but the extreme feelings you have now fade in only a few years. You sound worried, more than normal."

"Yeah, it's just…she wants to attend the Solstice Masquerade."

"That's wonderful, Matthew. I think you will enjoy yourself," he could practically hear her smiling.

"Will you be there?"

"Emilia and I will be attending the one in London, it is the largest and lasts over several nights. Are you going to the one in Washington?"

"Yes. But, I'm worried someone will recognize me and try to hurt her."

"Your face will be covered and no one there will harm a child as young as she is, no matter who the sire is. We value them. The incubi have given you a terrible view of us, your attendance will help you see us as we are. One moment."

Matthew heard someone entering whatever room Ascelina was in.

"There's an attack," Stolus said.

"There is another matter that requires my attention." Ascelina cut off the call abruptly.

Well, at least he got all the answers he was looking for. A guardian of the Blood God. He tossed the phone back to Devak, who caught it and slipped it into his pocket.

The idea that gods walked among people and sent down their soldiers stretched Matthew's beliefs to the limits. Maybe they were powerful beings, but *gods*?

And, why the hell would one care about Matthew? He was powerful, for sure, able to perform feats no other vampire could, but he was hardly the strongest creature around.

"At least now you know what a guardian is. I wish I could have been the one to tell you," Devak said.

Matthew wished the same. Trying to figure out these answers was frustrating at best.

****

An early winter snowstorm rolled through that night, keeping them indoors. The next night it cleared and Matthew took Samantha hunting for the first time.

She was so excited to go, even after he explained that she might kill the person she'd be feeding on.

Once in town, Matthew told her to pick a person. She spotted an attractive young man who looked close to her own age.

"Stay here, I'll bring him back," Matthew said and left her waiting in an empty area behind some shops. They were going to start slow, only feeding for now. He'd teach her how to compel and erase memories another night.

Matthew wrapped an emotional hold onto the boy, leaving him aware of his surroundings but calm. When the boy saw Samantha, he grinned and approached her.

He told Samantha how wonderful her smile was—yes, even with her fangs—and how beautiful she was. And after about five minutes of flirting, he leaned closer and kissed her.

Matthew found the entire situation hilarious and had to work to keep from laughing. He shouldn't have pushed the boy's emotions so much. And Samantha, who had been on the run since her early teens, had probably never caught the notice of a boy her entire life. She was nervous but enjoyed the attention.

Matthew could feel that deep down, she didn't believe that she was beautiful. While it was true she wasn't conventionally attractive, her features were framed in a fascinating way. Once she caught the eye, it was hard to look away until fully studied. He had a feeling that this wasn't the first man he'd be seeing her with.

Samantha broke away from the kiss and announced that she wouldn't be feeding on him, which Matthew had already gathered would happen.

The next time they tried, Matthew picked the prey, and it wasn't some cute young man either. He chose a squat old woman. Samantha leaned in to bite the woman, but pulled away at the last moment and began to cry.

"I don't want to," she said. She backed up into a pile of wooden pallets and collapsed onto the ground, burying her face in her hands.

Matthew released the woman. She walked off, her mind already forgetting what just happened.

"I'm a terrible vampire," Samantha sobbed.

Matthew took a seat next to her and pulled her into his chest. "You're a fine vampire."

"I'm broken. I don't even want to kill."

"You are not broken, and you don't have to kill if you don't want to." Matthew wonder if it was easier for her to control her vampire nature because she was weak or if it was just the bond. When he had been turned, he wasn't able to control anything. Just smelling a human would set him off. "There's no pressure here. If you don't want to try hunting again for a while, we don't have to. I don't care if it takes years."

Samantha trembled in his arms. "But I'm sure other vampires—"

"I don't give a flying fuck what other vampires do." Matthew was going to put a stop to that shit right now. "You're mine and if you don't want to kill, you won't."

That seemed to help...she wiped her eyes. "Okay."

He picked her up and carried her back to the cabin.

They stayed at the cabin for two weeks and their nights fell into a comfortable rhythm. When they woke, Samantha would feed from Matthew. If Samantha was having a vision-free day, the three of them would head into town.

Matthew would leave Samantha with Devak while he went and fed. She enjoyed going to bars or being around people for a while. Unlike when Matthew was a new vampire, she didn't feel the need to stalk humans that neared her, though she'd often get exhausted after a few hours of being around them and would want to retreat back to the cabin to read or just sit quietly for a while.

If Matthew wasn't done feeding by the time she was ready to go, because he got a little caught up pleasuring his partner or went looking for prey that would give him some chase, Devak would take her back early.

Matthew would rejoin them a few hours later and begin training with Devak.

Training wasn't quite what Matthew expected.

He found that while Devak was submissive around Matthew most of the time, that was not the case when it came to fighting.

"I have one condition—" Devak said to him before they started, "—when we begin a session I am your instructor and must have that authority. When the session ends, I will kneel before you and once again be yours."

Matthew agreed to his terms, though he didn't need the kneeling at the end but Devak insisted.

Over the next two weeks, Matthew found himself wishing several times that he hadn't made the agreement. To say Devak was a *demanding* instructor would be an understatement.

If Devak knocked Matthew down, he expected Matthew to be back on his feet again immediately. If Matthew took too long, he'd simply begin attacking him while he was prone.

If Matthew lost his temper, Devak ignored it and continued until Matthew mastered whatever they were working on, or until Matthew lost all control. In those cases, Devak would take to the air and fly out of his range, infuriating Matthew even more. But since there was nothing he could do about aerial targets, he'd roar and pace until he wore himself out. Then, Devak would land and continue the lesson.

After the session, Devak would kneel and ask for forgiveness, but never during.

Devak pushed Matthew hard, leaving him exhausted by sunrise. In truth, Matthew enjoyed it—it felt good to spar with someone who not only matched, but exceeded his own strength and speed.

After two weeks, Matthew found he enjoyed life again. It was nice staying in one place and getting to know his new companions. At the end of each night, the three of them—well, four, counting Jet—would gather in the living room of the cabin and just sit and talk about absolutely nothing important.

Devak—who Matthew was beginning to trust—didn't speak often, but Matthew more than made up for it. He'd chat about anything; history, food he used to enjoy, what the different states he visited during this past year were like, anything. Samantha would often talk about the books she had read or what was in the newspapers they picked up for her.

For the first time in a long time, Matthew found himself hopeful for the future. Maybe karma was finally rewarding him for the hardships and pain he had endured the past few years.

He tricked himself into believing it.

He should have known better.

Twelve

In a corner booth of a cozy local bar, Matthew and Devak sat with drinks in front of them.

Samantha was in a back booth with a young man who prattled on about whatever he was studying in college.

Matthew scanned the crowd, seeing if there was anyone he wanted to feed from tonight. He was eyeing a woman with dark, curly hair reading a romance novel.

He was considering giving her an erotic night she'd never forget when he noticed Devak actually drinking the beer they had ordered.

"You can drink that shit without getting sick?" Matthew asked.

Devak nodded. "It will not get me drunk but drinking it doesn't bother me."

Matthew made a face. Anything but blood or cum tasted terrible to him. "What do you feed on anyway? I've never seen you hunt."

"I need blood to make my wings but I draw my power from—" A low growl came from Devak as he tried to speak the words but they refused to form. He slammed his drink down in frustration.

"Curse?" Matthew asked.

"Yes." Devak swirled the liquid around in his glass, looking for something to say. "My memories were erased when I was cursed. Most are back, some I still struggle with. I spent many years living as a human, unaware of what I was."

"Really?"

"I was a banker."

Matthew laughed. "For real?"

Devak joined him with a smile. "It was strange that in eight years I never aged, but I thought it was good genetics." His smiled lingered for a moment before it dropped. "The curse stripped me of my abilities for a while. I am not even half as powerful as I should be."

"Jesus," Matthew breathed out. Devak was one of the stronger creatures he'd ever been around, he couldn't imagine what he'd be like at full power. "You're making me feel inadequate."

Devak eyed Matthew up and down. "I do not think you are inadequate in any way, my prince."

The flirtation wasn't lost on Matthew but he ignored it. Though it shamed him to admit it, his thoughts often wandered back to Tarrick, and he didn't want to get involved with someone else right now.

Devak pushed the drink away and looked into Matthew's silver eyes. "Around you, I am becoming stronger."

"Are you?"

"It is not the reason I am here but it is good to be...near you. It is hard to explain with the curse binding me."

Matthew put his hand on Devak's shoulder. "I give you my word that I will do everything in my power to break the curse."

Devak's eyes drifted to Matthew's hand, then followed his arm back to his body and to Matthew's face. He wore a look of longing coupled with gratitude. He dipped his head slightly. "Thank you."

A strange sensation washed over Matthew...something was wrong. He looked around.

"What is it?" Devak asked, already on his feet, his muscles taut and his body ready to fight if needed.

Matthew got to his feet. "Samantha...she's not here."

The boy she had been talking to was sitting alone in the booth, reading. Matthew stormed over to him and grabbed him by the arm. "The girl you were with, where is she?"

The boy tried to pull away. "No idea. She took off a few minutes ago."

Then it hit him like a tidal wave:

Thump.

Both Devak and Matthew raced out the back door.

"How come we didn't feel it before?" Matthew asked as the two of them ran to the source.

"The incubus was probably targeting only her. Once they realize she's a fledgling, they try to draw out her sire as well."

Matthew reached out through the bond and felt Samantha's calmness.

The two picked up speed.

As they neared the empty outskirts of the town, Devak pulled Matthew to a stop and they ducked behind a building.

At the edge of a wooded area stood a succubus dressed in warm clothes, except her neck was exposed. He recognized her from a party he had once attended; her name was Lady Naomi, a young succubus warrior.

No vamp trap was visible under the snow and dirt but Matthew knew it was there—as would be a team of six hunters.

Samantha stood in front of Naomi, who ran her hands through Samantha's hair. The two smiled and Naomi leaned in. "Pretty vampire, where is your sire?"

When Samantha pressed her body against the succubus, Matthew's vampire side ripped forward. He was going to kill that bitch for what she was doing to his child.

"I left him to come here. Do we need to talk about him? Can't you just kiss me instead?" Samantha asked.

Naomi leaned in and gently pressed her lips to Samantha's.

The succubus had a hold around Samantha and was feeding from her. Unlike Matthew, Samantha had no hope to break free from it.

Matthew began to stalk forward when Devak pulled him back sharply. "Clear your head, she will not kill Sam right away. She will feed for a while and try to draw you out. If you run in there, this place will be swarming with hunters and incubi."

Matthew calmed some of his rage. "You're right. I'll deal with this. Go back to the cabin and pack up, find Jet, and get us a new car. We'll have to get out of here fast."

He was surprised when Devak didn't object or fight his order. "Call my name if you need me, I'll hear it," Devak said, then turned and bolted away, disappearing from view.

Matthew considered how he wanted to handle the situation. The hunters had to be taken out first and for that he'd need patience. He pulled up the collar of his thick wool coat, kept to the shadows, and moved into the forested area where he knew they'd most likely be hiding. Then he waited.

Hunters could conceal themselves to vampires but only if they didn't move much. Spending all night in the cold was boring as hell and eventually they'd shift positions. All Matthew had to do was wait and watch.

He spotted the first up in a tree.

Lighter than a cat, he jumped up to the branch and ripped out the hunter's throat before he could make a sound or call for help, then he dropped down to the ground with the body and hid it in the snow.

His attention turned back to Samantha. She was kissing the succubus' neck. Naomi seductively pushed Samantha's jacket off and slipped her hand under her shirt. His child moaned as her eyes turned red and fangs came down.

Matthew pushed away the urge to run in and kill Naomi right then.

Instead, he waited out in the forest, watching and listening for the next hunter to move. Each time one would, he'd sneak up and kill the human. It took about half an hour to find and kill all of them.

By the time he was done, Samantha was half-naked and being pleasured by the succubus, whose hand had slipped into her pants. Urgent whines fell from Samantha's lips.

Every five minutes or so, Naomi sent out another *thump*. Matthew did his best to ignore them. She wasn't as strong as Tarrick so the feeling of desire didn't cripple him, but it still made him horny as hell.

He dug through the body of the last hunter he killed and found a piece of green chalk.

Thump.

Samantha shuddered as Naomi's hands traced her body and ended by squeezing the pink nipple of her small, exposed breast. "Please," Samantha whimpered.

"Call your sire to you and I'll give you more," Naomi said.

Matthew was on her before Sam could respond. He approached her from the back and put his arms around the succubus.

He felt her wrap a hold around him in an attempt to control him… he'd let her believe she was.

He brought his mouth close to her neck and took a deep breath in.

"You smell wonderful," he said, not allowing her to turn around and see who it was.

She backed up into him, pressing her ass into his hard cock. "I'm thrilled you've joined us. I was hoping I'd get two tonight."

Matthew ground his dick against her.

"Big boy," she said with a breathy moan.

Half of Matthew was tempted to roll his eyes, while the other half wanted to rip off the rest of her clothes and pound her right here in the snow. Not that he was sure he could with his cock being a traitorous bitch, but the desire was there.

"Father, are we going to take her together," Samantha asked, still trapped by lust.

"Mm, I would enjoy having both of you at once," Naomi said and reached behind his neck to draw him closer.

"I've missed fucking incubi," he said. He did.

"Have you fucked many of us?" she asked, moaning when Samantha and Matthew explored her body with their hands.

"Oh yes." Matthew broke away from the hold.

He felt Naomi pause in his arms as the invisible strands of energy snapped. She scanned the forest.

"If you're looking for your hunters, they're all dead," Matthew whispered.

Fear rose in the succubus. She pushed Samantha away before she kicked Matthew hard in the knee.

Matthew let her go and she ran out of the vamp trap. Naomi's eyes grew wide when she saw who it was that she had captured.

"Matthew..." she said. "All this searching for you and you get caught by a thumper trap?"

Matthew looked at Samantha, who stood topless in a trance. Naomi hadn't released her yet.

"Thumpers are my weakness, I guess." Matthew stalked towards her, stopping about a foot away. "But do you really think you've caught me?"

He held up the piece of green chalk. She looked down to see a single patch of dirt that had been pushed aside to expose the runes that made up a vamp trap. It had a line of chalk across it, breaking the magic.

Adrenaline surged through her and she dove for a loose mound of dirt. Matthew moved to the dirt pile before she could get close. He kicked the pile and exposed a wooden box. A vampire hunting kit.

"Are...are you going to kill me?" Her heart pounding loud in

Matthew's ears.

"Yes. I'll give you your weapon if you wish to die with it in your hand."

"Why? Why are you killing us? I thought you were fighting for us. We accepted you."

Matthew studied her. She had a soft face and a long neck. Her body was built to attract vampires, lure them out and kill them. A body that would have killed Samantha.

"After New Orleans, I was going to be caged again, punished, locked away alone. Used only as a weapon."

The shock that crossed her face told him that she hadn't known. What had they told their people about him? Had they branded him a traitor?

"And you made the mistake of trapping my child." He grabbed the back of her neck to hold her in place. "Answer my questions honestly."

Her will folded as he compelled her. Behind him, Samantha made a sound as the hold faded.

"Where is the nearest leystone to here?" Matthew asked.

"Twenty miles east."

"And how soon can backup arrive once they know I'm here?"

"Three minutes, if hunters push the range of their personal teleport," she said.

"How long until they send someone to check on you?"

"We have comm silence during traps, but we're due to check in at eleven." Damn. It was nearly eleven now.

"Unlock your phone and give it to me," he ordered.

She reached into her pocket and did as commanded. Matthew scrolled through the contact numbers until he saw the one he wanted and memorized it.

"Did you want your sword?" he asked.

Tears began to roll down her cheeks. "Can you make it painless?"

He could. Matthew reached up and snapped her neck, then smashed her phone under his heel.

"What was she doing to me?" Samantha asked, pulling her shirt back on. "I had no control. That sound...that feeling..."

"Some incubi can thump like that to lure vampires into traps and kill them."

"Oh. I'm sorry I wasn't able to resist it."

"You have nothing to be sorry for. When the incubi captured me, it was because of a trap just like this one. We have to go."

"Thank you for saving me."

"You don't have to thank me. I'll always save you."

"You'll always try."

Once she was dressed, he picked her up and sped back to the cabin.

Devak had acquired a four-wheel drive Jeep, which was all packed and ready to go. Jet sat on the hood and Devak leaned against the door.

"The succubus?" Devak asked.

"Dead. Let's get out of here. You drive," Matthew said.

"Where to?"

"The masquerade is in two weeks, might as well head out that way. Washington."

Matthew sat in the back with Samantha and Jet in the passenger seat, as Devak pulled away from the cabin.

Matthew stayed silent during the long drive. Thoughtful. The trap brought back a flood of memories that he wanted to forget. But they wouldn't leave him be.

They stopped at a motel, and Devak got them a room. "Is that phone untraceable? Even if I call someone?" Matthew asked once they were inside.

"Yes. Is everything okay?" Devak asked as he handed Matthew the phone.

"Yeah. I'm going out for a few minutes. I'll be back before sunrise," he said and left.

Through the closed door behind him, he heard Samantha say, "He's heartbroken."

Matthew went far away from them, past the buildings and into a forested area. He leaned against a tree and brought up the phone.

He punched in the numbers and stared at them for a while.

He shouldn't do this.

Matthew hit the call button anyway.

It rang.

"Yes. Who is this?" a deep voice answered. A voice that filled Matthew with such loathing and such desire. Tarrick.

Matthew closed his eyes and pressed his head back into the tree. He knew he should end the call. But he couldn't bring himself to.

"Hello?" Tarrick sounded irritated.

Why had he dialed the number? All he was doing was punishing himself. And what would he even say? He couldn't say what he wanted to: *Take me back.*

"Tarrick," Matthew whispered.

There was a pause, then, finally, "…Matthew?"

Matthew said nothing. He hoped Tarrick would talk. He wanted to hear his voice. He bit his lower lip to stop it from quivering.

"Matthew," Tarrick said again, this time with confidence. "What do you want?"

Matthew knew he should hang up. Tarrick was going to lash out and, as always, it was going to hurt, but he couldn't bring himself to hit the damn button.

"Do you wish to boast about how you killed Lady Sabine? She was unarmed and you ripped her to shreds. You know she stood with you, and even after your escape, she still advocated for you. Or perhaps you wish to talk about Lady Naomi and her hunters? How you snapped her neck and left her body in the snow? She didn't stand a chance against you. None of them did."

There it was. Matthew's claws came out and he dug one into the bark of the tree.

"They are not the reason…" Matthew said. "I…" his voice betrayed the ache he felt. He pulled the phone away from his ear and looked at the call information. *Hang up*, he told himself.

"Wait—" Tarrick said.

Matthew put the phone back to his ear and said nothing.

"Come back to me." There was an audible shift in Tarrick's voice. It lost the hard edge and became seductive. Alluring.

Matthew's eyes watered and he slid down the base of the tree, his ass hitting the hard ground. Those four words sounded so sweet.

"Come back. I promise you won't be punished for escaping. Or what you've done since." Tarrick sounded like a lover, warm and intimate.

A tear escaped and rolled down Matthew's face.

"You belong with us. With me," Tarrick said.

Matthew swallowed hard. None of what Tarrick said was real. It was all a ploy to get Matthew to turn himself over. But...he wanted to believe it, even if it was for just a few moments. Eventually, he worked up the courage to say something. "You always tell such beautiful lies."

He ended the call.

More tears escaped as he sat against the tree. The sky began to lighten but he couldn't bring himself to move.

Minutes before sunrise, Devak appeared before him. Matthew didn't have the willpower to speak. Instead, he just looked away... avoiding his gaze, avoiding the judgment.

But Devak didn't judge him. "I will make sure Sam is safe during the day."

Moments before the sun rose, Matthew sunk down into the ground and slept alone.

Thirteen

After his call to Tarrick, Matthew spent the next few nights in a depressed silence, only speaking when Samantha asked him a direct question. He was thankful Samantha and Devak gave him space. Jet, however, didn't leave his side.

They had set up in a house south of Seattle. The weather was wet and rainy and there had been no snow by mid-December.

By the third day, Matthew decided he had moped around enough and he announced that they would be going into the city to order tuxedos and get Samantha's dress fitted. Since the party was only a few weeks away they'd have to rush things.

The fittings went smoothly and they ordered masks too. Samantha picked them out.

The nights passed well enough as they settled into a similar routine to the one at the cabin. Since they were in an area that was far more populated, Matthew's training with Devak was limited. They would chase each other through forests working on speed, or Devak would teach him how to resist mind-altering effects.

It was during this time that Samantha had her first truly bad night. Sometimes she'd have a few hours here and there where she'd lose touch with reality but it was nothing like this.

Matthew had risen a few minutes before her and was grabbing some clothes to change into after his shower. He turned to set them down, only to find himself face to face with Samantha, standing on the edge of the bed. She reached her arm back and slapped Matthew across the face as hard as she could. The sound echoed in the room.

It didn't hurt but it did catch Matthew off-guard.

Jet, who normally slept at their feet, started barking.

Devak burst into the room, his eyes scanning the room for any dangers. "Is everything okay?"

"I don't know…Sam? Do you want to tell me why you slapped me?"

She looked as if she was possessed; more pale than normal and her eyes drifted, not focusing on anything. "My back still hurts from the blade."

Matthew walked around her and checked her back. Nothing was there.

"The galaxy will tremble when they see the blood," she continued. "They kneel and yet you still want more. Forgiveness carries a heavy price."

Alright…

She looked at Devak. "The traitor walks among us."

Matthew shot Devak a questioning glance.

Devak took a step back and bowed his head. "She is not wrong, but you are not the one I betrayed. I am loyal to you. I know it doesn't look good for me, but the curse prevents me from saying more."

"Hope fills him. The same now as the day he first held you in his arms and named you."

"What?" Matthew asked, bewildered by her words. Samantha continued to ramble but Matthew tuned her out as he watched Devak. "Is she talking about the past or the future?"

"The…" Devak's face twisted and he leaned against a dresser.

"Never mind, I'll add it to the damn list of questions I'm going to ask you once your tongue is untied."

Samantha leaped from the bed and began attacking Matthew. "The eyes in the dark."

Matthew dodged her claws.

The two men spent the rest of the night listening to her spout nonsense and moving away from her attacks while trying to take care of her.

Shortly before the sun rose, she collapsed on the bed just after smashing the vanity mirror. Matthew licked the cuts on her hand.

Her eyes fluttered and she whispered, "The singing, I can hear it."

"Can you?" Matthew asked. He longed to hear it as well.

"She's beautiful," was the last thing Samantha said before drifting off to sleep.

The next night, she only remembered small pieces of what she'd done. And she had a hard time interpreting anything she'd said.

She apologized to both men for attacking them. Matthew assured her that she had nothing to apologize for—neither was injured and it wasn't her fault. He didn't blame her for any of it, although he had no idea she could get so bad. He could see why the humans had thought she was mentally ill.

★★★★

A few days before the ball, when Matthew was sleeping, he woke during the day to find Devak standing over him. Devak's eyes were closed and he had a hand on Matthew's bare chest. Matthew could feel power stirring within him. It was…turning him on.

He tried to grab Devak's wrist and push him away but his body refused to respond to his commands, the sun making him weak and helpless.

"What are you doing?" Matthew asked, scowling and incapable of moving.

Devak's eyes snapped open and widened as he looked down at Matthew. "I am sorry, my prince, I did not mean to startle you. I didn't know you could wake during the day."

"Answer my question," Matthew growled and fought the urge to slip back to sleep.

"I…" Devak's chest began to heave and his muscles shook as he struggled against the curse that bound him. "Forgive me."

He left the room. Matthew—helpless to do anything else—went back to sleep.

When night fell, he ripped himself from the bed and marched into the living room, where Devak normally kept watch during the daytime.

He wasn't there.

"*Devak,*" Matthew snarled, his vampire side forward. He could smell him nearby. Devak came in from the kitchen. Was he hiding? He didn't make eye contact with Matthew before quietly falling on his knees before him. "Tell me what you were doing to me."

Devak bowed lower, his head on the ground but still said nothing. Matthew paced back and forth, his claws out.

"It must be convenient for you that you are unable to answer my most basic questions," Matthew growled. He wanted to sink his claws into Devak's skin and force the words out but he became distracted when he heard Samantha stir in the bed. "You're making it hard for me to trust you."

"I am sorry, my prince. I will stop."

"Stop? Have you been doing that every day?" His words were so loud he was practically yelling them.

Devak trembled. "I will accept any punishment you wish to impose, my prince."

"Stand up."

Devak rose to his feet but kept his head down. Samantha entered the room and plopped down on the couch. She didn't say anything as she rubbed sleep from her eyes.

Around you, I am becoming stronger, Devak had said.

Matthew stepped closer to him. "Now that I'm awake, show me what you were doing." If he couldn't talk about it, at least maybe Matthew could figure it out by watching him.

Devak reached out with shaky hands and placed them on Matthew—the brown skin a stark contrast to Matthew's pale chest.

The strangest sensation filled Matthew. It was as if power entered him from some unknown location, swirling through his body before moving on into Devak.

He had never felt anything like it.

Matthew closed his eyes and leaned his head back. Whatever Devak was doing made him feel strong, almost omnipotent. What was this? He'd ask, but he knew he wouldn't get any damn answers.

"Is he done feeding yet? I'm hungry too," Samantha asked.

Matthew opened his eyes and watched Devak, who removed his hands and took a step back. The feeling faded.

"How do you know he's feeding?" Matthew asked.

She shrugged. "How do I know anything? I just know."

Matthew let his anger subside. Whatever Devak had been doing didn't seem to drain Matthew so he saw no harm in letting Devak continue. "Alright, you can keep doing it. If you really are feeding, I don't want you to starve. But I want to be awake when it happens, understand?"

"Yes, my prince."

Matthew felt like a damned walking buffet.

The next night, wearing only boxers, he sat up and leaned against the headboard.

Samantha woke up shortly after him. She crawled up his side, pressing her body next to his, and sunk her teeth into his shoulder. She fed slow tonight, savoring his blood. Matthew wrapped an arm around her to keep her in place.

"Devak," Matthew whispered.

Devak came into the room a moment later and bowed. He wore the same black clothes with laces down the arms and front. They always seemed to be fresh and clean, though Matthew had no idea where they came from or how and when he cleaned them. Maybe he washed them during the day. The idea of Devak sitting around doing laundry made him smile.

"Hungry? Come." Matthew motioned to the free spot next to him.

Devak kneeled beside him on the mattress, facing Matthew. He reached out and held his hands inches above Matthew's skin. "Thank you, my prince."

Matthew nodded. Devak was back to saying 'my prince'...he always seemed to slip back to it when he thought he was in trouble or wanted to show his subservience. Matthew had done the same once, except the word he had used was 'master'.

"Feed," Matthew said.

Devak pressed his warm hands against Matthew's chest and the guardian's amber eyes rolled back into his head.

As the feeling of power returned to Matthew, he found his own eyes closing and focused on the sensation.

"Tastes so good..." Samantha muttered against his skin.

Feeding these two beings made Matthew feel as if he had complete dominion over them. He enjoyed the sensation more than he should have. He wasn't sure why, maybe it stemmed from how much he hated the loss of control...how much Tarrick had taken from him.

Tarrick.

The man he shouldn't love. It wasn't as if there had even been a romance between them...and yet...

As his thoughts wandered, he realized that having Samantha's fangs inside of him and having Devak's hands on his chest was a little too much.

His cock grew hard under his boxers, tenting them. He moaned.

Whimpers of pleasure escaped Samantha and she removed her fangs. He wasn't sure if it was the bond turning her on or something else, but after she licked the puncture marks she continued up his neck. Switching between frantic kisses and rough flicks of her tongue.

Devak, still feeding, responded by moving his hands lower across Matthew's abdomen. He traced Matthew's hard muscles and massaged the area right above his cock.

Matthew's eyes flew open. "Stop."

Devak pulled his hands away but remained kneeling beside him. Samantha didn't stop.

Matthew gently tugged on her brown hair and she looked up at him.

"Stop," he repeated, softer.

She looked hurt. "But don't you want it? Don't you want me?"

"Not this way."

She glared at Devak. "It's him you want? Alone?"

He could sense her jealousy. It was an ugly emotion on her.

Matthew should have realized sooner that she had a crush on him. She had done a good job of keeping it to herself but it made sense—he had turned her; they were bonded together. He was the first man to care for her in years. Hell, he was her first kiss, even if that was unintended. And being an incubus didn't help matters. "No, I don't want Devak either."

"I don't understand. You were enjoying it. I could feel that you want more," she said and tried to pull away from him. He tightened his arm and didn't let her go. He owed her an explanation.

It wasn't just sex that Samantha wanted. She wanted a lover and Matthew couldn't be that for her. Not right now. Not with his heart still fucking aching. He'd end up hurting her and since they were bound together for the next century, she wouldn't be able to run away or distance herself when the heartbreak happened. She needed someone else. Someone she could love and trust, someone she could explore with.

"Sam, please let me explain."

She struggled harder in his arm. "No, let me go."

Unwilling to hold her against her will, he released her and she stormed out of the room, slamming the door. Matthew listened to make sure she wasn't going to run out of the house.

He heard the shower of another bathroom turn on and his relief became pain when he heard her cry, feeling her distress as if it was his own. She had never known the sting of rejection before. It was a reminder to him of how new to all of this she was.

Matthew swung his legs around the side of the bed and sat on the edge. Devak hadn't moved.

"Are you waiting to be dismissed?" Matthew asked, irritated.

"No. I...may I speak openly?"

"Sure."

"I can understand why you stopped her. She is young, inexperienced. She clearly wants more than you can give. But I don't understand why you stopped me. I am not young, or inexperienced. I have been with many incubi and I know their desires. I can feed you and want nothing in return. Why do you not take from me?"

Matthew turned to face Devak. It was a fair question. Thoughts of unlacing his clothes and claiming his beautiful body danced across Matthew's brain. He pushed them away.

Unaware he was even doing it, Matthew reached up and rubbed the skin above his heart. He wasn't sure how to answer Devak.

"It's tempting. Last year..." He sighed. "Last year, I fell for an incubus I shouldn't have. Even after all this time I'm not over it. I don't want to put myself in a position where it could happen again." Devak opened his mouth to speak but Matthew raised his hand to stop him. "I know you are offering no strings attached but that's not how I work. If we were to meet in a bar and it was a one-night stand, sure, I'd bed you in a heartbeat. But we didn't and I don't want to have to send you away because I couldn't control my feelings. There are powerful beings after me and I can use your strength to help protect Sam. Hell, I could use your protection for myself."

Devak nodded, accepting the answer. "I had thought that maybe you didn't like me or my appearance wasn't pleasing to you."

Matthew chuckled. "That's most definitely not the case."

The edge of Devak's lip curled up a little, then dropped almost immediately. "The incubus you love, was it the one who held you captive?"

"Please don't start with the Stockholm shit, I'm well aware that—"

Devak shifted around on his knees. "No. That wasn't why I asked. I met him. I can see why you like him. He's powerful. And a strong leader. I also once fell for an incubus general. I think you and I are attracted to the same type of man."

"Wait. You met Tarrick?"

Devak nodded. "I was at his estate a few days after you had escaped, looking for you. At the time, I had thought you were there as a guest, not a prisoner. He tried to capture me, unsuccessfully, of course. They were all angry when I mentioned your name."

"Yeah, a lot of hunters were killed during my escape. And I'm not sure why you thought I'd be their guest, I'm a vampire after all."

"I hadn't realized the war was still going on. There was a time when the vampires and incubi of this world were at peace."

"And then you started the war?"

"I am the reason it started." Devak looked as if he wasn't going to say anymore. Matthew wouldn't push him. He stood and picked up a pair of jeans off the floor, pausing when Devak started to talk again.

"Many millennia ago, I was a companion to an incubus general. A human companion. I loved him. He was brilliant, ambitious… insatiable. He had many lovers, which didn't bother me. I understand incubi and their nature. I even took other lovers of my own, but we always returned to each other. That is until one of his lovers grew jealous of the attention he showed me. She gave him an ultimatum: choose between her or me. He chose me."

Devak, still on his knees, bowed his head down as he relived the painful memory. Matthew leaned against the dresser as he listened, worried that if he interrupted with questions Devak would end the story.

"She was a vampire, a powerful vampire, and in her rage, to punish him, she sired me. Because of the bond, I had no choice but to leave my love behind. I was so angry at her for what she had done, and furious at him for not finding a way to get me back, that when my Dominar abilities emerged I could think of nothing but destruction. The power fed those thoughts. I broke away from the bond and began a reign of terror, killing any that crossed my path, it didn't matter the species.

"That battle you saw, was just one of many. And I won them all.

My destruction spanned decades. During this time, the relations between vampires and incubi broke down, each blaming the other for my actions. When I killed their leaders, peace crumbled completely. In the end, I was seduced back by my love. I could never resist him… and when my guard lowered, he killed me."

Devak rubbed his neck. A thin line of scarring appeared across his skin but it was gone a moment later. He looked at Matthew.

"I want you to trust me, my prince. I am loyal to you. What happened to me was long ago and I've changed since that time. And he has too, I have no fealty to him."

Matthew cocked his head to the side. "Your general is still alive?" Tarrick wasn't old enough to be Devak's lover. Nor were any of the other generals currently serving.

"He is not a general anymore."

Matthew closed his eyes as understanding came to him. "Jesus. You were Malarath's lover? The fucking High King…"

Devak swallowed hard on hearing the name. "He was ambitious and when I wiped out the leaders, he took the throne and became their ruler. I haven't seen him since the night he killed me."

Matthew opened his eyes and rubbed his forehead. "And your sire, does she still live?"

"Yes, but there is no connection between us anymore."

"The sleeping Queen? That's why you asked about her?"

Devak nodded. "I can only assume that Malarath hasn't killed her yet because he wants her to watch as he wipes out all other vampires. Then, I think, he will end her."

"Is he stronger than her?"

"I think so. Thousands of years ago he was among the most powerful incubi. I can only imagine what he is today. You should know that neither of them would recognize me if they saw me. My appearance changed when I was made a guardian…"

Matthew went to stand by the bed, towering above Devak. He should be angry. Instead, he began to laugh.

Devak watched him, confused.

"Seems we both got fucked over by an incubus general. At least he hasn't managed to kill me yet," Matthew said.

Devak looked as if he wanted to smile but none appeared on his face.

Matthew set a hand on his guardian's shoulder. "I'm glad you told me. If I'd heard your story from someone else, it would have looked bad for you."

"Thank you for understanding, my—"

"Seriously, no more 'prince' stuff. If we're going to be around other vampires, I can't risk it."

Devak nodded. "Thank you."

Fourteen

The night of the masquerade was on them and Matthew felt Samantha wake the moment the sun set, which was a first for her. She was already feeding by the time he opened his eyes. Her hair was full of curlers. She drank fast, then peeled away to go get ready.

For the most part, she seemed to have forgiven Matthew for not wanting to sleep with her, but every time he tried to explain anything, she shut him down.

Not wanting to deal with a moody teen, Matthew dropped the matter. As a peace offering, he taught her to dance. Just the basics, working under the assumption that vampires danced the same as incubi...the two species were closer than either cared to admit, so he risked it.

She picked it up extraordinarily fast. Matthew was pleasantly surprised to learn that she was better at it than he was. It had taken him weeks to master the steps and he had months of training from Rosaline before he went to his first ball.

Devak, since telling his story to Matthew, seemed to be in an all-around better mood, as if a burden had been lifted from him. Matthew saw him smile once or twice each day, which was a vast improvement.

Devak fed from Matthew while Samantha showered and when the guardian was done he took his tux from the closet and left.

Matthew found himself disappointed that Devak hadn't changed in front of him. He wanted to see all of the man's beautiful body, and he wondered what it would be like to have such a powerful creature writhing under him in pleasure...taking all of Matthew into him...

Pushing the thought away with a grunt, Matthew ignored the incubus scratching under his skin; famished. He had gone out to feed yesterday and he was already hungry again. He adjusted his cock and frowned.

"Would it kill you to stay hard while I was fucking someone? You know I'm an incubus, right?" he asked it, then went about getting ready.

Twenty minutes later, both Devak and Matthew were dressed and waiting in the living room for Samantha. They both wore light pink ties that matched the color of Samantha's dress.

She had insisted.

And Matthew was a pushover when it came to her. At least she let them have grey—not pink—vests.

Devak's tie looked like a monkey had put it on him. Without thinking, Matthew ripped it off and began the process of retying it. Going to all those incubus parties had made him a pro.

He was nearly done when he noticed just how close they were standing to each other. Devak stood frozen in place, letting Matthew manhandle him. Matthew finished and took a step back.

"Sorry..." He wasn't really sure he was sorry but it seemed like the right thing to say.

"There is nothing to apologize for. I never had anyone teach me how to tie one. I've been winging it for years."

Matthew chuckled. "What? No ties in Heaven?" Well, wherever he was from. Matthew was just going to think of it as Vampire Heaven until someone told him differently.

"Something like that."

Finally, Samantha came down.

Matthew's jaw dropped.

She looked completely different from the night he had first seen her in the club.

The unexciting, average woman was gone and replaced by a vision of beauty. Her dress complemented her unblemished, smooth skin. Her brown curls cascaded down her neck, one side of her hair pinned back by white gems. She wore long jeweled earrings that drew the eye to her delicate neck.

It was the first time Matthew had ever seen her wearing makeup. It wasn't a lot, but it was flattering. She had added blush to her cheeks and outlined her eyes with kohl. A petite white mask, made of lace, sat elegantly on her face. It didn't cover much of her identity but they didn't need to hide it—no one would know who she was.

She stopped in front of Matthew. "You're both embarrassing me," she said after a long silence.

Devak came forward and took her by the hand. "You look stunning,

Sam."

"Gorgeous," Matthew said, trying to recover.

"Put them on!" Samantha pointed to the two boxes sitting on a side table.

Devak released her and opened his box. Inside was a Colombina rombi mask: diagonally checkered with bone, black, and gold coloring. Devak tied the ribbon at the back of his head. The mask suited him.

Matthew's mask was far more detailed. The center of the mask was bone porcelain and it had golden baroque detailing at the cheeks that went down each side of the face. The baroque pattern weaved upwards along the outer edges and pressed into fine points along the top, giving the mask the appearance of a crown. It wasn't the type of mask he would have chosen for himself but Samantha had insisted.

He put it on and caught Devak staring at him.

"It is quite fitting," Devak said, nodding his approval.

Samantha grabbed Matthew's hand and pulled. "Come on, let's go."

The three of them piled into the car—Devak driving, Samantha and Matthew in the back—and headed to the ball. At his feet, Matthew noticed the duffle bag was in the car.

"What's this doing here?"

"It's in case we have to barter for the offering. I packed some items that are worth a lot," Samantha said.

Matthew unzipped the duffle an inch and peeked inside. "And a sword I see."

Samantha just shrugged.

"Have either of you seen Jet since yesterday?" Matthew asked.

Devak glanced back in the rearview mirror. "I have not."

"He didn't sleep on the bed last night," Samantha said.

Matthew growled. He had told Jet that, 'No, a dog could not go to a party'. And then explained that vampires got nervous when gargoyles walk around, even if they did tolerate them sitting on the roof. Jet had huffed away.

Driving to the masquerade reminded Matthew of the drive onto Tarrick's estate. There was a hidden road they turned down; water drops splashed against the windshield as they drove through a canopy of trees.

They passed through what looked like a broken down gate. It was, of course, a magic shroud. Devak slowed the car as he approached and pulled up behind a long line of other limos and expensive look-at-me cars.

Once they passed through, an expansive estate unveiled before them. It looked reminiscent of Ashwood. It stood four stories high, stone, with high spires and angry looking gargoyles on the corners.

It was hardly surprising that it looked similar since vampires had built Ashwood. Tarrick had, as Matthew had come to understand it, sieged the estate and taken it for himself.

There were small glowing balls of soft light floating in the air, illumining the lush garden. They were alive but Matthew had no idea what kind of creature they were. Some sort of supernatural bug?

Matthew reached out with his senses and scanned the estate. He counted twenty-four living gargoyles on the roof. Including Jet. He sighed.

"Everything okay, Father?" Samantha asked.

"It's fine, Jet's here."

"Oh, good."

Matthew went back to scanning. He estimated there were already hundreds of vampires here and more were arriving. He wouldn't be able to distinguish between lords, children, and normal vampires until he was standing much closer to them. He could also sense shifters, though he couldn't determine their type, and witches.

If he was discovered, he'd be dead. No question. He could barely handle eight lords and this was far beyond that. He double checked to make sure his mask was secure, then he suppressed his aura further so it wouldn't tip anyone off.

Devak was scanning the area as well.

Matthew leaned forward to speak with him. "There are shifters and witches here. Humans too. Thralls, maybe?" He had assumed there would only be vampires here tonight.

Devak nodded.

Samantha put her hand to her temple and cried out with pain.

Matthew grabbed her. "What is it?"

"It's all pressing in on me."

She had never been around another vampire, let alone this many.

The power coming off them must have been tremendous for her.

Matthew touched her and used the bond to lend some of his strength. After a few moments, she was better and back to smiling.

Devak pulled the car up to a valet, got out, and opened Samantha's door for her.

"Bring the bag," Samantha said to Matthew as he got out.

He slung it over his shoulder and she held out her arms for Devak and Matthew to take, one on each side. Her eyes were huge with wonder as she took in the scene. Vampires of all different sizes and attitudes were streaming into the front entry. Many older ones had fledglings or thralls following them. Other vampires were locked arm and arm with a lover—some were human.

Large, double front doors were wide open; music and soft light poured out. A vampire wearing a mask that gave him the appearance of a devil was collecting invitations.

"You already collected ours," Matthew said with a smile, compelling him. The vampire struggled against him for just a moment before nodding and letting them in.

Vampires packed the foyer, grand staircase, and the balcony above. Gothic artwork and tapestries lined the walls, and dark roses filled vases on the tables. Every window—what few there were—had thick velvet drapery.

The undead wore a wide variety of formal attire. Most of the men were in some variation of a tuxedo, while women's dresses tended to vary by the age of the vampire. The younger they were, the more modern the dress. Corset dresses with big skirts were popular with the older vampires.

Every person wore a mask and they were as different as the number here tonight. There were full-face masks that made the wearer look like a porcelain doll, leather masks that bore a resemblance to wild animals, half masks adorned with flowers, jewels, or feathers. Masks made of metal, or paper, or glass. There were jesters, plague doctors, an arlecchino…it was a feast for the eyes.

Both Matthew and Devak wanted to take a few moments to absorb everything but Samantha was too eager. She pulled them onwards.

They brushed past the crowd, making their way towards the beautifully eerie music, into the packed ballroom. It was larger than the one in Tarrick's estate but nowhere near as large as Queen Agleea's. It had a high ceiling with an enormous candle-lit chandelier in the center. Long ribbons hung high on the ceiling, aerial performers twisting around them like snakes.

An orchestra played from the far end of the crowded room, and dancers filled the center, waltzing around. Most couples kept in step with the music but some would break away, disappearing and reappearing elsewhere.

A male vampire rushed by Samantha, pushing past her. Matthew pulled her in and growled at him but the vampire ignored them, moving on.

"Stop it," Samantha said.

Mathew released her. "Sorry."

Samantha led them to the edge of the dance floor and drank in the spectacle.

Matthew and Devak resumed scanning the room, taking note of numbers of people, exits, the biggest threats, artwork, and so on.

Above them, there were landings and balconies full of tables. Matthew could sense the more powerful and, most likely, important vampires up there. It was the opposite of how the incubi did it, where the higher up one went, the less important one was.

There were servants with trays full of tall glasses of blood. A human walked past him with unhealed bite marks running up and down her arms and neck as an open invitation to take a sip. Saliva pooled in Matthew's mouth when he saw her, but he didn't partake because he didn't know the rules and he wanted to avoid anything that would draw attention to himself.

Even with the human thralls, this party wasn't like the get-together in New Orleans. There were no incubi on display, nor were any of the humans near death or in pain. The masquerade was...civilized, far more than Matthew had expected.

"I want to dance," Samantha said and grabbed Matthew's hand.

Devak took the duffle from him. "I'll stow this."

Matthew led Samantha to the dance floor and took the lead. Any steps she didn't know, she picked up right away by following his lead. She was incredible.

He danced with her for a few songs until there was a swap in partners. She went twirling off into the arms of another vampire while Matthew ended up with a vampire lord.

She had long blonde hair and sharp features under her purple mask. Matthew could sense a great deal of power coming from her. Physically, she looked young, but power radiated off her. She was old. Extremely old.

"You're new," she said with a deliberate smile.

Matthew smiled back, hiding his nerves. "Are you certain? Do you know everyone here?"

She tilted her head slightly. "Anyone who matters."

"Even under the masks?"

She looked up at the vampires above them. "Most are here to show off and be seen, even with the masks."

"I'm just here to dance with beautiful women." He would have added 'and men' at the end but he noticed that there were no same-sex couples on the dance floor. There were a few sitting around but it seemed vampires weren't quite as open about it as incubi were.

"Is it the beautiful women that have you aroused?" She pressed her body into his but it wasn't his dick she was referring too. It was his red eyes.

Among the vampire community, there wasn't much information about the vampire that had attacked New Orleans—about Matthew—except that he had silver eyes. Not wanting to give himself away, he kept his eyes red. It would give the appearance that he was hungry or horny but it wouldn't be out of place. Looking around, many vampires here had red eyes and fangs out.

"As you said, I'm new."

They chatted about nothing important for the rest of the song until he found himself with a new partner. Heck, there seemed to be a line waiting for him. Matthew wondered if the same quality that drew incubi to him also attracted vampires.

An hour passed before he could break away and retreat to a darker corner alone. Both Samantha and Devak were still on the dance floor.

Devak's dancing was flawless. He and his partner glided from one step to the next so smoothly it looked as if the two of them were floating off the ground. The guardian talked with her and even smiled in his responses. He looked like he belonged here; as if the grim warrior was the mask, and tonight he removed it.

What had life been like for Devak as a companion to an incubus general? Had Devak even known how to fight when he had been human? It was clear he had mastered the art of navigating a social event. Matthew wished he was that skillful but he always found fighting easier than small talk. Devak only seemed to fight when he had to.

Matthew didn't need the bond to know that Samantha was in high spirits. He saw her in the arms of a vampire who wore a leather mask with stag horns rising from the top. The vampire's skin was a dark greyish coal color and his hair was curly and black. He looked to have been in his early thirties when he was turned but he was younger than a century, much younger. A child by vampire standards but, then again, Matthew wasn't one to judge...he was nine.

Samantha seemed enamored by him. Her body language made it clear she was flirting and he responded in kind. Matthew forced away the instinct to go over and growl at his daughter's suitor. He needed to leave the area or he'd end up attacking the man.

"Can you keep an eye on her?" Matthew said, his voice low, directed at Devak. Across the ballroom, over the music and loud conversation, Devak nodded. The movement was so slight that his partner didn't catch it.

After making sure Samantha would be safe, Matthew left the ballroom to explore the mansion in hopes of running across something that could be an offering, or at least memorizing where everything was so that he'd be able to locate it if a vision came to Samantha.

He studied the art he passed by, most of it had images of war and battle. There wasn't much in the way of human art either; the bulk of it showed vampire warriors through the ages, the rest featured other supernatural creatures: dragons, shifters, centaurs. One depicted a tree full of dead bodies—it was gruesome. He wondered just who owned this place.

Matthew made his way down the hall towards the gardens.

He froze when a man entered from the back door. He was large, and it looked as if his nose had been broken many times. He wore a tux but he looked out of place in it and he had an eye patch over his right eye. He was a shifter. A tiger.

And Matthew was the reason the tiger was missing that eye. He had stabbed it with a dagger during a battle—his first battle actually. One where he was fighting on the side of the incubi.

Matthew dodged down a different hallway and ducked into an empty bedroom as the shifter came to a stop and sniffed the air. Around him, sounds of sex and other depraved acts bled through the walls. He stopped breathing and waited. Getting into a fight with the tiger would be bad enough, it kicked his ass last time, but more than that—it would draw the attention of the vampires.

The shifter took a step down the other hallway, looked around, then moved on.

Matthew breathed a sigh of relief. He exited the room and started back to where he came from when he felt something tug him in another direction. He turned but found nothing there. He felt the tug again. It was a subtle thing, as if someone had tied a thread to his wrist and gently pulled on it.

His curiosity piqued and he followed the feeling. It led him down the empty hall to a set of dark wooden double doors. He could smell blood on the other side. There was another tug, and a whispered word:

Matthew.

That voice. He recognized it. He had heard it in New Orleans—it had saved his life.

He opened the doors and walked in.

Inside looked like a gothic church with a set of pews facing a thick stone altar, covered with bowls of blood. Lit candles lined the room, their red wax dripping down the walls and onto the floor. In the center of the altar stood a large marble statue of a skull that had ridged horns curling out the side and a mouthful of fangs. This was a place of worship. A temple to the Blood God.

Matthew shut the doors behind him, walked up to the altar, and studied the skull. The fangs were covered in dried blood.

Unsure why, he found himself lifting his hand and pressing his thumb against the fang, puncturing his skin. He removed his thumb and over one of the bowls he let a few drops fall in, then he licked the wound to seal it.

Within him, he flushed with power. It felt the same as when Devak fed on him: energy coming from an unknown source, filling him.

What was he doing?

Matthew pushed away from the altar and the feeling faded...then he realized he wasn't alone in here.

He turned and froze.

Before him stood a vampire. A male. Big. Wearing a white Bauta mask that covered his entire face except his stone grey eyes. His hands were gloved, a black cape covered his neck and body, and he wore a tricorn hat. A chill ran through Matthew. What was under all of that?

"I'm sorry, I thought I was alone in here," Matthew said.

The figure nodded once.

Matthew carefully walked past the vampire, whose stone eyes never left him.

When Matthew reached the door, a whisper floated past him: *Matthew.*

He whipped around and the vampire was gone. He was alone.

Another chill ran down Matthew's spine. He couldn't stay in here any longer. With haste, he made his way back to the ballroom. He didn't see Devak but he spotted Samantha sitting at a table on the second floor. She was still with the man in the stag mask, and several other vampires were at the table with them. They were laughing and drinking glasses of blood.

Matthew watched as the male rested his hand on the small of Samantha's back. Rage flashed through him. How *dare* that vampire touch his child. His.

From across the ballroom, Matthew surged forward to stand behind the group in the blink of an eye. Before they could move, he yanked Samantha up out of her seat and pushed her behind him. He snarled at the group, flashing his large fangs and claws. If any dared challenge him he'd destroy them.

The group of vampires leaped to their feet, their own guises coming forward.

"*Father,*" Samantha hissed.

Matthew looked back at her.

"What the hell are you doing?" she asked, her eyes narrowed.

What was he doing? The vampire had touched her, not hurt her. She was in no danger.

Devak appeared beside him...or maybe he had been there and

Matthew had only just noticed. The area around him became crowded with onlookers but no one made any moves to attack him.

"I...I'm sorry, Sam," he said and forced his claws away.

She narrowed her eyes at him, pushed away, and ran off into the crowd. Matthew started after her but Devak put a hand on his shoulder. "Give her a moment to cool down, I will watch over her."

Matthew said nothing as Devak went after her. He straightened up and turned to the group she had been sitting with. Clearing his throat he said, "My apologies."

One of the older vampires at the table, a male wearing a black mask, laughed. "No harm has been done." He placed his hand on a female vampire standing to his right. "When I turned her, I could not stand anyone touching her for a decade."

The situation defused, the onlookers returned to their own conversations, and the vampires returned to their human appearances. Matthew nodded to the group and slunk away into the crowd. He shouldn't have lost control.

Matthew walked for a bit, then came to rest against the railing overlooking the dance floor. He could sense that Samantha was still upset with him. He wanted to seek her out and tell her how sorry he was. A thought made him laugh at himself. He, of all people, shouldn't feel rage or jealousy if Samantha was getting a little action—he was an incubus for fuck's sake. Even still...the bond cranked his desire to protect her to a ridiculous extreme.

Something caught his eye and pulled him from his thoughts. Across the ballroom, also leaning against the railing was the last person he ever expected to see here:

Tarrick.

Fifteen

Matthew couldn't believe his eyes. Tarrick stood on the other side of the ballroom in a tuxedo and a horned mask. The incubus general flashed Matthew a devious smile.

How could he possibly be here? Vampires could sense incubi, and more than that, every vampire knew what Tarrick looked like; mask or no, he should be getting ripped to shreds right now.

Matthew looked around, no one else seemed to notice him. When Matthew looked back Tarrick was gone, but his scent of night and earth lingered in the air. It *had* been Tarrick.

Pulling power to his speed, he rushed over to where Tarrick had been standing. The scent trailed off behind a curtain. Matthew pushed it back and found a hallway behind it. He followed it up a flight of stairs to the fourth floor, then down a hallway that looked exactly like something found in Ashwood Estate—right down to the same tables and art.

At the end of the hall were thick double doors. Matthew pushed them open and entered.

It was Tarrick's room.

Everything—every detail—was the same. His weapons adorned the walls, a set of chains hung at the back, to the right was the open air shower, and before him the large bed with black silk sheets. The room was orderly and clean. A wooden desk had neat piles of reports on it.

And standing before him was Tarrick.

His sapphire eyes sensual, his dusty blond hair flawless, and his polished shoes didn't have a single scuff. He no longer had his mask on.

Matthew's chest tightened and his breath shortened. Even though he hadn't fed tonight, it felt like his heart was pounding against his ribs.

"What is this?" Matthew asked. Had Tarrick used magic to bring him here? There had been no green flash that normally accompanied teleportation.

When Tarrick stepped forward, Matthew backed up, bumping into the door, forcing it closed behind him.

Tarrick came closer. "I'm not going to hurt you."

Matthew's vampire emerged as he pressed against the door. He should attack Tarrick before the hunters showed up but he couldn't bring himself to move. Tarrick closed the gap between them. He was shorter than Matthew, but right now Matthew felt tiny in comparison. He had to resist the urge to kneel.

The incubus put his hand on Matthew's face then leaned in and claimed his mouth. Matthew couldn't believe this was happening. He was too shocked to respond to the kiss except to part his lips. Tarrick's aggressive tongue pushed into him, past his fangs, and took ownership.

When Tarrick finally pulled away, he kissed Matthew's chin, then trailed across his jaw, and down his neck. It was more than Matthew could handle—out of his mind, he let out short, desperate moans.

"I've missed you," Tarrick said, his lips tickling Matthew's skin as he spoke.

"Master..." Matthew whispered in response. This was too much. Matthew sank to his knees, away from Tarrick's lips. He pressed his palms onto the wooden floor and trembled.

He wanted this to be real but it couldn't be. None of it made sense.

He was at a vampire ball, and it was impossible for an incubus as powerful as Tarrick to show up undetected. He couldn't be here in Tarrick's room. And Tarrick wouldn't start making out with him— he'd call his hunters and have him shackled, or he'd pull a weapon from the wall and attack.

A gentle hand rested on his shoulder.

"I'm sorry, I thought you would enjoy this," a soft female voice said to him.

He looked up and saw a petite, young-looking vampire standing before him. She had smooth, brown hair and wore a corset and matching skirt. She had no mask on, though even if she had, Matthew would still have known who she was.

"Emilia..." Matthew said. Ascelina's child.

He looked around; the room had changed. They were in a decent-sized bedroom but it was nothing like Tarrick's suite. It had a bed with red satin sheets, a couch, and a heavy wooden dresser with a matching vanity.

Matthew pushed himself to his feet. He was doing his best to not take out his anger on Emilia but he couldn't hide how irate he was. He removed his mask and tossed it on the bed. She took a step away from him as he towered over her.

"I'm sorry," she repeated.

"Aren't you supposed to be in London with your mother?"

She lowered her head. "She told me you were coming here and I wanted to see you. I haven't seen you in over nine months."

"What were you doing to me?" he growled.

"Trying to feed you," she said.

"I don't need help feeding."

She stared at him. Matthew guessed that she knew he was having some issues.

Sometimes he forgot that she was a telepath. He threw up a defensive mental shield that Devak had taught him how to do but Matthew was still new at it and Emilia was one of the strongest telepaths around; she could probably break through it if she wanted.

Emilia frowned. "No one knows about your problem with feeding—" that was a nice way of summing up his erection issues, "— not even my mother. And I won't tell anyone."

"I thought you only had the ability to give people nightmares...I didn't know you could make something feel so...real."

"I only learned how to do it a few months ago. Please let me help you."

"Emilia." Matthew sighed. "I feed on sexual energy. What you're doing is fake...there'd be nothing for me to feed on."

"It would be real. I would, uh." She looked away, a bit shy. "I would be using you while you used me."

Matthew wasn't sure what she had planned but had always gotten the sense that she had wanted to sleep with him when they were locked in Tarrick's prison together. His suspicion was confirmed when he stayed at Ascelina's house for a few months after his escape. He always put her off, choosing instead to feed only on humans. They were less complicated.

She took a brave step closer and grabbed his hand. "Please. You took care of me once. Let me help you."

"No. Not this way."

She placed her other hand on his stomach. "You're so hungry."

"I'm fine. It's not empty, but even if it was, having an empty soavik won't kill me."

Matthew felt strong hands grab his waist from behind. He glanced over his shoulder to see Tarrick— fake Tarrick that is—pressed up against him. "But you're in pain. Let me feed you," he said in a deep, sexy tone.

Matthew turned to face Emilia but she had disappeared again.

"Emilia," he called out. "Please stop this."

Tarrick nipped at the back of Matthew's neck.

"Emilia," he said again, this time quieter. The nipping felt so good.

Tarrick's hands slid up Matthew's body, loosened his bow tie, and began to unbutton his vest.

"Please," Matthew begged. It was the last feeble attempt he made to get her to stop before he surrendered to the illusion. The part of him that wanted this won out and he was back in Tarrick's room.

"Undress," Tarrick commanded.

Helpless, Matthew did as ordered. He slipped out of his shirt, vest, and jacket, dropping them to the ground, then sat down on the bed to remove his socks and shoes.

"Everything," Tarrick said.

Matthew stood and undid his pants, pushing them down with his underwear. He stood in front of Tarrick, exposed, and so hard it was painful.

"Now me."

Matthew began to undress Tarrick. He went slow. His fingers trembled as he unknotted Tarrick's tie and worked his way down the buttons. Once undone, he pushed open the shirt and studied Tarrick's chest. The defined muscles were sinful. Matthew reached out to touch them but his shaking fingers stopped just short.

He pulled away. "This is wrong. I-I can't."

Tarrick peeled off his jacket and shirt, set them neatly on a chair, and then removed the rest of his clothing. Matthew licked his lips as Tarrick's hard cock sprung free.

When Tarrick took a step to him, Matthew backed away. God, he would give anything to spend another night with Tarrick but he couldn't do this. This wasn't healthy. This wouldn't help him heal.

"Emilia, stop," he said with a little more resolve this time.

Tarrick moved close and pressed his body into him. Matthew thought that he should try to get away but he couldn't move; his desire to stay close to Tarrick was too strong.

Tarrick planted rough kisses on Matthew's shoulder and began to move inwards. Matthew's body responded. He leaned in so that more of their skin touched and reached down to run his hand across Tarrick's hard sex. The heavy weight of it drove him crazy with desire.

Emilia wasn't going to stop and Matthew wasn't able to control his own body. He was too far gone to try and push her out mentally or even beg her to end this.

"Devak, help me," he said, it came out barely louder than a whisper as Tarrick grabbed Matthew's length and stroked it. Tarrick's hand felt like velvet. It always did.

Matthew could no longer resist what was happening—he wanted more. No. He *needed* more.

He wrapped his arms around Tarrick and pulled golden threads of sexual energy into himself, feeding. He moved his hand around the back of Tarrick's head, running his fingers through his hair, messing it up slightly. He smiled to himself, thinking of how much Tarrick hated having anything out of place.

Then a dark hand ripped Tarrick away from him. Tarrick's room faded away. And it took Matthew a moment to process what was going on.

Tarrick was gone and Devak was holding Emilia in the air by her neck. His hands were clawed and his eyes were deep pools of red. Emilia struggled to get away from him but he clamped down harder, crushing her larynx, making it impossible for her to speak.

"Put her down," Matthew ordered.

Devak released her but looked as if he was ready to attack her if she moved. It took her a moment to heal the damage Devak had inflicted.

Her eyes darted between Matthew, Devak, and the closed door behind her.

Matthew growled in warning. "Don't even think about trying to run—we're both faster than you."

"What is he?" she asked, her voice hoarse. She tried to take a step away from Devak but he gripped her shoulder, keeping her in place.

"He's not the one you should be worried about," Matthew said.

"I...Matthew, I'm sorry. I didn't mean for it to go so far. I can sense how hungry you are. I wanted to give back what you gave to me."

"I fucking told you to stop," he said.

Emilia bowed her head in shame. "I'm sorry. I got caught up in it. I was enjoying bringing you pleasure...I—"

Matthew held up his hand to cut her off. She fell silent. Matthew, still naked, but no longer sporting an erection, put his hand on Emilia's cheek. She looked up at him.

"I can forgive you this once. I understand what it's like to lose control to your powers, especially when they are new. But know this—" Matthew's voice turned dark, "—there will never be anything beyond a friendship between us. I am never going to sleep with you. And if you do this to me again, I don't care who your mother is, or what good deeds you two have done for me, I will kill you."

Tears ran down Emilia's cheeks.

"Do you understand?"

"Yes. I'm sorry, Matthew. I'm so sorry."

Matthew leaned down and kissed her on the head. "I know you are. Go rejoin the party."

She wiped her tears away and grabbed her mask sitting on the side table. She tied it on and left the room.

Matthew took a seat on the edge of the bed. He pushed away his vampire side, buried his face in his hands, and fought away the anguish he felt. Everything she had done to him had felt so real. Being so close to Tarrick again, even if he was only an illusion, made his heart hurt.

Devak, who was back to looking human, sat next to him, only a few inches between them. "You are very benevolent."

Matthew took a deep breath and released some of the tension that had built up in his muscles. "Thank you for stopping her."

"I will always come when summoned. I am yours."

Matthew looked at him and became conscious of just how close Devak was. Emilia had been right—he was in pain. No matter how much he tried to ignore it or push it away, he had spent the last year with a constant, throbbing ache deep within him.

Devak met his eyes, then the guardian's gaze drifted downwards across Matthew's naked body, settling on his groin. The smaller man's lips parted only just. One moment extended into another before he glanced back to Matthew's face.

Realizing what he had done, he stood. His stance tense and uneasy. "I did not mean to…" He trailed off for a moment. "It is obvious you were born an incubus…I mean that in only the best of ways…you are well put together, your body that is…not to say that you aren't also—" He snapped his mouth shut.

Matthew had never seen Devak trip over his words in such a way. He was usually concise, saying only what he needed to.

Devak, who seemed to realize his own loss of control, bowed. "I will return to watching Sam."

Matthew sat in silence, still processing what had just occurred. Emilia had nearly raped him and he had no power to stop it from happening. But Devak saved him. His guardian. Submissive and always following Matthew's command, always offering himself and expecting nothing in return. And he had offered his body many times for sex—feeding—with no strings.

Matthew felt weak…he had for a long time. He had a broken heart, a daughter to protect, an army after them…combined with not fully feeding, it wore him down. He wanted to feel strong again.

He needed something he could control. The desire to possess Devak coiled around him like steam rising from a hot spring.

His incubus side stirred. As Devak opened the door to leave, Matthew moved before he could change his mind. He slammed the door shut and blocked his path.

Devak froze in place, head bowed. "I apologize if I overstepped my station," he whispered, misreading Matthew's intent.

Matthew said nothing as he studied Devak's features: scintillant eyes, near-luminous bronze skin, full lips that looked made to be wrapped around a dick, and lean muscles obvious even under his tuxedo.

Matthew put his hand on Devak's chin, his fingers gentle on his jaw as his thumb stroked his fine cheekbone and moved to Devak's lips. They parted under the touch.

With his other hand, Matthew reached back and untied the ribbon that kept Devak's mask in place and it fell away.

He tilted Devak's head up, leaned over, and kissed the man he so desperately wanted right now. It was just a brush, a testing of waters, a first kiss that promised more. The kiss deepened and passion overtook them, turning aggressive with want and need.

Matthew broke away. Devak—no longer misreading the intent— raked his eyes over Matthew, pausing at his now-erect cock.

"I thought that you didn't—" Devak started to say but Matthew cut him off.

"Feed me," Matthew said, his voice firm and his desire clear. His fangs emerged as if to authenticate his need.

Devak took off his tie and began to unbutton his vest and shirt.

It was too slow. Matthew spun him around and pressed him against the door. He pulled the half-unbuttoned shirt away from the guardian's shoulder and explored his skin with his mouth. Devak moaned.

"May I..." Matthew started to ask for blood then stopped himself. He was the one in charge here. He didn't need to ask for Devak's blood, he could just take it. Matthew scratched the door with a claw in frustration as he struggled with the choice.

Devak looked up at him, eyes wide with confusion.

Matthew wrapped his clawed hand around the back of his neck to hold him in place, and sunk his teeth into his upper shoulder. He did it without asking. Knowing he could take blood again without permission felt...freeing.

Devak's head fell back, his own fangs coming down.

Blood filled Matthew, delicious and powerful. He drank greedily, his fangs deep in Devak's beautiful skin. Devak was his.

His to possess. His to own. His guardian.

A growl escaped him. And only once he took his fill of blood did he remove his fangs.

At some point, Devak had finished unbuttoning his top. Matthew pushed the clothes off and pulled him closer so that their chests pressed together. Carefully, Devak began kissing Matthew's neck. His movements seemed restrained, as if he was waiting for an invitation to take it further.

"Stop holding back," Matthew said.

With permission gained, Devak scraped his fangs against Matthew's neck, drawing thin lines of blood that he licked away with his delicate tongue. He worked his way down Matthew's chest with his lips and tongue and teeth, leaving no muscle ignored.

Devak dropped to his knees and looked up with big eyes. It was a tender pause in the frantic momentum that had been driving them. Devak's facade of confidence peeled away and before him was a vulnerable man: a subject kneeling before his ruler, needing his approval.

"My prince." The whispered words hung between them. It was a subtle request, one laced with desire.

Matthew touched his face. "I want you, Devak."

Those words seemed to have a profound effect on him. His mouth pulled up into a shy smile, his fangs went back into his gums, and his hands roamed up Matthew's muscular legs. He wrapped his lips around the crown of Matthew's cock and twisted his tongue against the head, lavishing it with attention.

Matthew grunted, leaned over and planted his palms against the door as his body trembled with pleasure. Heat welled in his belly and he focused on drawing in the sexual energy that rose from Devak.

Devak went slow, still only working the slit and crown. Matthew threw his head back and inhuman sounds escaped him. He rocked his hips forward wanting more but Devak was practiced in the art of sexual control. He manipulated Matthew's cock with his mouth like that of an expert.

Matthew dug his claws into the wood and another moan tore from his throat. His body craved a faster tempo.

He looked down at Devak. Seeing the first few inches of his cock stretching his guardian's lips had him trembling with need.

Amber eyes looked up and locked onto Matthew's gaze. Then, in one captivating motion, Devak pushed his mouth down on the erection. Matthew's large cock hit the back of Devak's throat and kept going.

"Oh my god," Matthew said and struggled to keep his eyes from rolling back into his head. Watching his cock disappear into the guardian's mouth was hot as hell, and it was rare that someone could take all of him like this.

Matthew placed a claw on Devak's shoulder and dug into the skin just deep enough to draw five points of blood, the scent filling the air.

He resisted the urge to take control of Devak's head and frantically fuck his mouth.

Devak withdrew, keeping his tongue pressed against the underside. A wonderful suction sound came from his mouth as Matthew's member popped out. Devak grabbed the base, holding it firm, and guided the cock back in. He began to blow him harder, faster.

Each journey down the shaft advanced Matthew towards the inevitable end. But whenever he drew close, the guardian changed things with a twist or a scrape, delaying the release. Matthew's balls drew up every time Devak came down on him, and his grunts grew needy.

Devak's skill with his mouth was unlike any he had ever encountered, and Matthew's muscles shook with expectancy. His whole body was primed for release, every touch sent shivers through him, and every flick of the tongue had him on the verge of begging.

When he could take it no more, Devak raised a hand to Matthew's stomach and dug sharp claws into his pale skin. As he raked the claws down Matthew's torso, drawing blood and pain, he cupped Matthew's balls with his other hand and continued a fast repetitive motion with his mouth.

The sensations were too much.

Matthew cried out as he came, intense color filled his vision and his entire body shuddered violently. Devak didn't let up, drawing out his pleasure for the entire orgasm, and swallowing every ounce of cum.

When, finally, Matthew could see again, he realized he had clamped down on Devak's shoulder, his claws digging deep, blood oozing around them. His own stomach had five long gashes, also bleeding.

Devak, with Matthew's cock still in his mouth, wasn't moving.

Matthew withdrew his claws from Devak's skin, but Devak stayed where he was, hard under his tuxedo pants and longing in his eyes. Matthew tapped his shoulder and fought back the urge to jerk when Devak removed his mouth from his dick. The guardian sat back on his knees, looking up.

"Stand up," Matthew ordered.

Devak made his way to his feet. On his way up, he licked Matthew's wounds, closing them. Matthew leaned down and did the same for Devak's shoulder but didn't stop there...he moved his lips to Devak's ear and tugged on his earlobe with his blunt teeth. Matthew wanted more. He wasn't sure he'd stay hard but he had to try.

"I'm still hungry," he said, his voice low and thick.

"My prince…" Devak said, his breath hitting Matthew's neck.

Matthew claimed his mouth, enslaving him with his ravenous hunger. Their kiss became desperate; demanding.

Reaching down, Matthew palmed Devak's hard length through the fabric of his pants. Devak broke away from the kiss and leaned into him, helpless.

"Do you enjoy that?" Matthew asked.

Devak gasped for air. "Yes."

Matthew slipped his hand inside and grabbed him. He squeezed the base, made his hand slick, and pushed pleasure into Devak. He began one tight, unhurried stroke up the shaft. Devak's mouth fell open and his knees trembled. Matthew locked his free arm around the smaller man so he wouldn't topple over.

"Finish undressing," Matthew whispered and removed his hand.

It took Devak a moment to move. He pulled his shoes off and pants down, his dick jutting out. It was a good size, not too large but not small either. Matthew grinned as he studied it.

Waiting for instructions, Devak stayed in place. Matthew grabbed his wrist and led him to the bed, where he guided Devak to lie on his back.

Matthew kneeled between his legs, pushing his thighs apart. Devak propped himself up on his elbows to watch his prince wrap fingers around his cock. Matthew smiled as it twitched under his hand, his own cock hardening once more.

Devak's eyes widened. "My prince, you don't have to…my pleasure is not important."

Matthew's brows knitted together. He wanted to take his own pleasure from him but he wasn't a greedy lover—he refused to leave his partner unsatisfied. Matthew crawled up Devak's body, forcing him back down on the bed and trapping him between his large frame and the red satin sheets. He leaned in close to his ear and whispered, "I want you to come for me."

Devak bit his bottom lip and closed his eyes. Matthew slid back onto his knees and looked at Devak sprawled out before him. His radiant skin irresistible, Matthew rubbed his hands along it, feeling his muscles flex below his fingers.

Tracing his hand along Devak's hipbone, Matthew followed the grooves to the juncture between hips and legs. He lightly teased Devak's cock once more, then continued past his balls and the area between until he reached the tight entrance.

Matthew focused and a velvety lube seeped from his fingers. While it wasn't his favorite incubus ability, he had to admit it was useful, and right now he was extremely thankful for it.

He teased and pushed a finger in, stretching him. Then a second finger and a third, curling them and ripping breathy sighs from Devak. When he was prepared, Matthew removed his fingers and pressed the head of his cock against the hole. Devak tilted his hips up and stilled, waiting.

Matthew hoped he wouldn't lose his erection, not right now. He needed this, he hungered for it. His desire for Devak grew every moment he let slip by. He rocked his hips forward and worked his way into Devak's tight passage. He went slow and careful. Devak responded by silently opening his mouth, arching his back off the mattress, and gripping the sheets. His scent of sweet wine and fragrant oil mixed with desire perfumed the air.

When Matthew was finally in, he leaned over and kissed Devak's chest. He drew in the sexual energy coming from him.

Matthew felt Devak's inner thigh glide up his body, followed by the pressure of his heels against his ass. He set a pace that would bring them both pleasure but wouldn't have Devak coming too soon. He fed again from Devak.

"Please, *yes*," Devak moaned.

Matthew dove deeper into him, hunger and need urging him on. He wrapped his arms around Devak, wanting to be as close as possible. The smaller man's body formed to his as if they were one. Matthew evoked pleasure through every point they connected.

Under him, Devak's muscles tensed as he neared climax. Matthew pushed himself up and sat back onto his knees, wanting to watch when Devak spent himself. He wanted to see all of what was his trembling with the pleasure that he brought.

He grabbed Devak's cock and began to stroke it while continuing his relentless pounding. Devak near the edge, his body tense and twitching, was a glorious sight. Matthew sent him over.

"My prince," he cried out—his words broken and strained, his hands tearing at the sheets. Thick strands of cum jetted out of him. The first of it landed on his chest, then, in the spasms that followed, on his abs.

It was a feast and Matthew ate every bit of it, filling himself with the pleasure.

Unable to hold back his own release any longer, heat ruptured within him as he came harder than he could ever remember.

Sixteen

Matthew and Devak showered in silence, both enjoying the post-coital haze. Matthew smiled when he bumped into Devak and the guardian moaned softly from the contact, then returned to washing himself.

Devak's jaw clenched, as if he wanted to say something but held back.

"If you wish to speak you don't need my permission. I've told you that before," Matthew said.

Devak stepped away from the water a bit to address him. "I know. It's just hard for me. There are rules and…this curse…"

Matthew set his hand on Devak's shoulder. "Sam will figure out where this offering is. We'll break the curse."

Devak nodded. "What made you change your mind? About… feeding."

"I was hungry and have been for a long time."

"Ah," Devak said with a slight nod and stepped back under the water. Understanding came to Matthew. The question was deeper than face value. What he had really been asking was 'did you want me or was it just an incubus need?'

Matthew watched the water run down Devak's attractive body. He wasn't sure how to answer that even to himself. He didn't love Devak, he hadn't allowed himself to think about anyone else that way…but maybe…there could be something if he let things progress.

Matthew wasn't sure he was ready for that, but now that he had tasted Devak, he wasn't sure he was ready to give it up either.

"It was more than that though," Matthew said, wanting to give him something. "I wanted you…I'm not sure how to proceed here. My heart still aches for another. I don't even fucking understand it. I was his slave and he deceived me. By all rights, I should hate him…and I do…and I don't. I don't know anymore. I don't even know why after a year I'm still thinking about it, or why I can't move on." He rubbed his hand across his scruff and laughed. "Maybe I'm just hung up on him because he was my first cock."

A half-smile crossed Devak's face. "Was he really?"

"Yeah. Only women before him. Nowadays, I like everything." And now it looked like things were working for him again. If he could high-five his dick, he would have with a 'we did it, buddy'.

Devak's smiled spread. "Incubus," he said, teasing.

Matthew laughed again. "You're over forty-five centuries old, don't tell me you haven't fucked just about everything."

"Mm," he said with a nod. His face became serious again. He raised his hand to place it on Matthew's cheek but he held back and instead rested it on his chest. "I have no expectations from you. I am here to serve you however you wish."

"But what do you desire?"

Devak looked away and removed his hand. Matthew caught it, not letting him retreat. Devak didn't fight him. "I...it is not my place to desire anything."

"I don't give a shit about whatever fucked up hierarchy you follow. I want to know what you want."

"My prince—"

"Matthew," he corrected him for the millionth time. He let Devak get away with it in bed because it was damned sexy—submissive—but that was over now and here, in this shower, he wanted to be called by his name. Not that Devak would say it—he had never actually called him by his name, not even once.

"—I've always been attracted to strong incubi. You are no exception."

"I don't get that, your power is ten times mine and you're still weakened. My strength is nothing compared to yours."

"For now. One day that'll—" Devak screamed and folded in half.

Matthew caught him in his arms before he hit the floor, worried that if his guardian kept trying to push the boundaries of the curse, it would kill him. Devak shook in his arms for a while until the pain subsided.

Matthew didn't release him until he was sure he could stand on his own. Even then, he stood close, water running down their bodies. "We'll fix this."

"I have faith you will," he strained.

The two of them finished showering and dressed. Matthew had just finished buttoning up his pants when he sensed Samantha coming down the hallway. Devak sensed her too and threw on his clothes quicker.

"Shit," Matthew said. There was no way she wasn't going to know what they had been up to. The room reeked of sex, Matthew's hair was still drying, and both of them were alone in here. And that's not even taking into account that she was an oracle who could see past events.

"Perhaps if you explain to her that it wasn't planned," Devak offered.

"You think she's going to listen to that? No matter what I say, she's going to be hurt that I'm not sleeping with her."

Devak struggled with his tie. "She just wants her first time to be with someone she trusts. If it's not going to be you, you need to find someone to fuck her so she gets it out of her system."

Matthew laughed. That was the most unguarded comment Devak had ever made. "You're always welcome to fuck her."

"Women don't interest me sexually. Besides, I wouldn't want you growling at me the whole time—it'd ruin the mood."

Matthew chuckled. He was right, that was going to be a problem for anyone she was with. Although he did find it interesting that he could now tolerate Devak touching Samantha without possessive rage surging through him.

Matthew brushed Devak's hands out of the way and fixed his tie for him. There was a sudden shift in Devak's body language. He seemed to grow uncertain with the easy banter that had formed between them and he fell back into his normal obedient posture, dipping his head. "But if you order me, I will obey the command."

"Jesus," Matthew said. "I'd never order you to fuck someone you didn't want to. Hell, I'm not even comfortable ordering you around as it is."

"I don't believe that, my prince."

Okay, maybe he did enjoy ordering Devak around a little, but before he could respond, Samantha opened the door. "Father, I think I know—" She froze. Her eyes darted between Matthew and Devak, then over to the bed and back to them. Her face twisted, more from pain than anger. "But you said 'no'. When I asked if you were going to sleep with him, you said 'no'."

"Sam—wait, please let me explain," Matthew said.

Samantha backed out of the room and ran down the hallway.

Matthew hissed. She was so god damn frustrating. He started after her but Devak grabbed him and held out the gold and white crowned mask. He put it on while Devak did the same with his own.

"I swear, if I were human she'd be giving me ulcers," Matthew growled.

"You can always summon her back to you."

"I don't like doing it against her will…besides, she'd find a way to punish me for it eventually."

The two of them went after her. They followed her scent back to the ballroom. Leaning against the first-floor railing, they scanned the area. She wasn't hard to spot. She had gone to a corner on the main floor to make out with some vampire. His hands wandered all over her. A low growl thundered in Matthew's chest.

"She's just doing that to piss you off," Devak said.

"It's working." Matthew tried to get ahold of himself. If she wanted to kiss every vampire here, that was her damn business. So long as they weren't hurting her.

"I think she was going to say something about the offering," Devak said.

"Yeah, I'll ask her once she's—"

"What the fuck did you do to my sister?" an angry male voice cut in.

Matthew turned and a fist went flying into his stomach with such force that he went over the railing and fell to the dance floor. He twisted and landed on his feet. His vampire side was out before he even touched the ground and he was ready to defend himself.

The man jumped over the railing and landed in front him.

Stolus.

Ascelina's other child. Emilia's protective little brother, though he looked older; somewhere in his mid-thirties, with long black hair (currently in a ponytail) and pale skin. The scars that Tarrick and Cullip had given him had long since healed.

He hated Matthew. Stolus had once ended up with a back full

of lashes just for talking to Matthew while they were imprisoned together. And he blamed Matthew for some of the harm that had come to Emilia.

Stolus was a capable warrior and he always tried to protect the people he loved—traits Matthew valued. But the fucker was a pain in the ass.

When Matthew stayed at Ascelina's house for a few months, there was no end to the derogatory comments he spewed out...although he never physically attacked Matthew.

Guess tonight was different.

Stolus ripped off his own mask and tossed it aside, his fangs and claws out—a clear challenge.

Around them, the musicians stopped playing and the dancers had moved out of the way. In fact, the entire place fell silent as vampires, and the other creatures, pressed next to the railings to see what was going on.

Matthew sighed. This seemed familiar...

Devak landed between the two of them, hunched over and growling, ready to attack Stolus if he made a move on Matthew.

Part of Matthew realized he needed to end this fight. If Devak showed his wings or eyes, they'd know he was something besides a vampire and they *might* attack him, but if they recognized Matthew—if his mask came off or Stolus revealed who he was—they *would* attack him for sure. Devak and Matthew couldn't take on all the lords here tonight. He guessed their numbers to be near forty, maybe more.

The other part of Matthew wanted to smack Stolus around a little for all the disrespectful shit that vomited from his mouth.

Matthew tapped Devak's shoulder and motioned for him to stand to the side. Devak moved away but he stayed ready to defend if he had to.

"I didn't do anything to her," Matthew said.

Stolus growled. "Really? She's bawling her eyes out and your scent is all over her."

"You need to go talk to her, then. I didn't do shit."

"Boys, I won't have any fighting in my home," a female voice sounded from far above them. Matthew looked up. It was the blond haired lord wearing the purple mask...the one Matthew had danced with. He wondered if she knew that he had crashed her party. She, along with a male lord, came down from the fourth floor balcony and landed gracefully beside them.

Stolus scowled at Matthew and forced his claws away. "I'm sorry, Gwenyth," Stolus said with a slight bow.

"No harm was done, darling. And them—" she turned to Matthew and Devak, "—my mystery guests. Do you know who he is, Stolus? We've been trying to figure it out all night long." She looked amused.

Matthew shot a glance to Samantha, who was on the far side of the room with many vampires between the two of them. If they wanted to kill her, any one of them could do it before he could make it to her. His gaze shifted to Stolus. If he told the lord who he was, it was over.

Stolus narrowed his eyes at Matthew then waved his hand in a dismissive gesture. "He's no one, a coward."

"No, this one I do not care about—he's just a child." She brushed Matthew off with a wave. Matthew huffed at the dismissive gesture. "I meant that one." She walked to Devak and studied him. "You lack any aura. Your heart doesn't beat but I'm not convinced that you are a vampire." She touched him on his neck. "You are too warm."

Matthew had been just as confused about Devak when he first saw him. He couldn't tell his age or much else about him. Devak opened his mouth and let his fangs come out as if to prove he was a vampire.

"Who are you?" she asked.

"Doesn't knowing that ruin the fun of a masquerade?" Devak answered.

Gwenyth said something to him but neither Devak nor Matthew heard her. Their attentions snapped elsewhere. Magic. Then heartbeats. Far, but approaching.

"Sam, come," Matthew commanded her. No one stopped her. She walked into Matthew's arm and he held her close, protecting her.

Cries brought their attention back to the ballroom. Jet, in full gargoyle form, landed beside Matthew. With the exception of Samantha, the younger vampires retreated to their sires. Awakened gargoyles were disturbing, especially to the newly turned.

"I know, we sensed them too," Matthew said as Jet looked up at him.

Matthew noticed that everyone gave Jet a wide berth. His pride was slightly wounded that no one seemed to consider him a threat.

"Sensed what?" a man with a deep voice asked from behind him. It was the vampire Matthew had pulled Samantha away from earlier, the one with dark skin and in the stag mask.

"Huunnnnnters," Jet hissed.

Many hunters. Incubi too. There was an attack incoming. None of the other vampires had sensed them. Not even the oldest ones.

"What does the gargoyle mean?" the vampire in the stag mask asked Matthew.

Matthew didn't want this.

"We're leaving." He grabbed Samantha's wrist and dragged her away. He was surprised when she resisted.

Samantha tugged on his arm. "Father, we have to stay or the offering won't be found."

Matthew looked at Devak, who was waiting for an order, but he looked as if he wanted to stay. And Matthew had promised that he'd break his curse. He hated going back on his word.

The situation was bad, but if he fought for the vampires there was no turning back. Even after killing the incubi and hunters, Matthew still held onto an unrealistic kernel of hope that he could rejoin incubus society. If he fought, it would be gone forever.

Tarrick would be gone forever.

Maybe that was a good thing. Maybe it was time to let him go. His chest ached at the idea. Every logical thought told him to move on and forget Tarrick, but no matter how he tried it wasn't happening.

And it wasn't like there weren't other reasons for not wanting to fight in their war. All he wanted was to find out who his sire and parents were. He didn't want to be a soldier, to fall in line and do what others ordered him to do. Selfish? Yes. But other than Ascelina, none of them had ever done anything for him.

"How many?" Stolus asked. For as much as Stolus pissed Matthew off, the vampire knew what he was capable of and never underestimated his abilities, and if Matthew said he sensed something, Stolus would believe it.

Matthew pushed Samantha behind him and stood tall. "There is a force of over a thousand hunters, incubi, and witches surrounding this area, they are still miles out. I give it eight minutes before they're in position and they start their attack." Matthew made sure his voice carried loud throughout the entire ballroom.

"Impossible, they've never attacked during the solstice. There is an agreement in place. And even if they did, I sense nothing out there," Gwenyth said.

"And what are you going to do?" Stolus asked Matthew, ignoring Gwenyth. "Will you stand and fight with us or will you flee like the coward you are?"

Matthew snarled at him. "Call me a coward one more time and I'll rip your fucking head off." That earned him several growls from the surrounding vampires.

"Why do you care about this child? Let him leave if he wishes," Gwenyth said and waved Matthew off in a dismissive gesture.

"He is no child—"

"Shut up, Stolus," Matthew growled.

"—he is—"

"No."

"—the reason we no longer have New Orleans. He destroyed House Moreau."

A deathly cold silence clung to the air. Matthew grabbed Samantha and backed away from the largest grouping of vampires but it would do him no good. Anger rolled off the vampires around him and he looked out into a sea of red eyes. Lords dropped from the higher levels, their fangs out and claws ready to strike.

The first two launched themselves at Matthew but they never reached him. Devak knocked a vampire from the air, sending him flying across the ballroom with a punch while Jet pounced on another, pinning him to the ground.

A third attacked. Devak's wings burst forward and a tendril of blood grabbed the vampire and smashed him against a wall. Matthew looked for any avenue to escape with Samantha but he saw none. He wouldn't need it, though. When Devak's wings came forward, the attacking vampires gave pause.

Devak floated several feet above the ground, releasing his aura— Matthew had never felt anything like it. It was overwhelming, even to him. Samantha clung to him tighter. For the first time ever, the significance and power of the guardian's age were real; before it had only been a number. A large number, yes, but still just a number. Matthew knew Devak was stronger than him but he had never realized how *astronomically* stronger.

Devak opened his mouth to speak and the entire estate shook with his voice. "The next creature that attacks will die painfully."

"A blood guardian…" Gwenyth gasped and dropped to her knees.

Others followed suit until most of the creatures in the ballroom kneeled before him. Even Stolus, whose eyes darted between Matthew and Devak in disbelief.

Well, this wasn't quite the reaction Matthew had expected.

The man in the stag mask, who hadn't kneeled, stepped forward and addressed Devak. "Are the incubi really about to attack?"

Again, Matthew was a little offended that he was ignored.

"Yes," Devak said, his voice a little less booming.

The man pulled off his mask and turned to address the entire ballroom. His features were stern, his confidence absolute. "I don't think the guardian is lying to us, which means in a few minutes we are going to have a battle on our hands. I give everyone a choice: leave now or stay and fight. But I very much doubt the incubi left any routes of escape."

Most of the vampires looked around, uncertain. They didn't seem to have any idea who this young vampire was that was issuing them orders.

Gwenyth, who seemed to be the next oldest in the room after Devak, stood. "I suppose it's time you stepped out of the shadows, General."

The man nodded. "We knew this was inevitable."

She turned to face the vampires filling the ballroom. "This is General Bryson. You will leave my house now or submit to his orders."

A wave of hushed whispers made its way through the crowd. Bryson was a child by vampire standards. No wonder he had been issuing orders from the shadows, older vampires would never follow his commands otherwise.

At least no vampires made a move to leave, which was smart of them because the approaching incubi forces would slaughter any that tried to flee.

"We're outnumbered almost two to one. Any children under a

decade will stay here. The rest fight." General Bryson turned and addressed a big, blond vampire with a military buzz. "I need a map of the surrounding areas. And get the armory open."

The vampire nodded and left to carry out the orders while Bryson organized vampires into groups and had the blood reserves brought out in preparation of injuries. The way he commanded the room reminded Matthew of Tarrick. Both men had the same authoritative presence.

"Donovan," Bryson addressed a large, hairy man—a wolf shifter. "Does your pack flee or fight?"

"We fight. But it'll cost ya," the alpha said. Shifters began ripping off their clothes and changing into their animal form—massive dire wolves. Matthew didn't see the tiger around.

"We'll settle after the battle. Tanya—"

A human stepped forward, her hair wild; her mask the shape of a flock of birds. "We will fight but our magic is limited here."

"Oh!" Samantha said, drawing the attention of the general and the witch. "I brought something for them."

"You knew this was going to happen, Sam?" Matthew asked.

She looked sheepish in his arm. Matthew made no effort to hide his displeasure, scowling at her.

"If you wish to leave," Bryson said to Matthew. "No one will stop you, but we could use you and the guardian."

Matthew sighed. Everyone wanted him to stay and fight. Even Devak's eyes betrayed him, no doubt wanting to find the offering, though he would never voice it. This wasn't Matthew's battle, but if he left then these vampires were doomed. There was no way Tarrick would send a force here unless he was sure he could win. But Tarrick didn't know that Matthew and Devak would be here. Their presence might be enough to shift the battle in the vampire's favor.

"My child is here," Matthew said, looking at Samantha. All his instincts screamed at him to run with her, to keep her safe.

"I can protect her."

"No offense but you're young and I doubt—"

Bryson ripped open his tux, revealing his chest: it was covered in silver-colored hunter runes. No wonder he was so adept at countering incubi strategy, an ex-hunter would know everything about the incubi.

No wonder the war was turning around for the vampires. "How often do people assume the same thing about you because of your age? I know how to fight if they break through. And I'll hold a few lords back for protection as well—you're not the only one here tonight with a child."

Matthew tore off his mask, tossing it on the floor and began removing his shirt. Beside him, Devak landed and undressed as well. Tuxedos were a bitch to fight in.

"I have a few conditions," Matthew said. "If any harm comes to my child, what I did in New Orleans will be nothing compared to the bloodbath I will bring down upon you. Also, you understand that this is a one-time thing, I am not your soldier nor do I have any interest in your war."

He can help us get to Delphi, Sam had once said.

"And you'll owe me a favor," Matthew added.

Bryson considered the terms carefully, then nodded.

"Go get the bag," Matthew ordered Devak, who disappeared and returned in the blink of an eye.

Bryson's attention turned to a table beside him, a map of the area spread out on it. The shifter alpha, the witch leader, and a half-dozen other important vampires, including Gwenyth, gathered at the table.

Matthew looked through the bag. Samantha had clearly expected this. In addition to the sword, she had packed the bracers, boots, and tactical pants along with a smattering of other items. No shirt, though. He wished Sam had packed a shirt.

Matthew ripped off his shoes and pants and changed right there, ignoring the stares, but it was hard to ignore the feelings of desire that rose in some of the vampires around him when he had stripped down to only his underwear.

Devak held up his hand. "La'mast. Na'mori."

"Are meteor's gonna come bursting through the roof?" Matthew asked as he finished pulling up his new pants.

"Not unless I want them to."

At the table, Matthew heard Bryson assign areas to different groups of vampires.

"The forest will force some to land but they'll still have aerial advantage," one of the vampires said.

"Jet—" Matthew called as he snapped the bracers around his forearms, "—get the other gargoyles into the battle, I don't care if you have to push them off the roof to do it. Tell them the castle will fall if they don't wake up. I need them to force the incubi out of the sky, rip their damn wings off."

Jet nodded and flew away. The group at the table stared at Matthew, who attached the sword and sheath to his hip

"What?" Matthew asked them.

Bryson frowned. "None of the reports I have on you mentioned that you were a gargoyle commander."

"I'm not."

The vampires at the table exchanged glances. They didn't believe him but Matthew wasn't going to argue with them about it.

A young vampire juggling several phones joined the table. "General, we just got word that London is under an attack. It started about five minutes ago."

Stolus, now armed with a round shield and a spear, approached with Emilia trailing behind him. "Our mother…?"

"No word on anyone yet," the one with the phones said.

Bryson kept focused on this battle. Matthew doubted there was much the general could do for London right now.

A streak of bright light flew in from the doorway and across the ballroom floor. Devak held out his hand and caught his maul with a heavy clang. The entryway began to glow and Devak leaped up into the air as beams of light smashed into him. Everyone covered their eyes and, when it cleared, Devak was fully clad in his black armor.

"You and I should go for their leaders. If we cut off the head it might force them to regroup or retreat," Devak said.

Matthew agreed. "Think Prescott will be here?"

The man with the phones answered the question. "The Argonauts have been reported in London."

Apprehension rose in the ballroom as the vampires finally began to sense the hunters approaching.

The windows of the ballroom, facing the front of the estate, lit with a fiery glow. A loud crashing sound echoed through the area as a ball of rock and fire impacted against the stone outer wall.

This was followed by five more fiery boulders soaring through the air towards them.

The seven witches, all gathered near their leader now, turned and held their hands out and chanted words in a language Matthew couldn't identify. Two of the fire boulders slammed into the estate, setting the upper levels ablaze, but the next three smashed into an invisible barrier. Did the incubi bring freaking siege engines?

"We can't keep this spell up for long," their leader, Tanya, said with a strained grunt.

"Oh, yeah!" Samantha reached into the bag and took out a rod with runes etched along it. It was the one she had taken from Sabine's closet. "Here," she said and handed it to Tanya.

Disbelief crossed Tanya face as she reached out and touched the rod. "Child, do you know what this is?"

"Yeah, I brought it for you to use," Samantha said. "I want it back after."

"What the hell is it?" Matthew asked.

"The Rod of Sioua. It's a power font. We can keep that shield up all day with this. Mother Earth, it will give us enough power for a counter attack."

"Then do it," Bryson said.

Matthew grabbed Samantha's shoulders and turned her to face him. "If you're in trouble, call for me or Devak. We'll hear you."

"I know. I'd tell you to be safe but I already know what happens." She looked worried. And maybe a little guilty.

"Care to share?"

"Nope," she said, then embraced Matthew. "Be safe anyway."

Outside, the sound of the first clash of battle erupted.

"Ready?" Matthew asked Devak.

"Always," Devak said.

"Let's go."

Matthew and Devak sped out of the keep together and into the fray.

Seventeen

The initial engagement had finished by the time Matthew and Devak burst out of the estate's heavy front doors. A wave of decaying vampires lay in the wet dirt just beyond the wall that surrounded the estate.

At the forest's edge, beyond the gardens and a clearing, were dozens of men and women. They didn't wear the normal black leather garb of hunters. Rather, they wore simple, loose-fitting robes and dresses.

Matthew watched as they spoke and magic sparked at the edge of their fingertips. A boulder ripped up from the ground and a swirling torrent of fire formed around the rock. The boulder flew through the air and smashed into the barrier.

Witches.

Around Matthew, vampires poured out of the estate, ready to fight, but stalled because the clearing between the wall and the forest was a death zone. Any vampire that tried to cross the exposed stretch met a hail of bolts and stakes.

The seven witches that were on their side came out and stood behind the vampires. Tanya chanted a few words and touched the ground. The dirt beneath her fingers began to move and continued forward like a ripple towards the incubi's witches. Thick roots exploded from the ground under them, wrapping around some like tentacles and scattering the rest.

From the forest, hundreds of glowing green eyes appeared. Hunters.

A wave of flying incubi rose above the trees. In response, vampire lords took to the air. Their bat-like wings unfurled behind them.

Devak, who was floating just a few inches off the ground beside Matthew, raised his hand and made his own near-invisible shield. An oversized metal ball smashed into it and broke apart. Hundreds of silver grenades flew out from the forest and exploded above them when they hit the witches' barrier. Fine particles of silver dust covered the area like a fog, forcing the vampires back.

"We need to scatter their front lines or they are going to pick us off one by one with their ranged weapons," Devak said.

"I agree. Let's end this quick."

Devak rose into the air. "I'll cover you from the sky."

Matthew glowered when he saw that none of the gargoyles had moved. In fact, Jet was sitting on a corner, as motionless as the others. He assumed Jet would have jumped at the chance to tear hunters apart. Gargoyles were strange…

"I'll be there in a moment. I have some gargoyles to yell at," Matthew said. Devak nodded and continued on to the battle.

Matthew scaled the outside wall up to the roof. A wave of heat rolled past him as a fiery boulder slammed into the barrier nearby.

"Alright you fucks—" Matthew said to the gargoyles, "—get off your stoney asses and go rip apart some incubi."

Nothing happened.

Matthew released his aura. *Death and destruction*. That's what he was told it felt like to others. The gargoyles all turned their heads to him. Slow and creepy. "Go. *Now*."

One by one they started to move and took to the air. Matthew smiled at his success.

He jumped off the roof. When he landed, the vampires around him cowered away. He suppressed his aura so they wouldn't feel it anymore, but a few flashed fangs at him. He ignored them and watched as a wave of gargoyles fell upon the incubi.

Skirting the cloud of silver dust, he leaped over the wall, pushing power into his speed so that he could dodge the onslaught of bolts as he crossed the clearing. Only one bolt had hit him in his arm by the time he made it to the tree line. He ripped it out. Behind him, the other vampires that had followed his lead weren't so lucky. Twenty had followed, only eight had made it.

But it was a start. Once his small group of vampires made contact with hunters, they were merciless in their attacks.

Matthew glanced back at the estate itself. It didn't look good. The upper floors were on fire and parts were collapsing in. Green outlines appeared as hunters teleported to the flanks to pick off vampires.

Above him, incubi, gargoyles, and vampire lords clashed, silhouetted against the nearly full moon. Devak hit an armored incubus warrior in the chest with his maul. The incubus went crashing into the ground. Matthew was on it before it could recover. He sliced off one of its wings with his sword, then clawed its neck open, blood sprayed the trees.

Hunters appeared around him, trying to get to the incubi to save him but they were too late. Matthew punched one and drove his sword into the chest of another. The rest teleported away from him.

Matthew ripped the comm and earpiece from the dead hunter at his feet and put them on so he could listen to the orders without the need to focus. He heard a familiar voice barking commands: Dennith. She was Tarrick's right-hand and if she was directing this battle, that meant Tarrick wasn't here tonight. He was either in London or overseeing both battles from his command center at Ashwood.

"Ghost, Ashwood Yellow and Red, and Helldogs, go to the south side. Vassu, if that really is a guardian we need it neutralized," she said.

"I'm heading to him now," a deep, bass voice replied.

"Devak," Matthew said. He couldn't see him through the trees but he knew Devak would hear. "You have a big incubus coming your way. He helped train me. He's great at anticipating moves, uses a double-bladed sword, and favors his right."

"I look forward to the challenge," Devak said from somewhere above him.

Matthew wished he could watch Devak take on Vassu—it'd no doubt be an epic fight—but he wasn't here to spectate. He dodged a grouping of bolts that flew at him and rushed at the hunters, on top of them before they could teleport away. He killed three with quick jabs of his sword and wounded two others.

More hunters teleported near him. In the comm he heard a gasp followed by, "Holy shit—Matthew's here."

Matthew turned to the man who had reported it and flashed a wicked smile, one that was sure to show off his fangs. The hunter teleported away and his vampire purred at the fear he had instilled.

A different hunter appeared in front of him and thrust a stake at his blood pouches. Matthew caught her wrist. It was a cadet he had trained with, though she was in full hunter attire. Maybe she had graduated.

"You'll have to do better than that, Kitty." He let her teleport away. He wouldn't kill her unless she forced him to. He liked her.

"Matthew is wearing one of our comms, he can hear everything we're saying," Kat reported.

Matthew raised the comm to his mouth. "I can hear everything you're saying anyway. This just makes it easier."

There was comm silence for a few moments before Dennith spoke. "Matthew...are you enjoying killing my hunters?"

He had to admit to himself that he was enjoying this battle. After spending most of the last year avoiding all this shit, being back in the thick of it was exhilarating. The monster inside of him didn't get many opportunities for such unbridled killing. It was as if there was a part of him that hungered for this just as badly as he hungered for blood or sex.

"I'll stop killing them if you tell me where you are, Dennith. You and I can throw down. It'll be like old times."

Dennith was an excellent warrior and she'd be a good challenge for him. He didn't want to kill her, but if it meant ending this battle and keeping Samantha safe, he'd do it.

"Maybe later, but I'll send some people your way to keep you entertained. All hunters swap to channel delta."

And with that Matthew could no longer talk to Dennith. He tossed the comm away.

The distant sound of rocks slamming into the shield reminded him that something needed to be done about those witches. Before he started moving, he heard a low predatory growl coming from the bushes.

A tiger leaped out at him.

Fuck. This wasn't a fight he could afford right now. Matthew ducked and rolled out of the way from the lightning fast tiger, bringing his arms up defensively.

Nothing happened. The tiger leaped past him, and swiped his claws in the air, hitting a hunter that had been waiting, invisible, for Matthew to pass by. The tiger ripped the hunter to shreds as Matthew stood and watched. When the one-eyed tiger finished with its victim, it turned and growled low, its mouth bloody.

Matthew took a step back and raised his sword. "Uh, I'm confused.

Are we fighting or no?"

The large cat chuffed, amused, and slipped back into the forest.

Okay. No fighting.

Good.

In the distance, he heard a pack of wolves howling. It sounded as if the shifters fighting with them had made it into the forest and were trying to break apart more of the front line.

Matthew made his way back to the clearing, cutting down two hunters on the way.

He spied the grouping of enemy witches, protected by at least thirty hunters and seven fully armored incubi warriors. The witches were using their magic to keep vampires away. The approach to them was a meat grinder.

Ash rained down as a vampire lord decomposed in the sky above him. He spotted Devak battling Vassu, the two trading heavy blows. Vassu, who was absolutely massive compared to the guardian, looked weary while Devak darted around him unscathed. Other incubi were approaching them to aid Vassu. Matthew wished he had a ranged weapon—or wings—so that he could join in.

With no way of getting to the witches either, he felt useless.

The estate was in bad shape. The fires had been put out, but the outer wall surrounding the gardens had been knocked down and hunters were approaching, forcing vampires to stand and fight in the open—where they were susceptible to silver grenades—or retreat.

The group of seven witches looked exhausted. To their credit, they were taking on four times their numbers in enemy witches and they still managed to keep their protective barrier up.

Hunters were pressing in from all fronts. The south side didn't have enough defending it and the vampires there were falling. It wouldn't be long now until they breached the walls.

Even though it was a terrible idea, Matthew needed to take out those witches.

Three incubi, in their full incubus forms, dropped down around him. Two of them—one male, one female—he didn't know, but the third he knew all too well: it was Tarrick's son, Tane.

Tane looked just like Tarrick, with dirty blond hair and violet eyes. Unlike his father, he was small for a warrior incubus—reaching only six feet in his incubus form. The other two incubi had at least a foot on him. Matthew knew not to underestimate him, though. He was fully armored and incredibly skilled with the large claymore he wielded.

Tane's lip curled up. "Nine."

Fuck Tane.

Matthew narrowed his eyes at him. "Seven," he said and surged at the male incubus standing by Tane's side. He caught the incubus off-guard with his speed and the warrior almost didn't get his sword up in time to block. The incubus deflected Matthew's swing but he lost his footing in the exchange. Kicking his opponent's knee, Matthew sent the incubus stumbling backwards and used the opening to drive his sword into the creature's face.

The incubus dropped, gurgled up blood, and expired.

Tane and the succubus were on Matthew before he could pull his sword from the body. Matthew raised his arm and blocked a swing from Tane with his bracer. The blow hit him with such force that he slid along the ground, dodging a swing from the female.

When he came to a stop, Matthew grinned at Tane. "Eight."

Tane snarled and pressed him. The only weapon Matthew had now was his claws, which didn't do all that well against armored foes. There was no way he would be able to face both of them. He'd have to acquire a weapon and return to this fight.

The idea of retreating from Tane hurt his pride, but he'd rather have a hurt pride than a broken body. He tried to retreat only to find he couldn't move.

What the hell?

He struggled against whatever invisible force was holding him and every muscle began to burn with pain. Matthew would have screamed but he couldn't move his lungs.

Tane and the succubus held their weapons ready but didn't attack.

"The High King wants you brought in alive, otherwise you'd be number ten for me," Tane said.

Hunters teleported into the area and looked to Tane for orders. Matthew tried to move again but he was stuck in place, trapped in his body.

Tane motioned to the hunters. "Shoot him a couple times—it'll make him compliant—then stake him and tie this bastard up. Use silver shackles. Oh, and don't forget the collar."

Silver bolts hit Matthew's chest with a thud and his vision began to blur as pain tore through him. A hunter appeared before him holding a box, housing a collar. Matthew panicked. He couldn't go back to being a prisoner, to wearing a collar. But his body wouldn't respond.

A pale woman, a human, wearing a tight black dress walked out from behind a tree. She was moving her hands like that of a puppeteer. She raised them higher and Matthew felt compelled to move forward. Tane laughed, cruel and heartless.

Before the hunter had a chance to snap the collar around Matthew, Devak appeared from out of the sky and smashed the human away with his maul.

The pale woman held up her hands to Devak and Matthew felt the hold over him diminish a bit but he still couldn't move. Devak marched at the woman, struggling against some unseen force holding him back. He growled at her.

Bolts went flying. Devak brought his shield of light up in time to block about half of them.

As Tane brought his sword down upon Devak, a new vampire joined the fray, jumping out of a tree and smashing a large shield across Tane's armored horns. Tane, staggered by the blow, stumbled backwards, tripping and falling to the ground. The vampire tossed a spear at the succubus, which impaled her through a weak point in her armor at the shoulder.

The vampire stood tall and lowered the shield. It was Stolus.

Stolus drew a Xiphos, a Greek short sword, from a sheath that hung under his left arm and swung at the pale woman, ignoring the hunters that were around him. She released whatever hold she had over Matthew and Devak, and instead focused on stopping Stolus.

Stolus froze in front of her. Now free, Matthew broke to the right and began taking out the hunters who were going to shackle and collar him, while Devak went left, working his way to the pale woman.

Tane shook off the blow he suffered and forced himself to his feet. Matthew surged at Tane, knocking him back down and kicking his sword away.

The succubus ripped the spear out of her shoulder only to suffer a rib-cracking hit to her back by Devak's maul. She slammed into a tree and slumped to the ground.

Tane rolled back to his feet. Matthew lunged at him, but his body felt as if it was stuck in syrup. The pale woman laughed as he struggled against her control. Tane, now outnumbered and unarmed, grabbed the woman around her waist and took off into the air with her. The surviving hunters in the area teleported away.

"What the fuck was she?" Matthew asked as he ripped the bolts from his body. Devak was removing the bolts that had hit him as well, though the silver didn't burn him.

"A necromancer. Controls dead and undead," Stolus said.

"Jesus."

"I didn't know I could be affected by one," Devak said.

"Well, you're dead aren't you?" Stolus asked and picked up his bloody spear from the ground. He stabbed it into the unconscious succubus' neck to finish her off.

Devak nodded.

Matthew studied Stolus, who was shirtless for seemingly no real reason other than to show off his abs. With the spear at his side and the massive round shield, he looked...silly. "What's with the Spartan getup? You look like something out of a cheesy action movie."

Stolus growled at Matthew and said nothing for a moment then muttered, "The film was not cheesy."

Matthew laughed and looked up at the night sky. "What happened with Vassu?"

"He retreated along with the others who thought they could best me," Devak said with a hint of pride.

"Good." Matthew heard explosions. "We need to stop those witches."

"Our forces are too scattered now. Do you expect the three of us to stop them?" Stolus asked.

"I don't think we have any other choice."

"Have you ever fought a witch? Magic wrecks us. And did you see the number of hunters and incubi they have surrounding them? Even with the guardian, there's no way we can break through that."

"Right, well, you can stay here and guard these dead bodies. Devak and I will go take them out." Matthew had just about had enough of Stolus tonight. As Matthew and Devak marched off towards the witches, Stolus grumbled and followed.

The three of them hid in the shadows of the trees and watched the impenetrable group of incubi, hunters, and witches attacking and killing vampires. Witches sent flaming rocks flying into the sky, aimed at vampire lords. One hit a lord, burning it to ash.

"There's no way we can pierce their defense," Stolus whispered.

Devak assessed the situation. "I can hold a shield up long enough for us to get to them. But I can't disagree that this will be a hard fight. Can you gather the gargoyles? We would have a better chance with them."

They were right. Matthew and Devak might get a few kills but then they'd be swarmed. And Stolus would go down right away. Even if the vampire was a shithead, it impressed Matthew that he decided to come along.

"I'll try summoning the gar—" Matthew didn't have a chance to finish his sentence.

What happened unfolded before him in slow motion.

He watched across the clearing as a group of assassin hunters teleported behind the seven witches still holding up the barrier. The hunters drove daggers into the witches and were gone before the vampires that were guarding them had a chance to react.

The barrier dropped.

The witches that fought for the incubi ripped up a massive boulder from the ground, set it ablaze, and launched it at the estate. Matthew watched it slam into the first level—*into the ballroom*—and explode inside.

His bond with Samantha severed instantly. She was dead.

All reason drained from Matthew and rage filled him. It was a blind, devastating fury. He roared and launched himself at the witches.

He would make them all pay with their blood.

That was his last thought before wrath consumed him.

Eighteen

Time had no meaning to Matthew. A dark insanity encompassed him; blinded him. He heard terrified cries and screams. The scent of fear surrounded him. The tangy taste of blood coated his tongue. Soft flesh yielded to his claws.

He was endless. Powerful. Unstoppable. An avatar of rage and destruction.

Every living thing would die.

That was all he knew now.

Forever.

That is until a hand touched his arm. He wanted to destroy it at first by ripping the hand from the body it was attached to. He wanted to hear the sweet cries of agony that would follow. Then…a voice.

"Father…"

It was quiet and yet it broke though the thoughts of violence. Matthew stilled himself and focused on the delicate hand. Its gentle brush against his skin calmed him.

"…come back…"

He blinked hard, clearing his mind and blurred vision.

Samantha was standing before him. Alive. She looked up at him with her big brown eyes, wearing worry on her face.

"You—" Matthew started to say but his throat was raw, as if burned by silver. He couldn't even choke out the word.

"I'm okay," she said.

Matthew fell to his knees and pulled her into him. He wrapped his big arms around her, nearly crushing her. She was alive. Their bond was as strong as ever. What had happened? He wanted to ask but couldn't speak.

As he held her, he came to realize that blood, dirt, and pieces of flesh and guts caked him; not a single inch of him was clean. There were wounds littering his body and they throbbed. Matthew was getting blood all over her pink dress.

His insides twisted and lurched inside of him. He pushed Samantha back, grabbed the damp ground with his palms, and expelled the contents of his stomach and blood pouches, heaving up dark blood for several minutes. Samantha rested her hand on his shoulder while he vomited.

"He's okay now," she said to someone.

Matthew couldn't tell who—his senses were too dull. He needed fresh blood. Strong hands reached down and began to pull silver bolts out of his body. They worked quick and were careful not to cause further pain.

He wiped his chin and looked up. It was Devak.

He was wingless but his armor was still on, scratched and dented in several places. What on earth had done that to him? Devak hadn't even broken a sweat in his fight with Vassu but now he looked exhausted.

Samantha's gentle tongue ran across the wounds on his arm, sealing them.

Matthew looked around the forest…it looked like a bomb had gone off. The trees surrounding them were smashed apart or toppled over. There were signs of burning, though nothing was currently on fire. Bolts, throwing stars, even longswords littered the area—along with many corpses. Dead hunters. It was impossible to tell how many because they had been ripped to pieces.

"You drank a lot of hunter blood. The poison is why you vomited. There's blood back at the mansion. I'd offer mine but you already took most of it," Devak said.

Had he? Matthew's eyebrows knitted together. He didn't remember any of that.

Matthew forced his vocal cords to repair. "The battle?" he asked, still hoarse.

"It's long over," Devak said.

Matthew forced his vampire side away and struggled to stand. Both Devak and Samantha helped him to his feet. Once he was up, he grabbed Samantha by her shoulders. "I thought I had lost you."

She looked away, avoiding his gaze. Matthew could sense she was guilty about something but he was too hungry right now to care. He was just happy she was alive.

He looked around the clearing again. "I did this?"

Devak nodded.

"And that too?" he asked, motioning to the long claw marks across Devak's armor.

"You weren't stopping after the incubi retreated. I was hoping you'd get tired if we battled for a while. It didn't work."

"Stopping? What the fuck did I do?" Matthew asked.

"Let's go back, you will see," Devak said. He released his maul and it crumbled away. His armor floated off him as well, disappearing into light. Underneath, he wore his normal lace outfit, also caked with the grime of battle.

Matthew held Samantha's hand as they returned to the estate. His muscles burned as if he had been pushing them to their limits for a long time. Glancing at the moon, it was a few hours until dawn. The attack had happened just before one a.m.; Matthew had lost three hours of time. What the hell was going on? What had he done?

As they walked through the forest, he couldn't believe what he was seeing: body parts sown across trees and dirt. It was mostly hunters but there were incubi and a few decomposing vampires as well. Deep claw marks were etched into the bark of several trees.

When they reached the clearing where the witches had been fighting, Matthew came to a stop. Death hung in the air and a red field of blood stretched out before him. Every enemy witch had been sliced beyond recognition. The incubi who had been guarding them were all dead—their armor peeled open and their weapons smashed. Dead hunters piled around them.

It was horrific, even for Matthew. There had been no mercy in any of these killings. Even those who looked as if they were trying to escape were dead on their bellies.

"Holy shit. Tell me I didn't do this."

Devak's and Samantha's silence spoke volumes.

"How is this possible? I don't remember anything..."

Devak opened his mouth as if he was going to answer but no words came. Matthew wasn't sure if it was the curse or if he was equally appalled by what he was seeing.

"When a sire loses the bond with their child, they are met with great pain," Devak finally said.

Matthew's eyes narrowed. "This is more than that. I've never lost control like this before. How the hell did I take them all on? I can barely keep up with you when we spar. Look at these people, I ripped them apart. I butchered them. And nothing could stop me?"

"I stopped you," Samantha said and squeezed his hand.

Would he still be lost in the rage if she hadn't been able to calm him? What would have happened when the sun rose?

He stroked her cheek. "Thank you," he said, then turned to Devak. "Tell me what happened. Details."

Devak motioned to the bodies before them. "When you lost control, you attacked the witches. You...I've never seen you move so fast or kill so unrestrained. They tried to stop you, but you healed or shrugged off everything they threw at you. When you had killed this group, you moved into the forest and everyone before you fell, including a few vampires and a wolf. Even those flying weren't safe from you—you were jumping and grabbing them out of the sky. Bryson figured out what was going on and ordered everyone to stay out of your way. Ten minutes later the incubi called for retreat. You had killed hundreds at that point."

"Ten minutes? But that was hours ago..."

Devak nodded.

Matthew looked back at the forest, half the damn trees had been knocked down. "You fought me for hours?"

"It was either that or you would have doubled back to the estate and slaughtered everyone in there."

"How did I become so unstoppable? I know I'm powerful but this... this wasn't me..."

Devak's face grimace. The curse.

"Four gifts from four parents," Samantha said.

"What the hell does that mean, Sam?"

She shrugged. "I don't know, I only count three: a mother, a father, and a sire. We'll find out the meaning one day."

Damn it. He hated her cryptic, half answers.

His stomach cramped, reminding him that he needed fresh blood and with dawn only a few hours away, they still needed to get to safety. And—maybe most importantly—he needed a freaking shower.

Matthew walked away from the gruesome mess and back to the estate. It was in shambles; the upper levels were gone and rubble surrounded the place. Matthew came to a stop. The ballroom was still intact; no fireball had hit it like he had seen.

He turned to Sam. "Explain how you are alive, now."

She looked up at him innocently.

"Now, Sam. That's an order."

She pressed her lips together but she wasn't able to fight the command for more than a few moments. "The witches aren't dead. I had Bryson order them to cast a spell, an illusion, where it looked like they died and...then...another spell on me to disrupt our bond for a few moments. The fire boulder was just an illusion."

Matthew growled. He released Samantha's hand and marched into the estate. Behind him, Samantha protested. "It was my idea, no one else's."

He didn't give a shit. She wasn't the one who gave the order.

The heavy wood doors to the ballroom were closed. He kicked them open and they went flying from their hinges, clattering across the floor. The room was full of vampires. Matthew zeroed in on the one he wanted.

Before any of them could move, he was on Bryson, grabbing him by his shirt and slamming him into the wall. Matthew's fangs were down and his eyes burned. "At what point did you think it was a good idea to make me believe my daughter had *died*?" Matthew roared.

Bryson tried to struggle free but Matthew held on to him tightly. Once the general realized he couldn't get away, he stopped moving and his face became hard. "I had no idea that would happen. But I don't regret giving the order, we were losing the battle."

"Father, please let him go," Samantha pleaded.

"It's obvious she's a seer, and she told me that doing it would win me the battle. I stand by what I did. And I would do it again given the choice. Kill me if you must."

"Oracle," Samantha corrected Bryson.

Bryson's head snapped to her. "Oracle? Impossible. No oracle keeps their powers after they are turned."

Matthew growled. How was it that Samantha always managed to hijack his conversations? Matthew let Bryson go. He wasn't going to kill him and there was little point in posturing.

He looked around. Devak stood near him, but the other vampires in the room had scattered, terrified. The witches and shifters stood back—they looked as if they had wanted to defend the general, but after seeing what Matthew had done, what he had become, none of them moved.

Matthew strode to the table with jugs of blood—stuff that had been intended for the masquerade—and ripped the lid off a gallon. He drained the jug in record time and tossed it away. He grabbed another and drank this one slower, savoring the flavor. It wasn't as good as blood from the vein but he wasn't too picky right now.

He raised an eyebrow when he realized that every vampire in the room was watching him drink. Gwenyth came forward. Matthew felt a little bad for her—her home had been ruined. She looked as if she had been fighting as well; her dress hung in shreds but she had already healed her wounds.

He lowered the jug from his lips. "What?"

"It's just that…none of us really believed the rumors we heard until tonight."

No one ever believed he was really an incubus turned vampire until they saw what he could do with their own eyes…especially creatures as old as her. "Let me guess, you'd like to scan me? Go ahead."

She paused, torn between curiosity and a sense of self-preservation.

"I'm in control of myself now. So long as my child is safe," he said.

Gwenyth looked back at Samantha. "Believe me. None of us would dare harm her."

Matthew did believe her, now that they knew what he was capable of. Matthew resumed drinking the blood and Gwenyth approached. She rested her hand on his bloody abdomen. It tickled as blood shifted around inside of him. Still hungry, he didn't stop drinking. Behind him, Devak was drinking as well. It was the first time he had ever seen him do so and it had him wondering what it would be like to go hunting with Devak. Fun, he guessed.

Gwenyth broke away from him. "A soavik…it's true. You are an incubus."

Matthew finished with the jug of blood. His senses were returning to him. Everything was louder, brighter, and sharper. "And a vampire," he reminded her.

"And a vampire," she repeated in agreement. "Four blood pouches and you aren't even a lord…we would have lost many more if not for you. Thank you, Matthew. And you as well, Guardian."

Matthew nodded and Devak bowed to her. A part of him liked that he had saved them. Maybe the vampires wouldn't all hate him now, but losing control like that...he could have hurt someone he cared about.

"Does the water still work?" He desperately wanted that shower.

Gwenyth pointed down a hallway. "The rooms on the right all have running water."

He left, heading in the direction she indicated, Samantha and Devak behind him. Vampires parted, giving him a wide berth.

Matthew. That voice again. Calling him.

Matthew paused in front of the door to a room.

"Is everything okay?" Devak asked.

"Go clean up. There's something I have to do real quick."

Devak looked concerned and Samantha confused.

"Do as I say and go shower. Don't worry, I'll be right back," Matthew said and walked down the hall, towards the back of the estate. Behind him, he heard Samantha and Devak obeying his order.

The halls were empty; not many creatures stuck around after the battle. He went down corridors until he was standing in front of the double doors that led to the temple of the Blood God.

He entered and closed the doors behind him. He didn't want anyone seeing what he was about to do. Matthew approached the altar and examined the horned skull statue.

"I guess I can't really ignore you anymore. I've been looking the other way because it's easier than facing the truth. It's easier to pretend that gods don't exist but they do, don't they?"

The statute gave him no answer.

"I shouldn't exist. It's impossible to turn an incubus into a vampire... that is unless you're a god. Then I'd imagine you could sire whatever the fuck you wanted."

Matthew couldn't feign ignorance any longer. Not after what he had just done.

There was a fucking guardian following him around calling him 'prince'. Victor had called him 'prince' as well. He knew he wasn't the son of the High King or any other incubus royalty, Tarrick would have told him. Nor was he the son of the vampire Queen, she wouldn't have broken the bond. And vampires would know if ancient ones were walking around.

He had four blood pouches and he could perform feats that no other vampire could…and he was only getting stronger. Strong enough to kill hundreds in minutes.

Still a child by vampire standards, he could take on lords, command gargoyles, and compel whatever the fuck he wanted.

And then there was the statue. It kept calling to him, both here and when he was in New Orleans.

All the evidence was right in front of him. The answer to 'who is my sire?' was obvious.

"Then answer it," a harsh, commanding voice said from behind him.

"The Blood God," Matthew said, then turned to face his sire.

Nineteen

The god was an exaggeration of everything vampires were. He was huge, much taller and wider than Matthew. He wore imposing black and red metal armor. His skin was a pale grey, he had long black hair, and his eyes were orbs of crimson, as if formed from blood. And like the skull found on the altar, black horns twisted from his head.

He looked exactly how Matthew imagined the god of vampires would—powerful and frightening. The god flexed his nightmarish claws and a pleased look crossed his face.

Matthew froze in place.

Until now, he had wanted to find his sire, face him, and ask why he had turned and then abandoned Matthew. But now that question was the last thing on his mind. What right did he have to demand anything from a god? In the god's presence, every thought seemed to vanish.

Matthew sunk to a knee and bowed to his maker.

The Blood God walked around him, studying Matthew with his red eyes. Matthew's muscles knotted with nervous anticipation. Shirtless and still coated with blood, he didn't look his best right now.

"Nonsense," the god said, his voice laced with an edge of danger, "you look like a warrior, as you should."

Matthew hadn't said anything. He looked up at his sire and the god smiled down at him, his mouth full of thin, terrifying fangs. Pride swelled within Matthew. Followed by dread, then confusion. This is what he had always wanted, and he couldn't even speak.

The Blood God touched Matthew's face and ran sharp claws down the jawline. Matthew's vampire side came ripping forward. He roared with the sudden pain of it and he had to struggle to not pull away from his sire.

"That's better." The god chuckled and dug the tips of his black claws further into Matthew's face. Drops of blood pooled at the points and dripped down. Matthew ground the back of his teeth, his fangs pierced the inside of his lip filling his mouth with a coppery tang.

The Blood God leaned in and pushed his claws deeper into

Matthew's flesh. "When you are worthy, you will be my champion and all will tremble before us."

Around them, the candles flared, red wax flowing like water. The blood in the bowls floated into the air, forming into long tendrils that reminded Matthew of Devak's wings. The tendrils encircled the two of them, writhing and twisting. Then they began to wrap around Matthew's right arm, starting at the shoulder and spiraling to his fingertips.

He held up his hand and watched as the blood was absorbed into his body. It began to affect Matthew like a drug.

His eyes rolled back and sanguine visions of death filled his thoughts. Pleasure pulsed through him as he saw himself standing in a field of blood, armored and invincible. At his feet lay the broken bodies of his foes and his warriors bowed down around him.

A loud bang ripped him away from the vision.

When Matthew looked up, his sire was gone. In fact, everything was how it was when he first entered; the candles burning in their usual fashion, the bowls of blood untouched. It was as if nothing had happened at all. As if there hadn't just been a god standing above him.

Matthew, still kneeling, blinked hard to clear his head and gather himself. The heavy doors to the temple were off their hinges—that must have been the noise that drew him out of the vision.

Standing just outside of the room was Devak. His vampire side was forward, his eyes red orbs. A blood guardian.

Matthew felt a sting of pain along his chin and neck where his sire had dug his claws in. He touched the wound just to be sure it was there, just to be sure it was real. It was. And his right arm was sore.

A single question had been answered and left in its place was a hundred more. What had he meant by 'champion'? And just what would Matthew need to do to prove himself worthy? And he still didn't know why. Why had he been turned into a vampire? Why him?

This was so fucking frustrating. He wished he had been able to talk to his sire but instead all he could do was bend a knee and revere the one who had made him.

He was sired by a god. He didn't know how to wrap his brain around that. It was too big. He wondered if other gods had (or in his case—*made*) children. Did he have siblings?

Stop. Just stop. Take it one step at a time.

Matthew forced his vampire aspect away and pushed himself up to his feet. Everything felt so surreal.

"Are you okay?" Devak growled, angry.

No. How could he be? Matthew's hand swept across the claw marks. "My sire…"

"He was here." Both stood in silence for a few moments then Devak added, "He wanted me to know."

"And there's nothing else you can say, is there?"

Devak's eyes returned to their honey brown and his claws melted back into his skin. Unlike Matthew, Devak was now clean and in fresh clothes. "I'd give anything to be able to tell you, my prince."

"Then let's go get that damned offering." Matthew needed someone to talk to. Someone who wasn't half-crazy like Samantha, someone who could understand all this and put it in perspective. He needed Devak's curse broken. Matthew started to leave but then he paused. "Are you unable to enter this room?"

Devak tried to say something but the words didn't form for him. He finally settled on: "It is sacred ground."

Since that was all Matthew was going to get, he nodded and the two of them walked back to the room with the shower—something Matthew was literally willing to kill for right now.

"Do you think Sam will know what just happened?" Matthew asked.

"She won't."

Matthew didn't bother asking Devak why she wouldn't know—Devak wouldn't be able to tell him. It seemed anything related to gods was off the table. "Good. I don't want her to know yet. I need to… come to terms with it."

Devak nodded.

Matthew laughed. It wasn't out of humor so much as a release of nerves. "At least now I know why you call me 'prince'."

Devak stopped walking and sunk down to his knees. "I am yours."

Matthew towered above him in the empty hallway. Devak kneeling was damn sexy. Stirring inside of what was left of his pants, his cock reminded him that the battle left him hungry for more than just blood. But his dick would have to wait. Shower first.

"Yes, Guardian. You're mine. Come."

When they entered the bedroom, Samantha was lying on the bed. Both the duffle bag and Jet—who was back in his Rottweiler form—next to her. Jet wagged his tail wildly when he saw Matthew, and Samantha pet him to try and calm him down.

"A black hole," she said.

"What?" Matthew asked while he toed off his boots and peeled out of his pants. Behind him, Devak sat down on a chair.

"Something has distressed you. I can feel it but all I see is black. Are you going to tell me?"

"Not yet. But I will, just give me a little bit of time."

She looked upset for a moment, then it passed. "Okay."

Matthew finished stripping at a record pace and made a beeline for the shower. He focused on the task of getting clean and once he was, he didn't linger. Dry, with a towel around his hips, he wrinkled his nose at his grimy pants, there was no way he'd put those back on. When he came out of the bathroom, Samantha tossed him his still-clean tuxedo.

"Do you just summon fresh clothes to you?" Matthew asked Devak while zipping up his pants and trying to ignore the growing need inside of them.

"Yes."

"That must be nice." Matthew peeled his bracers off and tossed them in the bag. His sword was long lost.

"It is convenient."

"Did you find the offering, Sam?" Matthew asked as she rooted through the duffle bag.

"Yeah, Gwenyth has it. She won't give it up freely but I have a plan."

"Then let's go get it," Matthew said.

When Matthew re-entered the ballroom he took a moment to fully survey everything before him. Most of the shifters were gone, only the alpha and two others remained. The witches were still around; they would probably teleport out together when they were done with whatever the hell they were doing. There were maybe thirty vampires in the keep consisting mostly of leaders, lords, and their companions or subordinates.

A group stood in the center of the ballroom, surrounding Bryson's makeshift command table. A passionate debate was well in progress.

Stolus glanced at Matthew. His eyes betrayed some fear, no doubt stemming from the terrible things he had witnessed Matthew do first hand, but he hid it and he returned to the argument. Emilia was standing behind him, tears streamed down her face.

"My mother is as good as dead if she's not rescued soon," Stolus said.

"What's happened to Ascelina?" Matthew asked. The vampires stopped their conversation when he spoke.

Bryson pinched the bridge of his nose. "London fell. We lost… hundreds…maybe thousands and many were captured, including Ascelina. We're not going to be able to keep any territories in Europe after tonight. Those who managed to get away are fleeing to Russia now."

Matthew rubbed his hands over his stubbled chin, then through his wet hair, pushing it back. If it were any other vampire he wouldn't give a shit but Ascelina was the one who had rescued him from the incubi…and helped him without asking for anything in return.

He looked back at Samantha and Devak. Somewhere along the way, he had started to form a family again. He hadn't meant for it to happen, and yet he had two people whose welfare he cared a great deal about. Three if he counted Jet. He valued him too.

All of it was made possible because Ascelina had saved him; because she guided him.

"God damn it. Is a rescue even possible?" he asked, then wondered if he should probably stop cussing to god. He decided he wouldn't stop because he doubted someone who went by the moniker 'Blood God' would care all that much.

"Not right now," Bryson said, "they've taken them all to a secure facility. We don't have the manpower to break through it but I have someone watching their movements. I have a feeling she'll be moved to Ashwood to be killed by Tarrick. The two of them have been fighting for a long time. He'll take his time with her, which is good news for us."

"'Good news'," Stolus repeated with a growl.

Gwenyth put his hand on Stolus' shoulder. "My child is strong. She will endure it."

"Wait. *You're* Ascelina's sire?" Matthew asked, his mouth hanging open.

Gwenyth nodded.

Emilia let out a sob and Samantha hugged her. "Don't worry," Samantha said. "My father is going to get her back."

Bryson lifted an eyebrow. "Are you?"

Matthew raised his hands in a defeated gesture. "I have no idea, but everything she's ever said about the future happens. I'm to the point where I just accept it. I owe Ascelina. She's known what I am for a long time and has never shunned me for it, and she rescued me from the incubi..." A thought occurred to Matthew. "You have someone on the inside, don't you? It's the only way she would have known I was being transported that night..."

Stolus, Bryson, and Gwenyth exchanged glances. Bryson then looked around at the other members of the room. It was clear he didn't want them overhearing.

"The sun rises in an hour. If you are serious about helping us, then we'll continue this tomorrow night. Call me with your address and I'll send a car for you and your companions." He motioned to Devak and Sam as well.

Devak shifted his weight from one foot to the other as if he wanted to say something, but he stayed silent. Matthew knew he was trying to be patient about the offering.

"I need something from you," Matthew said to Gwenyth.

"And that is?"

"I don't know—Sam?"

Samantha curled her fingers and held them up as if she was holding an invisible baseball. "A Night Stone."

"No," Gwenyth answered without even asking what they needed it for.

"We will give you this in exchange." Samantha reached into the duffle bag and pulled out a ring. It was the ring Matthew had seen when he first went through the bag.

Several of the vampires gasped, and the witches came over.

"Impossible," Gwenyth said and reached for the ring.

Samantha clasped her hand around it and pulled it away. "We need a Night Stone."

"Alright, well, I'm in the dark here. Sam, what the hell is the ring?" Matthew asked.

Gwenyth's jaw dropped. "Your child has had it the whole time and you don't know what it is?"

"It's a day ring," Devak answered. "The magic it holds allows a vampire to walk in the sun. There aren't many on this planet."

This planet. Such odd phrasing.

"There are only three in existence," Gwenyth said. "One the Queen has, one is used by the Viper, and the third is worn by Lord Skeld."

"And the fourth by you—" Samantha said with a slight smile, "—for the low, low cost of a Night Stone." She waved the ring in the air. The vampires all watched in envy—Matthew included. He'd love to see the sun again...feel it's warmth on his skin. Samantha and he were long overdue for a chat.

"The stone is not here. I keep it elsewhere," Gwenyth said.

"I know," Samantha said. "Bring it with you tomorrow." She slipped the ring back into the bag and zipped it up. "I'm tired."

Matthew scooped Samantha into his arms to carry her.

She tugged on his sleeve. "The witches still have the rod."

The witches all frowned. Tanya, the leader, stepped forward and held the rod out to Matthew, but there was a longing in her eyes.

"Do we really need a power font, Samantha? Will it be important to us at some point in the future?" Matthew asked.

"No. I guess not," she grumbled.

"Let them have it then," he said.

Pure joy, like that of a child, crossed Tanya's face and she bowed. "You give my coven a blessed gift. I will not forget it."

"Just promise you won't use it against me."

"You have my word."

Giving witches something so powerful might bite him in the ass but it might be a good idea to have some witches around who owed him. "Did our car survive or are we running home?"

Bryson motioned outside. "There are quite a few cars still in working condition. You are free to take any of them."

Matthew felt relieved. He was exhausted. "See you tomorrow then."

"Tomorrow," Bryson said with a nod.

Twenty

When they arrived back at the house, Matthew carried Samantha up to the bedroom, helped her change into pj's, and put her to sleep. Jet curled up by her feet.

Matthew dug through the duffle bag and retrieved the ring. He walked downstairs. Devak was sitting on an oversized recliner, his eyes drifting closed as if he hadn't expected Matthew to come back downstairs.

"Do you need sleep?" Matthew asked. He had never seen Devak actually sleep.

"In a way. I need to give my body time to fully recover. I'll need to be near you for a while tomorrow if you will permit it," he said, sitting forward.

Matthew looked at the closed curtains; the area around them was beginning to lighten as sunrise approached. He held up the ring. "How does it work?"

Devak stood. "There isn't much to it. Put it on and the sun no longer affects you. You can walk around during the day as if it was night. Your eyes will hurt until you get used to the brightness. I don't think your skin will tan unless you've fed recently, but I'm not sure. I've never really had that issue." He rubbed the top of his bronze skin.

"That's it?"

"You'll still need to rest so that your body can repair. Someone as young as you will need about eight to ten hours of sleep, but it gives you the freedom to choose those hours. The longer you wear the ring and the older you are, the less rest you need."

"Do witches make these?" Matthew asked. He studied the ring. It wasn't anything special, just a gold band with runes on it. It reminded him of a wedding band. This one wasn't very big and he wasn't sure it'd even fit him.

"Yes. But only one witch on this planet knows how to make them. And he—or she, I do not know his current gender, but he prefers male—does not make them often." Devak saw the confusion on

Matthew's face and added, "Powerful witches are reincarnated when they die."

"Ah," was all Matthew could muster. He didn't really care about witches right now. The heaviness of the night bore down on him. During the battle, he'd become something terrible and it had pleased the Blood God, but it didn't please him. It frightened him.

Devak must have picked up on Matthew's misery. "Put the ring on, my prince, and let's go watch the sunrise."

Matthew slipped it on his pinky and followed Devak outside. They both jumped up onto the roof and sat facing east. It wasn't the best view with trees and hills in the way, but it wouldn't be long before he saw the sun. At least he hoped—the sky was overcast right now.

His instincts were screaming at him to find shelter or sink into the ground. But he ignored them and continued to watch the east sky as the sun cracked the horizon. The clouds broke apart a bit, and Matthew's breath hitched as he watched the star continue to rise.

"I had forgotten what it looked like," Matthew said. It was a cold morning, but even still he could feel the world around him warming. Life stirred. It was so much louder with humans moving around in their houses and cars filling the streets. Everything was buzzing.

He sighed.

"You do not have to give up the ring if you do not wish to, my prince."

"I gave you my word that I would do everything in my power to break your curse. I keep my word," Matthew said.

"Perhaps there is a different offering or maybe we could find a different Night Stone. I've seen them before, I know others exist," Devak suggested.

"No. If there was another way, Sam would have mentioned it. And I won't steal the stone. The last thing I want to do is piss off more vampires." Matthew squinted his eyes, the world around him seemed to glow. "This is nice, but I am a creature of the night. And, who knows, maybe in the future I'll find another one of these. One that fits."

Devak brought his knees to his chest and hugged them. "It means a great deal to me that you would give up something you so obviously desire, my prince."

"I wish I could say it was completely selfless, but I don't think my sire is going to make another appearance anytime soon and you hold answers to questions I have waited my whole life to find out."

"The moment the curse is broken, I will tell you everything I know."

Matthew sat up. A small part of him feared that Devak wasn't what he seemed, that he was sent by the Blood God to trick him or manipulate him. Maybe it was all an act to guarantee Matthew's compliance. He worried that he might fall for the guardian only to have his heart betrayed, just as Tarrick had done to him. Matthew wouldn't be able to handle that again. He wasn't even handling it now.

He absentmindedly rubbed at the area above his heart.

"I do not seek to hurt you, my prince," Devak said.

Matthew shot him a questioning glance.

Devak motioned to Matthew's hand. "When you think of him, you rub your chest and you do not hide your facial expressions well. Your pain is obvious."

"Ah." Matthew lowered his hand. He didn't really want to talk about his pain right now. Instead, he looked at the ring. "Samantha had this ring the whole time and she didn't tell me. I could have been watching the sunrise for a month. It makes me wonder what else she keeps from me."

"She holds many secrets inside of her, but I don't think she keeps them from you intentionally. Her whole life she's been an outcast or alone. It is not something that changes overnight. I hope I don't overstep when I say that I think you should be patient with her. When you are upset with her, she seems to shut down and withdraw deeper inside."

Matthew had planned on chewing her out for some of the crap she had pulled tonight. He hated that he lost all of his control when he thought she had died. And she knew it would happen, but maybe Devak was right; yelling at her wasn't a way to build trust, and it might result in her keeping even more from him. He was still going to have a long talk with her, but he'd try not to raise his voice...much.

"You don't overstep. It's wise counsel," Matthew said. He lay down and looked up at the sky. Confusion about his sire churned inside him. What would he turn Matthew into? And would he even get a choice? Could he fight a god if it came down to it? He felt so lost. "Today, I feel very small."

Devak's eyes drifted across Matthew's body. "Nothing about you is small."

For a moment, Matthew's gloomy thoughts lifted as he studied Devak. He looked different in the daylight; his bronze skin was radiant. His amber eyes seemed lighter and inviting. The cold warrior's edge softened became seductive. Devak lounged on the roof, his body presenting itself to Matthew like an offering.

Matthew bit his lip. Damn it, he needed a release. He looked around to make sure they weren't in view of anyone. Then, he grabbed Devak by his arm and yanked, pulling the guardian on top of him so that their bodies pressed together, facing each other.

He slipped his hand behind Devak's neck and pulled him into a kiss. Devak melted on top of him as their lips clashed with urgency. Matthew's appetite turned savage as he felt Devak's erection pressing into his hip through their clothes. His own length stood hard with desire. He pushed Devak up and began pawing at the laces on his shirt. There were too many and it was taking too long. He brought out his claws with the intent of cutting the shirt away.

"I can unsummon my clothes," Devak said.

"Do it," Matthew growled and ripped his own shirt open, and began to work on his pants. He was so hungry.

Devak's clothes crumbled off him and dissolved into light.

Matthew pulled out his own cock. "I fucking need you right now." In a single, swift movement, he slipped out from under Devak and was behind him. Devak yelped when Matthew pulled up his hips, forcing him up on all fours.

Matthew pressed his throbbing cock against Devak's entrance. Normally, he'd want to take more time, let the pleasure build, prepare him, but not right now. Desire burned too hot within him. He rubbed his cock along Devak's skin, teasing the hole and wetting the area. He pressed in, going slow, listening and watching for any signs of protests from his partner.

There were none.

When Devak began moaning and moving his hips, Matthew wasn't able to keep going slow any longer. The sound drove Matthew crazy. He angled himself so that it would be pleasurable for Devak, then he impaled him with his length, driving his dick in hard. Devak shuddered.

Fuck, Matthew enjoyed this. He loved overwhelming Devak, feeling big on top of him. He loved being inside of the guardian's warm body. No, not warm. Hot. Blazing hot skin wrapped around his dick tighter than almost anyone he had ever been with.

The guardian's scent overwhelmed him, and Matthew's eyes rolled back as he slammed into Devak again and again. Cries of pleasure escaped them both.

Matthew leaned over, caging the submissive creature, and licked his neck. "Need your blood," Matthew said, his voice nearly unrecognizable with raw hunger.

"My prince...please...please..." Devak answered; desperate.

Matthew let his vampire take over and struck hard, his fangs sinking deep into Devak's perfect neck. He owned Devek right now. Wanted him. Needed him. The guardian's flesh and blood belonged to him. Both Matthew's vampire and incubus side growled in agreement.

Pulling in mouthfuls of hot liquid, Matthew nearly came. He wanted to hold his orgasm until Devak trembled below him but he wasn't sure he could. Not with this rapture of blood and body pleasuring him.

Matthew removed his fangs and gave Devak a command: "Touch yourself."

Devak obeyed without hesitation, gripping his own cock and stroking it hard.

"Come for me," Matthew growled into Devak's ear.

Devak's head rolled back and his muscles tightened. He was close.

"That's an order, Guardian." Matthew bit Devak again, this time on the back of his neck, taking more blood.

That sent the guardian over the edge. Below Matthew, Devak's muscles twitched, and his tight tunnel clamped as cum splashed on the roof tiles.

Matthew groaned, wrapped his thick muscled arms around Devak's chest, and rocked his hips forward, pushing himself deeper inside. He kept thrusting until the air froze in his lungs and every nerve ending exploded with pleasure. He pumped harder as he filled Devak, drinking in sex and blood. He didn't want it to end, but eventually it did.

Devak stilled.

Matthew removed his fangs and cock, and collapsed back onto the roof, rolling to his back, pulling Devak with him into an embrace.

A low purr came from deep within Matthew's chest and he nuzzled Devak's neck, brushing it with a kiss. Matthew's eyes dropped down to half-mast.

"Are we going to sleep up here?" Devak asked, his eyes drooping as well. "It'll be safer inside."

Matthew kissed his neck again, then released him. "You're right." Matthew could hear a human in the next house over, walking to their window and looking out the blinds. He chuckled. "I think we disturbed some of the neighbors."

Matthew grabbed his clothes but didn't bother to dress. He jumped off the roof and headed back inside. Devak—who had summoned pants when Matthew wasn't looking—started to return to his chair in the living room. Matthew grabbed his wrist to stop him. "Join me in the bed. You can feed while I sleep."

Devak eyes widened, then looked down. "But…what about Sam?"

"I'll handle her. Right now I want you in my bed." Matthew didn't wait for an answer. He tugged on Devak's wrist, pulling him along to the bedroom.

Devak didn't resist. Matthew slipped on some clean boxers and crawled into the middle of the bed. He wrapped one arm around Samantha and placed her head on his chest. Devak stood at the side of the bed, waiting.

Matthew reached out as an invitation. Devak hesitated. What was holding him back? Matthew dropped his arm. "If you don't want to, I won't force you."

"I want to." Devak bit the bottom of his lip and looked down. "I would fall on my blade for you if you wished it, but I failed you." Devak cried out as pain tore through him. "*No*. This curse…I have to tell you," he said, struggling with the words. His muscles strained.

"Stop, you're hurting yourself," Matthew said.

"But…"

Matthew gently slipped out from under Samantha and rushed to Devak's side. He put his hands around him. "Please, stop. Once you can speak about it, I'll listen."

Devak rested his head on Matthew's wide chest and Matthew stroked his guardian's neck to comfort him, nudging his emotions just a little to settle him down. Devak's muscles began to unlock beneath his touch. "It is wrong of me to desire you."

Matthew smiled and kissed the top of Devak's head. "Says who?"

Devak looked up, his face twisting.

"Don't you dare answer if it's going to cause you pain. Come." Matthew reclaimed his place in the center of the mattress. He placed Sam back in his arm and reached for Devak again. "This isn't an order, but it would please me if you slept here."

Devak's jaw tightened. He looked different. He wasn't the hardened warrior that rarely smiled; instead, he was a man who looked afraid of what was happening. When he spoke next, it was barely a whisper. "The last man I loved killed me."

Matthew wasn't sure he could love Devak, at least not in the way Devak desired, but right now Matthew wanted to feel the people he cared for around him. He needed it after what he had done and seen last night. What he had become…it was terrifying.

"I'm not Malarath. Had I been in his place, I would have done everything in my power to get you back. I would have found a way to save you."

Those must have been the right words because Devak lowered himself next to Matthew, settling into his arm. Matthew held both of them tight while Jet repositioned, resting his head on Matthew's legs.

Matthew's stomach felt warm. Content. He had no idea what the future held, but in this moment he had what he wanted. He had a family again and he swore that he would fight to keep them safe.

Twenty-One

Nightmares plagued Matthew while he slept. In them, he rained destruction, tearing apart every living creature that crossed his path. He saw flashes of terrified hunters trying to escape him and failing as he sunk his claws into their meaty bodies and tore them apart. Their screams haunted him. But the most horrendous part of the nightmares were that on some level he *enjoyed* hearing their pain.

The scent of blood filled his nose. Samantha's blood. Devak's blood.

His eyes snapped open.

Devak was straddling him, his hands were on his chest, pinning him down. Devak's arms and torso were shredded up by long claw marks. Samantha was in the corner of the room, clutching her bleeding arm.

Matthew shot up and looked around to locate what had harmed them.

"You are safe, my prince," Devak said, his hands still on Matthew's chest.

Matthew furrowed his eyebrows, confused. He raised his hands up...only to find them clawed and covered with blood. *He* had hurt them. "I did this."

"The wounds are not bad, minor scratches," Devak said, already healing. Samantha was not, though; claw marks ran down her arm. Matthew forced his vampire side away.

"What happened, Father?" she asked, shaking.

Matthew's thoughts were blurry. It took him a moment to sort them out; the sun had just set. He remembered he had fallen asleep with both of them in his arms. He sensed Jet leaving at one point to go keep watch on the roof. The ring. "I had a nightmare about the battle. I don't dream often when the sun is up, let alone have nightmares. Are you okay?" Her wounds were finally knitting together.

She nodded.

"It might be a side effect of the ring," Devak said, sitting back but still straddling Matthew.

Matthew ripped the ring off his pinky and set it on a side table. "I hope that's all it is. Did you get Samantha away from me?"

"Yes, my prince. I should have been quicker but I am still weakened."

From her corner, Samantha's eyes shot daggers at Devak. "Why was he half-naked in the bed anyway?"

"Because I asked him to be here," Matthew said. Devak slid off Matthew and scooted to the far side of the bed, distancing himself from Samantha. A forty-five hundred-year-old vampire guardian retreating from a month old fledgling...Matthew couldn't blame him.

Samantha's face scrunched with anger and her eyes narrowed. She stormed to the door.

"No. Samantha come here. I'm sick of you running off when we need to talk about this." Matthew stood up.

She didn't stop.

"That's a command."

She spun on her heels. Her shoulders heaved and eyes darkened as she stomped to Matthew, then sat on the bed, crossing her arms.

"I'll give you privacy." Devak bowed and left the room, shutting the door behind him.

Samantha's lips curled up, and her eyes glared red. When he tried to touch her, she pulled away and hissed at him, flashing her tiny fangs. It was almost endearing how she tried to be threatening. Matthew suppressed a smile. He dragged a chair over and sat facing her.

"Why do you always run?" he asked.

She pressed her lips together into a thin line and crossed her arms.

"Samantha—" He used her full name so that she realized just how angry he was right now. "—there are some things we need to discuss and we are going to talk about them whether you want to or not. I don't want to have to command you to answer, but make no mistake, I will."

Her eyes began to water and Matthew's heart broke. Maybe he shouldn't have said that. He shouldn't be so harsh with her. She was his child after all, not a damn prisoner.

"Sam..." he said, softer this time. "I just need to understand you. We need to actually talk to each other." She said nothing. "Please. I want to know why you are keeping things from me. You knew what would happen if I thought you had died...what I would turn into.

Did you even pause for a moment and think what it would do to me? I hate losing control and that…that was…did you do it to punish me for sleeping with Devak?"

Her eyes widened, horrified. "Your opinion of me is very low. I did it because that's what was supposed to happen."

"I don't have a low opinion of you. I assure you, it's the opposite."

She scoffed. "How can it be? You made me such a weak vampire."

"You know that wasn't intentional. I was trying to save your life. If I could go back and re-do it the correct way, I would."

"If you could go back, you wouldn't have turned me at all." She looked away and swallowed a few times, trying to hide her pain.

"Maybe not, but I don't regret that it happened. I like having you as my child—you fill me with joy and I find you fascinating."

Her head snapped to him. "Then why did you pick Devak and not me?"

"Sam…"

"Other vampires sleep with their children. I asked. It's common practice."

"But you aren't looking just to sleep with me, you want something deeper and I can't give that to you right now."

She opened her mouth to speak but Matthew held up his hand.

"Let me finish. I can feel that you want to fall in love with someone. I want that for you. I love you Sam, but I'm not romantically *in love* with you. Having sex with you right now would have catastrophic consequences. It wouldn't mean the same thing to me as it would to you and you aren't to the point where sex isn't just sex—not yet anyways. Maybe not ever. Some people aren't wired that way."

She sat in quiet contemplation. Finally, she nodded. "I think you're right."

Matthew smiled and carefully touched her arm, ready to withdraw in case she didn't want it. She let him. "I'll do anything in my power to make you happy."

Her lips curled into a half-smile. "Do you think we'll have meaningless sex one day?"

He laughed. "You're my sired child. I don't think I could. But then again, you're bound to me for a hundred years. That's a long time to be around an incubus and not bone them at least once…"

"Incupire," she corrected.

"Incupire," he repeated with a nod.

Samantha's smile dropped and her head fell forward. Matthew could feel through the bond that something else was weighing heavy on her heart. He cupped her cheek and lifted her head. "You know you can tell me anything. Talk to me."

She swallowed hard, forcing the lump in her throat down. "It's nothing."

When she looked away again, Matthew lowered his hand. She had more to say. He sat silently waiting for her to say it.

"It's just...I'm not used to this..." she said, trailing off until she found the courage to continue. "I never had any friends. I was always... different...and it only got worse as I got older. And when I lost my parents, I lost what little I had." Samantha wiped her eyes. "I was so lonely until you came along. I'm afraid you're going to leave me and I don't want to be alone anymore. Please don't leave me," she pleaded.

Matthew scooted from his chair to sit next to her on the bed. He pulled her into him, and a muffled sob escaped her. "I won't ever leave you, Sam. I'm also scared of being alone."

After he had been turned into a vampire he was alone for years. He never wanted to go back to that. Never. When Tarrick had captured him, it was the threat of being alone in a cage that he feared the most—more so than any other punishment.

His incubus side required companionship, but since he didn't know what he was until relatively recently, he just assumed he was a needy, extroverted male.

Samantha wiped away her tears and giggled a little. Not the reaction Matthew was expecting.

"I've seen you fight. I don't believe you're scared of anything," she said.

"Bullshit. I'm scared of many things." He held her tighter. "I'm scared of losing you, of losing myself, I worry I might never find the answers I seek, I'm frightened of being recaptured by the incubi." Matthew paused, and it took him a moment before he could continue. "I'm...terrified that my heart might never heal. As a human, I had a hard time letting go. As a vampire, it's magnified and...I loved him. Those feelings haven't faded like I thought they would."

Samantha wrapped her arms around him and rested her head on his shoulder. "I don't know what's going to happen to us, I've only seen small pieces and none of it makes sense yet. It's dark. Are you going to tell me what happened after the battle last night? I still can't see it."

"Yes. But not today." Matthew needed a little more time to come to terms with who sired him.

"Alright. But soon?"

"Soon. I promise."

She nodded, and he was thankful she didn't press the issue. Maybe she could feel what he needed through the bond. He sighed and changed topics. "It was selfish of me to invite Devak into the bed without even talking to you about it. I'm sorry."

Her body went stiff. "Is he going to keep sleeping with us?"

"I'd like him to, but if you aren't comfortable with it, then no."

She said nothing for a moment, then she relaxed. "I don't mind if he's here. I know you like him a lot. But I want something in return for agreeing to let him be in the bed."

Matthew wasn't quite sure what she had in mind. He was a little worried. "And that is…?"

"Once we break the curse, I want to find a home somewhere and stay put for a while. And I want you to take me out hunting."

Matthew raised an eyebrow. She wasn't able to feed before and she had expressed no interest since.

"I mean—" she started to clarify, "—I want to try blood from different humans and maybe even an incubus if you can catch one. You can, um, feed it to me. By, you know, kissing." She looked flustered. "Also, I want to learn to compel and sink into the dirt."

All of that sounded nice to Matthew. By then he'd have all the answers he wanted, and the idea of having some stability suited him just fine. "It's a deal."

There was a soft knock on the door and Devak enter fully clothed. "I am sorry for interrupting. I just got off the phone with General Bryson—the car will be here in 20 minutes. He warned that we will be blindfolded since the location is kept secret."

"Thanks. Have you fed?"

Devak nodded. "While you slept." He bowed and left the room.

With their talk done, Samantha fed, showered, and got the duffle bag packed. She was wearing tight black pants and a t-shirt that plunged deep, showcasing her small breasts. Matthew suspected it was because Bryson would be there. She seemed to enjoy his company quite a bit at the masquerade.

While she finished getting ready, Matthew told Jet that he wouldn't be coming with them tonight. Jet wasn't very happy about it, but Matthew didn't want to see someone die because they tried to stick a blindfold on a gargoyle.

Twenty minutes later, the three were ready to go when a black SUV pulled up. The driver was a large vampire wearing a white button-up shirt with black slacks. He was a lord but a younger one, maybe three hundred years old or so, Matthew guessed.

"I am Vikentiy," he said with a thick Russian accent as he approached. He held up the blindfolds in his hand. "You were told about blindfolds, yes?"

Matthew nodded.

"Good. Listen. Is important we keep location secure. Normally, if you pull blindfold off, I kill you, but I was there last night and there is no way I could kill you or guardian—" he said pointing at Matthew and Devak, "—and I don't dare touch her. So, I ask real nice, leave blindfolds on, okay?"

"We'll respect your wishes," Matthew said.

Vikentiy opened the door for them and they piled into the back. He handed them each a blindfold and waited until they were on before returning to the driver's seat. They were underway a few moments later.

"Are you really an incubus?" Vikentiy asked, breaking the silence.

"Yep." Matthew wasn't too worried about being attacked; he could smell and hear everything the other vampire was doing.

The large Russian vampire laughed. "I would love to meet motherfucker that turned you into vamp." *No, you wouldn't.* But Matthew didn't say anything. "I cannot believe guardian is here. You show up because Pit opened? I mean, that is what you do, yes? Fight demons."

"My reason for being here is not your concern," Devak said, his voice carrying a dark edge.

"Sorry, no offense. Is just I've never seen guardian before. I was up there fighting by you yesterday and you were knocking them out of the sky. I would kill to watch you fight incubus guardian, that would be something."

Devak began growling. It was a low warning. Matthew couldn't recall ever hearing Devak growl like that.

"I don't know why these blindfolds are needed," Samantha said.

"Because we want to keep locati—" Vikentiy began to explain again.

"I'm an oracle. The moment you came close to me I could see where we were going because you had been there."

Matthew suppressed a chuckle. Samantha was probably feeling left out of the praise that Vikentiy had given them and she wanted to show off.

Vikentiy drove in silence for a moment. "No oracle has ever retained their powers after turning vamp."

"Diana is still alive."

The car came to a screeching halt. Matthew pulled Samantha into him and was half-tempted to rip off the blindfold, but Vikentiy didn't move. Matthew could hear him gripping the wheel tight.

"Say again," the Russian said.

"Diana is still alive."

"Where?" he asked, his voice barely a whisper.

"House Petracca."

After a few minutes of silence, the car began moving again. Vikentiy had nothing else to say for the rest of the drive. About an hour later, the car came to a stop and the doors open. "You can take them off," the Russian said. Matthew peeled the blindfolds away and looked around.

They were underground in a cavern carved out of solid rock. Around them were many parked cars. Huge bunker doors were closing behind them. Matthew pulled red strands of energy into his hearing to extend it. There were three stories below them and some sort of structure above. The facility had just over seventy vampires in it right now and many humans—thralls most likely.

Matthew noticed that Vikentiy was eyeing Samantha. When he took a step towards her, Matthew growled and Devak moved between the large vampire and Samantha. Vikentiy backed off.

"I...thank you, little one," he said to Samantha, then walked away. "Follow me."

They were led down a sloping hallway until finally, Vikentiy stopped outside a set of metal doors.

"Wait here," the Russian said and walked into the room, shutting the door behind him. Matthew couldn't hear anything on the other side, meaning it was magically warded.

"Diana?" Matthew asked Samantha, not caring if the vampires in the room heard him. He felt certain that Vikentiy was reporting what had happened right now.

Her lips curled into a devious smile. Well, her version of devious. It was actually kind of cute. "His sister. She was captured a long time ago."

"Ah," Matthew said and leaned against the rocky wall while they waited. Devak shifted. "Something wrong?"

"I dislike being underground," he said with a frown.

"Claustrophobic?" Samantha asked, still smiling.

"I am not," he said, answering just a little too fast. "It's just that my weapon and armor will collapse the ceiling should I need to summon them."

Matthew laughed. Devak clearly didn't enjoy being in a confined space.

The doors opened and Vikentiy ushered them inside. The room was set up sort of like Tarrick's own command center. It had a wall of live feeds coming in from all over the world with dispatchers gathering reports. Important looking vampires watched situations unfold and gave orders.

Unlike the incubi command center, it wasn't as high tech and the vampires didn't look as disciplined as hunters were, but it got the job done. Oh, and there weren't any fucking thrones either.

Bryson, Gwenyth, and Stolus stood around the center table discussing something. When Matthew, Devak, and Samantha walked in, the room went quiet.

Bryson stepped forward. Samantha sucked in a breath when she saw him, eyeing his body. Even Matthew noticed he filled his grey wool pants and a button-up shirt well. There was no doubt about it, she had absolutely dressed with him in mind.

Matthew noticed there was a long leather jacket hanging nearby; it looked like standard issue hunter gear.

"Are you still interested in helping us rescue Ascelina?" Bryson asked, his voice deep and solemn.

"I am," Matthew said.

Bryson motioned for them to join him at the table and everyone else returned to their tasks. Vikentiy stood guard at the door. Matthew could sense some of the vampires in the room were nervous, but most seemed to be in awe of both him and Devak. Every once in a while, they'd look up from their work and steal a glance.

"Last night, you were right—" Bryson started.

"I don't think you should tell him," Stolus said, interrupting the general while scowling at Matthew.

Bryson growled. "You've already made your objections known. That conversation is long over." Stolus huffed but said nothing else. Bryson continued. "You were right. We do have someone inside. A lot of someones, actually. There are hunters who don't agree with how the incubi run the corps. Hunters who believe they should be an independent organization. And, there are some who dislike the incubi more than they dislike us. We provide them support in exchange for intel."

"I see." It was hardly surprising to learn they had spies. "Do you have a plan to rescue Ascelina?" Matthew asked, wondering what his role would be. He hoped it would be something more than just 'go kill everything in our path'.

Stolus fisted his hands. "No."

"We are working on it now," Gwenyth said and put a hand on Stolus to calm him. "We received confirmation that she was moved to Tarrick's keep, along with three other lords and seven non-lord vampires."

Matthew looked at the table, memorizing the contents on it: printouts of reports, a screen that displayed a map of the area around Tarrick's keep, and photos of Ascelina in chains taken from a distance with a telephoto lens. There were other photos, too, of other lords. Nothing on the table gave him any ideas. His eyes drifted to the monitors, and he noticed some of the screens had videos of hunters.

Vampires in the field must be following them around with a camera to keep tabs on them.

"I take it you can't teleport inside his keep anymore?" Matthew asked.

"No, Tarrick bolstered the wards." Bryson pointed to the map of the keep. "Right now, we don't know any weaknesses in the defenses. We've considered a direct assault but he's expecting it. Even with you and the guardian, we would lose too many. I'm not willing to sacrifice hundreds to save a few."

The more he interacted with Bryson, the more Matthew liked him. Bryson had the mind of a leader, even if he was younger than almost every other vampire in the room, save for himself and Samantha.

As Matthew watched the monitors, an idea came to him. He didn't have all the pieces yet, but the picture was forming all the same.

He was lost in thought for so long that Samantha asked Gwenyth if she wanted to trade the Night Stone for the daylight ring now. Samantha dug the ring from the duffle bag and Gwenyth had a human thrall bring a wooden box over to them. She opened it to reveal a beautiful palm-sized stone that looked as if it had a galaxy of stars trapped within it.

As Samantha held out the ring, Matthew grabbed her wrist. Devak looked puzzled, as did everyone else around the table.

"Do you no longer wish the trade?" Gwenyth asked.

"The trade will happen, but it's going to be delayed for a few nights." Matthew took the ring from Samantha. "I have a few questions I need answered. Do you ever track Tarrick's movements?"

Bryson shook his head. "We try, but he's careful. If he goes to feed, it's normally during the day or he'll bring his food back to his keep. He doesn't even go to parties that often, and he doesn't let anyone know his movements ahead of time. His hunters are on call twenty-four-seven because of it." He chuckled. "As someone who served as one of his personal guards, let me tell you, it was hell."

Bryson had served on the Wardens? Impressive. Matthew wondered just which vampire was ballsy enough to capture Bryson and turn him. But this was hardly the time for that conversation.

"Sam, if I brought you someone, how likely would it be that you could see a few days into their future?"

"It depends. I'd have to focus. If it's someone whose future is not intimately entwined with mine, it's easier. Also, it helps if I spend a little time near them, but not too long."

"Good." Matthew turned to Bryson. "How long would it take to get us to Pennsylvania?"

"We have private jets—we can be in the air within the hour. What are you thinking?" Bryson asked.

"How valuable do you think Tarrick is to the incubi?"

"After the High King, I'd say he's the most important incubus there is. Others outrank him but he's the one who keeps them alive. The other generals are good, he's better."

Matthew already suspected that was the case. "And how many vampires do you think they would trade for him?"

"Many. Wait…" Bryson was catching on. "You aren't suggesting—"

"Oh, yes, I am." Matthew lowered his voice to show just how serious he was. "We're going to capture High Lord General Tarrick."

Twenty-Two

The plan to capture Tarrick was far more complex and relied on way more luck than Matthew wanted. If one piece went wrong, it would crumble apart. But once he had explained his idea, all of the vampires agreed that it might just work. They rushed to put it in motion.

The flight on the private jet from Washington to Pennsylvania was mostly quiet. Inside, the chairs all faced inwards towards the center.

General Bryson was on his tablet, sending out orders and coordinating vampires. Vikentiy was up front piloting the plane while Stolus spent his time scowling at Matthew with his arms crossed over his chest. Matthew hadn't wanted Stolus to come along but he insisted being there when his mother was released.

Samantha spent the flight reading. Or rather, pretending to between stealing glances at Bryson whenever she could. When he noticed her looking at him, he shot her a friendly smile. Matthew had to suppress growls but he managed to keep himself together for her sake.

Devak sat quietly in a seat near the rear. He wasn't thrilled to be 'stuck in a tin when he could have flown out himself.' But Matthew insisted they stay together and there was no further objection. Gwenyth wasn't with them. She and the witches were on their way to Europe for their part in the plan.

Matthew didn't have time to get Jet so Bryson sent a vampire to the house to tell the gargoyle where they had gone. Matthew had no idea if Jet would join them. He had a feeling the gargoyle would show up again when he wanted to show up.

The long flight made Matthew miss traveling by leystones. Due to the time difference, when they finally set down in Pennsylvania the sun was less than an hour away from rising.

A car was waiting for them. They were driven (this time without blindfolds) to another underground bunker and escorted to a sparsely decorated room that had a queen bed. Matthew was surprised to find it had a bathroom with a shower. He'd assumed there'd be no plumbing underground. The adjacent room was provided for Devak.

After they were informed that the rooms were warded against sound in case he needed to talk about sensitive matters, they were left alone. Devak stood in the carved-stone hallway, not entering either room.

"Is there a problem?" Matthew asked.

Devak's eyes were wide. "The rooms are small. I will stand guard out here during the day."

Matthew smiled. "Does being underground really bother you so much?"

Devak clasped his hands in front of him and looked uneasy. "I never enjoyed it, even when I was a vampire. And, as a guardian, I no longer possess the ability to move earth."

"If you want to feed, you'll have to come in."

Devak clenched his jaw and stepped inside.

Samantha had already changed and was getting settled on the bed. She looked to Devak and said, "You're lucky we're both small, otherwise the bed wouldn't fit all of us."

Devak sent them a questioning glance.

"You don't have to join us but you're welcome to," Matthew said and motioned to the bed.

"You do not have an issue with it?" Devak asked Samantha, who was adjusting her pillows.

She cocked her head. "Didn't you overhear our conversation yesterday? I know your hearing is at least as good as Father's."

"Out of respect, I chose not to listen."

"Oh. Well then, no, I don't have a problem. So long as you don't hog the whole bed like he does," she said while pointing to Matthew.

Matthew frowned. "It's not my fault I'm a big guy."

A muffled moan escaped Devak, so quiet Matthew almost didn't catch it. He shot Devak a seductive half-smile then crawled into bed beside Sam. She lay her head down on his chest and fell asleep.

Devak hesitated for a moment then lowered himself down to the other side of Matthew, placing his hand on Matthew's tight abdomen. "I'll feed for a while tonight so that I am fully recovered by tomorrow."

Matthew nodded. Tomorrow night, if everything went as planned, was going to be busy. He slipped to sleep as the sun rose.

****

The closest town to Tarrick's keep was decently sized and never had vampires because it was used as a training ground for hunters.

Matthew crouched behind an AC unit on a snowy rooftop. His vampire guise was out. Devak kneeled beside him. The moon was fat, which worked against them.

"Be sure not to hurt her," Matthew said for the hundredth time.

"I assure you she will be unharmed, my prince," Devak said.

Below them, six cadet hunters weaved through buildings, practicing moving as a team. Overseeing them was Commander Silva, who looked bored out of her mind. The group she was training seemed to know what they were doing so her job was 'glorified babysitter' at the moment.

One of the advantages of training at Ashwood was that Matthew knew the routines of the various instructors. He knew Silva would be here. And right now, none of the hunters had any idea they were being stalked.

Matthew was having a lot of fun jumping from rooftop to rooftop, tracking the hunters. It had been a long while since he pursued a mark like this and his vampire side thoroughly enjoyed it. His body responded as if he was hunting prey. Even Devak seemed pleased; his fangs were out and he moved like a predator, agile and silent.

Devak, who took the lead because of the possibility of hidden vamp traps and wards, tried to anticipate where the team was going. He misjudged, moving a little faster than the team below them, and he and Matthew had to scramble down behind a parapet to avoid detection.

Matthew crouched behind Devak, pressing in close as the hunters approached in the street below. If any of them teleported up here, this was over. Unless, that is, he and Devak wanted to murder everyone. And Matthew had had his fill of killing hunters this week.

He rested his hand on Devak's hip and pulled him closer. Devak nodded at the hunters, warning Matthew to behave. Matthew smiled and leaned in close, brushing his lips against his guardian's ear.

Devak's chest vibrated with a silent purr.

As the team of vampire hunters came closer, both of them stilled, but Matthew kept his lips firmly wrapped around Devak's earlobe. One hunter appeared on an opposing rooftop but didn't see them. Matthew pressed his hardening cock against Devak's ass and he wished they didn't have layers of clothes on. Devak's chest vibrated again.

Once the hunters were far enough away, Matthew tackled Devak, spinning him so that he landed on his back. He slipped his hand behind Devak's neck and aggressively claimed his mouth.

"You should have fed before we came," Devak said when Matthew broke away.

"But this is much more fun."

Devak's face fell neutral, unamused.

Matthew dipped down to his ear and whispered, "Don't act like you don't enjoy it."

Devak half-moaned, half-growled, showing off his wonderfully long fangs. "My prince...we are on a schedule," he said, and slipped out from under Matthew, disappearing across the rooftops.

Matthew chuckled to himself. He really should stop teasing Devak, but when he tapped into his predatory side, he got turned on. He couldn't help it.

He pushed more power into his speed and tried to keep up. He had no hope of it; Devak could run laps around him if he wanted. Thankfully, he had waited for Matthew.

"Not nice," Matthew said when he caught up.

Devak's lips curled up into a slight smile for a brief moment, then he let it drop. "Are you ready?"

Matthew nodded. This next part would happen incredibly quick, and they had to execute it with perfection.

They were in a business district. Not many humans here this late, but there were enough for what they needed.

The hunters teleported down another alleyway and came to a stop. Before them was a still-warm body of a human male.

"Sir," one of the hunters called from below. "It's a vamp kill."

Silva joined them by the body. She touched it. "This is fresh. Follow me."

She took over the team and began tracking the vampire that had killed the human. Matthew and Devak knew where she was heading...

they helped set the trail after all. They moved past the hunters and got themselves into position on the rooftop of a two-story building.

The scent of blood filled the air as Devak's back began to bleed in preparation for his wings. Matthew readied himself, weaving red threads of blood energy throughout his body, leaving it coiled like a spring ready to release. Devak tensed as well.

A human screamed. The hunters rushed in that direction. As they neared, weapons out, a young woman ran into them. "Please help me! Oh god, it has claws," the panicked girl cried.

One of the hunters ushered her away while the rest moved forward. A large vampire appeared before the hunters and looked surprised. "Oh shit," Vikentiy said with his Russian accent. He turned and darted the other way, avoiding the bolts the hunters were firing at him.

As he ran away, Vikentiy kept himself slower than normal and didn't bring out his wings, pretending to be just a regular vampire, not a lord.

Silva pointed at the fleeing vampire. "The first to stake him has tomorrow night off. Get to it, cadets."

And with that, the cadets began their chase. Vikentiy would lead them all through the city, keeping them distracted for a while before he took off back to the base. The six cadets weren't a real threat to a vampire lord. If it were an elite team of hunters, that'd be a little different.

With the cadets gone, Silva brought her comm up to report.

Matthew nodded once then released the stored energy and bounded off the roof. Devak followed and grabbed Silva. The two ran at a breakneck pace out of the city and into the surrounding forest. To Silva, everything would look like a blur. She tried to teleport away but Devak drained her runes of magic before she could use them.

They came to a stop miles outside of the city. Devak released the commander, and before she could process what had happened, she had her crossbow out and shot off a bolt at Matthew. He knocked it from the air and stood before her.

"Matthew," Silva gasped, her brain catching up.

She moved to fire again but Devak grabbed her wrist and applied pressure, forcing her to drop the crossbow. He stomped on it, sliced off her sash of silver daggers, and began removing the rest of her weapons, tossing them far into the forest.

Helpless to do much else, she raised her comm again. "Dispatch—" was all she got out before Devak pried it from her and tossed it to Matthew, who closed the channel.

She looked up at Devak. "Hello again, little human," he said.

Silva narrowed her eyes. "Well, you've disarmed me and made my runes useless. Seems like a lot of effort just to kill me."

"We're not going to kill you, Silva," Matthew said.

"Then what do you want?"

From her earpiece, Matthew heard a dispatcher asking Silva to report in.

"I want you to tell dispatch to clear out Ashwood's eastern dorms." Matthew held the comm up to her mouth but didn't open the channel yet.

"And why would I do that?"

Matthew looked to Devak.

"La'mast." High in the night sky, a single blinding bright line of light cracked open and a meteor came careening to the earth. Its target was far from them, but it was still impressive.

Matthew pointed up. "Because I've killed enough hunters this week and I think the ones currently in the dorms would enjoy living."

"Hell's bells," she said. "You're destroying the leystone."

"Yeah. Don't tell dispatch I'm here. As much as I would enjoy having Prescott or Hiroto, or the other Argonauts all over me, I'm going to take a pass on them tonight."

Matthew pressed the button down on the comm.

"Dispatch—" Silva said, "—order all hunters out of Lincoln hall. That meteor is heading for the leystone."

Matthew crushed the comm before she could relay any more information, then removed the earpiece from her and tossed it away.

The sky grew brighter as the meteor streaked overhead.

"You're up," Matthew said to Devak, who nodded and launched himself into the air. His wings snapped out wide and he went chasing after the meteor, towards the academy, leaving Matthew alone with Silva. They were a ways out from Ashwood, but it wouldn't take Devak that long to get there. He could fly fast.

Silva stared at Matthew but didn't make any move to try to fight him. What would be the point? She was good but not at his level, and she knew it.

"What the hell are you doing, Matthew?" Silva asked, standing her ground. "And please don't say you are here to apologize again."

"Silva, I'd be on my knees begging if I thought for a moment you'd ever forgive me," Matthew looked down and sighed heavily, "but I know better."

Silva pressed her lips together and he heard her teeth grind from anger. "Good. Because you killed many of my friends the other night. I'm not in a forgiving mood."

Matthew rubbed his forehead. "We're in the middle of a fucking war. It's not like I went after them—"

"You did! I saw the damn footage. They were trying to run from you and you didn't let any of them go."

Matthew leaned against a tree. Everything she was saying hurt, but it wasn't anything he wasn't already beating himself up over. "I take it you were in London?"

She didn't say anything. Her weight shifted from one leg to the other, crunching leaves and snow under her feet.

"How many vampires did you let go when they tried to run from you?" he asked.

Out of habit, Silva reached for a weapon on her belt. When she found none she balled her fists.

"We're in the middle of a war," Matthew repeated.

"You've always been on their side, haven't you? You were always deceiving us."

Matthew lunged at her and his eyes burned with fury. "That's not true. *I* was the one deceived!"

She took a few steps away from him. Matthew took a deep breath to regain his control. He hadn't meant to scare her, but her words bit him. Digging a claw into the tree, he closed his eyes for a moment and forced them to return to silver. "That's not true," he repeated again, softer. "When I was first captured, it was my plan to stay until I was powerful enough to take on anyone. But somewhere along the way…" Matthew trailed off.

"You started believing you were one of them," she finished for him.

"That's the shitty part. I am one of them whether they accept me or not."

Silva almost looked as if she felt bad for him. "So why did you grab me? Are you going to compel me again?"

"No, I'm not going to compel you. I still regret doing that the first time. I guess...I just wanted to talk since I'm here anyway."

Silva stared at him for a moment, trying to figure out what was happening.

"Oh yeah, right, you wouldn't know. This is part of a massive coordinated attack that's taking place around the world." Matthew moved his index finger in a circular motion. "I volunteered to take the Ashwood stone but it's really Devak that's doing all the work."

She looked in the direction of Ashwood, worried. "Is he killing them?"

Matthew crossed his arms and leaned against the tree again. "Nah, I ordered him not to."

"You ordered a guardian? And he followed the order?"

"Yes," he said, but didn't give up any more information.

"How many stones are being attacked tonight?" she asked.

"Many. Most of the southeast states, Western Europe, Australia. Russia, of course. Oh, and Japan." There was no harm in telling her. Tarrick would know all this by now, and by the time she was back the attack would be over.

"There's no way you are going to get to all those teleport stones. We're prepared to counter an attack like this one."

Matthew shrugged. "I'm sure you are."

She eyed him. "What do you have up your sleeve?"

"Oh, nothing."

She glared at him.

"Okay, okay. Other than here and a few other choice locations, we didn't go after many of the big estates. The rest of the homes only have one or two teams of hunters stationed, and with no leystone that means no backup."

Silva didn't look impressed. "Most of those homes keep the leystones inside. And all those houses are warded. The first vampire to step through would get zapped. Backup can arrive long before the vampires can figure out a way into the house."

Matthew slumped against the tree a bit more and baited her with a, "If you say so."

"*Matthew*," she said, irate.

"Hm?" he asked with an innocent shrug.

"Tell me."

Matthew grinned, especially proud of this part of the plan. "I found out something interesting the other day. It turns out that even though vampires can't use or activate magic, magic can still protect us if we wear it."

She crossed her arms over her chest. "I know that."

"Right. But did you know that witches can make rings that make vampires immune to protection wards?"

"Sure, but there's only a handful around because they take a lot of power to create."

"Normally, yes. But if they have a power font? Enchanting a ring with that spell is so simple to cast that witches can empower, like, fifty at a time. And because only humans have thresholds, it means the entire vampire army can roll right into any incubus house. No death by zapping."

Silva rubbed at her belt were her crossbow normally hung. "The Rod of Sioua. The one you took from Sabine's house after you killed her...that's what they used during the battle?"

It turned out, having a bunch of witches owe him paid off much sooner than he thought it would. They used the rod to make the rings. And Bryson had rushed the rings out over the day so that they would be there waiting for the vampires when they woke. Bryson might not have Tarrick's experience and wealth, but he was resourceful and knew how to get shit done.

"Yeah. And, ironically enough, I got the idea for the rings from hunter runes. I know cadets get a protection rune with their first set of tats, meaning it has to be easy for a witch to cast, even if it does take a lot of power."

Her eyes widened. "This was your idea?"

Matthew smiled.

Her body shifted as if it had become heavier. As someone who had trained him, and been responsible for him the day he escaped, she probably blamed herself for everything Matthew had done since he got away. "You've joined the vampires then?" she asked, her voice low, almost sad.

Matthew ran his fingers through his hair. He stood up so that he was no longer slouched against the tree. "No. I just owed someone a favor."

Matthew approached her and put his hand on her shoulder. She didn't pull away. He cared for Silva, but they'd never be friends again and that pained him. "I really do just want to be left alone." His phone buzzed in his pocket letting him know the plan had worked. "If you are done pumping me for information, you're free to go."

"That's it?"

"Well, unless you want to fuck me. In that case, you better start undressing because I'm likely to slice through all that leather with my claws." He held up his hand and flexed.

Her lips curled up at the edges. "I told you once before, I don't fuck creatures that I might one day have to kill."

"But you're really cheating yourself out of all this," Matthew said with a joking smile and motioned up and down his body. She chuckled, and for just a moment it felt as if they had recaptured what they once had. Then it faded.

"You really are letting me go? This isn't some trick where you let me have hope then come chase me down and kill me?"

Matthew's face dropped. "Do you really think I would do that? If we were to fight, you'd have your weapons and your runes. I really hope it never happens. I might be *your* enemy, Silva, but I don't consider you mine."

She looked conflicted for a moment, then her face hardened. "I still don't understand why you grabbed me. You didn't need to be here for the guardian to destroy the stone. And you could have warned them to evacuate the building by calling if it really matters to you. I know you have Tarrick's phone number."

Matthew swallowed a lump and looked away.

"Oh. I see. You did come to apologize," she said.

"Silva…"

She held up her hand, unwilling to allow it.

Matthew met her eyes. "I wish there was no war. And more days than not, I wish I hadn't been turned. I always wonder what my life would have been like if I had simply been an incubus. Some days, I like to imagine we would have stayed friends."

She said nothing to him. Condensation from her breath hung between them. The silence hurt more than any words she could say.

Finally, she spoke. "Ascelina killed my whole team, you know? That night you escaped. I had served with some of them for decades, and your friend and her son ripped them apart in front of me. The war will end when all vampires are dead."

Matthew said nothing. He couldn't deny what had happened; her anger was justified. As was his. As was everyone's. They were all locked in an endless cycle of hate and destruction.

Silva took a step away. "Thank you for letting my hunters get out of the building." The words came out cold, as if she was distancing herself mentally from Matthew. It gave him hope that maybe deep down she cared for him, despite everything that had happened.

"Yeah. No problem. Your runes should be back up in about fifteen minutes."

She nodded then began to run back to the town without saying another word to him. Matthew closed his eyes while he waited in the dark forest. Devak would be breaking away from Ashwood right about now and flying the opposite direction. They'd meet up later.

Once he sensed that Silva was far enough away, Matthew reached down into the cold dirt below him. He willed the earth to split apart under his hand. Under the ground, Samantha grabbed him and he pulled her up.

Reflexes made her cough and she brushed the dirt off herself.

"Did it work?" Matthew asked.

An elated look crossed her face. "Yep. It was easy to read her future, and I know where Tarrick is going to be two days from now."

Twenty-Three

Once they were back in the bunker, Matthew sent Samantha off to shower while he headed to the command room. He passed Vikentiy on his way in. The Russian vampire affectionately punched his shoulder and told him just how much fun he had playing with the hunters.

When Matthew finally made it to the command room, he took a moment to study it. It was smaller than the one in Washington, but it had all the necessary equipment. Bryson, in dark slacks and a white button-up shirt that contrasted against his greyish-black skin, was all smiles. Hell, even Stolus looked happy.

"It went well?" Matthew asked, already knowing the answer from the looks on their faces.

Bryson looked up from a map. "The incubi had no idea what hit them. We destroyed almost three hundred leystones and our losses were minimal. This is really good for us—it'll be years before they can replace them all. What about on your end?"

"It worked. We know where Tarrick will be in two days."

Devak still wasn't back but Matthew wasn't too worried yet.

"You still sure you want to do it without any backup? I can get shifters…"

Matthew waved his hand. "I'm sure. Let's just stick to the plan." Mercenary shifters worked primarily for vampires but Matthew didn't trust them not to sell them out.

Bryson nodded and went back to work. No one kicked Matthew out, so he crossed his arms over his chest and leaned against a wall, watching the general do his job. Bryson rolled up his sleeves as he issued orders to vampires across the globe. As the night went on, and the vampires finished their various attacks, the room grew quieter.

"Do your hunter runes still work?" Matthew asked Bryson during a lull. He knew next to nothing about the general and had questions bouncing around his head.

Bryson looked up from his task. "Not really. Every couple of weeks, if I focus, I can activate one for a few moments."

"How old are you?"

"Thirty-three," he said. Matthew wasn't sure if he meant vampire years or if he was including his human ones. He opened his mouth to ask, but Bryson beat him to the punch. "I was twenty-nine when I was turned. So, sixty-two. I came from a family of hunters." The general sighed. Matthew knew that he had probably killed them all after he was turned. "I'm sure you've heard that my sire is gone."

Matthew nodded. "Do you think the incubi know who you are now?"

Bryson laughed and set down a folder. "I never expected you to be so talkative. I thought you were the quiet, brooding type. Then again, incubi love to chat."

Matthew smiled. "Yes, we do." None of the other vampires in the room seemed too happy at the reminder that Matthew was an incubus, especially Stolus, who wore a deep frown. But none voiced their opinion.

"I'm not sure if they know who I am. None saw me during the battle, but it's only a matter of time before Tarrick breaks a vampire and finds out. I'm done hiding." He clasped his hands behind his back. "Clear the room."

The order wasn't directed at Matthew, but rather the others. Stolus looked as if he was going to object but changed his mind when he saw how serious Bryson's expression had become. They filed out, leaving Matthew alone with Bryson.

Matthew, still against the wall, raised an eyebrow.

"What are your plans after we get Ascelina back?" Bryson asked.

"There's something I have to do in Greece. Delphi, to be exact. I might need your help there, but I'm not sure yet."

"Delphi? Then it's something to do with the oracle?"

"Yeah." Matthew didn't want to go into details until he knew exactly how the vampire general would be helping them.

"And after? Do you plan to choose a side?"

Matthew hadn't changed his mind about the war. If anything, his resolve to stay away had strengthened. "I thought I made it clear that—"

Bryson raised his hand to stop him. "I'm sorry. I know you don't want to fight. It's just that…we're losing this war."

"That's not what other vampires are saying."

Bryson shook his head. "That's because I don't want them to lose hope. It's propaganda. The vampires think I am just as skilled as Tarrick. But he has more than nine hundred years of experience on me. And I was raised to hunt vampires, not lead them. Getting even a handful to work together takes incredible effort. If we were even a fraction as organized as the incubi, we'd have won this war a long time ago."

He sighed again. "We're outnumbered and our losses are outpacing our victories. The incubi control vast sums of money, and they have technology I can only dream of. If you join the incubi, it'd be the breaking point—we wouldn't stand a chance. Not if you fight like you did the other night."

Matthew never—ever—wanted to lose control like that again. "You can rest easy. I don't plan to fight for them either. I was their prisoner, after all. They never trusted me. I'm not going to go running back to them, especially now that I have a vampire child."

Although, he had an incubus daughter, too. Lily. He hadn't seen her since the night he was turned. She was a child then and, as far as he knew, she still had no idea he was alive. He hoped she was safe…

"If it matters," Bryson said, "my goal isn't to eradicate the incubi. I just want them to surrender. Hell, I'd even settle for signing a peace treaty or armistice. I've read old tomes that speak of a time when incubi and vampires actually existed side by side. No war. And as someone who has been on both sides, I know for a fact that vampires love feeding from incubi and incubi absolutely love fucking us, even if everyone denies it."

Matthew found himself drawn to Bryson. Besides his charisma and good instincts, the two of them had a lot in common it seemed, having seen the war from each perspective. He could see why Samantha was quite taken with him, but his attempt to sway Matthew was obvious. He didn't blame him for trying, though. To be honest, part of Matthew was tempted, but he didn't want to be the weapon that beat the incubi into submission.

Bryson wasn't done with his pitch, though. "Our queen sleeps, and even if she were awake she doesn't lead us. We need a strong leader if we have any hope of lasting until the next century. Every vampire only makes one, maybe two children every hundred years, we're losing vampires faster than we're turning them."

"Then why don't you lead? You practically already do," Matthew asked.

Bryson motioned to the door, where the other vampires would be waiting outside. "There are some who can accept me as a leader, they understand what's at stake here, but most others only respond to strength. I can hold my own in a fight but I'm not a lord. Give me three centuries and maybe it could happen, but we need someone now."

Matthew wasn't sure what his point was at first, but then it came to him. "You want me to rule?"

"Yes. You'd be perfect."

Matthew slumped against the wall some more. When the incubi had captured him, he dreamed of having them kneel before him. But when he thought of Samantha or Devak that desire faded. He just wanted to be away from all this.

Matthew shook his head. "I'd be a puppet."

"No. You'd be a partner. Publicly, you'd be our leader, but the reality is that you'd be in charge of uniting our people and raising the army while I'd still be commanding it." Bryson motioned to the map in front of him. "Look at what the two of us accomplished tonight— you came up with the idea for the rings and I put the plan in motion. Together, we dealt a major blow to the incubi."

"And when the war is over, what would happen then?"

"I'd step back. I have no aspirations to be a king. Hell, I'll be the first to kneel before you."

Matthew paused. The King of Vampires...there was a time when he couldn't get close enough to a vampire to speak with one and now they wanted him as their ruler...he'd probably have to stop wearing jeans. "I don't know. Are you sure other vampires would accept me?"

"Most don't believe you're actually an incubus and even if they did, your vampire traits are your dominant ones. I won't lie, you'd have to participate in battles—and win—or the vampires won't respond to you. And even then, it might take house calls to make them fall in line, but you're strong enough to make it happen."

"Why not have Ascelina or Gwenyth lead? They're powerful," Matthew said. They were stronger than him and seemed like they would be perfect for the role.

Bryson shook his head. "Because they've made the wrong enemies over the years. There's too much bad blood between the older families. It's the same reason why the Zhirov family from Russia isn't ruling everyone, although I think it's only a matter of time before they step into the role. Some of them are good vamps. Vikentiy comes from them, but the rest...not so much." Bryson hesitated for a moment before continuing. "I'd rather it not be them. The only family you've pissed off, you wiped out. Vampires fear you for it, which works for us. And having a blood guardian by your side would only legitimize the claim."

Matthew ran his hand across his face. The offer sounded more tempting by the moment. He began to pace the room. "You know, Tarrick wants this war to end."

"Yeah. I assumed so." Bryson seemed a little confused by the comment: of course it was obvious Tarrick would want to end the war.

"No, I mean, he'd be satisfied with a peace treaty. He's tired of losing his children."

Bryson took a moment. "Did he tell you that?"

"Yes."

"That's...surprising. I guarded him for years and the only people he ever confided in were Cullip or Dennith or Holst. For an incubus, he keeps himself separated from his people for the most part. Oh, and the redhead, Rosaline." Bryson shook his head, smiling. "Yeah... Rosaline...let me tell you, every hunter in Ashwood wanted to..."

Matthew growled. "Careful."

Bryson cleared his throat. "As long as the High King lives, this war will only end when they've killed every last one of us. For some reason I don't understand, he won't accept anything less than our total annihilation. And Tarrick would never go against him. In fact, I think you are the only incubus still living that has ever gone against Malarath."

"Then why not just kill the High King?"

Bryson laughed. "Believe me, we would if we could. He's one of the oldest creatures still around. Rumor is that he's undergone five transformations and no other incubus has gone past three. I fear the day he decides to crawl out of High Tower and rejoin the war. We might not even last a decade at that point. Look, I'm not expecting an answer anytime soon. Just consider it."

"I will." Matthew wasn't sure what he wanted now. The power had its appeal but he had promised Samantha that they would settle down. Maybe everything would become clearer when Devak's curse was lifted. Maybe Devak could tell him just what it meant to be the Blood God's son. Maybe then he'd learn why he'd been abandoned so much in his life. Maybe, maybe, maybe.

He was so sick of 'maybe'.

Bryson took a deep breath—a young vampire's habit—and asked, "How was she?"

The question caught Matthew off-guard. At first he thought the vampire was asking about Samantha, but then it dawned on him... Silva. If Bryson had been a hunter guard for Tarrick he would have served with Silva. "Good. I think. It's hard to tell, she spent the whole time being pissed at me."

Bryson smiled. "That sounds like her. That woman can hold a grudge like no one else I know. For the smallest shit, too."

"Yeah, you're telling me." A thought came to Matthew. "Were you and her...together?" Maybe it was none of his business but he was curious as hell.

Bryson nodded. "We went through the academy together. The two of us were the best of our class, and every team we joined did exceptionally well. Cullip took notice and put us on his team." Bryson leaned forward, resting both of his hands on the table. "When I was turned, I wiped out my family and didn't feel a thing. I still don't. But in the thirty-three years since, not a day has passed that I don't think about her, and she doesn't even know I'm still around. I wish I could have seen her tonight."

Wow. Matthew wasn't sure what to say to that. He felt bad for Samantha because she wasn't going to find what she wanted from Bryson, but he felt even worse for Bryson. He knew what it was like to be separated from the woman he loved. And for the same damn reason—becoming a vampire.

"I guess I should stop trying to fuck Silva then," Matthew said.

Bryson laughed. "God damn it, incubus."

A chirping alarm drew Bryson's attention, ending their conversation.

Bryson ordered the vampires to rejoin them and Matthew excused himself. Devak had probably returned by now, and he wanted to spend some time with the people he cared for...with his family.

Twenty-Four

When Matthew opened the door to his underground room, club music assaulted his ears. Inside, Samantha danced to the beat and Devak moved right along with her.

They looked completely ridiculous, but neither of them seemed to give a shit. They were just enjoying the rhythm and moving their bodies along with the pounding *unch, unch, unch.*

The music blasted from an old stereo.

Samantha held out her hand as an invitation for Matthew to join. He laughed and accepted, moving his hips and body along with the beat. He tried to show off with a terrible moonwalk followed by a robot, but Devak showed him up by doing the same, only better. Perfect actually. The dude could have been a backup dancer for Jackson.

The song changed and still they danced. The impromptu party went on for about an hour. The entire event was awkward, embarrassing even, but totally fun. A release. A stolen hour used to forget all the heavy shit floating around them.

When they finally exhausted the CD, Samantha collapsed on the bed. Matthew wished they could stream songs but connecting to the internet was too dangerous. According to Bryson, it wasn't only phone companies the incubi controlled, and they had to be extra careful since they were in incubus territory.

"We should go to concerts," Matthew said, trying to remember the last one he went to. Foo Fighters, maybe? It hadn't been since before he was turned, that was for sure. He had a feeling that both he and Samantha would love the energy at one.

Samantha lit up. "I've never been to one." She wouldn't be able to go to one without him given the sheer number of humans that would be there. Matthew couldn't even stand being in a movie theater right after he had been turned, but the bond would protect her from that. Well, protect the humans from her at any rate.

"Oh!" she said. "I want to show you something." She hopped off the bed and went over to the carved dirt and stone wall. She closed her eyes and held her hand forward. A small chunk indented inward. "I moved it!"

The excitement that rolled off her was contagious and Matthew swelled with pride.

"Well done," Devak said. "But please be careful to maintain the structural integrity of this room."

Matthew laughed. "She moved like two inches of stone. I think we're safe."

"If you say so, my prince."

Matthew ran a hand through his hair to push it back. "Are you ever going to call me by my name?"

"Unlikely. Perhaps if you just accept it, it'd be easier for us both."

Well, someone was audacious tonight.

"Maybe I should just start calling you 'my guardian'," Matthew said.

Devak's eyes grew dark and his voice dropped an octave, dripping with lust. "You may call me whatever you wish, my prince."

It was a total turn on and both sets of Matthew's fangs came out and his pants grew a little tighter. Both his vampire and incubus were loud. Hungry.

But this wasn't the time. He turned his focus to Samantha, who was trying hard to return the wall to its previous state. "I'm proud of you."

She beamed.

Unable to help himself, he scooped her up into his arms and pulled her against his chest, her feet dangling off the ground. She wasn't as thin as she used to be but she was still small compared to him.

"You're crushing me," she said, her words muffled against his shirt.

"Yeah, just give me another minute."

She stilled for a minute then began to squirm. Matthew set her down and she flopped onto the bed. "I miss Jet."

Matthew did too. That pesky gargoyle had been his mostly silent companion for months, it didn't feel right with him missing. "He'll turn up eventually. He doesn't fly very fast so it might take him a bit to get here."

He turned his attention to Devak, who was re-lacing the top of his shirt, which had come undone during the dancing. "How did it go at

Ashwood?" Matthew asked.

Devak stopped lacing and his eyes lit up as if honored by the question. "It was a fine battle. The incubi were strong warriors and the hunters clever with their attacks. But none could best me."

"Did you kill any?"

"As you commanded, none died or suffered permanent injury."

Matthew felt relieved. Killing incubi and hunters en masse during a battle was bad enough, going to their home and wiping them out felt...dishonorable. Although, if he did take up the crown—not that he was going to, but if he did—taking out the training facilities for the vampire killers would be right at the top of his list.

Devak started lacing up the leather strings again.

Matthew reached out and grabbed his wrist to stop him. "You should leave it open."

Devak's eyes roamed up and down Matthew, and he stilled his movements as if longing for the touch to linger.

"You did well tonight," Matthew said.

The guardian looked lost for words. His chest puffed with pride while he bowed his head in humble deference. It was a beautiful contradiction.

Matthew rubbed his thumb across Devak's wrist; the skin fine and soft. He wanted to plant a tender kiss there and run his lips across the guardian's arm to his neck. The thought of sinking his fangs into his delicate flesh had him taking a step closer to Devak before he even realized that his feet were moving.

Unwilling to relinquish Devak's wrist, Matthew raised his other hand and began to unlace the front of the black shirt. He now understood the appeal of the laces—it was the slow unwrapping and revealing of a body that served to heighten the anticipation of what would come next.

Devak closed his eyes and tilted his head back, his lips parted.

Matthew's cock pressed against the inside of his jeans and he gripped Devak's wrist tighter as he leaned in close, their lips less than an inch away. He breathed in deep, the scent of sweet wine and fragrant oil filled his nostrils.

"No, it's cool, I have plans for the rest of the night," Samantha said and jumped off the bed.

Matthew planted his forehead against Devak's and snickered. He had been so focused on the moment that he had completely forgotten she was even in the room. Devak seemed equally amused.

"Fuck, I'm sorry," Matthew said and released Devak.

"Why? I knew you were going to bone him so I made plans," she said. Matthew faced her. She didn't look upset, nor could he feel any irritation coming from her through the bond.

"Uh, are you going in the other room?" Matthew hated kicking her out from their shared space but he was hungry. They'd need to come up with some other arrangement in the future.

He chastised himself for thinking of a future with Devak. He wasn't ready for anything beyond a physical liaison right now, a mutual scratching of their metaphorical itches. He had already made that clear to Devak, and, hell, Devak had offered as much.

No strings.

"And listen to you two going at it through the wall? No thanks," she said.

"Oooookay. What are you going to do then?" Matthew asked. It wasn't like there was anything to do here in the bunker, and he didn't want her wandering around alone. He also wanted to keep her away from Bryson so she wouldn't have to suffer the inevitable heartbreak he'd bring.

She looked at her arm as if to check the time but she didn't have a watch on. "Three...two...one..."

Samantha opened the door to the room and grabbed hold of Vikentiy's arm as he walked past. Not knowing what the hell was going on, Vikentiy froze.

The large Russian's eyes darted up and down Samantha, then to Devak, who appeared just outside of the room, then to Matthew, who filled most of the doorframe.

"Samantha—" Matthew started but was cut off when Devak grabbed Matthew's arm and pulled him into the hallway. "What the—?"

"We can't hear you if you stand there. The ward," the guardian explained.

Oh. Right.

"Samantha," Matthew started again. "Is this something you've planned with Vikentiy?"

Vikentiy took a step away but Samantha stayed right with him. The poor vampire looked terrified. He said something Russian that sounded like a curse word and tried to slip out of her grasp, but unless he used force, she wasn't going anywhere.

Samantha smiled and looked up at Vikentiy, who had frozen in place again, unsure of what he should do. The guy was taller than Matthew and nearly as wide, and one young woman had managed to shut him down.

"There are lower levels to this place that have been shut down for years. Vikentiy is going to explore them with me," she said with her usual confidence.

A low rumble erupted from Matthew's chest. "Is he now?"

Vikentiy said something else in Russian. Devak raised his eyebrow and replied.

"You speak Russian?" Matthew asked.

"I speak all languages," Devak said and motioned to Vikentiy. "He apologized, though he's not quite sure what for, but he really doesn't want you or me to attack him."

"Yes. That," Vikentiy managed in English.

Matthew closed his eyes for a moment. Seeing another man touch Samantha made him aggressive and it pissed him off that he had no control over the reaction.

"Please, Father, let me go with him," she pleaded.

"I don't know, Sam. What's even down there? It could be dangerous."

She grabbed tighter onto Vikentiy's arm. "Nothing's going to happen to me."

"You can't really see your own future, Sam."

"But I can see his. And he's still alive next week. Which means nothing happens to me because if something did, you'd kill him."

In a strange, fucked up way, the logic was sound. He'd rip Vikentiy apart if she returned with so much as a scrape.

Matthew sized up Vikentiy, who had given up trying to understand what was happening and stood in silence. He wondered if the Russian had plans for the rest of the night. If he had, they were shot now.

"Will you keep her safe?" Matthew asked him.

Vikentiy swallowed and looked down at Samantha then back at the two men who were ready to jump him if he showed any indication of wanting to hurt her. "I will. I enjoy all limbs I have."

"Alright, you can go. But you have to be back in an hour," Matthew said.

Samantha bounced over to Matthew and kissed him on the cheek.

"Two hours. Thank you!" She returned to Vikentiy, who looked at Matthew once more for approval. Matthew nodded and the two disappeared down the hall, Samantha dragging Vikentiy along and speaking excitedly to the vampire lord.

Devak frowned.

"What?" Matthew asked.

Devak's gaze slid over Matthew's body.

"What?" Matthew asked again, this time with a playful smile.

Devak stalked towards him. He was a predator on the hunt—his fangs grew long and his eyes red.

"Is something wrong, Devak?" Matthew asked, acting innocent and backed into the room as Devak advanced and slammed the door shut behind him.

"You've been teasing me all night," he said.

"Have I been?" Matthew's body betrayed his desire. He couldn't hide his growing bulge, nor his lengthening fangs.

"You're going to let me worship you, my prince." Devak's red eyes flared as he drank in the sight of Matthew.

"Am I now?"

Matthew found himself against the wall so fast that he jerked with the suddenness of it. His t-shirt was shredded and removed; the pieces fluttered to the ground.

"I'm going to venerate every inch of you," Devak whispered as he pressed his body against Matthew.

Leaning his head back, Matthew thought of all the things he'd let Devak do to him.

Devak took advantage of the opening and pressed his lips hard against Matthew's neck. He scraped his fangs along Matthew's jugular and ran his tongue against his Adam's apple.

Needing more, Matthew wrapped his arms around the guardian and pulled him in, crashing their lips together. His tongue invaded Devak's mouth and he intentionally pierced it on the guardian's fangs. Blood flavored the deepening kiss, the tangy life essence heightening both their need.

Devak pulled away, his normally cool and collected demeanor replaced by a man possessed by heated desire. He made quick work of Matthew's jeans and boots, while Matthew made no effort to resist. Moments later, he was naked—his fat cock painful and leaking.

The guardian grabbed Matthew's hips and turned him to face the wall. Matthew looked over his shoulder, confused as shit. He had been expecting a blowjob. Now he was a little worried. Since his escape, he never let anyone penetrate him. Tarrick was the only man that had ever been with him that way.

Matthew's ass clenched at the idea. He wasn't sure he was ready for it.

He jerked when Devak leaned in and began to kiss his spine.

"My prince, I would never enter you unless you asked for it. My preference is being the receptive partner."

Matthew tried to relax but found it difficult, still unsure of what was going to happen.

Devak resumed kissing Matthew's spine and worked downwards until he was on his knees, licking the top of Matthew's ass crack.

He tugged at Matthew's hips, encouraging him to bend over. Matthew pressed against the wall for stability and pushed his ass out. Devak spread his firm cheeks apart and moved farther down the split with his mouth.

Mother. Of. God.

Every nerve ending in Matthew's body exploded like fireworks as Devak ran his warm, wet tongue over his hole.

Holy—

Why had no one ever done this to him before? It felt incredible. His dick bobbed as more blood rushed to it.

"The more you relax, the better it will feel," Devak murmured against his skin, his hot breath hitting the sensitive area.

Matthew fought the urge to clench and instead relaxed against Devak's mouth. The swipes of his tongue had Matthew's whole body writhing with pleasure.

Devak hadn't been kidding about venerating every damn inch.

"Jesus," Matthew breathed out.

He felt the guardian chuckle, still with his face buried in Matthew's ass. Devak pressed in harder, swirling his tongue around the wrinkled flesh.

"More," Matthew begged. His reservations about Devak entering him now seemed a distant memory. At this moment, Devak could do any damn thing he wanted and Matthew would accept it.

Devak slid his hands between Matthew's thighs to encourage them apart. Taking a wider stance, Matthew leaned forward, exposing more of himself. A warm hand grabbed his balls and squeezed them just hard enough that the pain brought him down a little. He trembled as Devak's hand slid upwards and wrapped around the base of his length. The hand traveled up and down his shaft with slow, tight strokes.

"God, yes. Fuck, yes," Matthew panted.

"Are you enjoying this, my prince?" The question was playful. Teasing. Probably payback for everything Matthew had done while they were hunting Silva.

Matthew's abs contracted as he breathed out a forceful 'ha'. "Don't stop."

And, god, the seductive creature behind him didn't. Wetness prodded the sensitive area as if asking for permission to enter. Matthew pushed against him, wanting more.

Devak's warm tongue pressed its way inside and at the same time, he hurried the stroking of Matthew's cock. What the guardian was doing to him was new, erotic, and unexpected. This sort of act shouldn't turn Matthew on as much as it did...and yet...

"I—" He didn't finish the thought. His body jerked and thick cum shot out of him, hitting the wall and dripping to the ground. Devak held him in place, not relinquishing his hand nor tongue until the orgasm met completion. And even then he was slow to move away.

Once released, Matthew turned and leaned his upper back against the wall, avoiding the cum. Devak looked up at him wearing a cocky half-smile. His eyes were wide, red orbs.

Matthew reached down and ran his hand through Devak's short hair, stroking his head.

"Do you have the incubus ability to recover right away?" Devak ran a single finger across Matthew's softening shaft.

"Not quite as quick, but I can be up again in a few minutes." Matthew tilted his head forward, his eyes hooded. "Why?"

His answer came when Matthew blinked and found himself lying flat on the bed, chest up. Devak was on top of him, his hands planted on Matthew's broad shoulders, his legs straddling the sides of his hips, and his crotch bulging against the laces.

"Every time you move me around like that, it reminds me of how much stronger you are than me," Matthew said, enjoying having Devak on top of him.

Devak sat back and looked Matthew up and down, then bowed his head. "I am nothing compared to you, my prince."

"That's not true." Matthew put his hand under Devak's chin and forced him to meet his gaze. Devak's eyes faded from red swirling orbs back to their usual honey coloring.

I care about you. That's what Matthew wanted to say, but couldn't. The sentiment would herald deeper emotions than he was ready to embrace right now. And what if this all ended in betrayal?

Love is the easiest way to control someone. The painful words bounced around his head and stabbed at his heart.

No strings.

"Remove your clothes, Guardian."

With a wave of his hand, the clothes disappeared into light. Devak's dark body straddled Matthew's pale one, ass pressed on hips. The tip of Matthew's thick cock glistened with pre-cum.

There was a slow slide of hands as both explored each other; muscles corded in rippling response. Matthew grabbed Devak's perfect cheeks and forced him to rise onto his cock, aligning himself to his entrance.

Matthew looked down. It was incredibly sexy seeing the tip of his dick pressing against the hole and he couldn't wait to fill it. His thick shaft glistened as he produced lube. He paused. "Do you need me to prepare you? I don't want this to be painful for you…on the roof I was careless…"

Devak's mouth hung open, his fangs gleaming. "No, I enjoy the suddenness of you filling me."

Matthew clenched onto Devak's hips and pushed him down while thrusting into him.

Devak cried out, his pain wrapped in pleasure. He shifted his weight down onto Matthew and froze in place, letting his body adjust.

The faint tension of hard muscles trembled just beneath his soft skin, shifting with beautiful restraint.

He was so tight that every little adjustment had Matthew writhing. His claws dug hard into Devak's side and he began moving the guardian up and down his dick, using Devak's hole to satisfy both their needs.

Devak gasped with each lift and cried out with each fall, his hard sex bobbing and seeping pre-cum onto Matthew's taut abs, his head thrown back in rapture.

It wasn't long before Devak gasped, "Slow down. *Please.*"

The thought of watching his guardian lose control caused Matthew to disregard the request. Devak tried to slow his movement but Matthew pounded up into him, relentless. Honey eyes widened.

"My prince—" Devak gasped. His eyelids slammed shut right before his body pulsed and his hot seed banded across Matthew's chest.

The sexual energy was delicious.

Completely spent, Devak stilled, his mouth parted. He started to move again...if his intent was to finish Matthew, he was prevented from doing so by the firm grip on his hips.

His eyes opened at a leisurely pace.

Matthew smiled up at him. "How long does it take for you to recover?"

"I...with you it would not take long."

"Good. Bite me. Take my blood." Matthew tried not to make the words sound so needy but he couldn't help himself. He wanted it badly. The pain, the blood, the connection only vampires could truly feel.

Lust crossed Devak's face and his eyes turned red once again. "Are you certain, my prince?"

"Bite me," Matthew growled, his voice dropping a few octaves.

Devak leaned forward, the still-warm cum smearing both their chests, and licked Matthew's neck. His upper fangs eased into Matthew's jugular and he pulled on the blood.

Matthew adjusted his hips to keep them seated together. With his length inside of Devak and Devak's fangs inside of him, Matthew felt as if they were one. He was selfish and wanted more.

"Feed," he whispered into Devak's ear.

Devak's body grew taut as if he was unable to handle the excitement of the request. Without removing his fangs, he placed his hands on Matthew's chest and began to feed.

The feeling of power flooded Matthew and his hips rocked deeper into Devak. He curled his body upwards and his fangs elongated as much as they could. He planted a kiss on Devak's neck then sunk his fangs into the flesh, tasting the powerful blood. His head swam.

They went slow; feeding, exchanging blood, and fucking. It was intense. Matthew had never felt so completely joined to another than he did with Devak at this fleeting moment. Both began to move their hips. Devak's shaft—now hard again—was trapped between them.

Matthew focused and the sexual energy around them became visible. The golden threads danced along the air, enveloping them. With each unhurried movement of flesh, the strands pulsed and twisted together, merging into beautiful bright threads.

It was unlike anything Matthew had ever seen before.

Together the two of them built momentum, giving the other what they needed until they both found release in one another.

****

Two hours later, Matthew and Devak had both come a few more times, cleaned the messes they had left everywhere, showered, and collapsed naked into bed together. Matthew purred as he pulled Devak to him, cradling his body and smoothing his hand across Devak's skin. He loved how warm the guardian was all the time.

Exhausted, neither spoke. Matthew wished he knew what Devak had on his mind, judging by the furrowed brow, it seemed serious. He didn't ask, however, since he didn't want to risk invoking the curse and ruining the moment with their mutual frustrations.

Besides, Matthew had his own deep thoughts to dwell on—he was wondering what Gwenyth knew about the Blood God. She did, after all, have a temple for him in her house. Should he risk telling her who he was? What he was?

His thoughts were interrupted when he heard Samantha and Vikentiy returning from their excursion. Vikentiy was in the middle of regaling her with some tale of a vampire who lost her voice to save her love, only to lose him in the end. It was a super cheesy love story but Matthew could feel that Samantha was eating it up.

Devak pushed himself up but Matthew pinned him back in place, nibbling on his ear. "Stay."

"But, we aren't dressed and the Russian will see us, my prince. The vampires will know we are…copulating."

"I don't give a shit right now. Stay."

"We should at least get dressed. For Sam's sake."

Matthew groaned like a little kid and flopped across the bed to pick up some boxers that he'd left on the floor. By the time he had them on, Devak was already back in his black pants, laced and all—Matthew didn't even see how he had done it. One of these days he'd catch him in the act.

Matthew crawled under the sheets and dragged Devak back into him.

The door to the room opened wide, Vikentiy had finished with his story, and Samantha ran in. She leaped up and body slammed onto the two men. So much for cuddling.

Matthew feigned anger with, *"Sam!"*

At the door, Vikentiy froze. Being a few centuries old he could smell the sex in the room and his eyes scanned over the bed.

He smiled wide, said something in Russian, bowed, winked, and shut the door as he left.

Samantha wiggled her way under the sheets, taking up the spot between Devak and Matthew. Matthew, having no other choice, accepted her intrusion and wrapped an arm around her.

Devak scooted himself to the edge of the small bed to give her space. That is until she grabbed his arm and pulled it over her waist, forcing him near her. Devak adjusted in position so that he was close to Samantha without pressing into her. His arm draped over her stomach.

"Mm, so warm," she said and pulled him a little closer.

"Did you have fun, Sam?" Matthew asked.

"Yeah. But not as much fun as you two I think," she said with a wide grin.

Devak laughed so softly it reminded Matthew of a song. "That's what the Russian said."

It was wonderful to hear him laugh. And to have Samantha finally accepting their strange situation.

"Tell me about your adventure," Matthew prompted.

Samantha dove into a minute by minute recounting of her night. Vikentiy, as it turns out, was a perfect adventuring companion for her. He told her stories, showed off his wings, convinced her the place was haunted (which was why she was going to sleep in the middle), and took her through some off-limits areas that were, in the end, not all that exciting because they were just barren bunker rooms, but she still had fun.

While she was talking, Matthew caught Devak watching him. Matthew pushed away the desire to reach over and touch him.

He had to stop trying to be closer to Devak.

No strings.

Twenty-Five

Matthew brushed the snow off his head and the shoulders of a heavy coat he was wearing. He didn't need the coat, the cold didn't bother the dead, but he wore it in case they ran into any humans. He didn't want to stand out.

It was day but the sun was hidden behind a grey, overcast sky. Snow had been falling for the last few hours and it was only getting worse. Both he and Devak were on the roof of a quaint little house that neighbored a white wooden church with red doors. It was out in the middle of a quiet countryside.

Below them he could hear the owner of the house, one of the priests, making tea.

The other priest was inside the church pacing nervously about. He was waiting. Matthew could smell adrenaline course through the human.

"Maybe Sam got the time wrong?" Devak whispered.

Before Matthew could respond, a black sedan turned down the road and pulled up in front of the church. Matthew's insides jumped around as he focused his senses on the car. Silva was driving, and in the back seat was Tarrick. Though from this angle, Matthew couldn't actually see him yet.

"At least let me check the perimeter," he heard Silva say.

"Must we do this every time I go out?" Tarrick said, his voice short, tired of this discussion.

"Only when you won't let me protect you."

Tarrick sighed. "It's daytime, the Viper is in Europe, and if there were shifters around I'd smell them. It might astound you to learn that I survived centuries without hunters."

"I just wish you'd let me do my job, General," Silva huffed.

"You are, Commander. Return in an hour," he said and slipped out of the car. Matthew's breath hitched when he saw him. Not a single strand of Tarrick's dusty blond hair was out of place and his eyes were the most brilliant blue. He wore a thick, knee-length wool coat that hid most of his tailored suit.

Tarrick walked up the path and entered the church. Matthew, who was unable to peel his eyes away, flinched when Devak's firm hand rested on his shoulder, reminding him why they were here. Silva had already driven away and he hadn't even noticed her leave.

Matthew nodded once to Devak and the two of them jumped from the roof and crossed to the church. They paused at the red doors and listened.

"I thought you weren't coming," an unfamiliar voice said from inside. Matthew had caught a glimpse of the young priest earlier as he passed by a window. His body had been tense and his face was full of agony like that of a tortured man fighting a battle raging inside of him. Tarrick had that effect on people.

"Of course I came," Tarrick said. "I've thought of nothing but you for weeks." It was a lie. Tarrick was hunting right now with the goal to feed.

"I can't do this, you should leave," the priest said, his voice faltering.

"Please don't turn me away. I know you want this as bad as I do," Tarrick said. Matthew imagined that he was running his hand down the priest's face right now.

"This is…wrong. Can we at least leave? I can't do this here, not in front of Him." The priest was begging, but he had already lost this fight.

"Come here. Lean over," Tarrick said, his voice seductive.

"No, not there. I…" the priest's breath went ragged. "Please… please forgive me, Lord."

There was an unzipping of pants.

Matthew waited. He was giving Tarrick a chance to feed since he wouldn't be getting anything else for the next couple of days.

Inside, the panting and moaning grew louder.

Matthew's cock grew hard and he placed his hand on the small of Devak's back. Devak's muscles rippled under his touch but otherwise he stayed still, waiting for a command.

Matthew needed to get a hold of himself but hearing Tarrick fuck someone else was maddening. He wanted to be the one under him. He pushed the thought away, ashamed that he still desired Tarrick. What the hell was wrong with him?

Unable to listen any longer, he retrieved a syringe filled with white liquid from his pocket then tapped Devak once to let him know it was time. The two of them moved as one, shattering the doors open as they rushed into the church.

In a fraction of a second Matthew took in what was before him: The two men—both still mostly dressed—were fucking on top of the altar. The priest was belly down, lost in the throes of passion, pinned under Tarrick. A statue of Jesus, attached to a large crucifix, loomed above them.

Matthew was thankful vampires weren't actually burned by religious symbols and churches could be entered, although he stayed away from them for the most part. Being here felt disrespectful.

Devak made it to Tarrick first. He ripped the incubus off the priest and threw Tarrick at Matthew. Matthew caught him midair and jabbed the syringe into his neck.

Tarrick's claws came out and he struggled against Matthew. The priest cowered at the sight of the two vampires.

"Stop," Matthew said as he wrapped his claws around Tarrick's throat. "You aren't going to win this one and I don't want to hurt you more than I have to."

Tarrick elbowed him in his side and Matthew tossed him on the ground between him and Devak. The incubus leaped to his feet. Tarrick's eyes darted between Devak, Matthew, and the windows outside.

"I'm not chained up this time, Tarrick. You might be able to take me if you have a weapon but there's no way you'd be able to take on both me and a blood guardian at once."

"It's daytime…"

Matthew held up his pinky, showing off the daylight ring.

"A fourth? Impossible."

Seeing Tarrick caught off-guard was a rare event for Matthew. He savored it. "You should have let Silva check the perimeter."

Tarrick grabbed his neck where Matthew had injected him and stumbled backwards into a pew.

"What did you inject me with?" he asked, his words coming out sluggish as he struggled against the drug.

"A super dose of Propofol and some other stuff that should knock out an incubus. I hope it does because I really don't want to have to beat you unconscious."

Tarrick's horns came out and his body grew a few inches, but became restricted by his clothes. Matthew always wondered why warrior incubi didn't wear clothes that allowed them to shift into their full form. He suspected it was because incubi were vain motherfuckers who needed to wear designer…

"Demons," the priest cried when he saw Tarrick's horns.

Devak grabbed the man. "Calm yourself," he said, compelling the panicked priest. "You will forget everything you just saw. Your lover did not show up today. You are heartbroken but you will heal. Leave now."

The priest nodded and left the church.

Tarrick growled and lunged at Matthew. But he tripped over his own feet as the drug kicked in. Matthew caught him, pulling him in close.

Tarrick pressed his claws into Matthew's chest, cutting the skin and drawing blood, as a desperate attempt to break away. Matthew stood unflinching. Tarrick looked up at him, his irises purple, and, in a drugged haze, said, "My beautiful vampire warrior…" before his body went limp. Tarrick was out.

Matthew sighed. Why did he have to say that?

He picked up Tarrick and carried him out to the van they had come in. Matthew got in the back with Tarrick while Devak drove. Before they left, Matthew crushed Tarrick's phone and left it on the asphalt.

Once they were underway, Matthew tucked Tarrick's cock back into his pants and carefully closed the zipper. Then he peeled off Tarrick's coat and shirt, and ran his fingers across incubus' chest. His skin felt so warm, so inviting.

"I can do that if you'd rather drive," Devak offered. Matthew thought he detected just the smallest hint of jealousy in Devak's voice.

"No. I've got this. Just drive fast."

Matthew forced himself to stop touching Tarrick and opened a large box that was on the floor next to him. He pulled out a metal harness and slipped it onto Tarrick; it went over his shoulders and across his chest, wrapping around to the back, where it snapped shut and locked.

He then took out two shackle cuffs, which had loops to connect chains, and put them on Tarrick's wrists.

The last thing he removed from the box was a metal collar. Matthew's hands began to shake as he opened it and held it to Tarrick's neck.

He couldn't do it.

Not to Tarrick.

Not to anyone.

The harness and cuffs would have to be good enough. He put the collar back into the box.

Twenty minutes later Tarrick began to stir. Matthew injected him with more of the drug to keep him under.

When they arrived back at the bunker, Matthew carried him down to the prison. Every shifter they passed growled when they saw Tarrick. Matthew was thankful the other vampires were sleeping right now.

Outside the prison, Matthew dismissed the shifter guards and turned off the cameras. He asked Devak to keep watch outside the door.

Matthew stood in front of Tarrick's cell and waited. His eyes traced the masculine arcs of his body, watching his bare chest rhythmically rise and fall under the metal harness. His gaze traveled downwards across his unblemished skin to his sensual pelvis and the suit pants that hugged his waist. Matthew wanted to slip his hand down in there...

It wasn't long before Tarrick began to stir. He struggled to sit up as he fought against the drug. Scooting to the edge of the bed, his head lolled forward. Several moments passed before he brought his hands up to his chest, feeling the harness on him. He was moving as if he was stuck in a vat of molasses.

"If you try to go into your incubus form, you'll be crushed by it. You'll die. It won't let you bring out your wings, either."

"Yes, Matthew. I am aware," Tarrick said with some effort. He closed his eyes and continued to sit on the edge of the bed for a while. Incubi recovered faster than humans but they couldn't force poison out the same way vampires could.

Matthew regretted not putting a shirt back on Tarrick, watching his muscles shift about was tantalizing.

Finally, Tarrick stood. The grogginess had lifted and his strength was returning. He ran his hands through his hair, fixing it as he looked around the room, studying every feature. The barred cell had a shower, toilet, and bed. Nothing else. There were half a dozen other cells in this room, all empty.

"This is quite the role reversal," Tarrick said once he had memorized all of his surroundings. He stood up taller and clasped his hands behind his back. He looked like a general, even half-naked and behind bars.

"Not really," Matthew said. "I'm not going to make you beg for your food. And as long as you don't try to escape, you won't be hurt."

Tarrick exhaled a sharp, unbelieving laugh. "The vampires finally have me and you expect me to believe that I won't be tortured?"

"The vampires don't have you. I have you. You won't be tortured."

"You're going to compel information from me then?"

"No."

Tarrick raised an eyebrow. "The secrets I hold could win the vampires the war."

Matthew smiled. "Are you trying to talk me into doing it?"

Tarrick chuckled. Sexy. Soft. "No."

It wouldn't be easy to compel Tarrick beyond a simple command, his will was like iron. "I don't need to molest your mind to get what I need from you."

Tarrick's face looked stern and his eyes grew hard. Matthew knew that meant he was analyzing the situation; trying to figure out what was going on.

"You told Commander Silva you owed someone a favor." Then the incubus general put it together. "Prisoner exchange. You are trading me for Ascelina because she rescued you." It amazed him how quick Tarrick was able to figure shit out. It would take Matthew ten times as long to make the connection, assuming he made it at all.

"We're going to ask for more than just Ascelina."

"It pleases me to learn that I am worth more than one vampire lord." He studied Matthew. It was the first time in a while the two had seen each other when they weren't fighting. "How—" he started to ask something then fell silent.

Matthew waited for him to ask the question but it never came. If Tarrick didn't want to talk, he wouldn't. Guess they were done here.

Matthew forced himself to leave.

When he was nearly at the door, Tarrick spoke again. "How did you do it, Matthew?"

Matthew turned back. "Do what?"

"Decimate my army." Tarrick's jaw clenched. It must have been hard for him to admit he didn't know something.

"You've always known I was strong."

Tarrick shook his head. "Not like that. My warriors staked you and it did nothing. Drained your blood pouches and you kept going, filled you with enough silver to kill the damn Queen and you didn't stop. Devil, Matthew, how?"

The Blood God's child. He wanted to talk to Tarrick about it. Tell him how frightened he was and ask him his opinion on the matter. He was desperate to talk to someone about this. The curse prevented Devak from really talking to him, and Samantha became lost in her own mind half the time.

But no matter how strongly he desired it, he knew he couldn't tell Tarrick. He would find a way to use it against him. So instead he said nothing.

Frustration flashed across Tarrick's face. Matthew braced himself for the verbal lashing that was about to come.

"You were an out of control *monster.*" Tarrick's voice was rough and deliberate.

Even though he was expecting it, pain rippled through Matthew. His eyes began to burn red but he refused to let his fangs or claws out. Matthew tried to conceal his emotions but wasn't doing a good job of it. He averted his eyes and took a step backwards.

It was time to leave. Being here was a mistake.

"I'm sorry," Tarrick said, his voice changed to a softer cadence.

Matthew glared at him. "No, you're not. Every word you say is calculated. You wanted this reaction from me and you got it."

"You give me far more credit than I'm due."

Matthew couldn't be here anymore. He left. Or tried to. When his hand was on the door to exit, Tarrick spoke. "Would you like to know how Lily is?"

Matthew stopped. He reached his hand up to his neck and touched it. It felt as if he still had a collar on and Tarrick had just yanked it hard.

Of course he'd use his daughter against him. "You don't have any compassion in you do you?" Matthew asked, his back still to Tarrick.

"Not for vampires."

Matthew winced and dropped his head forward, thankful Tarrick couldn't see his face. Tarrick had always been the one to insist that he was an incubus. He was the one who had made Matthew embrace it.

"If you want to know how she is, all you have to do is ask," Tarrick said.

The imaginary collar on Matthew's neck got tighter and he balled his fists. Tarrick was the one standing in the fucking cage and yet Matthew felt as if it was him. His broad chest expanded as he took a single deep breath and turned once again to face Tarrick. "How is she?"

Tarrick, mercifully, didn't gloat that he had won this exchange. "She's doing well. Under Rosaline's guidance, she has excelled socially. Everyone who meets her is enamored by her. Her incubi powers are extremely advanced for her age. It leads to many questions about her lineage. Right now, only a handful of us knows she's your daughter. But, Matthew, I can't protect her forever."

Matthew's claws came forward and he growled. "Are you threatening her?" He'd rip the cell door off and beat him if he was.

"No," Tarrick said, "but others among us have no issues with using her to capture you. I've been able to hold them off but it gets harder every time you stand against us."

Matthew frowned. If he accepted Bryson's offer to rule them, he'd have to rescue Lily first. And even then, having a succubus among a bunch of vampires would be a disaster.

Damn it, he couldn't lead the vampires. It was too great of a risk to both his daughters. Lily was in their hands and Samantha was so fragile, all it would take was one vampire hunter to spot her, one moment where Matthew was distracted, and she'd be gone. He needed to protect his family. For the thousandth time since meeting Tarrick, he wished there was no war.

He forced his claws away and his eyes returned to luminous silver. He rubbed his forehead.

"What is it?" Tarrick asked, concerned, as if they were close friends.

"They offered me the crown."

Tarrick stood silent for a moment. "Don't take it."

"No?"

"You think I chase you now? Wait until you become a vampire king. Every resource would be used to track you down. I even think the High King would come after you personally."

Matthew had already made his decision but he liked seeing Tarrick squirm a bit. "Well, I'd have an army he'd have to cut through."

Tarrick shook his head. "Vampires don't have much of an army. Not anymore."

"They will if I lead them."

Tarrick rubbed his fingers over his mouth and chin. "Devil, I think the vampires would fear you enough that you could bring them together." Matthew could tell that he was already thinking of strategies to try to counter a new vampire army. "You are a good choice. But you are still new to this and I will kill you. Just as I have killed every vampire leader that has tried to unite—"

Matthew laughed and held up his hand. "You can relax. I'm going to turn it down."

Tarrick paced back and forth behind the iron bars of his cell, glancing at Matthew while he processed. Finally, he said, "For now."

For now? No, Matthew had made his choice. "I really do just want to be left alone, like I keep trying to tell you."

"No. You desire more. I've seen it in you. I've watched you struggle against your nature many times. You can't help it. You might say 'no' for now, but one day you'll embrace what you are and take what they are offering you. It might take you a few decades but, eventually, you'll realize that I'm right about this."

Matthew wasn't sure what to say. Tarrick was wrong. He had to be. But...the monster stirred inside of him. He tried to ignore it, control it, but it was getting harder for him. Still, he had to try. For the people he cared for.

"Get comfortable, you'll be here for a few nights," Matthew said and left the prison before Tarrick could say anything else.

Devak was waiting in the hall, his face blank and unreadable. Matthew breathed out a long sigh. Emotionally he felt as if he had just gone twelve rounds and lost. Devak's features softened as he grew concerned and he rested his hands on Matthew's chest.

Matthew pulled his lover into him, thankful that Devak accepted the embrace without resistance.

"He was using a hold on you," Devak said against Matthew's shirt.

"I know."

"Why didn't you break it?"

He said nothing, the answer shamed him. Devak wrapped his arms around Matthew and gently traced his fingers along his spine. The tender caress soothed him. They stayed that way for a while until they heard the shifter guards returning. "I'd like you to stay guard. I don't trust anyone here," Matthew said before the shifter guards came too close.

Devak gave a slight bow to the order and Matthew went back to their room. Even with the daylight ring, he still needed rest, and it was pushing into late afternoon at this point.

He found it too hard to sleep, his mind swimming with thoughts of Devak and Tarrick. Eventually, he removed the ring and slipped into darkness.

Twenty-Six

Matthew was up as soon as night fell. He felt much better. A liter of blood was delivered to his door and he gulped it down. Bottled blood tasted like shit but he didn't have time to go hunting.

Samantha still fed from him, since, as she put it, he tasted 'way better'.

After getting ready, Matthew left Samantha behind in the room and went to check on Devak, who reported that there had been no incidences during the day. Matthew nodded to a camera in the hall then motioned for Devak to follow him in.

Tarrick stood, moving the best he could with the uncomfortable harness on. He came to the front of the cage and clasped his hands behind his back.

"I see you brought your guardian as back up," he said, nodding to Devak. One side of his lip curled up into a seductive half-smile.

Not in the mood to spar with Tarrick right now, Matthew didn't say anything.

"Why is a guardian following you anyways?"

"I assume Dennith has the authority to negotiate for the exchange," Matthew said, leaving Tarrick's question unanswered.

"Ah, yes," Tarrick said in a serious tone, then began to chuckle. Matthew couldn't help but watch the tightening and flexing of his abdomen. He really should have put a shirt on Tarrick.

He broke away from his stare and glanced over at Devak, who had been watching Matthew. The edges of Devak's lips curled down before he looked away.

"Something funny?" Matthew asked Tarrick.

"Yes. Since the moment I became High General, not a single day has passed where my location wasn't accounted for by someone. This is the first break I've had in centuries."

Matthew tried to imagine Tarrick going on a vacation and every scenario he came up with was hilarious to him. Tarrick at the beach, trying to clean sand off everything. Tarrick at the Tower of Pisa, having a hunter take a picture of him holding up the leaning building. Tarrick at Disneyland, barking orders to the ride attendants, trying to get the front seat of the coaster.

Matthew laughed. "Enjoy it while you can. I'm sure Silva will be giving you a piece of her mind when you get back for not letting her do her job. Do you think she'll get a box to stand on so that she's eye to eye with you? Or will you shrink down to her size?"

"She is quite little, even compared to me," Devak said, nodding.

"Yes, I imagine I'll be hearing it from her for the next few months," Tarrick said.

"Months? Years more like," a new voice added.

Standing at the door was Bryson, dressed in a black outfit that could have been easily mistaken for a hunter's uniform. It had straps and laces that all seemed somewhat unnecessary but made him look imposing.

What was with everyone and laces lately? Was something wrong with just a plain t-shirt?

The room fell silent while Tarrick studied Bryson. Ever the master of his emotions, he showed no shock at seeing him. "William," he said, calling him by what Matthew could only assume was his first name. More silence passed between them. "It seems the reports of you dying in Russia weren't entirely inaccurate. Silva will be upset to learn you were turned."

Bryson straightened the sleeve of his shirt and frowned. "After thirty-three years? I'm sure she's gotten over it by now."

Tarrick didn't respond.

Bryson's face became a mask, trying to expose none of the feelings he had admitted to having for Silva. But it was near impossible to hide such strong feelings from an incubus as old as Tarrick and the slightest gleam of victory flickered in Tarrick's eyes.

Bryson pulled out a piece of paper and handed it to Matthew. "Here's the list of the people I want back. Actually, I'd like all my people back, but these are the ones I think they'd be willing to exchange for him."

Tarrick's eyes watched Bryson while he put together the puzzle. "You're the general."

It wasn't really a question but Bryson answered it anyway. "Yes."

"I had speculated that the vampire general was an ex-hunter. I didn't expect it to be one of my former bodyguards. And not someone so young. You've had me guessing for years. Well done."

"Thank you. It hasn't been easy hiding from you."

"Alright, Tarrick," Matthew said, interrupting their verbal jerk-off. "I'm putting the call on speaker because I'm sure they'll want proof that you're alive. Don't speak until I tell you to or I'll have Devak shut you up."

Devak looked more than willing to do it too. He wasn't in his armor nor did he have his maul, but he did have a sword sheathed on his hip.

Tarrick nodded once.

Matthew dialed a number. It rang once and a dispatcher answered. "Sentinel Consolidated, how may I direct your call?" Ah, nice and generic for those misdials.

"This is Matthew. Please put me through to Dennith." There was a pause on the other end of the line. "Did you need me to repeat that?"

"One moment, please," the dispatcher said and the call was put on hold.

"I could have given you her direct number," Tarrick said.

"Yeah, but it's way more dramatic to have a dispatcher shout that I'm on the line. And I thought I told you to stay quiet."

"The only way to shut an incubus up is to gag him," Bryson said.

Devak smiled at the comment, seemingly agreeing.

"We're not that bad," Matthew said. But really, sometimes they were.

The phone clicked. "Matthew," Dennith's harsh voice echoed in the room.

"Hello, Lady Dennith."

"I am not in the mood for games right now. What do you want?"

"Actually, I have something you want."

"And that is…?"

"Tarrick."

There was silence for a moment, then she said, "Prove it."

Matthew motioned to Tarrick.

Tarrick took a deep breath. "Matthew—and the vampires—have indeed captured me."

"Are you harmed?"

Tarrick raised an eyebrow at Matthew, who nodded, indicating he was free to answer the question. "No."

"And he won't be so long as you agree to what I want," Matthew said.

"Which is…?" Dennith asked.

"A prisoner exchange." Matthew read off the list of vampires Bryson had given him: Ascelina and five other lords.

"Fine," she said. "Release the High General and then we'll release the lords."

Matthew chuckled. "No, it's not going to happen that way."

"There's no other way to do it, Matthew. I don't trust you to release him once you get what you want."

Matthew didn't blame her but he wished she could trust him. "I have another solution that I think we can both agree upon. Do you know Brujo Moya?"

"Yes."

This part of the plan was actually Devak's idea. He suggested they find an entity both sides could trust. Bryson suggested the brujo, a witch that used spirit and ancestral magic instead of magic drawn from nature. "And can you agree that he and his coven are neutral in this war?"

"Yes."

"Good. The night after next, five of his people will arrive at Ashwood Estate, and five will arrive here. They'll be taking us to a location that he's picked. Neither of us will know it ahead of time. You can bring a team of hunters for every vampire you have to transport, along with ten total incubi warriors. We'll be bringing ten, well, nine vampires and one guardian."

"Even with the extra hunters, this exchange is weighted in your favor."

"It's forty-six to ten."

"And you alone killed hundreds of my people last week."

"I don't want to fight, Dennith, I just want Ascelina back. Oh, and don't try to bring that fucking necromancer, the witches won't teleport you to the location if you do."

She didn't say anything.

"You have some time to think on it, but if you don't show up to the exchange, I hand Tarrick over to the vampires." Matthew ended the call and looked at Tarrick, who was still standing near the iron bars with his hands clasped behind him.

"Think she'll show?" Matthew asked.

Tarrick gave a nod. "I do."

With nothing else to discuss—or rather nothing else Matthew wanted to talk about with Tarrick—he left. Devak returned to guarding while Bryson returned to whatever the vampire general was up to, something in the command room.

Matthew went to check on Samantha.

"How'd it go?" she asked before he was even in the door.

On the bed, lying practically in Samantha's lap, was Jet, in Rottweiler form, wagging his tail. "Good to see you, boy." Matthew sat down by the two of them and gave Jet an affectionate pat. "It went just like we thought it would. How are you doing? I'm sorry you have to stay in here," Matthew said. He couldn't risk Tarrick finding out about her.

"I'm sick of dirt walls and I'm running out of books, but I'll live." She paused to think. "Uh, I'll undead...?"

Matthew laughed and pressed a kiss on the top of her head. "This should be over soon. I'm hoping that by the end of next week the curse will be broken and our lives will go back to normal."

"I don't think our lives were ever normal but I know what you mean. I'm excited for it. Can Vikentiy stop by without you getting all growly?"

"I don't know if I can help the growling, but he's welcome to stop by if he wants. You into him?"

"Nah, he's just a friend. He's fun to talk to. Oh! Are you ever going to tell me what happened at the ball?"

"Yeah," Matthew shifted on the bed and pushed his hair back. "I met my sire."

Samantha shot up so fast that the book she had been holding dropped off the bed onto the floor. "No way. Who?"

Matthew suspected it was rare for her to be so in the dark about something. He didn't need the bond to sense her excitement. He cleared his throat. "The Blood God."

Sam's shoulders slouched over. "Oh. Yeah, okay, that makes sense." She reached down backwards, nearly slipping from the bed, to grab her book then went back to reading.

"Wait. That's it? My sire is a god and that's all I get?" Matthew asked, half disbelieving, half finding her reaction hilarious.

"Um. What should I say?"

"I don't know, maybe, 'holy shit your sire is a fucking god'?"

She shrugged. And when Matthew accepted that she wasn't going to give him anything else, she looked over her book and giggled at him.

"Ah, I see. You're messing with me. Very funny, Sam." He tried to look stern but couldn't help but crack a smile; her laugh was infectious.

"So what was he like?" she asked once she was done laughing.

"Terrifying. I hope you never meet him."

"I don't know if I will, I never see gods in my visions unless they want me to. Oh, and, you should bring me to the exchange."

"No." It was non-negotiable. Having her there was far too much of a liability, for himself and for her, and now that Jet was back, he could watch her while he was away. Matthew had the feeling Jet liked Samantha more than him anyways.

"Okay. But you're going to wish I was there."

"Care to tell me why?"

"I don't know yet. I just know at some point you'll wish I was there."

Well, that was all he was going to get on the matter. He gave her another kiss and apologized again for keeping her in the room. She gave him a dismissive wave and turned back to her book. Matthew busied himself by joining Bryson in the command center.

He spent the night watching Bryson work, getting a feel for what type of general he was. His style was different than Tarrick's, it was rougher, like a field medic trying to patch wounds on the fly while Tarrick was like a surgeon, planned and precise. Matthew wondered what Bryson could do if he had Tarrick's resources.

A few of the monitors displayed a stream of Tarrick in his prison cell. He was sitting on the bed, not moving, his face betraying no emotions. Matthew found his eyes drifting to the monitor more than a few times.

Later in the night, Gwenyth entered, back from Europe where she had led the attacks against the leystones. Matthew had learned that she normally didn't get involved with the war directly but the destruction of her estate and capture of her daughter had changed that.

"The plan worked well," Gwenyth said with a nod. Her gaze dropped to the daylight ring on his pinky.

Matthew touched the ring with his other hand. "Don't worry, once the exchange is done, it's yours."

She looked relieved. "I was concerned you might have changed your mind."

"Nope."

Two hours before dawn, he ducked out of the room to spend a little more time with Samantha, who was drooped over Jet, using him like a pillow under her stomach.

"You should dress for rain," she said without looking up from her book.

"I'm not going out."

"Most definitely rain. I'll pack you an umbrella." And with that, she was done speaking to him for the rest of the night.

Matthew rolled his eyes while he stripped down to his boxers and lay next to her, enjoying the feeling of comfort the bond brought to him. When the sun rose, Matthew had to peel Samantha off Jet and put her in bed correctly. Jet licked his arm.

"If you were an actual dog she would have smooshed you," Matthew said as he took his place next to her on the queen bed. With Jet here, the only way Devak would fit was if he slept practically on top of Matthew. He smiled at the idea.

It was getting crowded in his bed these days and he loved it. "Thank you for watching over her," he said to Jet then drifted off to sleep… only to wake a few moments later.

He heard a scream and his right arm began to throb as if someone had run a hot poker down the side of it. At first he thought he was having another nightmare since he was wearing the ring, but the second scream told him it was no nightmare.

He shot up and checked Samantha. She was asleep, uninjured.

The smell of blood reached his nostrils.

Night and earth.

Tarrick's blood.

Twenty-Seven

Matthew bolted from the room, not even stopping to throw on clothes.

In the hallway were two shifters—in their human form—about to enter his room.

They carried stakes, sent to neutralize Matthew while he was sleeping.

They weren't prepared for how fast Matthew was as he snapped the arm of one and kneed the other in the chest, breaking his ribs and sending him flying into the dirt wall. Behind him, Jet leaped out of the room, still in his dog form, and latched his mouth onto the neck of the one with the broken ribs.

Matthew clawed the other one across his belly, and the shifter's insides spilled out. He didn't wait around to see if the shifter would survive, Jet would kill it if it managed to heal.

A fraction of a moment later, Matthew was at the door to the jail. It was sealed shut. The hallway cameras were off, Devak was missing, and he could smell shifter blood along with Tarrick's on the other side.

Without stopping, he reached down inside himself and pulled up strands of red energy coiled within him, pushing it into his muscles. The hinges on the reinforced metal door ripped away like paper under his power.

Inside, blood smeared the floor.

Dragged from his cage, Tarrick was on the ground bleeding from gaping wounds and bite marks that littered his skin. He was still conscious but he wasn't moving except to take pained, gasping breaths.

A pack of shifters—seven still alive and in their massive wolf forms—loomed above him, ready to go in for the kill. A shifter lay dead on the ground, reverted back to her human form. Incubus claw marks raked her body. Tarrick had tried to fight off the rest the best he could, but he was no match for them while he was unarmed and prevented from shifting form.

Seeing Tarrick beaten and broken on the ground sent Matthew into a rage. He was unrelenting in his attacks, showing them no mercy, ripping the shifters apart with his long claws.

They worked as a pack, flanking him, but each wolf that lunged close ended up dead. Some managed to bite him but he ignored the pain and kept going until he stood victorious over their bodies.

When the exchange was over, Matthew pushed power into healing his wounds and wiped the blood off his chin. The throbbing feeling he had felt in his right arm began to die down. He had no idea what caused it to hurt like that, maybe his body was finally punishing him for the constant abuse he put it through.

He stood over Tarrick, who looked up at him.

Tarrick tried to speak but only a gurgled, choking sound escaped.

Unable to put his vampire form away—the blood all over the place was too alluring—Matthew had to be extremely careful not to cut Tarrick with his claws as he scooped him up and carried him over to the bed inside of the open cell.

Another gurgling sound came from Tarrick's mouth. Matthew lay him down and gently ran his knuckles down Tarrick's face. "Shhh," he said, then leaned in and kissed him.

He pulled up golden energy from his soavik and used the kiss to send it into Tarrick. At first, Tarrick didn't respond but Matthew didn't let up.

Then, Tarrick began to heal.

Matthew felt Tarrick's hold wrap around him. It was like a warm hug, influencing his emotions. Incubi placed holds on prey instinctually when this badly wounded, so Matthew didn't fight against it. Their kiss deepened—Tarrick feeding with desperate greed—and Matthew didn't resist, letting him take whatever he needed.

Tarrick's missing skin and muscles reformed, knitting whole. He slipped his arms around Matthew, their skin pressed together, the cold harness digging into both of them.

Matthew's hands began to wander up the side of Tarrick's body, avoiding the healing wounds. The skin felt warm and welcoming under his touch. Tarrick stopped feeding but their lips stayed locked together, their kiss was electric with desire, firing every nerve Matthew had.

His soavik, nearly empty now thanks to the feeding, cramped with pain, but it was nothing compared to the emotional conflict squeezing his insides. He wished he could simply will his feelings away; longing for the incubus had brought him nothing but heartache.

He pulled back. When he looked down, his jaw dropped: scars littered Tarrick's body. And not just the ones from today...these scars were old.

He had never seen them before; Tarrick's skin had always been flawless and smooth. The man he was looking at now had the skin of a warrior.

Tarrick idly opened his eyes; they were glowing violet as they often did when he was horny, angry, or ready to fight. Right now he looked like he was experiencing all three emotions. He watched as Matthew studied him.

Matthew, finally able to force his claws away, ran his fingers over Tarrick's skin, tracing the scars.

Tarrick frowned and the scars began to fade away.

"Don't," Matthew said. "I want to see them."

Tarrick looked away, as if embarrassed. The scars returned. Matthew dipped down and began to explore them with his mouth and tongue. He started at a deep cut on Tarrick's shoulder and worked his way downwards, across his abs, then near his hips.

Tarrick's back lifted from the bed and he moaned. Then he swallowed hard and his face fell serious. "Enjoying yourself?"

Matthew stopped. What was he doing? He ripped himself away. "Remove your hold from me."

Tarrick removed it, the feeling of warm buttery tendrils melted away. Matthew checked to make sure Tarrick didn't have a second hold on him, tricking him. He didn't seem to. But even with the hold gone, Matthew wanted to return to licking Tarrick's body. And that was the problem that was eating away at his heart every fucking moment.

Tarrick looked extremely un-Tarrick-like right now. His pants were ripped, blood was smeared across his skin, he had a day's worth of stubble on his face, and his hair was a mess.

Matthew focused on the scars again. How had he never seen these before? He had been around Tarrick near death once before and he hadn't noticed them then. Then again, his attention was elsewhere at the time.

The scars made Tarrick look…flawed, but no less alluring. They were a visual reminder that Tarrick was a fighter who sacrificed for his people.

It was damned sexy.

Matthew reached out and touched a deep groove that started at Tarrick's chin and trailed over his neck, going all the way down the arm before ending at the left wrist.

He knew that most incubi could glamor, make minor changes to their body to make themselves more appealing in order to attract prey, but he hadn't known Tarrick was covering up so much.

"I didn't know incubi could scar. I assumed you were like vampires and it healed back eventually."

"Vampires can scar under the right circumstances," Tarrick said, sounding severe. Matthew wondered how bad the wound would have to be to scar a vampire. He'd had some terrible injuries but all of the marks on his skin had faded eventually.

"Why do you hide them?"

Tarrick brushed Matthew's hand away. "They are blemishes."

"They're beautiful," Matthew said, admiring them.

The scars faded and Tarrick sat up. "Yes. Of course you'd think so, vampire."

Vampire. Such hatred laced the word. Matthew took a step away from him. "Stop. I just saved your life, and not for the first time. You don't need to be so—" Matthew didn't finish the thought. Being here was borderline torturous. And dangerous. "Never mind."

Matthew's insides were in knots and his chest felt tight as he fought to keep his emotions under control. He raised his hand to his chest and scratched at the area above his heart.

Tarrick got to his feet and looked around at the rest of the prison. His cell door was still open, Matthew hadn't bothered to close it; blood, fur, and flesh smeared across the floor.

"What were you going to say?" Tarrick asked.

"Nothing. It's nothing."

Tarrick took a step closer to him. Matthew backed away. Right now, more than anything, he wanted to be close to Tarrick, but he fought it.

The general didn't stop coming at him, and Matthew retreated backwards. But Tarrick kept coming forward with another step. And another. And another. Until Matthew's back hit the steel bars of the cell.

Tarrick stood inches away. Matthew could feel the heat coming from the incubus' body and he became painfully aware that neither of them wore much: boxers and shredded pants.

"What were you going to say?" Tarrick repeated, his voice commanding.

This was ridiculous. Matthew was stronger, faster, larger...and yet right now he was helpless.

"Stop," he said. The word was meant to come out as forceful, but it escaped his lips as a plea.

Tarrick rested his hands on Matthew's chest and they began a slow slide downwards towards his boxers. Matthew's length jumped in response to the touch.

"Tell me," Tarrick ordered.

"*Heartless*. You don't need to be so heartless."

Tarrick's hands moved lower down Matthew's skin and disappeared into his boxers. "And why shouldn't I be? You are murdering my people." Before Matthew could answer, Tarrick gripped the base of his cock. Matthew let out a gasp and gripped the metal bars so tight that his knuckles turned white.

"I didn't want that," he managed to say.

The incubus closed the gap between them and pressed wet lips against Matthew's collarbone. "What do you want, Matthew?"

"I want to be left alone," Matthew panted as Tarrick began to glide his silky hand up and down Matthew's dick.

"No, you don't. Tell me what you want."

Matthew closed his eyes. The slow, steady stroke was driving him crazy. "I can't have the things I want." Matthew struggled to keep his voice from breaking. Tarrick squeezed, applying more pressure to the erection.

Matthew tilted his head upwards and a loud moan escaped him. When Tarrick began nipping at his neck it was too much. His fangs grew longer and a deep yearning pulled at his heart...and cock. Fuck, he needed release.

But Tarrick was never going to give him what he wanted emotionally. Hell, he probably wasn't even going to give him release physically. Chances were he was going to bring Matthew right to the edge then make him beg, make him kneel, make him call him *Master*.

"I can't have the things I want," he repeated. Needing to regain his control, he grabbed Tarrick's wrist and yanked it off his cock. "No."

Tarrick flashed a sinful smile and nipped at him again, hard enough to leave behind bruises before they faded away. Matthew let out a feral snarl and lowered his mouth to Tarrick's neck, resting his fangs against the flesh. He wanted the incubus' blood inside of him and his cock throbbed with need.

With his hand captured, Tarrick ground his body against Matthew. He could feel Tarrick's equally hard length through the thin material separating them. Just imagining touching Tarrick's cock made it almost impossible for him to fight the urge to thrust his pelvis forward and sink his fangs into his warm flesh.

Almost.

Matthew pulled back, pressing once more against the cell bars. "Stop." This time, the word came out the way he intended, commanding.

Tarrick stopped. His shining purple eyes looked up into Matthew's red ones. "This is what you want."

Matthew shook his head. "No. It's not."

"This is what I want," Tarrick said and resumed stroking Matthew's chest. Those words…so enticing. He released Tarrick's wrist and shook his head. "I wish I could believe that all you wanted right now was to fuck me but it's never that simple with you."

Tarrick took a step away. He looked hurt—just for a moment—before he concealed all emotions from his face. "Maybe if you had let me finish with the priest—"

"That has nothing to do with this. I'm so tired of your lies."

Tarrick kept backing away, and before Matthew even processed what was happening, he had stepped out of the cell, slamming the sliding door closed.

Shit. In reaction, Matthew surged at him, slipping his hand between the door and the bars before it could lock shut. The bones in his hand shattered with a sickening *crunch* but he had prevented himself from being locked in the cage.

Matthew pushed the door open, grabbed Tarrick by his harness, and tossed him back into the cell. Tarrick hit the back bars with such force that bones cracked. He slid to the ground, gritting his teeth as he cried out.

"What the fuck are you doing?" Matthew yelled at him and focused on healing his hand. "I've never seen you act like such an idiot before."

"You really think I wouldn't try to escape?" Tarrick asked between pained grunts. Was that what this was all about? Using sex to try and make a break for it? It had felt like it might have been more…

Matthew walked over to Tarrick and stood over the incubus. He could hear the bones inside of Tarrick's body mending—as were his own—and briefly considered giving him some blood to help the process along, but he was more than a little pissed off and Tarrick could use some suffering right now.

"Yeah?" Matthew asked. "How were you going to make it past the other packs of wolves prowling the upper levels? Do you know the protocols to open the bunker doors? Because you sure as hell aren't going to be breaking through two feet of solid metal. So stop with this bullshit—you get to go home tomorrow."

"I don't believe that you or the vampires will let me go. I wouldn't if I had their general—"

"*I'm not you, Tarrick,*" he yelled so loud that Tarrick flinched. "I don't have some ulterior motive. This isn't a trick. I want to trade you for Ascelina. That's it."

Tarrick pushed himself up into a sitting position and watched Matthew for a moment. Then his eyes fell to the dead shifters outside the cell. "And them?"

"The wolves were a mistake. I trusted someone I shouldn't have to guard you, but I can assure you that no one else here will touch you."

Tarrick said nothing for a long moment then, "What do you want, Matthew?"

"Why do you keep asking? Why the fuck do you want to know so bad?"

"Because you are a riddle that has plagued me since the day I met you." Tarrick struggled to his feet to face Matthew. "You are the impossible, sired by the unknown. And you act in unpredictable, baffling ways and I want to understand what it is you are seeking."

At least Tarrick didn't know who his sire was. Matthew wondered how he would react when he found out. Would he actually be awed?

"Fine. You want to know what I want? You're right, I don't want to be left alone. And I do enjoy fighting, and killing, and fucking. I want those things and more. But it's secondary to protecting my daughters and the people I care for. I want to know a world without this war and I dream of finding peace from the turmoil that is constantly ripping me apart. I'm stuck in the middle of two species and I hate it. What I want..."

Matthew swallowed hard and closed his eyes for a moment. "What I want is to feel what it's like to be around you when you aren't trying to control me. I love you and I want you to love me back."

"No," Tarrick said. "It's just an obsession. Lust. You don't love me."

Matthew's heart shattered to bits and fury overwhelmed him. He rushed at Tarrick and held him up off the ground, one clawed hand on the harness, the other around his neck, choking him. *"You motherfucker!* Stop. Saying. That."

God, it would be so easy to squeeze the life out of him. If he wasn't around to love anymore, maybe what he felt would fade away.

Matthew's hand tightened around the incubus' neck.

Tarrick clawed and kicked at him but he might as well have been trying to fight off a two-ton statue for all the good it did. Tarrick's face began to turn blue and his arms slacked down to his side.

Matthew released the man, who fell to his knees gasping. He loomed over him, trying to rein in the monster that had escaped.

"If it's true," he whispered, "and this is just an obsession...lust... then how do I stop feeling this way? Please tell me, so that I can move on." Hot tears pricked at his eyes. "I beg you."

Realizing the danger he was in, or just how close he had come to death, Tarrick stayed on the ground, but pity crossed his face. Matthew hated pity. He turned and left, slamming the cell door shut behind him.

Barefoot, he carefully stepped over the blood and bodies of the shifters. There was no way to re-attach the metal doors Matthew had torn off...and it was still early in the day.

His plan was to stand guard until nightfall, yell at Bryson a bit for what the shifters had done, and then ask Gwenyth to stay guard while he got some sleep. He could trust her not to kill Tarrick since she wanted her daughter back more than she cared about hurting the incubus general.

Oh, and deal with Devak, who had failed miserably at the task given to him.

Matthew was about to step out into the hall when Tarrick spoke. "What do you mean...'daughters'?"

Twenty-Eight

No. Matthew froze. He had been careless.

Behind him, Tarrick stood in the cage. "You said, 'it is secondary to protecting my daughters'. Plural."

Matthew turned. His fangs and claws grew longer, his eyes burned a deep red. He hunched over and a predacious growl came from deep within him. His right arm felt hot, the blood inside of it was stirring under the skin.

Tarrick, who was standing in the center of his cell rubbing the front of his neck, fell silent as an eerie chill crossed the room.

Matthew continued to growl. A single wrong move, a single threatening word, and he'd rip the cell door away and kill Tarrick. He had no choice right now. He would protect Samantha.

He fought to regain control but his instincts fought harder against him. Tarrick was going to figure it out. He could already see him putting it together.

The general had seen Matthew take Samantha from Chicago. He had the footage from the car garage of him leaving the hospital with her. Hunters had seen Matthew carry her when they used the stones to escape. It would only take Tarrick moments to piece it together.

Less actually.

"You turned the oracle, didn't you, Matthew?"

Matthew didn't answer.

Tarrick looked down at the ground, thinking. "Why would you have done that? You had to have known that having another child would be a huge risk...oh," he said looking up as he figured it out. "It was an accident. You gave her blood to try and heal her from those bolt wounds. But it didn't work. That's why you brought her to the hospital. You hadn't realized she was turned. I never taught you about the venom that would prevent it."

Tarrick looked proud of himself. He rubbed his hands over his chin. "I've been trying to figure out why you killed Sabine, an ally, so violently. But she saw that you had a child and you killed her to hide it from me. And I'll bet your daughter was caught in that thumper trap.

"And the masquerade…you brought her there. That's why you fought. That illusion spell that made it look like the keep was destroyed…for days I've been trying to figure out why your own witches would have cast that…it happened seconds before you lost control. You thought your child was dead. Devil. It all makes sense. Everything you've been doing is because you sired a vampire. Tell me, is she as powerful as you are? Can she compel other vampires or break an incubus hold like you can?"

He almost seemed excited by the idea of Matthew siring a child. It was as if he wanted to study her. A cold rage crept through Matthew.

He entered the guardroom and hit the button to unlock Tarrick's cell.

"She is precious to me and I would do anything to protect her. Anything. Even kill you."

Tarrick backed away as he approached him. Then screamed as he instinctively tried to slip into his incubus form, only to be crushed by the harness, falling to the ground, heaving in pain.

Matthew could smell his fear as he reopened the cell, pulled up Tarrick, and looked into his eyes. "You will forget any mention of a second child. As far as you are concerned I only have one, Lily, and no other," he said, trying to erase his memories. He wasn't sure it would work on someone so old.

Tarrick's breath slowed and the smell of fear lessened. The general grasped at his chest. "I thought my wounds had healed," he said, wincing in pain. "I can only remember half of our conversation… you've erased my memory."

"Yes."

Tarrick looked Matthew up and down. "Why?"

"Because I'd have to kill you otherwise."

"Oh." His face twisted, bewildered, as he tried to figure out what Matthew had removed. "Whatever it is, I am certain that I will figure it out eventually."

"I'm sure you will, but for your sake, I hope not."

And again, Matthew locked Tarrick in the cage and went out to the hallway to stand guard.

"I don't know where you are Devak but if you can hear me get your ass over here," he growled.

Matthew didn't have to wait long. Devak appeared, moving at an impossible speed and coming to a standstill beside him. Wearing his usual black laced up outfit, he looked...content. For a moment. Then he smelled the shifter's blood and his face dropped.

He looked into the prison, studied the carnage for a moment, then backed away so that Tarrick could no longer see him and kneeled down before Matthew. He was trembling.

Matthew grabbed Devak by his arm, his claws digging deep into his flesh, and dragged the smaller man down the hallway. He kicked open the door of an empty room and tossed Devak inside, who tumbled along the rock ground until he slid to a stop. He rolled onto both of his knees and bowed, prostrating himself before Matthew.

Matthew slammed the door closed.

"Where were you?" he asked, trying to keep his voice as even as possible, but it did nothing to hide the anger that was boiling inside of him.

Devak closed his eyes and bowed lower. "My prince..." he started. Then lost his nerve and fell silent.

"I'm racking my brain for a reason you wouldn't be guarding Tarrick like I ordered you to and everything I'm coming up with looks bad for you. Were you part of the attack?"

"No, my prince."

"You are jealous of him," Matthew said, pointing and spitting out the accusation.

Devak said nothing, his body shaking.

Matthew's muscles tensed as he resisted the urge to physically punish the guardian. *"Answer me."*

Devak looked up, then cowered back down after seeing just how enraged Matthew was. His shoulders dropped, his body submissive. "I am...envious," he said, the confession leaving him exposed.

Matthew's anger only grew. His right arm aching. "And you left him to die!"

Devak bowed deeper. "I did not intend to do so, my prince."

He was avoiding the questions and it was making Matthew furious. Matthew grabbed Devak by his shirt, pulled him up, and slammed him against the stone wall, coming inches away from his face.

"You have three seconds to start explaining before I hurt you," Matthew snarled.

Devak was unable to meet Matthew's gaze. He looked as if something was weighing heavily on him. "My prince...my intention was to return before the sun rose. I knew that the general would have watched over him until then...I lost track of time...I've failed you."

"Yes, you have."

Devak winced as if he had been punched in the gut.

"Tell me where you went. *Now*."

"I flew a few miles away for some privacy," Devak said.

"WHY?" Matthew roared, frustrated at having to pry the information out of Devak.

"I am your servant, my prince, your guardian. But being on this realm is not always easy for me. I needed time to reflect. To pray. I needed guidance."

Matthew's eyes darkened. "Is that what my sire does—gives you guidance? Because he sure as hell hasn't ever given me any."

Devak shook his head, distraught. "I did not receive the guidance I sought. I haven't for a long time." His voice was weak, timid.

Matthew took a moment. His monster was taking control of this situation and he didn't want that to happen. He owed Devak more than this. He released him and took a step away.

Devak fell back onto his knees. He seemed sincere but his actions had nearly cost Tarrick his life. Matthew would have never thought he would be so careless.

"What guidance could you possibly need?" Matthew asked, keeping his voice even.

Devak looked up at Matthew. "I..." he started to say, struggling to get out the answer.

"The curse?"

"No, my prince, it is not the curse...I am ashamed." He bowed over, keeping his head close to the floor. Matthew stayed silent, waiting for Devak to continue. "Please, my prince...please don't make me. I am humiliated."

"You will tell me." Matthew needed to know what was so important that it had Devak abandoning his duty.

Devak let a long moment pass before he looked up. He looked

awful, his face twisted like a man fighting inner demons. "I am falling for you. And I envy the love you give to Tarrick, knowing that you are unable to give it to me, my prince."

He waited, kneeling, for the rejection. His eyes were large, pleading almost, for kindness.

Matthew wasn't sure what to say. He wanted to protect his own heart. He couldn't truly trust Devak because he was sent by someone who had abandoned him. But the guardian had shown none of the same traits his sire had. He had always been there for Matthew when he needed him. He had protected him and tried his best to explain what he could, even with the curse.

Matthew pushed his hair back and rubbed his chin. He cared for Devak, no question. But love? Damn it. *No strings,* he repeated to himself.

"I've always been honest with you about my intentions...and you said you expected nothing from me in return."

"I know." Devak swallowed hard. "I am not asking for anything... but that doesn't mean I don't desire more. It has been thousands of years since I have fallen for someone. I didn't expect it. I thought I could ignore my feelings, but I am not as strong as I thought I was. Please forgive me, my prince."

Matthew's anger melted and he returned to his human guise. The pain in his right arm subsided. Before him, Devak looked so lost, so meek. No wonder he had left to try to find guidance.

"We aren't going to sleep together anymore. You can continue to feed from me. I intend to keep my word to break the curse, but once you answer my questions I can't guarantee that I won't send you away. And you are no longer on guard duty. You'll come to the exchange, but I need your word that you will follow each and every one of my orders."

Devak's face twisted with agony. "I give you my word. I am your servant." He struggled to get out the words as his chest heaved with pain. His body began to tremble again and tears started to fall. "But please, my prince, don't send me away. Please. Please."

It was hard for Matthew to see him like this. "Devak..."

"I am sorry for the way I feel. I will not mention it again, but I beg you, don't make me go. I have to stay or..."

Devak twisted as the curse silenced him.

Matthew sighed. There was an endless maelstrom churning within him and he needed to find some calm…which wasn't likely to happen anytime soon. Everything weighed down upon him—he had a child to protect, a curse to break, a sire to figure out, birth parents to find…a heart that refused to mend.

He had grown to think of Devak as part of his family and had come to rely on his advice. Maybe he did care for Devak more than he wanted to admit right now. But he needed time.

"Stand up," Matthew said. Devak got to his feet. Matthew grabbed him by the shoulder. "You've fought for me many times, and I appreciate it. I won't be unfair to you. I'll listen to everything you have to say once the curse is broken, but I can't promise anything beyond that. Not right now."

Unable to say anything, Devak nodded.

"Go back to the room and wait there."

Devak bowed and left.

Matthew went back to the hallway to make sure no one else tried to take a shot at Tarrick. The alpha of a different mercenary pack came by at one point. He shook his head and told Matthew that his wolves would never have done such a thing. Matthew was indifferent; if they tried to hurt Tarrick he'd kill them all.

The alpha did, however, order all the other wolves away from the level. Seeing the dead shifters might rile them up too much.

Bryson and Gwenyth, drawn to the smell of blood, appeared beside him moments after nightfall. Vikentiy was right behind them.

"Shit," Bryson said looking at the bloodbath inside the prison.

"We should not have trusted that pack," Gwenyth said.

Bryson balled his fists. "I thought the money would keep them in line."

Matthew's plans of yelling at Bryson changed, he was too tired and the blame did not lie entirely with the general. "Gwenyth, can you keep watch on Tarrick tonight? For Ascelina's sake we need to make sure no one else tries to off him."

"No one will touch him."

"I'm going out," Matthew said to Bryson, so he knew to open the doors when he got to them.

Matthew took a car and went to the closest town. He found a married couple that he convinced to sleep with him. He didn't bother to learn their names; he didn't want to. He wanted faceless, uncomplicated sex to feed. Halfway through the sexual marathon he realized that he wished he was feeding with Tarrick or Devak, or even Rosaline. He missed her. Feeding with any one of them was much more fulfilling.

When he returned to the room, Samantha shot death glares at him. Devak rose from a chair in the corner and bowed. Jet was wagging his tail. At least one of them seemed happy to see him.

He ignored Samantha and tore off his shirt.

"You smell like sex," she said.

"I'm an incubus," he reminded her, pulling off his boots.

"You hurt him a lot."

Matthew glanced at Devak. It wasn't meant to be an accusation, but Devak took it that way.

"I have told her nothing, my prince," he said in his own defense.

"I didn't think you did. I'm not in the mood, Sam," Matthew said and began unbuttoning his jeans as he walked into the bathroom.

"By the time you realize you love him it'll be too late."

Matthew paused in the doorframe, his back to her. He balled his fists for a moment then stepped into the bathroom and slammed the door behind him. Not wanting to face them, he spent a long time in the shower.

But he couldn't hide in there all night. Eventually he turned off the water, dried off, slipped a fresh pair of boxers on, and exited. Devak stood again. And bowed again. Samantha was still frowning.

Matthew slipped into the bed beside her.

"Wake me up before sunrise. You both can feed on me while I'm sleeping."

He closed his eyes, but it took a while before sleep came to him.

Twenty-Nine

Hiroto sat cross-legged with his hands resting atop his knees, his eyes closed. Incense rose around him as he meditated, wearing only black pants. The five scars Matthew had given him were nearly gone, just faint pink marks now. His fluffy white fox ears twitched and he gradually opened his brown eyes.

Matthew was sitting in front of him, mirroring his pose.

"What are you doing here, Matthew?" Hiroto asked.

Matthew sighed and slumped. "I don't know."

"I haven't been able to enter your mind for weeks. And I certainly didn't invite you into mine, and yet here you are."

The 'room' in Hiroto's mind was mostly dark except for a soft, source-less light that surrounded the two of them.

"I have no idea why I ended up here. I should be sleeping right now. I'll leave," Matthew said and stood. He was fairly certain that Hiroto couldn't track him anymore, but that didn't mean it was safe here.

"Wait. You don't have to leave. Is everything okay?" Hiroto motioned to the ground in front of him.

Matthew sat back down. "No," he said, but didn't elaborate.

Silence passed between them until Hiroto asked, "Is General Tarrick hurt?"

"He's fine. Will you be there tomorrow?"

"I can't tell you."

"You'll be there. Along with Prescott. I really don't want a fight tomorrow."

"No?"

"No." Matthew rubbed his hand across his face. "Maybe if it works out, some small amount of trust could be built between the two sides. Maybe other prisoner exchanges can happen. I know both sides have people they want back."

"Maybe," Hiroto said but didn't sound convinced.

Matthew sat silent for a moment, letting the incense calm him. Then questions began to bubble in his mind. "I read a little about kitsune after you told me you were one. If you are a messenger for a god, why are you working as an assassin for the incubi?" he asked. There hadn't been a ton of information in the book that Matthew had tracked down.

Hiroto's ears twitched. "Do you believe in the gods?"

Matthew laughed. If only the fox knew… "I do now."

Hiroto fidgeted, bringing his knees to his chest and wrapping his arms around them. He looked so small. "I…no longer work for Inari. I displeased her and was abandoned on this world. The High King saved my life. I owe him a debt."

"How many tails do you have?" He had read that they gained more tails as they became more powerful. Up to a possible nine.

"Seven."

"Can I see?"

Hiroto smiled. "If you tell me why you are here."

Matthew didn't want to talk about it so he looked around the dark space they were in. "Your mind is kind of boring."

Hiroto motioned around him. "Well, I was meditating. I don't need stuff cluttering up my mind when I'm trying to focus. I can always bring the bathtub back if you want."

Matthew groaned. "You just had to pick that fantasy out of all of them. It's one of my favorites."

"It was the strongest, it's why I was able to latch onto it." Hiroto stood and came over to him. He wasn't much taller than Matthew while sitting down. "Why are you here, Matthew?"

Matthew grabbed Hiroto by his hips and pulled him into his lap, holding him like a doll. He was so tiny compared to Matthew's large frame.

Matthew stroked his face and ran his fingers through his white hair and his soft ears. He couldn't help but touch them. He sighed. "I should go."

Hiroto fondled Matthew's chest. "You don't have to."

"Why? You hoping I'll stay and sex you, little fox?"

Hiroto shot him a sly smile and wiggled in Matthew's lap. "Maybe."

Matthew laughed and pulled Hiroto closer to his chest. "You know, if we did it, it would be a literal mind fuck."

Hiroto snorted out a giggle. "It'd be fun," he said, then turned thoughtful. "How did you get in here? Neither vampires or incubi can enter a mind like this."

"Really? How many things can I do that others can't?"

"I guess that's true."

Matthew held onto Hiroto tighter and said nothing else for a while. The incense continued to calm him. Being here was soothing.

"Did you come here just to cuddle?" Hiroto asked, half joking.

"I think maybe I did," Matthew said, not joking at all. "Or maybe… just to talk. You're easy to talk to."

"It's the big ears. Makes me a good listener."

Matthew once again ran his fingers over the fox ears. "I wish we weren't on opposite sides of this war."

"Me too."

"Are you a good assassin?"

"Yes."

"It's hard for me to imagine you killing people. Sneaking into a room at night and slicing their neck open or however you do it."

Hiroto pressed himself harder into Matthew's chest. Then suddenly he was gone and there was a burning at Matthew's neck as Hiroto appeared behind him with a dagger pressed into his skin.

"You shouldn't let your guard down around me. I really am one of the best."

"That's not fair, this is a dream," Matthew said.

"Doesn't mean I couldn't hurt you in here."

"So why don't you?"

The dagger was removed from his neck and Hiroto ran his small hand through Matthew's hair, sending chills down his spine.

"Two reasons. One, I think you are probably the only reason General Tarrick is unharmed. The vampires would never pass up the opportunity to torture him if they could. And two, your guardian is trying to break in. He'll be here in a moment, and I really don't want him blasting me again. It was really painful."

Matthew heaved himself up to his feet, towering over Hiroto. "I have to go now. But thank you. This was…nice."

"Matthew?"

"Yes, little fox?"

"I'm serious—don't let your guard down around me. I have orders to bring you in and I will follow them."

Matthew ran his hand down Hiroto's face. "I won't."

"Don't come back here either. One slip and I'll be able to track you."

Matthew nodded.

There was a flash of light and Devak was standing behind them. Matthew let his hand fall away from Hiroto's face.

"I'm not in any danger," Matthew said.

Devak, who kept his face unreadable, studied Matthew to make sure he was okay, then looked at Hiroto. "I thought maybe he had pulled you in again."

"No."

"The sun is almost up," Devak said.

Hiroto approached Devak and walked around him. Devak raised an eyebrow. "You cannot harm me, fallen messenger."

With his hand, Hiroto made a sweeping motion across Devak's body. Barbed chains appeared, becoming visible by whatever Hiroto had done. They were tightly wrapped around Devak, covering almost every part of him. They looked more than just uncomfortable, they looked excruciating.

"He's cursed," Hiroto said.

Matthew's jaw dropped. He had no idea that the curse looked like that.

Devak growled a warning. "Back away from me, *fox*."

"I've never seen one of Lysandros' guardians up close before," Hiroto said, still standing near Devak, looking him over with wide-eyed curiosity.

Devak scowled at him.

"Lysandros?" Matthew asked.

Hiroto nodded. "Vampires call him the Blood God."

"He has—" Devak started to say but the chains on him constricted. He cried out in pain as the barbs dug into his skin.

Hiroto frowned. "You must have pissed off someone powerful to get such a terrible curse on you." He turned to Matthew. "I think he was going to say that Lysandros has many different names across many worlds."

"Wait. Worlds?" Matthew asked.

Hiroto laughed. "Worlds."

"Um, the vampires don't know much about the Blood God. Would you say he's, uh, you know, a powerful god?" Smooth.

Devak shot him a worried glance but said nothing.

"Yeah. He's one of the strongest. He has many domains. My god always avoided challenging him." Hiroto dared to come a little closer to Devak, his eyes wide with admiration. "Blood guardians are among the most powerful. They're terrifying. Hard to stop. Normally if I knew one was in the area, I'd hide until it was finished with its mission. But you," he said to Devak, "your powers are weakened, aren't they?"

Devak said nothing.

Matthew wanted to ask Hiroto a thousand more questions but he didn't want Hiroto to start to suspect who his sire was. He'd just have to wait and hope Devak could answer his questions for him once he was free of the curse.

"Why does he call you 'prince'? Were you turned by an ancient one?" Hiroto asked.

"Alright, let's go." Matthew grabbed Devak and a bright light surrounded them.

When Matthew woke, Devak was sitting next to him on the bed, holding his hand. He broke away and took several steps back, then kneeled down. Samantha was sitting in the chair in the corner, her feet resting on Jet.

"I didn't mean to intrude, my prince," he said.

"No. It's okay. I shouldn't have gone, it was too risky," Matthew said as he sat up. His neck stung where Hiroto had pressed the dagger into him. He rubbed the area and found he had a small, healing cut.

"Where did you go?" Samantha asked.

"To visit a fox," Matthew said.

"The one with the fluffy white ears? I want to pet them one day."

Matthew laughed. "Come to bed, the sun is about to rise."

She crawled into bed and put her hand on his face. "She loved you very much."

"I know," Matthew said, not wanting to dwell on the reason Samantha had just said that to him.

Once she was asleep, Matthew ordered Devak to stay with her during the day while he went down to keep guard over Tarrick. He stayed in the observation room.

Today, no one came down. No one dared. The mess had been cleaned up and no doubt word of what had happened had traveled through the bunker.

Tarrick sat on the bed in the cell and said nothing for a few hours. Finally, he stood and walked forward into the cage. "Since we're both here all day, why not come talk?"

Both had heightened hearing so Matthew didn't bother to move out of the guardroom. "No thanks. I'm good," he said, leaning back in his chair.

"I know you enjoy talking to me..."

"I spent a while as a slave to this douche canoe who kept me imprisoned with no one to speak to for weeks on end. Nowadays I don't mind the silence."

"Sounds awful."

"You have no idea."

"I don't suppose you'd turn on the shower for me..."

Tarrick did look terrible and could use a shower, or maybe three. And he needed new clothes and a shave.

Without explaining anything to Tarrick, Matthew left the small room. He checked the other rooms on the hall—they were empty right now but looked as if they were normally meant to house sleeping guards. Quite a few had full bathrooms. Matthew poked around the bunker until he found a pair of slacks, socks, and a white button-up shirt that would fit Tarrick. He placed them in one of the rooms.

When he walked back into the prison, Tarrick had returned to sitting on the bed.

"If I take you out to shower are you going to behave?"

"I won't try to escape again."

Good enough. Matthew unlocked the cell and pulled Tarrick out of it. He led him by his arm down the hall and into one of the rooms. He ushered Tarrick into the bathroom and waited by the door.

"Going to watch?" Tarrick asked as he stripped out of what was left of his pants.

"I'm not letting you out of my sight. But if you try to seduce me I'm going to toss you back into the cell, I don't care if you're naked and soapy. I'm not in the mood for your shit today."

Tarrick nodded and got into the shower to wash off the dried blood and grime that had collected on him. To his credit, he didn't try to mess with Matthew even once.

Which was good because Matthew wasn't really paying attention to the incubus. Instead, his thoughts fell to Devak and what Samantha had said: *By the time you realize you love him it'll be too late.* Everything she had told him about the future had come to pass. Did he love Devak? He had been resisting the idea for so long…it was hard to love someone that he couldn't confide in…but there was something there he couldn't deny or ignore.

Even still, he didn't want to deal with it. Not now. He did his best to shove the thoughts away and ignore them. Today had another meaning for him.

Matthew let out a heavy sigh. His life had become so complicated. "Matthew?"

Matthew looked up. "Hm?"

Tarrick was already shaved and had just finished buttoning the shirt over his harness. "Are you well?"

The question seemed caring, but Matthew knew it was just a prelude to a verbal dance that he didn't want to engage in. "Back to your cell."

Tarrick didn't resist. Once Matthew had locked him in, he returned to watching from the guardroom, leaning his head on his hand.

The two remained silent as the day inched on. Matthew zoned out for a while and when he came back to it, Tarrick was standing, watching him through the bars.

"Need something?" Matthew asked.

"No. But it looks like you do."

Matthew rubbed his face with both his hands. "I'm not used to being awake all day long."

"You are still a terrible liar."

It wasn't exactly a lie. But Tarrick was right, that wasn't the problem right now. Matthew turned off the cameras then went to go stand in the door-less doorway.

"I found my sire." Matthew wasn't sure why he told him. There wasn't a hold or any manipulation on Tarrick's part. It just slipped out. Actually, he did know why. He was using the topic as a distraction from other thoughts.

"Did you? Is he or she still around?"

"Oh yeah." Matthew idly rubbed his right arm.

"Who is it?"

"I'm not going to tell you, but I'm sure you'll put it together sometime soon. I figured it out and I have half your brains."

"Half? That's quite generous." Tarrick smiled. That fucking, damn sexy, playful smile that always turned Matthew on.

"I concede. You're far smarter than me." Matthew grabbed his ring finger...searching for a ring that was no longer there. "Have you ever been married?"

Tarrick shook his head. "Incubi take mates, we don't marry. Well, not often. Sometimes if we're with a human and they insist...I've had three mates, all dead now. Why do you ask?"

Matthew shrugged. "Women? Men?"

"Two women, they bore most of my children, and one man. Not all at the same time. I've had other companions over the years, but those were the three I had wanted to share my life with—and would have if it wasn't for vampires. What's going on Matthew?"

Matthew looked down at his hand. His heart ached.

"Ah," Tarrick said. "Today would have been your anniversary with Alyssa. You two had a winter wedding. I've seen the photos from the event, she was very lovely."

She really was. He had met Alyssa in college. He was there on a football scholarship and she was there because she was brilliant. A violinist who had graduated valedictorian and Matthew, a frat boy who almost didn't even make it out of high school.

From the moment he saw her in the cafeteria he was head over heels in love. And she wanted nothing to do with him. Rightfully so, she was way out of his league. But Matthew wasn't one to give up so easily. He pursued her relentlessly. None of his buddies understood it because he could have any other girl he wanted. Hell, they practically threw themselves at his feet, but he wanted Alyssa and every damn day he flirted with her until she finally agreed to go out with him just to shut him up.

And what do you know, she actually had fun with him.

A few months later, she told him she was pregnant and that she was going to keep the baby. That night Matthew asked her to marry him and she said yes. It wasn't because 'it was the right thing to do'—fuck that shit—he married her because he wanted to marry her.

God, they were dumb kids. Nothing about them should have worked out. Nothing. She was so far above him it was ridiculous. He was a party boy orphan who grew up with nothing while she grew up privileged with a drive to improve herself. It was something that rubbed off on Matthew.

Over the years, she taught him to appreciate music, art, and even got him to start reading books because he wanted to, not because he had to. It turned out he had a brain once she showed him how to use it; no one else had ever bothered to take the time.

To this day, he had no idea what she saw in him.

Matthew's entire body ached with anguish. He left the prison and walked out into the hall to be alone. He leaned against the wall and slid down to a squatting position. It had been nine years since he had last seen his wife, and four since she died, and he still missed her. He still loved her. And he loved Tarrick and his feelings for Devak were stronger than he let himself believe. There were strings all over the fucking place.

He was a mess.

Thirty

Matthew stayed in the hallway until about twenty minutes before the sun set. Then he re-entered the observation room and turned the cameras back on. Out of what Matthew could only assume was compassion or sympathy, Tarrick said nothing.

Once the sun set, Gwenyth took over guarding Tarrick. Matthew went back to the room to feed Samantha and pack the duffle bag with a sword and bracers. While he gathered his items, Samantha slipped an umbrella into the bag but made no comment about it.

"Jet," Matthew said to the dog after downing a pack of blood. "You better take care of her while I'm gone."

"Caaare," Jet said and licked his hand. No matter how many times he had heard the gargoyle speak, it still tripped him out. Especially when he was in dog form.

Matthew kissed Samantha on the head. "Stay safe."

He and Devak—who wasn't wearing his armor nor wielding his sword because Matthew didn't want them showing up looking aggressive—made their way down to the prison area. Waiting there was Bryson, Gwenyth, Vikentiy, Stolus, and four other vampires, all lords, that Matthew recognized but didn't know personally. Unlike Matthew and Devak, they all had weapons and armor. Matthew had been unable to convince them not to wear them.

Bryson's leather outfit looked like the male version of Silva's uniform, except his weapons weren't silvered and he had no stakes. Stolus had his shield and spear, but at least he was fully clothed this time, while the other vampires wore a mix of flexible leather armor and heavier metal pieces. None as ornate as the armor incubi warriors wore.

"They're here," Bryson said, looking at a text on his phone.

Matthew pulled Tarrick from the cell and secured his cuffs together so that his hands were bound in front of him.

"I like him in the cage. It suits him," Stolus growled.

Tarrick opened his mouth to reply but Matthew squeezed his

upper arm so hard that he grunted in pain. "Let's do this without the shit talking."

Escorted by a vampire, the five witches sent by Brujo Moya entered the room. They smelled different than the other witches Matthew had encountered in the past. These ones dressed in normal clothes instead of loose-fitting woven outfits. Other witches always smelled like trees or wildlife, these smelled like decay and death. It gave Matthew a chill.

"Ready?" Bryson asked, putting up the hood of his cloak. Everyone scooted closer together and the witches circled around them. They chanted a few words and darkness enveloped them.

When the darkness cleared they were standing in the center of a dense jungle. They must have been on the other side of the world because Matthew could sense the sun was much closer to rising than it had been back in Pennsylvania.

The trees surrounding the group were lush, green, and so thick Matthew couldn't see the sky. Moss clung to everything and the wild night noises of bugs and animals filled the air. Everything was wet and smelled clean.

"Where the hell are we?" Matthew asked.

"Africa. Congo," Tarrick said.

"You're shitting me. We're in the fucking rainforest?" A smile spread wide across his face. "I've never been here before."

"This isn't a vacation, Matthew," Bryson said and motioned for the other vampires to take up strategic positions in the trees.

As the vampires moved, the five witches disappeared into the jungle. Matthew assumed they were dropping back to go wait until this was over and they were needed again.

"If you ever end up in my care again, I'm going to have to break you of your constant cussing," Tarrick said.

Matthew frowned. "I won't be ending up in your 'care' again and you'll never break me of that habit, I enjoy cussing far too much." He really did. Alyssa had always tried to rid him of the habit but the best he could do was watch his mouth around Lily. Over time she reluctantly accepted it.

The vampires stilled when the smell of incubi and humans hit them, still maybe a quarter mile out.

Matthew slung the duffle over his shoulder and grabbed Tarrick's elbow. They walked towards the incubi. Behind him was Devak, whose back was bleeding in case he needed his wings. To his side, clinging to the shadows, was Bryson. He moved like a cat through the jungle, far more graceful than Matthew would have thought for a man his size and structure. Stolus took up the rear while the other vampires followed along in the trees, jumping through them without making a sound or even disturbing a branch.

They came forward to a place where a few trees had fallen recently, creating a small clearing. Matthew came to a stop at the edge, gripping Tarrick's arm, and tossed the duffle on the damp ground.

He watched as hunters appeared above him in the trees and disappeared as their runes made them invisible. On the opposite edge of the clearing, the incubi stepped into view. Dennith was accompanied by Tane, and his oldest brother Tarquin, Vassu, and six other warrior incubi. All the incubi were armored and in their full forms—tall and imposing. The smallest was Tane at six feet and the tallest was the black behemoth, Vassu, who was just over ten feet.

At Dennith's side stood Prescott and Silva, who looked miniature standing next to the incubi. Hunters tossed out flares into the clearing.

Matthew blinked hard as his eyes adjusted to the light.

Dennith studied Matthew and Tarrick for a moment, then her eyes scanned the trees for the other vampires. Matthew felt a twinge of pain as the incubi looked at him with such seething hatred. Standing there were the people who trained him, fought beside him, and, for a time, called him friend.

Well, not Tane.

Fuck Tane.

"I brought mine, why don't you show me yours," Matthew said, since no one else was talking.

Dennith gripped a polearm she was holding. "I'd like to make sure the High General isn't under a compulsion first."

Matthew looked at Tarrick. "You have a way to test for compulsions?"

Tarrick gave a nod. "Sort of, Hiroto can tell. It's never been a concern for incubi until you."

"Ah," Matthew said and looked at Dennith. "Sure. Hiroto can come on over."

Dennith motioned her weapon forward, and—and in a silvery

white light—Hiroto teleported in front of Matthew wearing a red mask and black hood. He nodded respectfully to Tarrick and pulled off the glove on his hand. He reached up, touched Tarrick's forehead, and closed his eyes. After a moment he opened his eyes again and stepped back.

"He's not compelled," he said and teleported away.

"Alright, bring them forward," Dennith ordered.

Six vampire prisoners came forward with their hunter escorts. The vampire lords didn't look in as bad of shape as Matthew thought they would. Some had minor silver burns but they had been fed. Most, including Ascelina, had a metal muzzle over their mouth, their hands were chained behind their back, and they wore a metal harness around their chest, similar to the one Tarrick had, to prevent their wings from coming out.

One was different—he had a plastic-esqe cage with no holes or gaps, carried by hunters.

Matthew, come to my rescue? Ascelina's voice appeared in his head. Matthew smiled at her.

"We'll take three, release Tarrick, then you'll release the other three," Bryson said, still in the shadows. Matthew was happy he spoke up because he wasn't really sure how to do this part.

Dennith nodded and pointed at three vampires; the one in the cage and two others Matthew didn't know. She was holding back Ascelina. Smart.

The clear cage was opened and the male vampire, a tall pale man who would look right at home with a top hat and cane, turned into a swarm of bats and flew behind Matthew. He reformed and snarled at Tarrick.

Matthew shot him a warning and he backed away. The other two vampires walked over. Vikentiy appeared and removed their restraints. Once they were free, he grabbed one, a male, behind the neck and Matthew heard him whisper 'brother' before the three of them disappeared again into the jungle.

Matthew pulled two keys from his pocket and forced Tarrick to face him. "Please don't turn this into a blood bath. I really don't want to kill anyone here."

Tarrick stuck out his arms, and Matthew unlocked the cuffs, letting them fall to the ground. Tarrick rubbed his wrists, then his hand shot out and he grabbed Matthew's arm. It wasn't an attack; his grip wasn't strong.

It struck Matthew that this was probably the last time they'd ever touch unless they were fighting each other. Having Tarrick as a prisoner made one thing exceedingly clear: no matter how he felt, he could never be with Tarrick again.

Matthew wasn't sure why Tarrick had grabbed him, but a moment passed between them. A mourning, maybe, for what they were losing—or perhaps what might have been. It was so subtle that no outsider would have noticed it. Tarrick's arm dropped away when Matthew handed him the second key for the harness. The locking mechanism was on the back, one of his own people would have to take it off once he was over there since Matthew wasn't going to do it.

Tarrick walked across the clearing, his march confident as all eyes fell on him. When he reached the other side, Dennith nodded as a relinquishment of command. Tarrick stripped out of his shirt and Silva unlocked the harness.

Matthew did his best not to eye-fuck Tarrick's chest as the incubus rolled his shoulders once he was free. It'd be somewhat awkward to unintentionally start throwing out pheromones, letting everyone know that he desired Tarrick.

Tarrick went into his incubus form but didn't grow in size. His claws and horns—one still healing—came out, his eyes turned purple, and his ears pressed into pointed tips. Behind him, wings unfurled and stretched, and his pointed tail snaked upwards.

A hunter brought him his kanabō; the sight of it sent chills through Matthew, but he kept his face blank. Silva brought him the chest plate of his armor. She held it up to his body and said a few words in a language Matthew didn't recognize. The armor expanded around Tarrick until he was in his full set of iridescent plate.

Silva fell to his side as two other hunters worked on attaching a metal spike to the tip of his tail and the top of his wings.

Fully armored, he grew taller and wider, finishing his transformation into his warrior incubus form.

He looked valiant. Commanding. A paradigm of leadership.

Unfamiliar animal cries from the jungle pierced the silence.

Everyone waited for the High Lord General's order. Tarrick could decide right now if this was going to be a fight, and if he did carnage and death would follow. Matthew hoped that he would choose to release the last three and end this. He wanted to be on his way to Delphi tomorrow night.

Tarrick took a step forward. "Do you want to be the one to tell her, General, or shall I?"

That wasn't exactly what Matthew had expected him to say.

The incubi all looked incredibly interested since none knew who the vampire general was, or that he was even here. Matthew and Devak were the only two vampires standing in the open right now.

Bryson took a deep breath in and held it for a moment. Then he stood up straight and came out from the shadows, but didn't quite enter the clearing. His hood was still up, his face concealed by it. "You should have told her privately, but you've always been an asshole."

"I don't think she would believe me unless she saw it with her own eyes. I don't think any of them would." Tarrick motioned to the other hunters.

"You know, this won't stop her from yelling at you for sending her away," Bryson said.

Matthew watched Silva's hand drop uneasily to her crossbow when she realized the conversation was about her. Hell, every hunter had their hands near their weapons. This whole situation was a damn powder keg ready to blow. At least the hunters were disciplined.

Bryson stepped into the light of the flares, reached up, and pulled his hood back.

"Impossible," Silva gasped and a plethora of emotions crossed her face in the span of a second: confusion, shock, angst, and then hate.

She wasn't the only one who looked shocked. Bryson would have been well-known in the corps, and most of the hunters here tonight were elite, older, those whose lifespans were extended by the incubi. Most had probably known him personally.

Matthew knew that, to a hunter, becoming a vampire was something they feared most. They took extreme measures to ensure it wouldn't happen, up to and including killing themselves before the change could take place.

Right now, Bryson was doing a good job of keeping his face

unreadable, but Matthew could sense sorrow coming from him as he watched Silva.

"You're their general?" she asked, her voice laced with disgust.

"Yes, dear."

Silva's jaw clenched, her hand still resting on the crossbow at her hip. She was doing her best to hide her pain but it was there.

Tension pulled the air as each side waited for the other to make a move. Every hunter, incubus, and vampire poised to attack.

Tarrick dispelled the tension by a wave of his hand—the hunters lowered their weapons at his silent order. Even Silva obeyed and took her hand away from her crossbow. It always awed Matthew just how much authority Tarrick could wield with a flick of his wrist.

"What's your plan here, Tarrick? We going to finish this and go our separate ways or are we going to fight?" Bryson asked.

The three remaining chained up vampires looked eager to get out of there.

Tarrick's eyes flicked to Matthew and Devak, then they traced the outlines of the dark trees. He raised his hand, about to give his order when lightning arched across the sky and rain began to dump down on them. The water was hot and sticky, even at night.

Then the ground began to shake.

"Bastards. That's magic," Stolus said from somewhere off to Matthew's right.

"This isn't us," Dennith said to Tarrick.

"This is a trap, we should kill them now," an unseen vampire hissed from his hiding spot.

The hunters all had their weapons up. Bryson backed away, putting Matthew and Devak between him and the hunters. The vampire general was fully aware that he was one of the weaker creatures here today. Even Stolus was older than him.

Tane raised his claymore. "They must have made a deal with Moya."

Accusations flew from both sides but their words faded away in the rain, replaced by foul whispers carried on the wind. Creatures called to Matthew, begging for freedom. They wanted to break into this world. If they could only have his help, they'd be here sooner.

Listening to the whispers, he fell into a trance until he felt Devak's hand was on his shoulder, breaking him out of it.

This wasn't either side betraying each other. This was something worse.

"*STOP,*" Matthew roared. His voice cut through the shouts and downpour. He was surprised when each side shut the hell up and looked at him. Even Tarrick.

"In Chicago—what did you call it?—a demonic incursion? Because I can hear a whole mess of demons trying to break through into this world right now. And it's not just one portal this time. I can sense three of them opening around us. And we are grossly outnumbered. Oh, and those witches that each side trusted to teleport us here? They're gone. We're seriously fucked right now."

E veryone watched Matthew, looking at him like he was crazy. Then
Devak must have sensed something because, without a word, he
took off into the air, his wings snapping out behind him. The tendrils
looked as if they were constantly melting and reforming as the rain
beat down on them, but it didn't seem to affect his flying.

He disappeared above the trees.

"If there was an incursion about to happen, we would feel it.
There's always a warning," Imperator Prescott said from under his
dark armor.

"And what possible reason would Moya's coven have to betray us?"
Dennith asked. "They have never taken a side in the war before."

Silva gave a silent command to a team of hunters who disappeared
into the jungle to verify the incursion.

A few nasty verbal exchanges between the hunters and the vampires
later, Devak came smashing through the canopy of trees and moss
and landed hard in the center of the clearing, facing Matthew.

"You are correct, there are three portals. They all have some sort of
magic preventing me from approaching. We will have to find a way to
break through the barrier if I am to close them."

"You can close portals?" Matthew asked.

"I was built to fight demons, my prince. Closing and opening
portals to the Pit is part of that."

Damn it, he was really hoping Devak wouldn't call him 'prince'
right now. He wasn't sure who knew on the incubus side, but he had
somehow avoided saying it around the vampires.

Prince? I see you did find a blood guardian. Ascelina said to him
telepathically. Matthew didn't respond. He'd talk to her once she was
free and they were out of here.

Tarrick tapped his claws against his armor while he took a moment
to think, then motioned around him. "Look at who is here tonight.
Some of the oldest, most powerful vampires, the strongest incubi
warriors, and our best hunters. Brujo Moya saw an opportunity to

weaken both our factions and he's taken it. It seems he has picked a side in this war—his own."

Power washed through the area like an oppressive wave of heat and the rain subsided just a bit.

An uneasy silence washed over both forces. Except Matthew wasn't uneasy. He was about to fight demons for the first time. He was stoked. "Do you feel the incursion now?" he yelled over the rain to Prescott, laughing.

The leader of the Hunter Corps dismissed his silver battleaxe and summoned the golden blade with Ilertha's holy symbols on it. It was the same one he summoned in Chicago, so it was probably good at killing demons.

Devak eyed the weapon and took an uneasy step away from Prescott, but said nothing else.

"This isn't really something you should be joking about, Matthew," Silva yelled back, chastising him.

Matthew smiled. He opened his duffle bag, not really caring what everyone else chose to do. He and Devak had some demons to kill. This was the first time he'd be in a battle where he wouldn't be killing his own people. There'd be no guilt, no holding back. He could hardly contain his excitement.

He slapped on the bracers, grabbed his sword, and attached it to his belt. He stripped out of his t-shirt too, since it always ended up shredded and in the way.

"Our satellite phone is down," Vikentiy said, appearing beside Bryson. "No ride out of here. No reinforcements either."

A hunter on the other side reported the same to Tarrick. The incubi and most of the vampires had the ability to fly out of here but that would leave three open demon portals in Africa. And the hunters would be left behind. Their teleport rune had limits, or so Matthew had been told.

Another wave of power rushed through the area. Bodies tensed, waiting for a command.

The two generals faced each other.

Tarrick spoke first. "We can't leave the portals open. The demons will get to the humans, then we'll have a whole new set of problems we can ill afford."

"I agree. But Matthew's right, we're outmanned if there's three portals opening. That's—"

"—possibly thousands," Tarrick said cutting him off. "And that's assuming they don't have pit commanders."

"Pit commanders?" Matthew asked. Both Tarrick and Bryson shot him an irritated glance. Matthew made a mental note to never interrupt the generals again. The two of them went back to talking. Matthew hoped this would end with them agreeing to work together. It sounded as if their conversation was going that way since right now they had no other choice.

"Pit commanders are leaders of the demonic forces. You saw the hand of one of them in Chicago but we closed that portal before it could come through," a friendly voice answered in his ear. Matthew turned and, crouched on a tree branch, not even two feet away, was Hiroto. Damn, Matthew had no idea he was there.

Matthew lowered his voice. "I don't want to interrupt their generals' powwow but maybe someone should tell them that I can sense three of the big ones trying to break through."

Tarrick's, Bryson's, and Devak's heads all snapped to Matthew.

"Three, my prince?" Devak asked.

Bryson cussed.

"The demons were prepared for this then. If we survive this, I'm going to kill those witches myself," Tarrick said.

Without any further acknowledgment of Matthew, the generals went back to their conversation.

"So how do I kill one?" Matthew asked.

"It's not that easy, my prince. Even I cannot take one alone."

"But you aren't alone. Let me guess, massive damage? Cut off its head? That seems to kill most things."

Devak nodded. "Each one is different, but yes, massive damage will usually do it...assuming you can slice through its armored outer skin. The easiest way is with a holy weapon, but right now we only have two. Mine and his—" Devak pointed to Prescott who was across the way barking orders to hunters, "—and my bludgeoning weapon has its limitations."

"I have blessed weapons as well but my daggers won't do much against those beasties," Hiroto said, patting his cloak, his daggers hidden underneath.

Matthew wished he could see the daggers. "Really? Your maul is a *holy* weapon?"

A devious glint flashed in Devak's eyes. "Yes. Were you expecting it to be a bit shinier? Maybe with superfluous decoration all over it? A fancy glow?"

Matthew smiled. Devak knew him too well. "Um, well, yeah. It's a *holy* weapon."

Devak shook his head, amused, then turned to the sky. "La'mast and Na'mori." Bright light broke through the canopy and filled the area. He flew up to meet his armor midair; it hit him with a clang and wrapped around his body. Grabbing his maul, he floated back down. He looked damned impressive.

Matthew looked down at his own body and sighed. He didn't have badass armor or a glorious weapon. Just jeans and a run-of-the-mill longsword. He was feeling a little left out of the I'm-a-badass club.

In the middle of the clearing, Tarrick and Bryson shook hands. It seemed the generals had made their decision.

"Alright, listen up," Tarrick said, his voice carried as he addressed both sides. Everyone fell silent. "We're stuck here with three portals opening. Our comms are down, and we have no other way to call for backup. We're working on resolving that but in the meantime we're going to have to fight. General Bryson and I have agreed on a temporary truce. There is a precedent that exists for situations like this one. From now until the sun rises in four hours we are allies. Anyone, incubus or hunter, that hurts a vampire during this time will be executed."

Tarrick looked at Bryson, who in turned looked at Matthew, who was apparently in the role of enforcer now. Bryson was going to be really disappointed when Matthew officially turned down the crown.

"Yeah. I'll fucking kill any vamp that doesn't follow his rules," Matthew said, pointing at Bryson. He released his aura so they knew he was serious.

All the vampires, except the oldest, Gwenyth, moved away from him. He suppressed his aura again. That seemed to satisfy Tarrick, but Bryson's fangs were out and he was growling. Given his age, it wasn't a response he could control.

He recovered a moment later and acted as if nothing had happened.

"Release them," Tarrick said and pointed to the three vampires still chained up on the incubus side of the clearing. Ascelina glared at Tarrick once she was free, but she moved past him and went to her son. Gwenyth appeared beside her as well.

"We have a new chain of command," Tarrick said. "I'm in charge, followed by General Bryson, then the vampire Gwenyth, Lady Dennith, and Imperator Prescott."

Matthew couldn't help but notice the sour look that formed on Tarquin's face when his name wasn't called. Tarquin was actually a general in Russia, but probably fell low on the totem pole when outside of his territory.

The incubus was big, nearly eight feet with forward curving horns, and his wings ended in dark green tips. His armor was gold and silver. In the center was an engraving of a shield with a starburst pattern. Behind the shield were two swords and a crossbow, and incubus wings expanded out to the sides—the symbol of House Tarrick.

Tarquin was a shining star of his people. As Tarrick's eldest, he was practically a prince, heir to Tarrick's estates and the military. More than once, Matthew caught Tane watching his brother with adoration...maybe envy.

Matthew noticed Tarquin and Vikentiy sizing each other up.

"Since our comms are down—" Tarrick continued, "—vampires will have to relay orders."

"We're going to move together, take out a portal, then move to the next," Bryson said. "We'll start at the northern one and move clockwise. Our main priority is clearing a path and closing each portal before the pit commander comes through."

Bryson and Tarrick issued more orders to the group. They were splitting up teams based on skill, sending incubi and vampires who could fly into the air, figuring out what they would do with wounded. There were a million things they had to consider but it was happening fast and both generals knew what they were doing.

Bryson's training as a hunter made it easy for him to fall in a rhythm with Tarrick. It was actually sort of frightening how well they commanded together.

Matthew was worried. They had a quality force on their side but they were lacking in quantity. Sixty-three of them (broken down into thirty-six hunters, eleven incubi, fifteen vampires, and one blood guardian) facing a thousand or more. As excited as he was at the prospect of fighting a new foe, and facing a new challenge, he knew that people were going to die.

"*Matthew*," Bryson said, he had been calling to him but Matthew hadn't heard it…he had been listening to the demons, which were a few minutes away from breaking through.

"Yeah? Sorry."

"You and Devak won't be assigned to a team, we'll tell you where to go," Bryson said.

"Alright, General."

"I know I have no right to ask—" Devak said, "—but please, my prince, don't drink any of the demon blood. And if any demons identify you, don't let them retreat back into the portal."

"Is demon blood toxic or something?" Matthew asked.

"It's—" Devak screamed in pain as he tried to speak past his curse. Hiroto, of all people, appeared beside Devak and grabbed him before he fell over.

"You probably should stop pissing off that curse of yours," the assassin said, pushing Devak back to his feet. "I've seen vamps drink demon blood before. Makes them get all crazy. I'm not sure why it's important the demons don't report back who you are. Do you know?"

Devak growled a warning and Hiroto backed away.

Matthew gripped his guardian's shoulder to steady him, and said, "We might have a four-hour truce, little fox, but we're not on the same side here. I half expect you to try and stab me during the fight."

Hiroto narrowed his eyes, he was no doubt frowning under his red mask. "The High General's word is law right now. The truce will hold and none of us will break it. I'm not so sure about the vampires."

"Don't worry about us. We'll do what General Bryson says."

"I hope so. Fight well, Matthew," Hiroto said then teleported away to join up with the Argonauts, who would be taking point for the hunters.

Still holding onto Devak's shoulder, Matthew squeezed it. "Alright, no demon blood, and I planned to kill all the demons anyway."

"Me too. And I am excellent at it. I'll serve you well this night, my prince." Devak's chest puffed out with pride. He looked down at Matthew's hand on his shoulder and smiled, thrilled that he was being touched.

"I have no doubt," Matthew said. Part of him wanted to kiss him right then but he was still confused...and mad at him...and Tarrick was nearby...and everyone would see. Matthew was still a little shy in front of a big audience.

"Let's go," Tarrick called the order. Green flashes filled the area as hunters teleported north.

Matthew let his vampire out and surged forward. Above him, a handful of hunters used chains to move from tree to tree, propelling themselves forward with the skill of aerial acrobats.

The only vampires on the ground right now were Stolus, Bryson, and Matthew. The rest were lords who could fly in some fashion and would come down when they needed to relay orders. The incubi were in the air as well. Every now and then, through the canopy, Matthew would catch a glimpse of Tarrick or Devak flying. They looked awesome.

Matthew really wished he had wings as well. Maybe after this was done, he'd ask Devak if he could fly him around...just so he could see what it was like. Gah, he was being a child right now.

He moved up to Silva to keep pace with her. She rolled her eyes and teleported forward but he was already there when she materialized on top of a moss-covered log. Her hand dropped to a stake. Matthew planted a kiss on her cheek, then winked and sped away before she could react.

The terrain went uphill. The trees thinned and shorter bushes covered the area.

Then—through the rain and foliage—he saw the black portal hanging in the air.

He watched as the portal expanded to nearly the size of a house and dark, twisted creatures burst through. The demons crawled out of the portal at a frightening speed, covering the jungle in a sea of obsidian. Above them, winged monsters took to the air.

Matthew surged ahead of everyone, brought up his sword, and crashed into the mass of demons.

Thirty-Two

Bodies smashed against the wave of grotesque creatures. Bolts buzzed, weapons tore into flesh, and green runic magic sizzled the air.

Hunters flanked the sides, picking off any demons that they could separate from the swarm. Flyers were struck down by the incubi or vampire lords.

Stolus and Bryson took up positions beside Matthew. In the air, Matthew noticed Ascelina keeping an eye on her son as she ripped demons apart. He wondered what it would be like for her if Stolus died. Was their bond as strong as his was with Samantha? Stolus was almost old enough to leave her and go off on his own.

Fighting demons was different than fighting vampires or incubi. As far as Matthew could tell, the swarm that was coming through the portal was full of low level, cannon fodder. The demons weren't exactly pushovers, but they weren't nearly as terrifying as everyone made them out to be.

Although not too strong, they were fast suckers depending on their structure. Unlike the demons that came out of the portal in Chicago, many of these demons weren't humanoid. Some were on four legs, some on six, others were like demonic millipedes, grotesque and twisted. Just looking at them made Matthew's skin crawl. He had no idea why these ones looked so different from the ones he had seen before.

And the sounds they made…clicking and screeching; it was unnerving.

A four-legged demon holding a crude spear charged at Matthew. Black saliva oozed out of its mouth like crude oil as it snarled, showing off rows of jagged sharp teeth. Matthew blocked with his bracer and countered by driving his sword into its chest. The demon's black body was hard, like a carapace, and Matthew thoroughly enjoyed the tearing sound it made as he sliced it in half.

He killed another demon by driving his sword into its eye and cutting upwards. Two dead demons became fourteen as he worked through them. These were far easier to kill than he had expected.

The Argonauts teleported nearby and helped cut a path through the sea of fiends.

"Don't get cocky," Hiroto said as he severed the back of a demon's legs. Matthew finished it off as it toppled over. "These are just Pit bugs. Vermin. They're sent to demoralize and weaken defenses. The real challenge will be coming soon."

Matthew watched as a demon 'bug' grabbed a hunter in its pinchers and cut the human in half. Matthew's fangs itched as the smell of blood filled the air. He pushed forward, punching a demon with his free hand and following up with a slash to its torso.

The group made it to the barrier that prevented them from getting closer to the portal. The hunters set up explosive charges around the runes. Matthew wondered *why* they had explosives on hand...

"Clear the area around the portal," Tarrick ordered. He was currently flying at the back of the battle, issuing commands to various groups and keeping an eye on the other portals.

Matthew could feel more demons pouring through. There must have been hundreds filling the jungle around them. With the loud detonation of charges, the spell was broken.

Devak swooped down out of the sky and landed next to the portal. He smashed a demon with his maul as it came out, then sank his fingers into the hole hanging in the air. It began to shrink.

Before he was able to finish closing the portal, a large demon backhanded Devak across his chest, knocking him away. Gwenyth and Tarquin dove in to assist.

Matthew had never seen Gwenyth fight before. She was fast—faster than him—and she didn't bother with a weapon, ripping apart demons with her claws. Their black blood coated her. It was brutal.

At her side, using a longsword and shield, Tarquin bashed and sliced his way through the demonic bugs with ease.

Devak flew back to the portal and finished closing it.

That was one down. The order went out to move to the next portal, leaving the vermin behind for a later cleanup.

Over the sound of rain and battle, Matthew heard casualty reports. Four hunters dead, five wounded, and one incubus grounded from injuries. Not too bad.

Matthew started running to the next portal but before he could get close, demons came flowing around the trees. Claws, blades, and fangs flashed as the battle group cut down the demonic bugs and pushed into the actual demon soldiers.

Now Matthew could see what it was everyone feared. The 'real' demons were huge, armed, and had skin that was as thick as armor. Most had wings, which was an issue because they only had twenty-two vampires and incubi in the air.

As he fought, Matthew's right arm began to ache. Or maybe it had been hurting for a while and he just hadn't noticed. But whatever the case, it felt as if something below the skin was shifting his blood around.

He scratched at the bracer he had on and tried to heal whatever wound this was but there was no change. The constant, dull throbbing wouldn't go away, but he did his best to ignore it for now and resolved to ask Devak about it after the battle.

Beside him, hunters were shooting chains up at the flying demons to pull them down for a kill. One hunter, desperately clinging to a chain, went flying past Matthew. Matthew jumped up and grabbed the chain, yanking the demon down, sending all three of them toppling to the ground. The hunter teleported away at the last moment, leaving Matthew in a mess of silver chains with a demon—his sword lost and his skin burning away at each place the chain touched.

Matthew roared and pushed power into healing, doing his best to ignore the burning, but silver would drain him fast. He raked his claws along the demon's face, forcing it to close its black eyes. It blindly clawed right back at Matthew's much softer and fleshy skin.

The demon cut Matthew's jugular and, because he had fed today, his blood sprayed the trees like a damn hose. Matthew poured power into his strength and punched the demon in its ugly, scarred face. It didn't do much more than stun him for a moment.

But that's all it took for Silva to appear behind the demon and drive her sword through its neck, up into its brain. It fell limp. Matthew began to try and claw off the chain that was wrapped around him but he was only making it worse.

"Stop moving," Silva said.

Matthew stilled as she unwrapped him. "How'd you manage this?" she asked.

"Trying to save one of your hunters."

"Well, I'm not getting you another set of gloves. That ship has sailed," she said and finished freeing him.

Matthew smiled as he forced his wounds to close. He'd have to be careful using his power since there wasn't any fresh, non-poisoned blood for him. Unless he started drinking the incubi, but he had a feeling they might take issue with that.

"Watch out!" someone yelled from nearby.

Bryson appeared beside Silva and knocked her out of the way. For his effort, a spear went flying into his chest.

Matthew yanked the spear out of the general and rejoined the fighting, keeping the weapon. Behind him, he could hear Bryson asking if Silva was okay. And her blowing him off.

But not even a few minutes later Matthew watched as the two of them leaped out of a tree and took down a demon together, fighting as if they were one. As if thirty-three years of being apart were nothing.

A vampire general and a vampire hunter commander...lovers that could never be. Matthew felt bad for them.

He tore himself away from watching them and thrust his newly acquired spear into a perverse looking demon that had legs of a bull and six tits. The demon broke the spear in two and charged with massive horns forward. Matthew leaped up into a tree only to be knocked out of it when the bull-demon-six-boob-thing hit the trunk with the top of its head.

It began to charge again. Matthew scrambled to his feet and ran out of the way. He cussed. He wasn't sure where their weak spots were and he needed a weapon besides his claws. Having armor beyond just bracers would be nice too...

A bright light flashed in the sky. Matthew covered his eyes and felt dozens of demons dying all at once.

What the hell was that?

He didn't have any time to figure it out as the demon came at him again. Guess it was time to try something he had been putting off. He grappled the demon by the horns and held its head still. The demon sliced into his abdomen but Matthew ignored it.

"Stop attacking me and kill other demons," Matthew said, trying to compel it.

It stopped. Actually, that was far easier than he thought it would be. Maybe demons didn't have all that great of will power? They didn't seem particularly intelligent.

That meant Matthew could compel more. He released the demon and it charged off. Matthew rested on a rock and focused on sealing his wounds. He licked the small cuts on his arms to help the healing along.

The rain abruptly stopped.

"I've been told that you are a skilled warrior, but every time I've come to face you, you've run off," an even voice said above him.

Standing over him was Imperator Prescott, fully armored and face covered by his horned helmet as always. Dark demon blood dripped off the golden blade of his longsword.

"I run because you bring a team of bad-asses with you and you wear armor that makes you invincible. Even I know my limits." Matthew licked a wound on his forearm.

"I don't think you do. Were I without my armor, or my team, you still would not stand a chance. Your technique is novice at best and your tactics are amateurish. Luck has kept you alive more times than not, and you will eventually run out of it."

"Did you just come over here to shit talk?" Matthew asked and stood up. His healing wounds itched like crazy.

"No. When you abducted our High Lord General all of my other responsibilities were pushed to someone else. Capturing you is now my top priority. I thought it only fair to give you a warning. Even the guardian that calls you 'prince' will not be able to save you from me."

"I won't be as easy to bring in as you think."

A single "humph" came from under the helmet. "I hope you're right. I look forward to the challenge." Prescott held out his free hand and a longsword appeared in it with a green flash. He flipped it over and held the hilt out to Matthew. "Don't lose this one, I won't give you another."

Matthew cautiously took the longsword and Prescott teleported back to the battle.

As Matthew went to rejoin the fight he saw Tarrick go shooting across the night sky and land not far off from him. Matthew changed course to see what was going on.

He smelled Tane's blood as he neared and a demon went flying into a tree next to him, its head bashed in, thick purplish blood oozing out of it.

Tane lay on the muddy ground, belly up and badly wounded; his arm and neck were mangled, blood pouring out, and his wings were crushed. His heartbeat was slowing.

The demon that had injured him was on the ground—bludgeoned to death. Tarrick stood over his son, protecting him, and swinging his kanabō into another demon, its chest caving in with a nauseating *thuck*.

Matthew's breath hitched as he watched Tarrick fight. Under his thick iridescent armor was a wall of muscle that transferred immense strength into each of his weapon swings. He wielded the kanabō like it was an extension of his own arm.

Having been on the receiving end of that weapon, Matthew knew just how painful getting hit by it was. How easily it shattered bone and devastated the body. The memory of it crushing him caused his skin to go numb with fear.

That is until he sensed more than a dozen demons heading their way, maybe picking up the scent of incubus blood. Matthew singled out one and compelled it to fight for him, then took care of two more while Tarrick beat back any that came near Tane.

Matthew backed up next to Tarrick as more demons advanced.

"You run, I'll fly him out of here," Tarrick said.

"He'll die, his heart's too slow."

Tarrick growled in frustration.

Matthew swung at a demon to force it to back off. "What do you have Devak doing right now?"

"He needs to close this portal before the pit commander gets through."

Above them, the sky burned with a bright golden light and the source of the light shot into the area like a comet. A wave of force slammed all of the nearby demons backwards. They went tumbling through the air and didn't stand back up once they fell to the ground.

The light faded and when Matthew's eyes adjusted Devak was

standing beside them. "I heard my name," he said. He looked exhausted.

"What the hell was that?" Matthew asked. He'd never seen anything like that before.

"It is…" Devak fell silent, the curse tying his tongue.

"He was channeling his god's energy," Tarrick explained "Which you should stop doing, blood guardian, since it's obviously weakening you and you are the only one we have that can close the portals. Unless you can close them, Matthew."

Matthew shrugged. "Probably. I was able to expand the one in Chicago."

"We'll test it only if the guardian dies." Tarrick pointed down at Tane. "Heal my son."

Matthew looked to Tarrick, then Tane, then Tarrick again. "Are you kidding me? I'm not kissing Tane."

"It wasn't a request, Matthew. Heal him."

Matthew growled.

"I can heal him," Devak offered.

"No, go close the portal," Tarrick ordered.

Devak looked to Matthew. Matthew sighed. "Do what he says, close the portal."

Devak nodded and flew away.

Matthew scowled. "I'm not touching his dick if he needs more."

"You will if I order you to."

Matthew grumbled. He didn't care what Tarrick said, he was not touching Tane's cock for any reason. This was bad enough. He kneeled down next to Tane, who was falling in and out of consciousness. He leaned in and squashed down the urge to vomit as he pressed his lips to the dying incubus.

He forced golden threads of energy up from his soavik, through the kiss, and into Tane. Tane was slow to respond but eventually his lips began to move. He wrapped his arms around Matthew, holding him in place and his kiss became aggressive. Tane's wounds closed and his wings formed back into their normal shape as he sucked energy out of Matthew. Matthew, for his part, let it happen.

Tane's eyes fluttered, then they snapped wide when he saw who it was in his arms. He pushed Matthew away from him and scrambled backwards.

"*What the fuck?*"

"It wasn't my choice either." Matthew looked over at Tarrick who was still slaughtering demons.

Tane wiped his mouth and stood up. "Disgusting. Never do that again."

"Believe me, next time I'll be happy to let you die. And if it makes you feel better, I'll be in crippling pain from my soavik being damn near empty for the rest of this battle."

"Yes. That does make me feel a bit better." Tane grabbed his claymore from off the ground and took to the air.

Matthew heard reports that the second portal was closed, followed by reports of casualties. "Did you hear those updates?" he asked Tarrick, who was fending off a demon. The demon sliced him across his armored torso. Tarrick grabbed the demon's arm and yanked it into him while kicking the demon in the ribs with his huge hoof. He finished it off with a kanabō swing to its neck.

"No. Repeat them."

"Portal two is closed, three vampires down, Ascelina lost her arm, one of the Argonauts fell, also another seven hunters are dead, and two incubi. Fuck, Vassu is reporting that Dennith is badly injured." Their band of sixty-two warriors was now forty-five, and seven were reported injured, leaving just thirty-eight that could fight.

Tarrick deliberated for a moment. "How many demons do you sense nearby?"

Matthew closed his eyes and did a quick estimate. "Just over two hundred coming at us from the direction of the remaining portal and fiftyish around the one we just closed. And I'm sensing lots of those bug things scattered around the jungle. It's hard to pinpoint a number."

"And the remaining pit commander?"

"It's almost through. And I can feel…more commanders on the other side. It feels like they are waiting on something. Does that make sense?"

"Yeah. Let me tell you what is about to happen. That pit commander is going to break through and with him, he'll be bringing his elite demons: deathguards, bodyjumpers, stalkers, terrorbelchers that are bred to level whole cities, the list goes on and on…they're the intelligent demons, not like ones we've been fighting. Pit commanders will open more and more portals. It'll be a snowball effect that's near impossible to contain."

"Okay…why are you telling me this? Not that I don't appreciate learning about it."

"Whatever you did during the masquerade attack, I need you to do it again. I need you to be unstoppable and kill the demons for me."

Matthew rubbed at his still aching arm. "It's not like that. I can't just turn it on and off." Samantha did say that he was going to wish she was here. As much as he was relieved she was nowhere near this place, it would make things much easier if he thought she was threatened.

Tarrick swung his weapon over his shoulder, resting it on a pauldron. "If you can't find a way to get to that place again, then you were correct: we're seriously fucked right now."

Thirty-Three

Tarrick ordered everyone to fall back to a clearing. It only took a few moments for the group to collapse in together.

An oppressive wave of heat rolled through the area and the rain began to fall again. The pit commander had broken through. Matthew climbed to the top of a tree to take a look at it. Even from a far distance, it was hard to miss. The colossal demon was easily seven or eight stories tall. The trees in its path fell as it lumbered towards them on four hooved legs. Its torso curved upwards like a demonic centaur, and in its hand it held a massive spiked mace.

The demon had long jagged tusks and enormous horns protruded from its head. A strip of fire ran down its spine to the end of its long tail, burning like superheated lava. The rain did nothing to douse the flames.

Expansive frayed wings stretched out behind it as it pointed forward with its weapon, directing the other demons. From the portal, waves of flying demons poured through. Big fuckers with armor and huge weapons. Groups of them flew together in tight formations.

Below him, Matthew heard Tarrick and Bryson talking.

"We can't fight it, not with what we have," Bryson said.

"We have little choice," Tarrick said.

"Maybe we could outrun it." Bryson pointed in the direction opposite the demonic force. "Maybe get a message through to call for reinforcements. Or we fight, die, and the whole damn planet will know soon enough."

The flying demons were nearly on them. They were out of time.

Matthew dropped down out of the tree, landing in a crouch on the muddy ground. Around him, the injured humans were drinking their vials of vampire blood to heal. One was actually getting blood directly from a vampire, which surprised the shit out of Matthew. He expected the vampires to keep on one side of the area and the incubi forces on the other, but it seemed the life and death situation had brought them together. For now, anyway.

Dennith was in her human form, cradled in Vassu's massive arm. She was alive but covered in wounds. Matthew could hear her broken bones scraping together each time she moved. Vassu was giving her vampire blood as well since they didn't have time for sex right now. The blood wasn't as effective on incubi as on humans but it should keep her stable.

Ascelina's arm was missing from the elbow. It wasn't bleeding and she showed no signs of being in pain. She looked annoyed at its loss more than anything else. She kept close to Stolus whose skin was webbed with wounds.

Anyone fit enough to fight formed a tight perimeter, killing any demons that came close, but their side was slowing. Nearly everyone had injuries of some sort and they all looked worn.

"Incoming," a hunter yelled.

Before Tarrick had time to issue any new orders the first wave of flying demons broke through the treetop canopy and dove at the group.

Three of them crashed against a wall of golden light and incinerated on impact. The remaining demons flapped their wings furiously and veered off before hitting the shield.

On the ground, Devak was kneeling in the center of their group, eyes closed and head lowered. He held his maul against the ground and his body was glowing, his blood wings floating long behind him, twisting in the air.

Centered on him and expanding outwards were radiant golden lines. They formed a circle around the group, creating the shield, protecting them.

Another wave of demons attacked and again they were consumed by the barrier, dying with painful screams. Devak strained, gripping the handle of his maul tight, his teeth clenched.

"How long do you think he can keep that up?" Bryson asked no one in particular.

Hiroto pushed down his red mask and hopped down out of a tree. "I'm not sure, I didn't think blood guardians had this ability. My guess is a few more waves."

Matthew walked to the edge of the shield and looked in the direction of the pit commander. He couldn't see it through the dense foliage but the ground shook with each step the monstrous creature took.

There was no way they were going to be able to outrun these demons. They had no idea where the nearest civilization even was, and when the sun rose the vampires would be forced to sink into the earth, where the demons would no doubt dig them up or lie in wait until nightfall.

The demons were going to kill the people he cared about. People he loved.

A deep guttural sound of frustration came from Matthew.

He needed power. He needed to lose control again, no matter how terrified he was of it. But he had no idea how to access that invincible monster that lurked deep within him.

But if he did nothing they were all dead.

Matthew closed his eyes and focused.

He tried to let go but nothing happened. He let his rage come to the front of his mind, and still nothing. He imagined Devak and Tarrick dying by demon blades, and while the idea brought him great pain, he didn't lose control.

This wasn't going to work.

Prescott was right, he was a novice that survived off luck. Many of the creatures around him had centuries of experience. What was he compared to them? A child playing with power he barely understood.

He wished his sire had taught him how to use his abilities. Or given him anything other than a life that was all but guaranteed to be full of torment.

Matthew's right arm flared with pain.

The pain.

Since the night the Blood God came to him, his arm had been burning every fight he had been in. There's no way it was a coincidence.

He focused within himself. He could feel *something* inside, entangled around the bone, merged with his blood. Part of him. It called to him, begging for release.

Accept me. A dark voice said. It wasn't his sire's voice; it was something else.

Matthew ripped the bracer off his right arm and tossed it to the ground.

"No, my prince," Devak cried out. "It's a curse, not a gift. Once you take it, you will carry the burden for all eternity. Refuse it." Devak howled in pain as he struggled to keep the shield up as another group of kamikaze demons threw themselves against the golden light.

Accept me. The voice said again.

Matthew opened his eyes, his back was to the group as they all watched him. He looked down at his arm. Blood flowed from cuts that had scored themselves across the skin of his right arm. The blood pooled at his hand, defying gravity; not a single drop fell to the ground.

"Is he a Sanguine Dominar?" Vassu asked.

Devak strained and managed a, "No."

"I've never seen this before," Prescott said.

Tarrick took a step forward. "Matthew…"

Matthew grunted as the pain increased and blood poured out of him, pooling in his hand. It was waiting for him.

Behind him, Devak screamed, unable to hold the shield against the waves of flying monsters pelting it. The shield dissipated and he passed out from the strain.

Fury swelled inside of Matthew. He tilted his head to the heavens and yelled, "I accept."

The world around him melted away and time stood still.

Deep red tattoos made of blood appeared under the bleeding cuts, glowing bright, and patterned like the tendrils of Devak's wings; twisting and coiling from his fingers up to his shoulder.

The blood formed into the shape of a large double-headed battleaxe, and became solid in his hand. It changed color to a dark grey metal. In the center of the two sharp blades was a skull with fangs and horns twisting out from it. Blood continually poured out of the mouth and empty eye sockets of the skull.

And there was more to this gift.

Matthew's body began to change. His fangs and claws grew longer, his eyes burned, and his muscles bulged like braided rope, nearly breaking through the skin. Power surged within him. The urge to fight and kill overwhelmed him.

Time returned to him as demons poured down from the sky.

He released his aura and let out a terrifying roar.

The demons turned their focus to him. Good. Matthew couldn't fly, but once they dropped below the tree line they were *his*. Matthew sprung into the air and swung his battleaxe into the closest demon.

The demon let out a high-pitched wail the moment the axe touched him and sliced through its body. Its solid black eyes flickered with a red light and the screaming stopped. As the two halves of the demon's body fell to the ground a black smoke rose from its exposed innards.

More. Give me more. The dark voice whispered to him.

Matthew smiled, happy to oblige. He hit the ground and leaped back up, killing another demon in the same fashion. And then another and another.

He didn't register the fighting around him. Bolts whizzed by towards the demons and Matthew's only thought was that he hoped the demons would live so that he could be the one to deal the final blow.

And with each kill, power rushed into Matthew's arm, making him stronger. Stronger than he had ever felt before, the axe was feeding on the blood…and it was power he could access.

The tattoos spread up his shoulder and neck, burning its way through his skin.

The weapon hummed with pleasure. It was part of him now, as much as his claws or eyes or fangs.

Wave after wave of demons fell before him. The bodies of his foes were in pieces.

When there was a break in the fighting, he landed back on the ground and looked at the axe in his hand.

More.

Greedy fucker.

More.

There's plenty more.

"Matthew—" Tarrick's voice tore his attention away from the axe.

Matthew turned and faced the group: hunters, incubi, vampires, all staring at him. Devak was kneeling on the ground, half-conscious. He was trying to hide his exhaustion the best he could but his eyes kept falling shut. He was probably ashamed by his condition, but the guardian had already closed two portals and taken out more demons than anyone else. There wasn't anything for him to be ashamed of.

"Holy shit," Bryson gasped.

"His eyes—" a hunter said.

Matthew didn't need to see them to know they were completely red...just like Devak's; just like his sire's. His tattoos burned and the axe was eager to kill again.

"I'm going to go close that portal." Matthew's voice sounded rougher than normal.

"My prince—" Devak said with great effort, "—let me..."

That wasn't happening; he couldn't even stand.

A new wave of demons approached. They had run out of time.

"I'm going to go close the portal," Matthew repeated, "then I'm going to go kill that pit commander."

He rushed out of the area, not waiting to hear the objections.

Thirty-Four

M atthew ran past the demonic foot soldiers and avoided the ones flying in the air.

He cut down any demons that stood in his way, the axe fueling him, making him stronger with each kill. And faster. He ran up a hillside then scaled a tree to survey the area.

The pit commander had left a trail of destruction in its wake. No trees or animals had survived and parts of the jungle had caught fire, despite the rain.

Far behind the gigantic demon was the black swirling portal. It stretched from the ground to high in the air, hundreds of feet tall now. Demons were pouring through. And beyond the portal he could hear thousands more, eager to join the fight.

Even if Matthew took down the massive creature, they'd have to contend with that mess after. Damn it. It'd be nice to catch a break.

He pushed power into his speed, moving faster than he had ever run before. The demons didn't even notice him as he ran by, that is until he stopped in front of the portal. There were hundreds there.

The demons closest to him charged. The first that came close lost its arm, the next its head, and the third's body was split in half.

This axe was damn formidable. So long as he was killing, he had near-endless amounts of energy. The power stored in Matthew's blood pouches went unused as he tapped into what the axe was giving him.

A demon sliced him across the back while another pierced his lungs with a spear. His wounds healed in the blink of an eye. Around him, bodies piled up and their thick black blood stained the ground.

Unsatisfied, he needed more. A group of demons emerged from the portal and Matthew jumped into the middle of them, slaying them before they even had a chance to gather their surroundings.

More. The dark voice whispered to him.

Yeah. Working on it.

Wait.

He was here for a reason.

Ah, that's right. The portal. He had come to close it.

Feed me.

The red tattoos expanded, creeping across his chest. And as they grew, Matthew felt his will failing him. The weapon was taking over and wanted him to think of nothing but blood and death.

Devak had warned him that it was a curse, not a gift. And now Matthew could see why—he was no longer wielding the axe: *it was wielding him.*

As Matthew fought for control, more demons fell upon his weapon.

"No. I am your master, not your slave. Obey me," Matthew said to it.

The axe sunk deep into the gut of a nasty looking demon. Matthew grinned as it fell to the ground before him, feeding him more energy. Then he scowled upon realizing that the axe's control over him hadn't diminished.

Fuck this. He wasn't going to be a slave to anyone—or anything—ever again. He tossed the axe away, sending it flying far across the jungle battlefield. In the air it turned back into blood and fell to the ground, soaking into the earth.

Pain flared across his body and the tattoos split open again. Blood dripped back down to his hand and reformed into the metal battleaxe.

"You've got to be kidding me," he said as he killed another demon. "Alright, fine. Obey me or I'll cut my arm off."

The threat had the opposite effect. Instead of giving him control, he kept killing and the tattoos slithered down his abs, towards his legs. He was going to be furious if they wrapped around his junk. The idea of them searing him in such a sensitive area sent him into a panic.

Matthew picked up one of the many demon swords that littered the ground around him. He brought it up, ready to dismember himself. It'd hurt, no doubt, but at least he'd be in control again.

The tattoos retreated, shrinking back to only his right arm, and blind thirst to murder everything died down. It wasn't gone entirely but Matthew always felt that way during a fight, axe or no. At least he could think straight again.

He held the axe up and glared at it. "Good. Behave yourself." Blood continued to drip from the skull in the center but it said nothing to him. Maybe it was throwing a fit.

Back in control, Matthew cut a path to the portal. He could feel immense power on the other side of it. He touched the black swirling mass and focused on closing it.

Demons pushed in on his position to stop him. Vassu, Gwenyth, and Vikentiy showed up, landing beside him.

"We have your back, close portal," Vikentiy said while Vassu and Gwenyth tore into the demons. The three of them kept the horde back and bought him the time he needed to collapse the portal. It shrank into nothing and was gone.

Around them, there were still hundreds of demon's left. Three more hunters were dead, two more vampires, and he watched as the pit commander grabbed an incubus from the air and crush it in his hand.

His temporary bodyguards took to the sky as demons began to overrun their position. Matthew pushed power into his speed and ran at the pit commander, following the line of fallen trees and ash. He stopped before it and gripped his axe tight.

The behemoth looked down at him.

"Do you think you can stop me, puny creature?" Its echoing voice boomed across the jungle.

"I'm going to try," Matthew said.

It...smiled? What it did with its lips looked kind of like a smile. It was hard to tell with the black drool and thick tusks.

"Closing the portal was a futile labor. I will open many more and unmake this world as I have countless others."

"That's not what's going to happen." Matthew charged at it. His plan was to hamstring its back leg to slow it, then climb up the fucker, run up its back, and sink his axe into its spine. No matter its size, that should disable it.

He didn't get the chance. The pit commander swung its spiked mace. The 'spikes' looked more like crude black nails coming out of it, except those 'nails' were as long as a man.

Matthew changed his path, trying to dodge out of the way, only to be slapped by the pit commander's empty hand and launched into the air.

The pit commander brought his mace upwards and impaled Matthew through his back, piercing his lower abdomen. The thick metal spike was nearly a foot in diameter.

Skewered, blood poured from his body.

Using the power from the axe, he swung at the spike, trying to cut it down so he could pull himself off. But it was an awkward angle and he couldn't build enough momentum to cut through it.

The pit commander brought his weapon up to his face so that he could look at Matthew. Its molten breath smelled like rotting eggs.

"We are unsealed," it said.

He plucked Matthew off the spike and held him, the giant hand engulfed his body.

Matthew tried to move but the bottom half of his body wouldn't budge. It dawned on him that his lower spinal cord was no longer there.

The demon crushed him in his hand, breaking nearly all his bones, then threw Matthew the seventy feet or so to the ground. Matthew hit hard and bounced, landing on his back. The force ripped the axe from his hand and it melted into a spray of blood. A replacement axe didn't appear. He didn't have the blood left to reform it and he no longer had any blood pouches, only a hole in his stomach where they should be.

An enormous hoof came down on him and crushed his body into the mud, breaking him in new places. Then the pit commander continued onwards, leaving Matthew behind to die.

Matthew's nose was broken, along with his jaw, and he was pretty sure his skull was fractured in several places. And that was just his head. His legs were bent the wrong way; he could feel ribs sticking out of his skin but couldn't turn his head down to look. A small blessing.

Having no way to heal this, he was trapped, dying, in the mud. Hell, he should be dead already—damage this severe normally would kill a vampire, no matter the age.

The clouds above him thundered and the rain picked up. Black pushed in at the edges of his vision. It wouldn't be long before a demon came along and finished him off.

Between the waves of pain, Matthew laughed at himself. Maybe, *just maybe*, going after the pit commander alone wasn't his best idea ever.

He thought of Samantha. God, he didn't want to leave her behind. What would happen to her if none of them returned? She was smart and had survived on her own before. She could again. That gave him some comfort.

Lightning arced the sky and more thunder shook the area.

The raindrops turned warm. A fat drop of rain hit Matthew square in the eye, blurring everything with a red tint.

Strange. Rain isn't normally red. Drops fell into his mouth.

It wasn't water…it was blood.

Blood was falling everywhere. The few trees in Matthew's field of view began to turn red as the sanguine liquid coated them.

Then he saw Devak, fully armored and wings long, descend from the clouds. But he had a black sword in his hand, not his maul. And then a second Devak appeared from out of the clouds. And a third. And a forth.

What?

That made no sense.

He must have more damage to his brain than he thought.

But…

Holy shit, he thought as it dawned on him—they were blood guardians.

And not just four…more dropped out of the clouds…there were twenty…thirty, no, fifty, no, more. Matthew lost count.

The first landed near Matthew. He was huge—his armor thick and black with red runes, his wings double the size of Devak's, his sword enormous. Dark horns twisted out of the top of his head. He looked as if he was their leader. He stood over Matthew, his all-red eyes judging. The blood rain slicked his pale skin.

"My prince," he said in a harsh, mocking, tone. His mouth full of fangs.

He raised his sword then disappeared from view.

As Matthew lost consciousness, he could hear the demons dying around him.

It was a beautiful sound.

****

Blood filled Matthew's mouth. It was strong. And the drugged out, erotic feeling told him it was from an incubus.

Instinct took over and he sunk his fangs into the flesh pressed against his lips. Matthew couldn't feel his blood pouches or his soavik. Why were they missing? He couldn't remember.

And he couldn't move, couldn't hear, or see, or smell. But the blood helped push away some of the pain. He focused on healing his jaw, neck, and ears.

"That's enough, Matthew." It was Tarrick. His voice commanding but not harsh.

The wrist—Tarrick's wrist—was ripped out of his mouth.

"Thank you, Master," Matthew whispered, his voice rough. He still couldn't see but at least he could speak and hear.

"Matthew—"

"Hm?"

"You aren't in my prison right now."

"You didn't do this to me?" Matthew was confused. Hadn't Tarrick beat the shit out of him? Wasn't this a punishment?

Tarrick answered with a pained, "No." He touched Matthew's chest and his anxiety floated away as the incubus flooded him with pleasure. It was a kindness.

"Oh yeah," said Matthew as the events came back to him, but his brain wasn't firing quite right yet. "I escaped from you. I remember now. Demons. Are they dead? Or are we?"

"They're dead."

"And the angels?" he asked. "They looked glorious falling from the sky."

"The guardians are gone. Are you able to see?" Tarrick asked softly. At least the sun hadn't risen yet, so there was still a truce. Tarrick wouldn't hurt him.

"No. Can't move either."

"Don't try. General Bryson is going to take you home."

Home. To Sam. With Devak.

"I'm standing right here, Matthew," Bryson said. "We'll get you healed once we're away from here, we had to stabilize you first."

"The angels...did you see them, Tarrick? My father sent them."

"That's impossible. If Matthew is a demigod, the Judge would have come for him," a different voice said. It took Matthew a moment to recognize it as Hiroto's.

"The Blood God is his sire?" someone asked. Matthew wasn't sure who. There were other comments of astonishment.

Matthew swallowed hard a few times, trying to wet his throat. "Have you ever met a god, Tarrick?"

"I can't say I have."

"Even you would tremble."

"Lord General—" Silva's voice interrupted, "—the vampires' witches just arrived. Ours will be here in two."

"Devak?" Matthew asked, more memories returning to him. No one answered. He grew distressed when he couldn't sense him close by. He wanted Devak. Needed him. "Where's my guardian?"

Strong hands wrapped around Matthew and lifted him up. "We will tell you when we are away from the incubi," Vikentiy said, his Russian accent thick as ever. "Rest easy, the good witches have come to take us home."

Matthew wasn't sure what happened next. He was in and out of it. They must have teleported back to some bunker because the next thing he knew Samantha was curled up on his chest. He couldn't see her but he could feel her. Having her close brought him comfort.

He could feel warm blood flowing into his arm. An IV drip. He relished the feeling of Samantha for a bit before fatigue overcame him.

"You didn't use the umbrella," she said right before he fell asleep.

Thirty-Five

Fractured pieces of the world returned to Matthew at a sluggish pace. There was something heavy pressing down on his feet. Friendly voices, low and muffled, were nearby. The delicate aroma of parchment and vanilla mixed with sweet wine and fragrant oil drifted across his nose.

A warm feeling spread across his chest as blood filled him, coming in from an IV attached to his arm. He ached but it wasn't unbearable. Whatever he was lying on was soft and plush.

Matthew focused on his body. A single blood pouch had healed, the rest in various states of repair. Typical. His soavik was back, though empty and aching. All good signs.

He risked opening his eyes, keeping it slow because his eyelids felt as if they weighed a thousand pounds each. The lights in the room were dim and it took a moment for his eyes to focus on anything.

He looked down. A thin sheet covered his hips and stopped there. His right arm was still covered in swirling tattoos but they were black in color. He flexed his hands and was thrilled when they both worked.

He tried to move his feet but couldn't. Jet, who weighed a ton even in his dog form, was lying on top of Matthew's legs. He raised his head and whimpered.

"I'm okay, boy," Matthew said, his voice hoarse.

Jet's tail thumped against the sheet.

"Father!" Samantha said and leaped at him. She hit the king-sized bed and planted herself on his chest, her arms wrapped around him.

Matthew held her against him. "My daughter."

Vikentiy came to stand beside the bed. "How do you feel?"

"Better," Matthew said. "How long since the battle?"

"Two weeks."

Damn. "Where are we?"

"Washington bunker," Samantha muttered into his chest.

"Do you want human?" asked the Russian. "I can have one brought in."

"Maybe in a few hours when I can move a little more. Can you turn up the IV drip?"

Vikentiy increased the flow of blood for him. "Need anything? I can acquire whatever you desire."

"I'm good. Just give me another night to rest, then I'll be up."

Vikentiy nodded and stood silent, but he looked as if he wanted to say more. Matthew looked around the room. There was a table set up with cards on it; it seemed the Russian and Samantha were in the middle of a game. Devak wasn't in the room, but judging by his scent he was standing guard outside the door.

"How should we address you?" Vikentiy finally asked.

Samantha groaned. "I already told you, he's not going to like that question."

Matthew's eyebrows knitted. "What do you mean 'address'?"

Samantha slipped out of his arms and sat up on the bed next to him. "He's going to be mad."

"You are son of Blood God. The—"

"Don't say it," Samantha warned.

"—prince."

Matthew rolled his eyes and pressed his head back into the soft pillow. "Fucking hell."

Samantha wagged a finger at Vikentiy. "I told you."

"Matthew. Call me Matthew. And if anyone other than Devak tries this 'my prince' bullshit I'll rip their tongue out."

"Okay, Matthew." Vikentiy took out a phone and set it on the nightstand. "I will let others know you'll be up tomorrow night. Call if you need anything, number is in there. I will give privacy." He paused. It looked like he was going to bow, then decided against it, and instead said something in Russian to Samantha.

And she responded to him. He smiled and left the room.

"You speak Russian?" Matthew asked.

"He's been teaching me. My memory is nearly perfect since becoming a vampire, so it's easy. I can teach you if you want."

Learning other languages hadn't really been a priority for him; incubi all knew English because the High King lived in New York. But most of them spoke quite a few other languages as well.

Samantha sat in silence for a few moments. "This room is warded.

No one can hear us."

"You look like you have something important to say."

She nodded. "We should forget about Delphi. We should go find a house, and you and me and Devak and Jet should live together. You should finish teaching me how to move dirt around and you should let me watch you hunt so that I can learn. And Devak can get back to training you to fight. We could study all the languages together. We would be happy there."

Matthew took her hand in his. "Have you had a vision? Does something happen in Delphi?"

"Not a vision…a bad feeling. And it scares me. It feels like something is lurking in the shadows, about to change everything."

He wasn't sure what to say to her. He had given Devak his word, and breaking his curse meant getting answers to questions that had plagued him all his life. Who were his parents? What did his sire expect from him?

And he had a billion other questions. Did he have a soul? How did Devak become a guardian? What was Heaven like? What happened to people when they died? How long had Devak been watching over him? Would he ever see Alyssa again? The list was endless.

"We have to go, sweetie. I need these answers. But I promise that I'll do everything in my power to protect you, okay?"

She nodded.

"Be kind to Devak," Samantha said, laying a hand on his chest. "He's been beating himself up these last two weeks. He thinks he's failed you again."

Matthew couldn't see how he failed, Devak had fought hard against the demons. Maybe he blamed himself for Matthew's injuries.

Samantha slipped off the bed and ducked out into the hallway. When she came back, Devak was trailing behind her. He looked terrible. His skin had dark bruises and he was thinner than normal, almost gaunt. Even his clothes looked wrinkled and unkempt.

He fell to his knees as soon as he saw Matthew.

"Christ. You look like shit. Come here and feed," Matthew said.

Devak bowed his head deeper.

"My prince—"

"I don't care what you think you did wrong. Come here and feed for fuck's sake."

"—I was not able to save you," he said.

No, his sire had saved him. By all rights, he should have died. "I didn't expect you to. I made my own foolish choices and paid the price for them. I won't be trying to take on a pit commander alone anytime soon."

"I abandoned you. I ran."

Ah, so that's why he was missing. "Why?"

"I didn't want them to see me. I—" The curse reared its ugly head and pain racked Devak's now fragile body.

Matthew could understand that he didn't want his fellow blood guardian's to see him weakened. Devak was as proud as he was humble even if he tried to hide it.

Matthew pushed himself up to a sitting position. He motioned for Jet to get off the bed, and the dog jumped down. He started to remove his IV when Samantha grabbed his hand.

"Father, what are you doing? You need that to heal."

"If he's not going to come over here and feed I'm going to go to him even if it feels like half my insides are still liquid and I might have to crawl because I'm not sure I can stand."

Devak looked up. "I—"

"If you don't get over here I'll find a happy moment in your future and change it to be a sad one," Samantha said, her eyes narrowed at Devak.

He acquiesced and came to the bed. Matthew scooted over to make room—Samantha on one side, Devak on the other.

The guardian sat down next to him and placed his hands on Matthew's chest. He closed his eyes and began to feed.

"Whose blood have you been feeding on?" Matthew asked Samantha. Being fed on by Devak was alleviating some of his pain.

"I've been drinking bottled blood. It's nasty but I didn't want to kill. Vikentiy offered to let me drink from him but it didn't feel right."

"He seems like a nice guy."

"He's a lot like you, he'll do anything to protect his family, even if it causes him pain." Samantha abruptly jumped off the bed. "I'm going into the next room."

Matthew frowned. "What? Why?"

She pointed to his crotch, the sheet there was propped up. "Because you haven't had sex in over two weeks. Come on, Jet." She was already closing the door to the adjacent room before he could object. Jet plodding along after her.

Devak removed his hands. His bruises were fading but he needed to feed more. "I will go acquire a human for you, or a vampire if you desire. Now that they know who you are, none would turn down the request." His voice was remote, distant. He kept his eyes averted, unwilling to look Matthew in the face.

Matthew didn't want a human or a vampire. What he wanted was sitting right next to him.

Somewhere along the way, he had developed feelings for Devak. They had been there for a while…a slow burn, pulling at his heart the longer they were together. The man served him, warmed his bed, gave his blood, protected him…how could he even think that he could ignore this?

But the answers he got in Delphi might change everything between them and that scared him. He couldn't walk away from this losing another lover. The strings were tightening around his chest and he was sick of fighting them.

"No, Devak. Keep feeding, it feels good. I don't want—"

"I'll get you a vampire, my prince." Devak stood to leave, heading for the door.

"I don't want a vampire."

Devak turned back. "A human then."

"Devak—"

"Male or female?"

"Please—"

"I will bring you one of each."

"Don't—"

"You need to have sex. It'll help you heal. And help you manage your pain."

Matthew let loose a vehement howl. Agony shot through his body and soul.

Devak fell silent.

"What I want is—" Matthew started only to be cut off. *Again.*

"Please don't." Devak went back on his knees. "The rejection would be too painful for me and I don't want to risk being sent away. Please let me get these humans for you. My prince...I beg you."

Matthew closed his eyes and swallowed back a lump that was forming in his throat. He wanted Devak. He wanted to feel the weight of his body on top of him, his warm skin heating him. He wanted to hear Devak's cries of pleasure as he came. He took a moment to gather himself.

Maybe Devak was right. Maybe Matthew would push him away. Maybe his desire was nothing more than his soavik driving him to seek out food. And maybe Matthew wouldn't be able to ignore the small voice inside of him that sowed doubt:

Devak will break your heart. He is manipulating you. He will leave you, it said to him. *You will be abandoned.*

It wasn't a voice of reason but it wouldn't leave him alone. He needed to actually be able to talk to Devak without the curse. Then the voice might fade. Until then, he had to protect them both.

"One human," Matthew said after some time. "A woman. Someone who wants sex. I won't rape anyone."

Devak left without another word and half an hour later returned with a woman in tow. She was a young thing, a beauty that looked like she had been out clubbing. She shook her head as if chasing away cobwebs—a compulsion. Devak probably had her believing this was a mansion, not some underground bunker full of vampires.

"That's my friend I told you about," Devak said to her and motioned to Matthew. She eyed Matthew up and down and liked what she saw. He could smell the desire on her and he shot her a 'hey there, I'd like to fuck you' smile. It was fake, she wasn't the one he wanted to fuck, but she ate it up.

"You must be gentle because he's still recovering from that motorcycle accident," Devak said.

"Don't worry, I'll take good care of him." She started to cross the room to Matthew when she paused and looked Devak up and down. "Sure you don't want to join us?"

Devak flashed a charming smile. It was just as fake as Matthew's but she was fooled. "If I didn't have some other business to take care of..." He looked at her as if he wanted her. "Have fun, dear."

Not only was Devak attractive enough to pass as an incubus, he could lie like one too.

Devak left and Matthew fucked the woman, or rather she did most the work, but he made sure it was pleasurable for her. After, he took some of her blood and wiped the events from her memory.

At least his soavik was happy, even if he felt like an empty piece of shit.

He called Vikentiy and asked him to take her away. "And tell Devak to feed on me during the day when I'm asleep," he ordered.

He didn't want to see Devak right now. Couldn't.

Matthew was a coward.

Samantha kept him company the rest of the night and, for once, didn't chastise him for his actions. He spent the time healing what he could.

The next night he was well enough to remove the IV and walk around without pain. He went into the bathroom, intent on taking a shower, but his reflection in the mirror gave him pause.

Someone had cleaned him while he was unconscious but he looked ragged. There were bags under his silver eyes, his scruff looked a little longer, even though he hadn't forced any hair to grow—he'd have to shave for the first time in years, but what really drew his notice were the tattoos.

They were like long black tendrils that twisted from his hand to the top of his right shoulder. Matthew focused on the arm and could feel *it* inside of him still. He called it forward.

The tattoos turned red and his skin split open, the blood dropped down into his hand and the battleaxe took shape.

Blood. Feed me, the dark voice whispered to him.

"Not today."

Matthew focused on bringing the axe back into him. The weapon resisted him, pulling against him like a dog unwilling to relinquish a rope. His tattoos burned hotter, searing his skin. They fought in a battle of wills, and since he had full control of himself right now, Matthew won.

The battleaxe melted into blood and flowed upwards back into his skin. The gashes stitched together and the tats faded from red to black. It wouldn't be so easy to control during combat, he needed to practice and teach it who was in charge here.

Maybe Devak could help him. It felt as if ages had passed since the last time he and Devak trained together.

Matthew rubbed his face, then closed his eyes, and leaned over the sink, his weight on his hands.

Delphi tomorrow night, if possible. It needed to be soon. He felt as if his soul was ripping in half and he couldn't take much more of this. Thoughts of Devak wouldn't leave him.

He thought of Tarrick, in an effort to stop obsessing about the guardian, but it didn't help. All he felt was pain and torment. Tarrick... the burning inferno. It was time to let go.

"You can never get rid of it," Samantha said from the doorway.

Matthew looked up at her reflection in the mirror. "Rid of what?"

"Bloodreaver, Harbinger of Ruin."

"Uh..."

She came over to him and ran her hand down his tattoos. "That's its name."

"You named it?"

"No. It named it." She sighed. "When I was younger I saw a vision of you. You were fighting something and you were using the axe. It's part of you. Always will be. You'll find another one day."

"Great. I'm going to have two of them?"

She shrugged. "Be careful when you use it, it will always try to rule you."

Matthew flexed his hand. "Lovely."

Samantha leaned her butt against the countertop and crossed her arms. "What does it look like when a guy cums?"

Matthew snorted, actually snorted, trying to not laugh at the question and failing miserably. "Samantha...I don't know, it just... haven't you ever watched a porn?"

She shook her head. "No. Watching porn was sinful."

"Alright, when we're done in Delphi I'll set you up with a computer, we'll dim the monitor so it won't bother you and you can spend all night watching porn."

She smiled, but then it dropped and she looked away. He put his hand on her shoulder. "What's wrong, dear?"

"Why did you dump Devak?"

"We weren't together."

"Yes, you were. I miss him in the bed. He's warm like the sun. You don't have to tell me but, you know, I feel all your emotions. I know you want to be with him." She pushed off the countertop and walked out of the bathroom. "I'm going to go tell Bryson that you'll be out in an hour, they want to talk with you."

"Sam?"

She popped her head back in. "Yeah?"

"You know I love you, right?"

She smiled. "Of course. I'm an oracle."

Of course.

Thirty-Six

An hour later Matthew felt like a new man. Well, new vampire anyway. He had showered, shaved, and downed a gallon of blood. Externally most of his wounds were pink scars.

Samantha spent a good two minutes rubbing his now-smooth face because she had never felt it without the slight stubble he had honed. Then she fed from him, delighted to be drinking something fresh.

"They're waiting for us in the command room," she said as she licked blood from her lips.

Devak was back to standing guard in the hallway and bowed as Matthew exited the room, Samantha and Jet trailing behind him.

He still looked like shit. It was hard to see him this way. Every part of Matthew's being wanted to carry him back into the room and take care of him. "You didn't feed on me during the day, did you?" Matthew growled.

"No, I—"

"I gave you an order."

Devak took a step back and looked lost. "I—"

"I don't want to hear it. You'll feed after this meeting. Don't disobey me again. You are supposed to be my guardian and right now you look like something Samantha could beat up."

He squared his shoulders to make himself look stronger. "I assure you I am not that weak, my prince."

"Hey! I'm standing right here," Samantha said.

Devak bowed to her. "My apologies, my princess. You hold great power, but it is not physical."

She scoffed, even though she knew it was true.

Matthew raised an eyebrow. "Princess?"

"It was her request," Devak said.

Matthew shot a hard glance at Samantha.

She folded her arms. "If you're a prince then I am a princess."

He rubbed his forehead. "For fuck's sake."

"I do not mind it," Devak said.

"Fine. Whatever you want to call each other is between the two of you but, Samantha, if you start acting like a prima donna we're going to have words. Strong words." Matthew turned and continued down the bunker hall. "Come on, we're late."

"Yeah, we wouldn't want a second prima donna around here, would we?" she said under her breath. "Maybe Devak should call *you* princess."

Matthew kept walking. "Could we reign in the sass a little?"

She scowled at him, her nose scrunched and lips pressed together.

He didn't chastise her more because he knew she was just upset at what was happening between him and Devak. Fuck, he was upset by it, too.

Matthew pushed open the door to the command room.

It sounded like a busy night. Bryson was shouting orders while Vikentiy relayed them in Russian into a phone. Gwenyth and Ascelina were sitting in two chairs in the corner of the room. Ascelina's arm had grown back but it was pinkish in color, and her shiny black hair was pinned up, showcasing her long, pale neck. No Stolus. Matthew couldn't smell him either; he had probably been sent home to his sister.

There were eight other vampires in the room, all busy with work.

When they noticed Matthew, everyone fell silent except for Vikentiy, who was yelling at the phone in Russian. Eventually, he hung up with a few choice words. Matthew didn't need to know Russian to know he was cussing someone out. Then Vikentiy fell silent too.

Bryson dismissed the nonessentials from the room. Vikentiy stayed, as did Gwenyth and Ascelina, who joined Bryson at the table. Devak took up a spot in the corner while Jet stayed with Samantha behind Matthew, standing opposite the other vampires.

A moment of silence stretched as the group studied him.

Matthew cleared his throat. "Thank you for caring for me the past few weeks."

Bryson nodded.

"I have been filled in on everything that was done to rescue me, Matthew," Ascelina said. "I owe you a great debt."

"Well, it didn't go exactly as planned and I'd like to think we're even now. You did do the same for me, after all."

"Are you certain that you do not wish us to call you 'prince'?" Ascelina asked.

"I'm certain."

"Then how about 'king'?" Bryson asked.

Matthew looked over to Samantha, then to Devak. No matter what happened between him and Devak, he was going to give Samantha the house she wanted. "I can't right now. I have some promises I need to make good on. Which reminds me…did you do the swap for the ring while I was out?"

"We were waiting on you," Gwenyth said.

Shit. Matthew didn't even know where the ring was right now, he didn't have it on. Then Samantha held it out and Gwenyth produced the wooden box that housed a Night Stone.

"Be careful—" Matthew warned as they made the trade, "—it gave me all sorts of nightmares."

"To see the sun again after so long, I will risk nightmares," Gwenyth said as she slipped it on. It fit her ring finger perfectly.

Samantha pocketed the stone, leaving the box behind.

"You should reconsider," Bryson said. "You should be the one ruling us. You're a demigod. Even the Russian families would submit to you, Matthew."

"I'm still trying to understand what being a demigod means."

Vikentiy cupped his hand in the air. "It means you have big brass balls. We faced defeat and you were fearless," the Russian said with a nod of respect. "What did you say to it?"

"It? You mean the pit commander?"

"Da."

"Uh, I just told it I was going to kick its ass, but that didn't work out so well for me."

Vikentiy did a little dance. "Ha! I win!"

"Win?"

Gwenyth shook her head with disapproval and Bryson laughed. "We had a little bet going. None of us speak any of the demonic languages so we had to guess what you said to it."

Matthew just stared at him. "Um, what?"

They looked confused by his confusion. Devak stepped close to him to explain. "You were speaking to it in its tongue, my prince."

"Ah." He could understand the demons when they whispered beyond the portal…he had never thought about it but it didn't really make sense for them to be speaking in English.

Bryson motioned to Samantha. "You know in the long run, fighting the incubi is the only way you're going to be able to keep your daughter alive. I know you've given your answer but I'm not going to stop asking. We need you."

Bryson played Matthew's weaknesses well, but it wasn't enough to convince him to change his mind right now.

"Fair enough, but don't expect a different answer anytime soon." Matthew studied the table in front of him—it was filled with reports of recent clashes with the incubi. "What happened at the end of the battle?"

"Which part?" Bryson asked.

"The blood guardians…I saw them show up and was out after that."

Bryson laughed. "You know I'm an atheist? Now I'm not so sure. The incubi teach hunters about the gods but I thought it was all bullshit." He pointed at Devak. "I thought he was just some sort of old super vamp."

Devak frowned. Gwenyth too.

"Sorry," Bryson said to them. "The guardians showed up, murdered everything, and left. They didn't stop to talk to us."

Gwenyth pushed back a loose strand of her blonde hair. "When we last battled demons, over two thousand years ago, guardians often showed up to help in battles. Never in such numbers, three was the most I have ever seen at once."

Bryson pulled out a folder and slid it over to Matthew. Inside were photos of Brujo Moya's witches, all dead, propped up in gruesome poses.

"You did this?" Matthew asked.

"I wish I could claim credit. I sent a team down as soon as night fell but the incubi got there first. Tarrick doesn't take betrayal well. Look at the wounds. It was nice of him to not leave a hunter team behind to take my guys out."

Matthew studied the photos closer; some of the witches had been bludgeoned to death by a weapon with square metal spikes. Tarrick's kanabō. He had gone there personally to kill them.

"We didn't find their leader among the bodies but I don't think he got away. I think Tarrick wants to take his time killing him."

Good. The evil bastard deserved it.

"I need that favor now," Matthew said to Bryson.

"Delphi?"

"Yeah, all I need is transportation there. As soon as possible."

"Tanya's witches can bring you close, but because of the time difference, you can't get to Greece until tomorrow. It's day there right now. Vikentiy's volunteered to go with you. If you need help he can get in touch with me right away and he's resourceful if you need anything."

Vikentiy wore a wide smile.

"You can join us in Greece—" Matthew said, "—but what we're doing in Delphi is private."

"We'd accompany you." Bryson motioned to himself, Ascelina, and Gwenyth. "But the incubi have been active in their attacks the past few nights."

"It's not necessary, but thank you."

Ascelina appeared beside him. She took his hand. *You have a lovely child, Matthew. When you are done in Delphi you should consider staying with me, I would enjoy hosting you again, and your family.* Seems Samantha made all sorts of friends while he was out. *And I apologize for the actions of my own child during the masquerade; I assure you that it will not happen again.*

Emilia had really messed with him by creating the illusion of Tarrick, but that felt so long ago that he didn't give it much thought anymore. And he had forgiven her anyways.

Bryson sent a message to the witches and informed everyone that they would be there in thirty. After saying goodbyes and Ascelina thanking him once more, they returned to the room to get ready.

Matthew had Devak feed while Samantha packed for them. She had a new duffle bag—a Christmas gift from Vikentiy—this one black and pink with her name embroidered on the side. Matthew wouldn't be using it too often. Pink wasn't really his color.

They arrived at a safe house in Portugal right before the sun rose, and the next night they were in Greece. Vikentiy was quiet for most of the trip, watching Matthew with reverence. It made Matthew a little uncomfortable.

After waiting a few hours to be sure that the tourists and workers would be long gone from the ruins, Matthew sent Devak ahead to compel any security guards that might be there.

Matthew set out for the ruins, carrying Samantha while Vikentiy ran behind them. Jet circled overhead. They ran over the hills, avoiding the roads.

"Stay here," Matthew ordered Vikentiy when they were a mile away. "Samantha, I want you to run to him if there is any trouble, okay?"

She nodded and they continued without the Russian.

The ruins were breathtaking. Nestled on a rocky slope, surrounded by green bushes and the occasional tree, the moonlight lit what was left of the once-great buildings. But for all its beauty, it was out in the open. The hills would make it easy for anyone to approach unnoticed.

Matthew kept all his senses on high alert.

Devak appeared beside him. His wings were out and he had his maul but he wasn't in his armor. Samantha insisted that he not wear it. "The humans have been dealt with, they will not be back tonight."

"Let's go," Samantha said, shifting the duffle bag to her side.

She led the march, her two protectors vigilant behind her. She walked past the Temple of Apollo, which was only a limestone foundation surrounded by a few free-standing Doric pillars, and headed over to what was left of the Altar of the Chians, a tall—over ten feet by Matthew's estimate—square, structure of worked stone.

She climbed on top of it, unzipped her bag, and took out the jeweled dagger with the gold handle and silver blade—it was the same one she used on the Chicago rooftop to open the portal.

She set it down, then retrieved a shallow copper bowl and placed the Night Stone inside of it. From the bag, she also picked up a glass vial with clear liquid, broke the wax seal, and poured the contents into the bowl, coating the stone.

"Well?" she said to Devak. Devak set his maul down against a stone and flew up to the altar. She directed him to lie down; as he did so, his wings withdrew back into him.

"This is going to hurt a little," she said.

Devak smiled. "I am ready."

So was Matthew. It was time to finally get some answers.

With a flick of her lighter, she set the contents of the bowl aflame. The stone melted away and black smoke rose high in the air as she began to chant in a language Matthew didn't know. Her eyes turned completely white.

At the apex of her chanting, she picked up the dagger, dipped it into the liquid, and plunged it into Devak's chest.

Devak screamed.

The barbed chains of the curse became visible, wrapped tightly around him.

Samantha kept chanting and Devak's body rose high into the air, the end of the chains floating as if unaffected by gravity. They began to turn from metal into blood and melt away.

When the last link disappeared, Devak plunged down to the ground. Matthew rushed over and caught him in his arms.

"I'm free," Devak whispered, his eyes rolled back and he passed out.

Matthew pulled the dagger out of him, tossed it away, and sat down at the base of the altar, cradling Devak in his lap.

Samantha crawled off the altar and sat down beside them, leaning against Matthew's shoulder, exhausted.

He brushed his fingers against Devak's cheek and his eyes fluttered, and opened. The warm honey color melted Matthew's soul and in that moment all doubt faded away.

"My prince."

"My guardian."

Devak smiled wide. "Where should I start?"

"I—I have no idea. I have so many questions."

"Help me up, I want to stand, and run around a little. Those chains were heavy. I feel light right now."

Matthew pushed him up, standing with him.

Samantha crawled a few feet away onto some grass and she whistled. Jet, in his frightening gargoyle form, came over. He had been hiding among the marble, his stone-looking skin was now white instead of its normal black.

"Are you alright, Sam?" Matthew asked.

"Yeah. Tired. I'll be right here," she said using Jet as a rocky pillow.

Devak took a deep, cleansing breath and ran. Matthew spotted him on a rock across a valley, then, a few minutes later, he was standing next to Matthew again.

"Having fun?"

Devak brought his wings out again, stretching them behind him. "I have been cursed for nine years and it felt as if it was nine hundred. There's so much I want to tell you." He put his hand on Matthew's upper arm. "I am not what you think either—I've wanted to tell you for so long."

"Then tell me. Because I'm dying here." Matthew needed him to start talking about anything—he was desperate for any answers.

"I am not a guardian of Lysandros."

Matthew blinked once. Slow. "What?"

"I am not a blood guardian. It was the reason I couldn't enter the temple in Gwenyth's keep and it's the reason I ran when the blood guardians showed up—they would have killed me if they had seen me."

Matthew stood stunned as his entire perception of Devak shifted. He was a vampire during his life, he had said as much, and right now his blood wings floated behind him in gorgeous array. How was he not a servant of the god of vampires, the Blood God?

Devak reached up and caressed Matthew's face. "I was there the day of your birth. I named you. Took you to the hospital."

"And abandoned me." Matthew's eyes narrowed. He had been dropped off with no information and grew up an orphan, bouncing from foster home to foster home.

Devak dropped his hand. He looked horrified. "No. Never. I've watched over you most of your life, but I had to keep my distance so that no one would know what you were."

"What I was? An incubus?"

"You're not just any incubus, my prince."

"Oh!" Samantha said from the grass behind them. "That's so cool."

Devak laughed. "You've jumped the gun, princess, I have not told him yet."

A growl of frustration rumbled from Matthew's chest. "Would someone please tell me?"

"I was sent by your mother."

"My mother?"

"I am a guardian of Ilertha. A pleasure guardian."

"T-the incubus goddess?" he stuttered out. It was a dumb question, but at least Devak didn't mock him for it.

Devak nodded.

Matthew wasn't sure what to say as a dozen emotions slammed him at once. His mother was Ilertha? Was that why he could hear singing when he was close to her statues? And if his mother was a god, why had she sent him to a human hospital? If she couldn't keep him for some reason, why not just drop him off with an incubus family where he would have at least been raised as one of them?

He wanted to ask Devak all of this but instead spat out: "But—but you look like a blood guardian."

"Because he was one before he betrayed me for that whore," the Blood God said from behind them.

Thirty-Seven

Devak's eyes widened. "Na'mori," he said, then moved fast, picking up his maul.

Matthew turned. Lysandros, the Blood God, his sire, was standing in the center of the Temple of Apollo's ruins. He was huge, wearing spiked black and red armor. A constant stream of swirling black vapor shed off him and pooled at his feet.

Devak placed himself between Matthew and Lysandros. He held up his maul, ready to attack. Bright light flared as Devak's armor came down from the sky and donned itself onto the guardian's body.

Jet sprung forward, snarling at the god.

Lysandros raised his finger to his mouth. "Shhh."

Jet sat down and froze into a statue.

Matthew wasn't sure what to do here, or who to trust. Should he be kneeling to his sire? Devak looked ready to fight the god. Should he back him up?

"I won't let you take him," Devak growled.

"I already have him," the god said, his voice filling the area.

Devak's body tensed. "He has a choice of which throne he serves. It is his choice."

The god curled his lips, showing off a mouth full of frightening long fangs. Like a fast moving fog, power filled the area and pressed in on them.

Samantha whimpered and passed out on the grass. Whatever was happening between his sire and Devak suddenly wasn't important to him. Matthew scooped her up.

"I don't know what's going on," he said to his sire, "but can you please suppress your aura? She's only a few months old and can't handle this."

The god took a step forward and Devak hissed in response, blocking the path to Matthew and Samantha.

"Show your true form and I will make it bearable for her," said Lysandros. Matthew wasn't going to argue with the god—he let his vampire free. A sound of approval came from his sire.

The oppressive waves of power died down and Samantha stirred in his arms.

"He's terrifying," she muttered, her eyes fluttering.

"Stay here, honey," Matthew said as he gently set her down on the grass, then looked at Devak and his sire. "I'd really like to know what's going on."

Lysandros and Devak continued their stare down without saying a word.

"Please?" Maybe being polite might get him somewhere.

"Do you wish to fight me again, Cel'ii? It didn't end well for you last time," Lysandros said, smirking. Matthew might as well have been invisible.

"I do not go by that name any longer."

"And why not? It fits you so well, Cel'ii. *Traitor.*"

"I am Devak—*Trusted.*"

Matthew approached Devak, walking around his wings, and placed his hand on his shoulder.

The guardian looked at him. "I tried to stop him."

"Stop him?" Matthew glanced at his sire, who looked amused by the situation.

"From turning you into a vampire. I fought him that night. I lost. My goddess assigned me above all others to protect her son and I failed. And for my failure, he cursed me and wiped my memories so I couldn't guard you anymore." Devak's face twisted with anger. "If I had been able to watch over you, I would have made sure the incubi knew that you are their goddess' son, a prince. They would never have treated you so poorly."

Matthew looked at Lysandros again. He stood there, saying nothing. Wasn't his sire worried about what Devak would say to him? That it would sway his opinions?

The corners of the god's mouth twisted up. "I am not worried. You belong to me. Nothing he says will change that."

Okay, so he *could* read Matthew's thoughts. Fun.

"Kill him," the words slithered from Lysandros' mouth like a poisonous snake.

"...What?" Matthew asked, not sure if he had heard correctly.

Lysandros nodded to Devak.

"What the fuck? I'm not going to kill Devak."

The Blood God's red eyes narrowed. "You are."

Lysandros wasn't displaying all the grandeur he had the first time he appeared in the temple but Matthew wasn't fooled, he was impossibly powerful and Samantha was right—he was terrifying. But, even still, he wasn't going to kill Devak. He didn't have all the answers yet but Devak was ready to take on a god to protect him. Hell, he already had and got cursed for the effort. That was good enough for Matthew to trust him.

Matthew studied the guardian. *His* guardian.

He had fallen for Devak. It frightened him to admit it; it made him vulnerable, but there it was. Those strings he had tried to ignore were tangled around his body. He was in love. There was no doubt now.

"He is not the only one who has watched over you all these years, my son. I sent my guardians to save you from the demons, did I not?"

"Yeah…and thanks for that but, I'm not going to kill Devak."

Lysandros motioned to the night sky. "Kill him, and I will give you a hundred guardians to command. With them you could rule this planet."

"That's not what I want."

"Then take them and do what you wish. They would be yours."

"Yeah, I think you're missing the po—"

Lysandros was so fast that Matthew didn't even see him move. One moment he was in the center of the ruins, the next he was towering beside him. The god brought his armored hand up and slapped Matthew so hard he went flying into the altar, shattering the stone around him.

A couple of Matthew's back teeth were knocked out and his ribs were broken. He pushed healing into repairing the ribs; the teeth would have to wait.

Devak lunged at Lysandros, swinging his maul. It never made contact. Lysandros raised his hand and Devak's blood wings reformed, wrapping around him like rope and squeezing him tight. Devak's maul went tumbling away as he was lifted into the air, floating a few feet off the ground.

The god looked down at Matthew. "You will learn that disobeying me is not an option," he said, his voice full of dark intentions.

Matthew pushed himself to his feet, coming face to face with Lysandros. He spat his loose teeth and blood out onto the ground. "I refuse to kill someone I love."

Devak stopped struggling against his blood prison and his eyes went wide upon hearing Matthew's words.

"There is another here you love." Lysandros looked at Samantha, who had been watching silently from the grass. Still sitting, she scooted back, looking to Matthew for reassurance. He had none to offer her; he was too enraged that Lysandros would dare bring her into this. His tattoos turned red and the blood collected in his palm.

In a dismissive motion, Lysandros waved his hand and the blood fell away, the axe failing to take shape.

"I am the God of Blood, and that is the weapon I gifted to you. Do not dare to think you can use it against me."

Shit. Matthew had no idea how to fight him. If he couldn't take on a pit commander, there was no way he could take on a *god*. But it seemed either Devak or Samantha was dying tonight. He couldn't let that happen; he had to save them.

"What kind of fucked up father are you? You left me a vampire with no instructions, forcing me to abandon my family. You fucking made it so I couldn't even finish my incubus transformation. And now you want me to kill someone I care for?" Matthew's eyes were burning with rage.

Lysandros set his hand on the back of Matthew's neck and dug his claws into his skin. Matthew grunted at the searing pain.

"I want you to be powerful, my son. I want you to rise and take your place beside me. Is that not what all parents desire—to see their children grow strong?"

Matthew wanted that for both Lily and Samantha but there was more to it. "And we want them to be happy."

"You are destined to rule. With the world at your feet, you could shape any future you desired." He motioned to Devak. "You haven't known him long enough to love him. Kill the traitor. You will recover from the loss and be all the stronger for it."

Matthew was getting sick of people telling him who he did or did not love. He knew his own damned heart.

Lysandros tightened his grip on Matthew's neck and leaned in. "You are young."

Matthew was sick of hearing that too.

"My prince—" Devak said, struggling to get the words out, "—you have a choice."

A deep, sickening laugh came from Lysandros.

"There are rules," Devak said. "He is vulnerable in this realm."

Lysandros released Matthew's neck, then raised his hand and squeezed it closed. The blood swirling around Devak tightened. His bones began to pop under the pressure. Devak cried out in pain and Samantha sobbed, tears flowing from her eyes.

Matthew lost it.

He pushed all his power into his speed, kicked up Devak's maul from the ground and swung it as hard as he could into his sire's chest.

It hit with a resounding *clang* and Lysandros went soaring, smashing through columns before sliding to a stop across the ruins. The blood holding Devak fell away and he dropped to the ground.

Lysandros rose up and the realization of what Matthew had just done hit him like a car crash. He was fucked.

Devak grabbed Matthew's shoulder. "He can't stay here much longer, it'll draw the attention of other gods who will come and try to kill him on this realm."

"Get Samantha out of here."

"If I don't help you fight him, he'll kill you."

"You gave me your word that if the choice was between Sam or me, you'd save her. Get her out of here. Take her to Vikentiy."

Power pulsed around them, drawing Matthew's attention back to his sire. Lysandros' eyes were glowing. Blood seeped out from between the joints in his armor and twisted in the air around him.

Matthew could smell despair coming from Devak. He grabbed his guardian by the shoulder and pulled him into a kiss. Devak's soft lips moved desperately against his, and Matthew felt as if a firestorm erupted between them.

The kiss was brief, it had to be, but the moment held more passion than Matthew had ever felt in his entire life.

Neither wanted to break it, but both knew they had no time.

"I love you," Matthew said.

"And I you, my prince."

Matthew looked at his daughter. Her tears had turned to blood. "I love you both."

"Survive," she said. "Don't let him break you."

And then they were gone, Devak carrying her to safety. At least Matthew hoped it was safety. How does one hide from a god? *There are rules.* Matthew hoped one of those rules would keep them safe. It wouldn't help him though; he knew he was about to get his ass kicked.

Lysandros stalked forward, blood floating around him. He grinned and a small portion of the blood formed into sharp spears and went flying at Matthew.

As he dodged them, Matthew wondered why the fuck the Blood God didn't just rip the blood out of his body. He obviously could control it. Maybe it was a rule…or maybe he was playing with him.

Whatever the reason, it wasn't something he had time to worry about right now…he ran down the hill into the theater. There were over thirty tiers of limestone seats that, in its day, could hold over five-thousand people. If he weren't in the middle of a fight he would have enjoyed being here. He loved history.

But right now, it was the farthest thing on his mind.

He reached the center of the amphitheater and held up the maul. He didn't really have much of a plan beyond 'survive as long as he could'. There was only one way this was going to end. No amount of luck could change it. Even if he wasn't running on just one blood pouch right now, his abilities couldn't stack up to a god's. That didn't mean he was giving up, he was just being realistic for once.

Matthew didn't see Lysandros anywhere. He couldn't sense him either.

Had he left? No way this ended that easy.

Then Lysandros was in front of him, again moving too quick to see. Matthew swung at his head but the god caught the handle of the maul, stopping it mid-swing. He yanked it away from Matthew and dropped it on the ground.

Matthew backed away. Attacking any armored foe with his claws was foolish, attacking Lysandros would probably mean he'd have no more hands after.

The god looked unimpressed. "You disappoint me. But you are

brave."

"Yeah, well, lately that hasn't gotten me anywhere."

"I am not going to kill you."

"No?"

"No." Lysandros crossed the gap between them and placed his hand on Matthew's shoulder. Blood and black mist surrounded them. "You are my son. Mine. And, despite what you believe, I have never abandoned you." His voice was almost affectionate.

Matthew laughed. It wasn't because he found anything funny, it was because he didn't think he was going to be alive much longer and his body needed a release of the tension.

"You are not going to go unpunished." Lysandros' claws sunk deep into Matthew's shoulder and the blood inside of him began to feel as if it was on fire. Every inch, agony. He fell to his knees, unable to pull air into his lungs to scream.

The pain died down. He had no idea what was being done to him but he felt weak. He collapsed to the stone ground, falling on his back, unable to move.

Lysandros looked down at him, his face unkind.

Matthew sucked in air and asked, "What have you done to me?"

"You will see."

A faint green outline traced air behind the god and an armored hunter appeared. Imperator Prescott. In his hand was the gold sword, Ilertha's runes glowed brightly. He plunged the blade into a weak point in Lysandros armor, sinking it into his rib cage.

The god turned and smacked Prescott in his chest. The leader of the Hunter Corps went into the stands, stone breaking apart when he hit it, sending a cloud of dust into the air.

Lysandros pulled the blade from his side as if it was a minor annoyance and tossed it away.

Matthew reached out with his senses the best he could. They were surrounded. There were hunters everywhere in the hills, and more were showing up, keeping their distance.

Prescott stood. No human, even a hunter, should have survived an impact like that. Guess his armor really did make him invincible.

"Do not attack me again. You do not possess the means to kill me," Lysandros warned.

Prescott pulled off his helmet and Matthew saw his face for the first time ever. He wasn't what he expected at all. The Imperator was young, early twenties, short dark hair, and a groomed beard. Greek origins.

Prescott nodded and held out his hand—with a flash of green he was holding the golden sword again.

Lysandros turned his attention back to Matthew. He kneeled down and, setting his hand on Matthew's chest, whispered to him.

"It is time you saw the true face of your mother. She is revealed through her people, just as I am through mine. The traitor guardian was correct: you do have a choice. In the end, you will choose my throne to bow before. When you do, I will forgive you."

His sire was going to leave him for the incubi. God, what they were going to do to him—he'd rather die. "Don't leave me like this…" Matthew begged.

"Grow strong my son."

"No. Father. Please."

But Lysandros vanished.

Matthew tried to move as Prescott approached, but he couldn't.

Prescott stood over him with a frown. "Shame we didn't get to fight. I was looking forward to it. Where is your guardian?"

Many hunters teleported around them. Hiroto approached, holding a box in his hands.

He wondered how long the hunters had been waiting. He prayed, well, he hoped anyway, praying was off the table right now, that they hadn't seen Samantha and that she was long gone by now.

"My guardian is gone. How did you know I'd be here tonight?"

"Vikentiy sold you out in exchange for his sister's release," Prescott answered.

"He wouldn't do that." Matthew refused to believe it. He had seen how Vikentiy was around Samantha, he cared for her. And he was Bryson's right-hand man, he'd never betray the vampires.

Prescott shrugged. "I don't think the Russian vampires want you as their king. I can't say I blame them."

Was this just a political move? Matthew howled. Betrayed. And he had sent Samantha to Vikentiy.

Silver shackles with chains were snapped onto Matthew's arms and legs. Hiroto opened the box he was holding. Inside was a thick metal collar, covered in runes and sparkling with magic.

"Little fox, please, no," Matthew begged, tears stinging his eyes. Not another collar. "Please." Hiroto's red mask covered most his face but his eyes were full of pity. For once, Matthew didn't mind the pity. He knew what was coming. He knew what the collar meant.

A flash of light streaked across the sky, accompanied with a high-pitched shrill. Devak landed in the center of the theater. He snatched up his maul from the ground and slammed it into the nearest hunter, sending the poor human soaring across the ruins.

The hunters attacked. Devak took out the first few with ease.

Hiroto dropped the collar and teleported behind Devak, stabbed him in the back of his knee, then teleported away. Bolts went flying at the guardian but he deflected them with a protective shield.

Devak stood above Matthew. His skin began to glow a bright gold color. Light from him expanded and burst outwards in a pulse, knocking away every hunter that didn't get out of its path.

Except Prescott. He shrugged off the hit and moved in, swinging his golden longsword. He and Devak traded blows. With each exchange, Devak looked weaker. Slower. The wound Hiroto had dealt had blistered and turned black.

"Run," Matthew cried, "get out of here."

Devak continued fighting and Matthew was helpless to save him.

Around him, the other hunters stayed back, watching their leader battle.

Prescott was skilled with his sword; the best Matthew had ever seen actually. He allowed one of Devak's blows to hit him, the armor he wore absorbed the impact and it created an opening for him to counter. He punched Devak with his free hand, then kicked him with his heavy boot.

Thrown off balance, Devak stumbled, and Prescott took advantage of it by slamming against him with his body. The hunter didn't let up. He swung, and Devak, expecting a blow to his left side, brought up his maul to block it, but it was a feint. Prescott spun and drove the sword through Devak's armor and deep into his chest.

The guardian staggered, then fell to his knees. He looked down at the sword, confused by its location. Then he accepted it and looked at Matthew.

"Forgive me, my..." He swallowed hard and repeated the words. "Forgive me, Matthew."

He tilted his head back to the sky. A loud humming filled the air and his mouth fell open. Bright beams of light shot out from every orifice as if his soul was escaping him. The light exploded and his body slumped to the ground.

Devak was dead.

Prescott yanked the sword from out of the guardian's corpse, then pierced Matthew's blood pouches several times. Hiroto picked up the collar from the ground and snapped it around Matthew's neck.

Matthew didn't notice. He was watching Devak's body decay, turning to ash. And no one else here seemed to care.

Devak was dead.

His eyes stung as bloody tears filled them.

Devak was dead.

Loss filled him.

Devak was dead.

He screamed.

Devak was dead.

Matthew was still screaming as blackness consumed him.

Thirty-Eight

Blood filled Matthew's mouth. He was unable to move except to swallow, and even that took tremendous effort. Thick metal restraints pressed against his neck, wrists, and legs, suspending his limbs in the air.

The flow of blood into his mouth stopped and an indeterminate amount of time passed, maybe days, as his body healed what it could.

He was able to move his head a little, and hours later he was able to smell again. The scent of jasmine and frozen air enveloped him. A single directional lamp hanging above him took shape as his eyes healed. Beyond where the light fell was darkness. Pitch black nothingness. Dread.

A while later he realized there was a man in the room with him. He was standing just outside the circle of light. Matthew squinted, but it didn't help. How long had the man been standing there, watching him?

The figure stepped into the light, moving with such grace he seemed to be floating. He was tall and thin with high, arrogant cheekbones. He had smooth, golden hair that fell long past his shoulders. His eyes were the palest blue Matthew had ever seen.

He wore a long embroidered blue and white robe that flattered every angle of his body.

He was beautiful.

Matthew desired him and, upon realizing who he was facing, his stomach lurched with disgust.

"Do you know who I am?" the man asked. His voice was alluring.

"High King Malarath," he said, his throat raw. Rosaline had been right; Matthew didn't need a photo.

"No." A cruel smile crept across Malarath's face. "From now until the end of your days, you will call me *Master*."

Matthew returns in Broken: Beautiful Monsters Vol. III

Meet the hunters of Ashwood Red in 2017

About the Author

Jex enjoys writing about hidden worlds full of vampire hunters, epic battles, steamy sex, and, of course, beautiful monsters. Find updates for new releases at: www.JexLane.com